W9-BDR-003

Revelations

ALSO BY SOPHY BURNHAM

Nonfiction
The Art Crowd
The Landed Gentry
A Book of Angels
Angel Letters

Fiction
Buccaneer
The Dogwalker

Plays
Penelope
The Study
A Warrior
The Witch's Tale

Revelations

Sophy Burnham

BALLANTINE BOOKS

NEW YORK

Copyright © 1992 by Sophy Burnham

All rights reserved under International and
Pan-American Copyright Conventions. Published in the
United States by Ballantine Books, a division of Random House,
Inc., New York, and simultaneously in Canada by
Random House of Canada Limited, Toronto.

Library of Congress Cataloging-in--Publication Data
Burnham, Sophy.
    Revelations / Sophy Burnham. — 1st ed.
        p.   cm.
    ISBN 0-345-37233-6
    I. Title
PS3552.U73242R48   1992
813'.54—dc20   92-53192
                                                       CIP

Design by Holly Johnson

Manufactured in the United States of America

First Edition: September 1992

On every page a bill come due;
On every page a billet-doux
To all the men and women too
Whom I have loved and seen love true,
And then to God, and then to You.

SB

A lamp am I to those who perceive me;
A mirror am I to those who know me.

APOCHRYPHAL ACTS OF JOHN

This project was supported in part by a grant from the D.C. Commission on the Arts and Humanities and by the Helene Wurlitzer Foundation of Taos, New Mexico.

Revelations

1

HOW MANY TIMES HAVE I FOLLOWED THE ROAD DOWN THE MOUN-
tain we call Big Top, steep and curved enough to make the
gravel trucks shift groaning into first, and twist past Middleman, which is hardly bigger than five houses set back in the
woods. They are tarpaper shacks with sagging front porches and
broken boards, and in the yard a dirty baby, his diapers drooping to his chubby knees and one finger maybe up his nose. The
yard is full of tires. A yellow dog lounges in the speckled sun,
scrawny and mean, and you're glad you're not on foot, though
you'd only have to lean down and knuckle the dirt to make it
turn with a hunted backwards look, tail tucked and scurrying
from the expected stone.

A quarter-mile farther on you plunge into a maze of U- and
hairpin turns, and here is Storey Lunt's house, which played
such a part in this account, and then down and out into the
sweet, lush, green, flat Valley. Today there's a bypass at Four
Corners that takes the truckers round, but in those days all
traffic ran right through the farmland into Naughton and out
the other side, following the valley floor according to property
lines and never cutting straight and irresponsibly as roads do
now across our best and fertile fields.

It was on that road that Tom drove in, rocking into Naughton in his black Plymouth with its rusting left fender. He was trying to be discreet. He'd lost his muffler on the mountain and he lurched into one pothole and bounced to the shoulder, raising a cloud of dust behind. From floor to ceiling the car was jammed with boxes of books and kitchen gear. Clothes swayed on hangers at the windows, while on the roof a mattress slipped from its lashings and leaned over the windshield like a hat over one eye. A tipsy sailor weaving down the road. Inside, the Reverend Thomas Lewis Buckford grit his teeth on the dust of shame and on an anger as righteous as fiery hell. He felt like an Okie in his worn-out car, now exploding, muffler-free, in thunderous announcement of his arrival, and the difference between his own poverty and the wealth of the area he had come to serve sat sour in his mouth. The taste did not disappear.

The next day as he stood on a ladder at the rectory in the unseasonable October heat, the hot wind in his hair and the sweat running down his back, he attacked the broken windowsill, hacking at the wood as if it were the Valley itself.

He had not wanted this parish. That was the first thing to be said. He felt diminished by the lushness of the land, the white-fenced estates with their grazing horses and brown fields raked and harvested, by pseudo-Georgian manor houses perched on hilltops and stone walls that meandered right into the woods.

It was Priscilla who had insisted on accepting this call. He would have turned it down. What did he know about the landed aristocracy of a Virginia rural community? His interests ran to the plain, the poor, what Priscilla called "the man of mediocrity." That cold sneer in her voice invariably had power over him. She had pointed out the advantages of a daughter now

fifteen being offered a scholarship at Miss Eugenia's, one of the
most fashionable boarding schools in the country. She had
pointed out the higher salary the parish offered and his reverse
snobbery that declined to serve the Lord among the rich.
Weren't the well-off just as beloved by Christ as the poor? But
Tom had liked his modest city parish, with its lack of money
or pretension. He hated leaving his home of eight years, his
friends. And he recognized as well his conflicting feelings of
fear and shame at being thrown into a parish whose members
could buy and sell him without noticing the change of income
either way.

There was more. Months earlier a desolation had come
creeping over him, a darkening of the soul. His joy in life had
disappeared. There were words for it in the Christian litany: He
had lost his believing hope. At times it came back—glimmers
of vitality. But more often, as now, standing on the ladder at
this upper window, looking out across the fall of hills, the sca-
brous oaks against corn-stubble fields, a sense of dullness filled
his heart as hard and cold as the line of Priscilla's mouth.

With his chisel he pried at the rotting wood, the heat beating on his back in waves, unseasonable scorching heat. After a
time he laid his tools on the window ledge, pulled off his shirt,
wiped it across his forehead, scrubbed his wet chest and watched
it drop, a limp sail, to the grass below. Soon in work the black
mood began to lift. He found a perverse pleasure in standing
on a ladder twenty feet above the ground, between earth and
sky as it were, and not in either, attacking the rot. There were
several reasons for doing so. One was to avoid Priscilla's acid
tongue, which would find enough fault with this house. Another was to escape the charge of souls he did not want to

know. A third was simply to roast in this October furnace, to feel the hot air scorching his lungs and the gnats in his eyes and the sweat bubbling on his skin.

He was concentrating so hard that he did not hear the two-tone green Buick purr slowly up the drive and stop, fins streaming, at the rectory door. Or see Emily Carter, who was so small that, even propped on pillows, she could hardly see over the steering wheel. She heaved her weight against the Buick's heavy door. She had come to bring a cake for the new minister, who was to arrive that night. She stepped out of the car, cast a practiced eye around the rectory grounds, and took in with surprise the ancient black car at the kitchen door, then the workman on the ladder. She could not remember the vestry authorizing work. The carpenter, bare to the waist, was absorbed in the window. She tried not to look at the muscles working in his back. "Is the rector in?" she called up.

Tom Buckford looked down in surprise. He had not seen the tentative approach of this woman, a toad, a galleon, almost as wide as square.

"No, he's out." He gave a bitter laugh, for that was true in more ways than one, including the fact that here he was outdoors in the clean blue air. He did not notice Emily's startled look.

"Out?" she murmured, glancing at the open door. "Oh dear." It was not just the workman, but anyone at all could walk into the rectory! What had John Woods been thinking of to let a perfect stranger come repair the house without a soul to supervise? Why, he could take anything—the silver tray that she herself had donated to the rectory, or the pretty little red lacquer Oriental boxes that sat on the reproduction Queen Anne table beside the fireplace. Or the odd pieces of flat silver in the dining room. It was then that she noticed the carpenter climbing down the ladder toward her. His bare chest gleamed with sweat. Without a second's hesitation she stepped inside and shut the rectory door.

"Wait!" she heard. But she had thrown the lock. Good God! The man was almost naked. She stood uncertainly in the hall, then jumped, remembering the kitchen door. She reached it just before the man did and slammed it in his face. She could hear him bang on it in exasperation, a hollow thumping that sent chills through her. Was she safe? *I must think. Think,* she thought. The windows were all shut. No. The window he was working on; and she paced heavily up the stairs to the front bedroom, sweating by now and breathing hard by the time she arrived. The window was open. She slammed it shut and locked it, because, thank heavens, he had not done so much work that the window was right out of the frame. Then she drew the curtains tight on every window in the room.

For a moment she leaned against the wall, heart floundering from her run. She hardly knew what she should do. Stay until the rector came? *Oh dear,* she thought with indecision, for when would that be? She crept softly away from the dangerous window and out of the room, shutting the door behind her. Now the workman could not see her anyway. Then she sat on the top step of the stairs and tried to collect herself, thinking how fortunate it was that she had come along just when she did. And fortunate that she had taken such command. That man . . . half-naked in October . . . what if he had already stolen the silver and stashed it in his car?

She couldn't bear to go downstairs, to expose herself to his peeping face peering at her through the ground-floor windows. Her heart was beating hard. *Be brave, Emily,* she exhorted herself. *You are a middle-aged woman, a pinnacle of the Church, and there is no one here to help you but your God, Who will look after you. Surely you were Sent,* she reminded herself, *to do something about just this situation.* And considering the matter, she had to admit that only she herself would have qualified for the command.

First, as a member of the vestry, she knew who worked for the church and who did not, and this man she had never seen in her entire life. From outside came the sound of his banging on the door. She covered both ears with her hands to thrust the sound away. First, as a member of the vestry . . . Second— she had forgotten what was second. Indeed she had forgotten what she had been counting.

"Count to ten," she said thoughtfully. Her father often used to say to her, "Emily, just slow down, count to ten and get control of your nerves. Then you'll know what to do next." She sat, therefore, counting slowly up to ten. Then to calm herself, she watched her bosom rise and fall, breathing in and breathing out. In a moment she would have to creep downstairs, in the face of all those windows, and make a quick inventory of what had been taken from the house.

Yes, second—she remembered now. Second, she knew every stick of furniture in the rectory. Many of the pieces were donations from her own house, given in memory of her mother. There was the silver tray in the pantry, and the lacquer boxes, and the two Oriental scatter rugs that always lay in the living room. She was all aflutter. *Get ahold of yourself, Emily,* she dictated firmly, as her mind considered her own things possibly abducted from the house, sequestered in that hideous black car she had seen parked behind the boxbushes. All the man had to do was to put on his shirt and drive away, and he could have taken everything already.

She had to reach the telephone. She crept downstairs. Already, with all the doors and windows closed, she could feel the house sweltering under the ninety-degree sun.

Meanwhile Tom Buckford, the rector, sat on the bottom rung of the ladder to think the matter over. He had picked up his shirt as a matter of courtesy to the old lady, thinking that perhaps he'd frightened her, but when she refused to open the door to his insistent knocking, he let it drop again. How long would she stay inside? Since he didn't know her name, it was rather difficult to call out anything and remain polite. What did one say in Virginia? "Hey you"? "Lady"? His Pennsylvania tongue toyed with "ma'am." He wanted to burst out laughing. The longer he thought about it, the funnier it became.

It did not occur to him that he ought to take the situation seriously, nor to wonder what Emily was feeling, trapped in that sweatbox of a house, or how she would feel when she came out and discovered she had locked the rector out. He did not stop to wonder at any of the problems about to confront him in his ministry, or the effect of making enemies. Instead he went back up the ladder and saw, to his irritation, that she had locked shut the window that he'd been working on. He was so annoyed he began to rip the whole frame out.

Emily, inside, could hear him tearing at the window. Terrified, she crawled downstairs to telephone me, John Woods.

So now about me, who's telling this story. And if you're as skeptical as my wife, you're like to ask why, too—why I sit at my rolltop desk, me, seventy-nine years of age next month and poring over memories of a single ugly event buried years ago.

There. I wrote that down, then sat for twenty minutes puzzling over it. I'm no writer. In my youth I tried my hand at a novel, pretentious drivel, and burned it, as it deserved, but this is a true account. Why am I recording this?

Part of the answer lies in my age. Next month I'm entering what's probably the last decade of my life. I want to finish things. Then, too, I'm retired now, and that was voluntary I should say, a couple years ago. I didn't wait to be asked by John III to move over. I pretended not to see his questioning glance when I'd get cramped sometimes and couldn't rise from my chair as fast as he thought I should. But he never asked me to retire, and I never missed a day of work in my life out of slackness or senility. No, I retired by myself, when I saw it was time, and there won't be another word said on that score, except to note that it's not right to have a son almost fifty who's never been the boss.

So I left that spring. We went through the farewell parties, everyone all teary that things'll never be the same without me, and I came home and began to putter about the house. Getting underfoot. Standing around. Looking out the windows and making life miserable for Margaret, my wife. And then I saw in the Richmond papers one day that Thomas Buckford had been killed, and it hit me like a spike in the chest. I almost cried aloud. All these years that business with the church had been haunting me. I was senior warden of the vestry then, and I may be the only one who knows the whole story, so maybe it's out of duty that I'm trying to make a record of the facts. Or maybe it's some pitiful attempt to atone. Because I'm not proud of the way I acted then. There are times I'd change the clock back and do it all over—the vote, the trial, my part.

I couldn't throw the obit away. "Tom Buckford's died," I announced to Margaret.

"Goodness."

"Shot in Guatemala. By the death squads."

"No!" She took the paper from my hand, holding it at her own arm's length. "Lend me your eyes," she said, reaching for my specs. Then: "Shot by the roadside. No mention of his family."

"Nmf."

"I'll write Elizabeth." Then she gave me a queer, sharp look. "Or, maybe you should be the one to write." She left the room.

I sat there at the dining room table reading those two short paragraphs over. Captured and shot during the fighting. No mention of his work with Indians in Peru. No mention of Elizabeth, or the heresy trial. No mention of his wife or his two children. Only the fact of death declared—a Protestant priest assassinated in a Catholic country in a petty war. Was he tortured too? Was he stripped and whipped, perhaps the skin torn off his face? Oh, we'd heard of the savagery there. It made me sick. What was Tom to them? I could see his joyous smile. I wanted to cry. Unconscionable! After a time I wandered out to the glass porch and sat at my desk, staring out through the louvered glass panes to the garden beyond. I wrote Elizabeth.

Two weeks later Trinity had a memorial service for Tom. The Bishop gave the eulogy—a new bishop, not Crowley. I was filled with rage at seeing the whole town turn out. Carolyn was there in a black mantilla (Dutton, her husband, having died), and Emily, and Miz Reischetz, and then General Shriver, hobbling on two canes, and all the others who had hounded Tom. Lizzie flew in, of course. I sat there listening to this new young Bishop praising Tom's work with the Indians and his vision, his generosity, his warmth and optimism, his contributions to Naughton—how in one short year he had left us changed. Yet hardly a word about what happened. Carolyn gave a reception afterwards at Walnut Grove, and it turned my stomach to hear Emily and Butch Shriver bickering about him still. After all those years.

In the hallway, as she was putting on her coat to leave, Elizabeth came up to me, gray hair flying round her face. I noticed worry lines at her forehead now, her wide mouth a little pinched with the look of command.

"Here, John, I brought something for you." She took my arm, pulling me along to the door.

"What?"

"Come to the car with me."

We walked out on the crunchy tan pebble drive, her hand tucked under my arm in that old companionable way, and my heart felt full.

At the car: "I promised you these once and never wanted to part with them." From the seat she took four notebooks. "My diaries," she said, "from then. You're the only one left who'd care." Her eyes were glistening with tears.

I turned them in my hand, plain blue-bound notebooks with lined pages. I couldn't speak.

"Do whatever you want with them," she said shortly, brushing it off. "Burn them if you wish." She patted my arm, then brusquely threw herself in the car. "I've got meetings in New York."

The following week I read them all, and now I've begun this account.

Out in the kitchen I can hear my wife moving around, doing Lord-knows-what-all. She never stops. The house, the garden. Round and round like a hound turning in his bed, nose following tail, until he suddenly flops down dead out and is asleep.

I write on lined yellow legal pads, using my favorite Waterman pen. I have some letters of Tom's to Elizabeth and now her diaries, Tom's notebooks, erratic as they are, and my memories of the trial. I have years of conversations with Angus, who has the gift of blab, and I'll add parts that were told to me by Carolyn and Emily and Angie Reischetz and the other people involved. I can't promise better than that. Maybe I'll make some up. It's the prerogative of age, to wander back and forth across time, recounting and reconstructing events, in a search for reality. What's the Shakespeare line? "The stuff that dreams are made of"; and maybe if I get it all down in one place it will make sense to me finally, create order out of chaos.

For that matter I don't even know who I'm writing this for. Who's going to read it? I use the second person singular. "You," I write, without even knowing who you are. ARE YOU THERE? WHO ARE YOU? Or am I writing to my own void soul? Or to my God? If there's any difference in the two.

I can't imagine anyone reading this, but I write pretending it's to someone else. To you. Who might be me. They say when you discover your own self, you find God. Well, I guess I've never found my self, and that's the most important thing that I could tell you about me, John Woods, who has lived in this community for seventy-nine years and whose family has lived here for three generations before that; who has run his feed business and bank and timber interests as honestly as he has known how and never to his knowledge cheated anyone. Who has served his church as vestryman as faithfully as he could.

And who has not seen God.

I know people who have.

Or say they have.

I envy them.

Well, it was never given to me to see God, as it was to some people, but I have trudged through my life and raised money for the church and done my ethical and civic duty as best I could. And I don't see how I could be expected to do more.

But maybe I'll know the answer to that, too, by the time I finish this account.

Emily telephoned me from the rectory. I was out of the feed store at the time. I hadn't been back two shakes when my secretary told me Miss Emily had called, not once but four times, she'd been that scared, locked in the sweltering parsonage on the hottest day of the year with a strange man taking out the upstairs window. I didn't know all that at first.

I stuffed my pipe in my mouth and went on back to my big desk that had been my grandfather's just after the Civil War and then was my father's when he established Woods Grain and Feeds, which is what we call the business. Strangers sometimes think it sells wood, grains, and feed, and I like to lead them on and let them think I'd sell them lumber, too, but actually the Woods part comes from our last name: John Woods, Jr., which was me, the son of my father and father of my own son, Johnnie, who is now the head. I eased into my tip-back wooden chair with its sagging wicker seat (also a hand-me-down from Grandfather) and I called Emily right off, curious as a cat.

She whispered into the phone. I had trouble hearing her.

"Get over here," she said. "Don't ask any questions, just

come quick. I'm alone in the rectory, and there's a man trying to break in."

"Did you call the police?"

"You don't want the police," she said, her voice trembling like water. "Just get over here now. I'm holding him off. But hurry."

I thought momentarily about calling the police myself. I stared at the phone for a second or two, then got to my feet and decided to check things out for myself.

I figured I'd be able to handle most anything Emily had thought up for me. Because I couldn't for the life of me imagine a burglar at the rectory. A burglar could have any mansion in the area to choose from, places like the Strong farm on Laurel Hollow Road, built of fieldstone and belligerence. Whenever the contractor asked for two-by-fours to build the house, Mr. Strong had changed the order to four-by-eights. That was the kind of man he was. The place was full of priceless treasures and overpriced junk, things to make William Randolph Hearst turn around and stare. Or, if you were a clever burglar, you could choose the French antiques at the Clark estate on River Road, or the painting collection that Judge Hideroff and his child bride, Jane, had put together. She was the college room-mate of his own daughter. He had met Jane when she'd come home for a weekend with her roommate. Within six months, the old man and Jane had married. Everyone in the Valley had predicted they would split up inside of a year, and each year the prediction had grown weaker. They'd been married for twenty years now and might have been the happiest couple in the Valley. They both loved to travel and they loved to collect art. So that kept them busy. The house was usually closed.

I'm off the subject. My point is that any burglar worth his
salt could find a lot of places worth more than the shabby little
rectory with its hand-me-downs and castoffs from the gentry. I
was mystified—the more so when I saw the new rector climb
down his ladder as my car pulled up. He grinned and wiped the
palms of his hands on his khaki workpants. He had no shirt on,
and his bare chest glistened with sweat. Buckford was in his
forties, his hair a brindle gray. He had a tight, muscular body,
tanned and well-built. He had a strong neck too. I remember
that especially, because it was evident even in his clothes, that
wide, muscled neck rising from his clerical collar. He had a
forward stoop that gave him an attractive stance, as if he were
plunging forward into life, and sometimes—later—he would
stand, bending to listen to one of the elderly ladies in the parish
with a little smile dancing at the edges of his lips and his green
eyes sparkling. I know he set some hearts alight.

Which was probably one of the problems with Emily. For
there she was locked in the house with this man projecting that
naked-to-the-waist masculinity, standing on the ladder and talking out loud to the sill. I've known Emily most of my life, and
I've never met a shyer person. She never married. She couldn't
cope with sex. When we were teenagers, we used to double
over laughing when we'd dare one of the boys to plant a kiss
on little Emily Carter. No one wanted to, of course. She was
called Effie. Or Fats. Later she settled into her mother's house
and raised her dogs. Her mother got older and more senile and
was finally settled in the nursing home, and Emily's house got
darker and dingier and dirtier. It became a joke in the community. At one time she had nineteen dogs—Shetland sheep
dogs and German shepherds, they were. Most were kept in the

kennels out behind the stables, but she always had five or six favorites that she let sleep in the house and sometimes took in the car with her. She would feed them little delicacies from the table and talk out loud to them in baby talk. The dog hairs blew around the house, the parrot screeched in its cage, and the smells got higher until it was a real decision whether you wanted to go to her house for tea. On the one hand the food was delicious, her cook being the best in the county, and on the other hand you were sure to pick one of those Shetland dog hairs out of your teacup, and you couldn't avoid noticing the gentle layer of dust that had settled into the Orientals and lay over the black finish of the piano and the bronzes on the mantelpiece.

At the rectory a boxbush hedge hides the cars so that from inside you can't see who's coming in. All Emily knew was that the man had stopped prying at the window frame when my car drove up. Tom and I stood talking at the car door for a few minutes.

"Fixing a window?" I nodded at the ladder, and he smiled with what I thought was a little grimace and shook his head.

"I thought I'd try to get the sill repaired," he said. "My wife's arriving next week, and I'd like to have the place in as good shape as possible." He looked serious for a moment, rubbing his hands together. "Well, it's hard, I guess, moving to new homes. And then the houses are never quite yours." He smiled. "I'd invite you in, but I'm locked out."

I thought it was tactful of him not to mention the problem.

"Well, that's what I heard." We stood together looking over at the house like old friends. I felt comfortable with him, as if he emanated a quiet harmony. "Emily Carter telephoned me," I said after a minute, for there was no hurry in figuring out what to do about the situation. "She said she'd locked herself in to keep out a burglar who was breaking in."

"That was me." He sighed and grinned both at once. "I was up on the ladder and this little woman trotted up and asked if the rector was in. I said he was out." He shifted in embarrassment. "Because I was, technically. The next thing I knew she'd rushed into the house and locked the door. I tried to tell her who I was, but . . ."

"Well, let's get her out of there." Em's on the vestry and a dedicated Christian, but she'd been in Florida and hadn't met the new rector yet.

I knocked on the door and saw her peek out the curtains. "It's me, Emily. John."

"Oh, I'm so glad." She threw open the door. I thought she was going to slam it shut again when she spotted Tom behind me. Her jaw dropped.

"It's all right, Emily," I said. "This is the Reverend Thomas Buckford, the new minister."

She was a sight. Her face was flushed deep red; sweat ran down the grooves in her cheeks, dropping off her chin, and her hair had wilted.

"How do you do." The chill in her voice could have done any member of the Valley proud. She had lived here all her life. She knew how to cut a person when she wished.

Tom's face fell. He was astonished by her reception. After all, as far as he was concerned, he hadn't done anything. He pulled back his outstretched hand.

"Would you like to come in?" she asked. Queenly—as if it were her own house. "I am not accustomed to a naked minister," she added.

"Oh, now, Emily," I interrupted.

But he jerked as if he'd been hit. He went dark for a moment and then turned without a word and walked to the ladder to fetch his shirt.

"Come off it, Emily," I coaxed her, whispering. "It's a misunderstanding."

"The man I pay to minister to me," she said, still on her high horse, "should have the manners to introduce himself."

"Well, but you locked him out of his own—"

"There was no need for him to behave," she continued, "as if I didn't exist."

I just snorted with disgust because there was nothing to say to Emily once she got into one of her hurt-feelings moods.

"He could have told me who he was. I came to pay a decent call."

"Now, come on. Let's open some windows," said I, doing just that. "And have a social visit. We're going to be working with the man."

"I'm sorry, John," she said. "I have far too many things to do to sit around and talk. I've wasted half an afternoon. . . ."

By now I could see she was close to tears of shame and humiliation. Tom was coming back, tucking in his shirt and smiling over at us, and I knew if he spoke to her, she would crumble. All that coldness was just a cover for her own heat and unhappiness. She pushed past me with her chins in the air, all three of them, her head high, waddling to her car on those inexpressibly tiny feet. They always reminded me of the feet of a Chinese doll I once saw in a museum, the bound feet of the nobility.

"Miss Carter—"

She had already plopped onto her cushions in the big Buick. Beside her the cake had melted on the seat. She reached out and slammed the door with a solid *thunk*. Tom stood a moment, indecisive, looking from me to her. I turned away and shrugged. I didn't know what to do. There was no doubt that she was offended, but it being by her own doing, I couldn't see what move he could make now to ease the situation. He looked down at his hands again, and up, and by then she'd turned on the motor and was backing slowly out. We both moved into the house together, neither of us having any idea that this little tiff, an infinitesimal misunderstanding, would come circling back like a medieval mace on a chain and hit him on the head.

We went inside and had powdered tea from a jar. The tea was already sweetened with sugar and had lemon flavoring added to it. We drank out of jelly glasses, which was all we could find on the shelves, little fairy glasses with a blue-check design. You get them at the Woolworth's in town. It was then that he told me some of what I've written here.

2

THOMAS LEWIS BUCKFORD NEVER IMAGINED HE'D MAKE AN ENEMY his first full day in Naughton. Just as we never thought he'd split the community, create scandal—open warfare.

He was a family man: married eighteen years with a daughter fifteen and a boy about twelve. His wife was the second cousin once removed of Kitty Spalding, who's been in braces with polio since she was a child. She plays golf, drives a car, swears like a soldier, smokes those tiny cigars that pass for black cigarettes. Everyone admires Miss Kitty's spunk, and if Buckford's wife was related to her, that stood for a lot with the search committee. Then there was his own background, which couldn't be faulted. He was a Lewis of Virginia, raised in Pennsylvania, out in the country. Everyone felt comfortable with that, although his father, a businessman, had gone bankrupt at one time. Originally Tom had thought to be a vet. That was another point in his favor, most people in the Valley looking to their dogs and horses as they look to people, only with more affection. Moreover he had changed his profession as a mature man, so we knew he wasn't one of those spineless, incompetent types you sometimes find in the Church. Spiritual fairies. I don't know why it is that the Episcopal church has a way of attracting the weakest sort of men, meek, henpecked creatures with their docile eyes. One of our criteria was someone with a little "fire" in him.

Also we wanted a low churchman. The parish had a list of qualifications. We wanted sermons people could relate to: no surprises. Of course we wanted good readings of the texts, but we don't like religion stuffed down our throats. A good holiday service, and the consensus is that the best sermons are the ones we've heard before.

I don't want to leave the impression we're stuffy. It's just that we know what we like. But we also wanted someone different from Dr. Ellis, who had served Trinity Church for nearly fifteen years before he died. Dr. Ellis had become so much a part of the Valley that it was hard to tell he was our clergyman. He raised basset hounds for showing. He liked his drinks before dinner and he danced at the deb parties. There were some in the Trinity congregation who felt he paid too much attention to our richest members. So there was a move afoot for someone who would direct his eye to the middle class, add new contributing members to the rolls, and attract a younger membership. Because the membership had declined under Dr. Ellis. So had the income. We took a poll of the parish. We decided we wanted candidates with fighting-cock qualities: "game" men, good "cutters," ones with stamina and "bottom," which is strength.

The choice came down to two men, Tom Buckford and Bill Wentworth. Bill was the Bishop's boy. Both men came in to meet the vestry on the same day, Bill in the morning and Tom in the afternoon. There was no question Bill could talk. A tall, rangy man from a Rocky Mountain state, he just spouted Godly sayings. Every third word was a quotation from literature or philosophy, and he impressed us, I admit. I mean, we all *noticed*

Bill. He had Presence. For one thing you had to look up till you got a crick in your neck just to meet his eyes. Tom, on the other hand, sat at the conference table, his elbows on his knees and his hands clasped. He didn't say much of anything. He just listened and nodded, very serious, except twice when he broke into an engaging smile and his whole face lit up. We felt at ease with him. Elizabeth once called it vibrations, but I have no patience with that kind of talk. We couldn't put our finger on it exactly. Bill dazzled us. Tom was just there, and when it came to a vote, we were all taken by surprise.

Mimi Foster pushed for Tom. She felt sorry for him, thinking he had paid his dues to God after living in Schenectady. She thought Priscilla and Tom should be rewarded with our parish.

General G. Scully "Butch" Shriver, retired now and a breeder of Black Angus and prize Charolais cattle, didn't actually cast his vote for Tom so much as against Bill Wentworth, who made the mistake of upstaging him. Butch prided himself on obscure quotations.

" 'Say not, the struggle naught availeth,' " the General said, quoting Arthur Hugh Clough. " 'The labour and the works are vain.' "

"Wounds," said Wentworth callously.

"What?"

"The labour and the *wounds* are vain," he repeated.

"Say not, the struggle naught availeth,
The labour and the wounds are vain,
The enemy faints not, nor faileth,
And as things have been so things remain.
If hopes were dupes, fears may be liars;

It may be, in yon smoke conceal'd,
Your comrades chase e'en now the fliers,
And, but for you, possess the field."

"Yes, well," General Shriver said savagely.

"It *is* the Christian message," boomed Wentworth. "Faith! The struggle is not for naught!"

"We hope it's for Naughton." I laughed to emphasize the joke. In a way it was unfair that a similar opportunity didn't present itself with Tom. No one quoted poetry at him.

Mimi Foster liked Tom's looks. That was clear immediately. She could hardly keep from touching him. Her warmth, however, brought down Esther Ratcliffe's spinster wrath.

"What in heaven's name did you have to go and tell him that for?" Esther whispered in her emotion, and brushed back her gray hair nervously.

"Tell him what?" Mimi answered, taken aback.

"Tell him about US. Tell him our biggest problem is alcoholism."

"Well, it's true."

"It's no business of his. You don't just go telling everyone all over Virginia and every state of the Union that. . . . Don't you have any pride at all?"

"Esther, if he's going to be our priest—"

"And don't use that word. You sound like a *Catholic*."

"It's a perfectly good Episcopal word." Mimi stuck to her guns. She and Esther had been fighting on the vestry for years, and it was still a draw. "I suppose you'd have the poor man come into the parish and not know anything about it?"

"I just think it's undignified, that's all. It's embarrassing. What if he's not elected, then what?"

"Then what?" Mimi returned blankly.

"Well, then he would know all about us, that's all. You just have no discretion."

"Now, now, Esther." Julian put one comforting arm on her Liberty-print shoulder. "I'm sure he wouldn't tell anybody, and it doesn't hurt. Mimi's right. We should probably have been more open with Dr. Wentworth, too, for that matter."

"God forbid." Esther shuddered. "It just puts enormous pressure on us all to vote for him. It's not fair." Which explained her reluctant vote for Tom.

"It really doesn't," said Julian. "You'll see, it won't make any difference. Don't worry."

"Well, it's not my worry," she answered, her voice rising. "I'm not alcoholic, and neither is anyone in my family, but it's just not something that you all go around—"

"General," I murmured, "are you ready for the meeting? I think it's time to discuss the pros and cons of the two candidates. We can have a half an hour and then we ought to vote."

It says something about the state of Trinity Church that the twelve-man vestry was reduced to seven in that year. Emily Carter was in Florida and couldn't vote. Of the rest, Esther, Mimi, and Butch chose to vote for Tom, and the other four of us stood up for Bill. Anne Adams wanted an intellectual and was choosing Wentworth for that. Julian and Rod thought his fund-raising experience an asset. I decided I liked Bill's directness and that energy that flashed out in the impatient shake of his heavy mane. I thought he'd have more flair, and, given our declining enrollment and the dispirited pledges from the last "Every Member" canvass, flair carried weight. So it was Bill's appointment four to three, I thought.

Voice vote would have done, but at the last moment Butch

Shriver insisted on a secret ballot. He handed out slips he'd officiously prepared. We all scratched our ballots, and then the General collected them. I remember watching the backs of his freckled hands as he counted them one by one. The light struck against his sandy hairs, darkened with liver spots. "Wentworth . . . Buckford . . . Buckford." He glared with satisfaction around the table. "Wentworth . . . Wentworth . . . Buckford."

He put down the last ballot and grinned around his cigar. "Buckford," he announced triumphantly.

There was a little pause—an infinitesimal electric shock.

"It's Mr. Buckford?" inquired Esther.

"No, no," Rod Cameron interrupted. "You must mean Wentworth."

"Let me see." I was so taken aback, I literally ripped the ballots from Shriver's hand.

"Why, I couldn't be more surprised," Esther was saying. "That takes care of the problem."

I riffled through the ballots, and there, sure enough, next to Tom Buckford's name was my own firm mark in the green ink from my Waterman pen. I could hardly believe my eyes. I was sure I'd marked the lower box. I returned the papers to Butch without a word.

"Well, that's nice."

"He'll be very good."

"I couldn't be more surprised."

We rose, closing file folders and shuffling papers together. Everyone was looking at the vote. They must have known I'd changed mine.

"Well," I said stiffly, and made an elaborate show of stuffing my pipe. "A good day's work. I will draw up a letter of notification in the morning."

Meetings of this sort don't break up easily. It's as if a herd instinct has overtaken the group. It has become an organism in its own right and cannot bear to separate into individual cells. We stood around longer, musing over what it meant and assuring each other the choice was fine, that with two such men no choice was wrong, and eventually we reached the arched doorway of the parish hall, built in 1736, and stood in the sweet June sun.

The light glittered on the front walk, with its high mica content, and cast rich shadows on the red-brick church. We looked over at it, a comfortable and stable early colonial structure with its low roof and fine row of stained-glass windows; plain as pie, and in its unpretentious simplicity more beautiful than any of the churches that are built today—those in the shape of a fish or a wedding cake or the ones where the steeple shoots too high for its squatty hall. On that fine summer day Trinity Church nestled comfortably into the soft Virginia landscape with the crepe myrtle waving shadows on the wall. I felt my heart lift, I loved it so. I shrugged off the fact I hadn't voted for the man I'd chosen. Trinity had survived a long time, and who could imagine that a single man would threaten that?

Three days after his encounter with Emily, Tom made a worse enemy out of Carolyn Page. Still we didn't take it seriously. It all had a faintly ridiculous tone, beginning in the way that Carolyn, as soon as she heard about the episode with Emily, rushed immediately up to the parish hall with the other Rectory Rats to satisfy her curiosity about the handsome minister. She returned home triumphant, having invited him to her luncheon the following Sunday afternoon. She decided he would help them start the school.

3

It was a formal lunch, the kind you read about from the 1930s but didn't expect to find at the end of the 1950s. The Pages were not the only couple in Naughton to keep up standards, but they did it best, and when Margaret and I walked in, I gave a grunt of appreciation. "May I rest your wraps?" asked the maid politely—a manner of speech I've remembered with admiration all these years. We gave her our hats and coats to rest and glanced into the dining room with its shining mahogany table laid out with lace placemats and a silver basket of fresh flowers as the centerpiece. At each setting stood a little silver cigarette cup, holding that guest's favorite brand. At each place stood a tiny silver ashtray and silver salt and peppers, and a placecard among a dazzling array of Waterford crystal and silver forks and spoons and knives.

"John! Margaret!" Carolyn swept us up with gracious hospitality and led us into the living room, her hawk eyes scanning the room for imperfections in the furnishings or guests. The house had been constructed in the 1920s in the romantic Renaissance style of Shakespearean balconies and leaded diamond-paned windows. There were bowls of fresh flowers on the tables, and the silver-framed photos of the children on the piano gleamed in the light. The usual antiques and probably the most beautiful Oushak rug I've had the pleasure of stepping on. We were the last to arrive except for Tom. Dutton Page was pouring bourbon at the bar, and since everyone in the room knew each other, the voices lifted in the usual topics of conversation—how the Valley was changing, the Jews moving in, the absence of servants, the intrusion of gov'ment, putting us all out of business with its paperwork and regulations. We got our drinks and joined the ritual. Time ticked by.

I looked around and saw the party was taking its own course, the conversation rising to the pleasures and paranoia of the comfortably rich, including the social escapades of the more interesting of our set. I learned, for example, that the beautiful Mrs. Billy Tyler had dropped her twenty-two-year-old poet for a seventy-year-old Texas oilman.

At one point Carolyn accosted me: "Do you think your cleric's forgotten?" Her eyes glinted like glass, and I noticed he had already become "mine," so that I shared in his guilt. I've known Carolyn all my life. She's a cousin, and I am godfather to Elizabeth. She's a woman to hold a grudge.

"Now, now, he'll be here any minute," I said, and then to soothe her, "It's his first Sunday. There's a lot of business." Carolyn was not one to be crossed.

"I would have thought, John, you would have warned him to cut the service short. Didn't you tell him what the lunch is about?"

"No, didn't you?"

Tom's lateness was partly due to doubt. Ignorant of the implications of his invitation, he had stood for a time after church wondering whether to dress in a regular shirt and tie or in his black priest's rabat; and he had forgotten to ask. Eventually he decided on the clerical collar on the lonely assumption that he was invited not for himself but as the rector of Trinity. He chose reluctantly, however, aware that the uniform of Christ, while it confers privilege, also isolates. He already felt alienated; and indeed on spotting him at the door, Billy Tyler turned with an irritated toss of her head: "My God, why do they always have to flaunt their black?"

He stood a moment in the doorway, surveying the crowd with a gallant smile, and then he was swept into the maelstrom.

"Mr. Buckford." Carolyn descended on him with all the appearances of cordiality. "What a pleasure to see you. We were just getting concerned. Was there a problem?"

"No." Was it the luxury that made him hunch his neck? The women wore silk dresses with strands of pearls, and their ears and fingers were heavy with diamonds and chunks of gold. The men sported lightweight plaid-wool trousers with blue jackets, or else gray flannels and tweeds—informal, country dress. They wore moccasins with tassels.

"No problem!" cried Carolyn with such clarity of diction that he wondered if she were affecting airs. "Why, I was sure there must have been an accident, or you would certainly not have been forty minutes late." Having made her point, she took his arm with social expertise. "But do come get a drink. You'll have to carry it with you. We're going in to lunch right away."

"That's all right," he murmured.

"I want you to meet your host. Dutton, this is Mr. Buckford, our new minister . . . my husband, Dutton Page."

"Well, well. Glad to have you aboard," said Dut. "Do you count the sun as over the yardarm?"

I was watching with interest our new minister's entry into Naughton society.

"There's hardly time for one short drink," Carolyn intervened. "He'll have to carry it in to lunch." Having done the honors, she turned away, bumping into her son-in-law with his empty glass, but Dut grabbed hold of him, relieved to find help in entertaining the rector.

"Angus," he said. "You know the Reverend Brockworth?"

"Buckford," said Tom. "Tom Buckford."

"Oh, excuse me. Buckford. This is my son-in-law, Angus McEwen."

A meaty paw appeared. Angus, burly, brown-skinned, heavy in the jowls and now going to lard, wore bright orange slacks. His eyes sank into the good-natured folds of his face.

"Glad to meet you, Reverend," he said, and Tom's lips twitched with annoyance, for to call a priest a "reverend" to his face is a courtesy only in the Negro ministries. In our church it's a term reserved for an envelope.

"I never trust a man who doesn't drink! Come on, Dut." His voice carried to the corners of the room. "The padre wants a proper belt." With that, he poured liberally from the bottle into a glass, threw in one ice cube, and with a high, wide smile handed the drink to Tom.

"Well, a little water." Tom had met these types before, the kind who take pleasure in getting the clergyman drunk. But Angus had turned the bottle cavalierly over his own glass too.

"There was a young man named Ossle,—Do you know this one?

"Who found a remarkable fossil.
He could tell by the trend
of the bend at the end
t'was the peter of Paul the Apostle."

He gave a guffaw, slapped Tom's back, and disappeared into the crowd.

Tom told me afterwards how he was suddenly aware of how dingy his shoes appeared against the magnificent blues and orange of the rug. He listened to Dutton proudly showing off his collection of harness brasses displayed inside the bar. Around him the conversations rose in an ocean of sound, a joyous roar on which periodically a single phrase leapt up like spume on the crest of a wave.

"You know who he married! An orthodox Jewess!"

"My father had twenty-eight first cousins." A female, Southern drawl. "And my mother had sixty-three, counting second-generation."

"What, play you? You cheat!" And peals of laughter.

It was that kind of party.

Dutton took Tom cordially by the arm. "This is a good opportunity for you to meet the community." He smiled. "Over there's Bradley Schley. He was ambassador to the Dominican Republic. Damned fine guy. That's his wife talking to Margie and John Woods; you know them, of course."

I joined them at this point and listened to Dutton's explanations.

"And Angus you met. In a way this is Angus' affair. We're giving it to help him out."

"Oh?"

"Angus is big in town politics. I suppose there's one in every family." Dut laughed. "Whereas I was brought up to believe a gentleman wouldn't go near politics. But Angus is doing very well. He's fallen in with this Anthony Reischetz, who's in the chamber of commerce." He gave a choked giggle. " 'Rye shits.' Why he doesn't change his name I can't imagine. Anyway the school is his idea, and Angus is helping to promote it."

"I haven't heard about the school."

"That's what this little get-together is about. This is a business lunch, really, a fund-raiser to open a new school in Naughton. One that can provide a first-class proper education for the best and brightest kids."

Tom nodded.

"So we told Angus," continued Dut, "we'd get these people together. Rye shits will be along after lunch. You'll understand then why we didn't invite him to eat with us. Don't you agree, John? I mean, he's just not . . . Now, that's Mikey Jackson standing at the mantel," he continued. "He owns the *Naughton News*." He dropped his voice confidentially. "I wouldn't waste any time with him. He's a lightweight. Inherited a pile of money. His father, see, married three times. The first was a teenage discretion. That one was annulled. His second wife was from a Very Fine Family. Big Money. Alcoholic, though. Affair with the chauffeur. Auto accident. Classic story. All her money went to her husband, and when he married for the third time and finally had a son, it all settled onto little Mikey. Now, the woman he's talking to is Mrs. Billy Tyler. A great lady. Always rides sidesaddle in the hunting field. You'll love her. Her money's in mines. Mikey . . . Billy . . ." He interrupted the two, who turned politely. "I want you to meet our new minister at Trinity. Mr. . . . um . . ."

"Tom Buckford." He spoke up quickly.

"How nice to meet you." Billy nodded. "I do hope you'll enjoy yourself. Mikey and I"—she turned, shining her full attention to Dutton, ignoring Tom—"were just talking about Didi Ferrari. It's like something out of a movie."

"You know who she's caught!" said Mikey. "A genuine English lord!"

"What's the name of that family, Dut? We were just racking our brains. I remember visiting their castle in Ireland once. She was married first," she explained politely to Buckford, "to some goddamn Wop no one had ever heard of. It didn't last. How could it? He was so totally different. They had two darling children. You can't miss them. They each have those long Eyetalian noses."

"Roman," Dut and Mikey said at the same time.

"Well, they're Catholic, so you probably won't see them, but there was poor Didi anyway, and none of us thought she'd ever remarry. She'd let herself get enormously fat. She slumped around like a common char. And now out of the blue she lands this wonderful man."

"Well, let's hope she'll be very happy," said Tom. He stared into his drink.

"I can't see how she'd miss. He's enormously rich."

I laughed and ducked off at this point. I record the next events from our later conversations, Tom's and mine.

Around us the voices rose. The din was deafening. The women tilted on their high heels, sophisticated and charming, and the men stood foursquare on planted legs, roaring in each other's faces like lions. Dut pulled back Tom's attention.

"That's 'Cougar' Roen. We served in the war together. A hell of a fighter. You'll love him," he added generously. "He's talking to my daughter, Elizabeth."

Tom's eyes flickered dutifully to the Cougar in his tweeds, but the jolt was for Elizabeth. She stood with her weight on one hip, head tilted at Roen playfully, and one hand toying

with the necklace at her throat. Tom took in her dark curls.
At that moment, as if feeling his gaze, she looked up. For one
moment she met his eyes, then pulled away. Dutton was recounting a war story concerning the Cougar's true heroism, but Tom
could hardly listen. His attention strayed to Elizabeth. He shifted
impatiently, waiting for the promised introduction and hoping she
would remain a moment longer at Roen's side. Just then Mikey's
wife, Buffie, grabbed Dutton away. Tom was left alone.

He slid along the wall. If he were a better person (he supposed), he would mingle gracefully, but he felt so removed it
was questionable if there was common ground on which to meet
these people.

"Reverend!" It was Angus. "You look like you need another drink."

"No, no." But Angus slipped the glass neatly from his hand
and vanished toward the bar, leaving him even more annoyed
with himself. Why not just say he didn't like to drink? Why
not correct the ignorant form of address? Was it a slur on himself or on the Church? Twice he had missed the opportunity.
As for what it said about himself, his integrity—

"Do you always talk to yourself?" Elizabeth was smiling up
at him wickedly, washing him with her warm laugh. "Practic-
ing a sermon perhaps?"

"One to myself." He laughed into those gray eyes.

"Here's your drink," Angus said. "Oh, I see you've met
my wife." He put one arm around her shoulder, and Tom noted
the almost imperceptible stiffening of her body. "Elizabeth, this
is the new minister at Trinity."

"I know." Then to Tom: "I don't know your name."

"Thomas Buckford."

"Gonna reform us all, eh?" laughed Angus. "You got a big job ahead."

"Oh, I doubt if I can reform anyone, Mr. McEwen." He smiled at Angus. "I'm not too good at reforms."

"What do you do?" Elizabeth asked.

"What?" The question caught him unawares.

"What *do* you do?"

"Well, I'm the rector. At Trinity."

"Yes, but what do you *do*?" Her voice took on an insistent, rising tone. He backed away a step, uncertain under her attack. She was looking up at him with passionate intensity, and he laughed, embarrassed.

"I serve the Church." He shrugged helplessly. "I minister."

"Yes, well, what does that mean? Nothing! I mean, what do you *do*?"

"He's a goddamn minister, for Christ's sake," said Angus, oblivious to the pun. "You gotta excuse my wife, Reverend. She's not too bright sometimes." Elizabeth stopped as if struck, stared from one to the other, then turned on her heel and left.

"Son of a bitch, I'm sorry. She gets odd sometimes." Angus dropped his voice. "I think it's because she can't have children, you know?" His forehead wrinkled with his own pain. "I mean, we have a boy. He's in a mental institution, though. Retarded. And she's had two miscarriages. That's hard on a woman, you know?" He glanced for approval at Tom. "One day she's nice and calm and happy, and the next for no reason at all she breaks out like that." He laughed. "Imagine, asking what you do, as if she's never been in church. I mean, not that we *go* to church, you understand," he confided. "I mean, I wouldn't want to lead you astray, make you think that we're part of your, um, flock. I don't have much truck with the church myself."

Tom held up one hand to interrupt, but Angus didn't seem to notice in the outpouring of his confession. "I mean, we were married in church," he was saying, "and my son was baptized. I stand by the forms, Christ. But to *go* there, like some people do every Sunday, and sing off-key to a dreary organ. And then all the people in church are so old. Have you noticed that? Old people go to church. I've thought about that a lot," he said, gulping his drink. "I think it's cuz they're suddenly aware they're going to die. See, when you're young and healthy, you don't have any need for church. You have years and years to go yet, and unless you're hit by a car or have a hunting accident like my friend Bob Dillinby had last month—God, that was tragic—blew off his head with a shotgun. And he was only thirty-two, only four years younger than me. It wasn't suicide. I'm sure."

"Yes, well."

"Anyway, what I was meaning to say is—" He paused, overcome by feeling. "I mean, I think you guys do a great job. Great. You do a real service in the world, taking care of weddings and funerals and giving sermons all the time and comforting people who are dying. God knows, it can't be pleasant! Jesus!" He looked soberly at Tom. When he shook his head, his heavy jowls shivered. "So." He laughed, clapping Tom good-naturedly on the back. "Keep up the good work."

"Well, thank you." Tom could hardly suppress a laugh, though whether it was at Angus or himself he didn't know.

"Can I freshen your drink?" asked Angus. "It's good bourbon. Nothing but the best for my father-in-law."

"No, thank you. You'd drink me right under the table, and that wouldn't look so good."

Angus beamed with pleasure at the compliment. "Well, I won't press you," he said generously. "It's true I can drink all night, and no one'd know. But that's just"—he struck his stomach with satisfaction—"*constitution.*" He leaned forward, causing Tom to step back at his breath. "Then I'll just get meself a wee draught."

Again Tom was alone. To his left, off a short hall, he could see the conservatory. No one would miss him. The conservatory, with its red-tile floor and arched glass, was filled with tubs of gardenias and small star-shaped ivy, geraniums, and camellias. Cool and damp, the place smelled of moisture and earth.

From the conservatory he opened the door to the lawns, for which Walnut Grove is known. Behind him rose the roar of voices, in which a single laugh erupted, a dazzlement dancing on the flood of their hilarity.

Autumn is a fickle time. In one day the weather had turned from July heat to winter cold. Tom had walked out in only his jacket, and that's the only explanation any of us could come up with later for what he did. It must have been that, plain and simple: he'd gotten cold, though when I once asked him about it, he threw back his head, roared with laughter and allowed as how he'd always been a forgetful guy. Did he do it purposely? He said he'd just circled back to the house and didn't notice, as he pushed open the door, that it led into the kitchen; and when he had stepped inside, assailed by warmth and the delicious odors from steaming pots, he gave a smile surpassing sweet at the astonished faces of the two black women there.

"Good afternoon," he said.

Meanwhile Elizabeth was furious with herself. She stalked out
of the living room, one fist clenched. She felt like bursting into
tears. Whatever had gotten into her, to attack a perfect stranger
with such stupid questions! As if everyone didn't know what a
minister did! Elizabeth, who had not set foot in church for
years, viewed religion with contempt. To her, it was a corporate
bureaucracy, the major purpose of which was identical to that
of any bureaucracy: its own perpetuation. Its main function (she
had often argued over the dinner table) was the acquisition of
wealth, and the fact that the Church displayed its gilt and gold
in its Bishops' robes ("Oh, come now, Lizzie, you—") and that
it acquired wealth by using its hierophants to prey (her voice
rising above the dissent) on those weakened by sorrow and
pain—was no better than witchcraft! Yes! Compliance wrung
out with duplicitous promises of eternal bliss! Psychic subjugation is no less reprehensible (she would be shouting over the
howls by now) than the crushing of a people by military might!
    Religion, God—yes, and God's treatment of her little son—
Elizabeth left to others. All this was racing through her mind
in a single chord, one resonant organ note swelled by her cut
at Angus' hands. She could feel a throb in her chest, like a
small animal burrowing. She knew she was reacting out of all
proportion to the cause, but she had no intention of sitting
during lunch next to that man. Her high heels cracked like
whips against the hardwood floors as she made her way to the
dining room.
    When she picked up her placecard, she was surprised to
find that her fingers were shaking. She circled the table, noting
her mother's formal seating, protocol-proper. She became in-

creasingly annoyed. Why were things so fixed? The next moment she was plucking at the cards. It was the work of only a
few minutes to change the seating of almost every person at
the table. As she left, she glanced back with malicious delight.
The former ambassador, the guest of honor, was buried mid-
table, with no distinction; Cougar Roen was next to Elizabeth,
while Mr. Buckford was as far from her as it was possible for
two people to be when lunching at an oval table for fourteen.

Her mother found her in the hallway.

"Dear, have you seen Mr. Buckford?"

"I certainly have," answered Lizzie with a toss of her head.
"And what a mouse!"

Carolyn was not amused. "Lunch is an hour late and he's
gone off, God knows where. Dear—" She put one arm around
her daughter's shoulder. "I thought I saw him, I can't imagine
why, walking across the lawn. I could have been mistaken, but
do be a darling and run outside and see if he's there. I'm going
to the kitchen. I can't imagine what's holding things up," she
continued, her voice rising with strain. "There's an angel," she
finished, pushing Elizabeth toward the front door, and having
delegated that responsibility, she directed her forthright steps
toward the kitchen with no idea that she would find Tom sitting comfortably at the round worktable, talking to the colored
servants of her house.

Carolyn took it hard. Why not? It was a slap in the face.
Here she was trying as hard as she could to do the right thing
in the right way, to give a nice lunch, a gift, as it were, to
everyone there; and especially it was being done for Angus and
Elizabeth. And what did she find but that no one was cooper-
ating. Angus himself was on the edge of sloshed. Elizabeth had

gone looking for the minister, himself so rude that he preferred the servants to the hosts. It was more than she could bear.

Dutton tried to calm her down. "He's just a minister, Carolyn; you can't expect him to know right from wrong." She laughed, as he had intended, and got herself enough under control to lead her guests with an evil grin to the dining room . . . where she discovered the seating all mixed up. Elizabeth was nowhere to be found, and Angus was holding the chair for Buffie Jackson, leaning over her just a trifle too solicitously. She'd thought little enough of Angus when he and Elizabeth had eloped—a playboy; and as the years passed she had felt confirmed in her awful judgment. It was hard for her to know which to feel—satisfaction at having been proved right or sorrow at her daughter's life.

She tried to straighten out the table seating with imperious commands, set protocol to rights, but though she managed to move the former ambassador properly to her right, the other guests took matters into their own hands, and all sat down wherever.

"Charlie!" she cried to Cougar Roen, who was supposed to be on her other side, and turning to me, she cried loudly, "I don't want you there!" But it was too late. The war hero had seated himself with happy informality halfway down the table, and I ended up on Carolyn's left.

She sat stiffly at the table, therefore, back straight, her hooded eyes avoiding Thomas seated at the far end of the table between my wife, Margaret, and Cissie Roen, she was that angry with him. She addressed Bradley Schley on her right:

"It sounds so much better to call it *potage parmentier*, don't you think, than just potato soup?" Her back was turned completely against me. At the time I thought it was because I was sitting where I shouldn't have; I didn't know it was because as senior warden I shared complicity in Tom's behavior.

And Elizabeth? She was down in the pasture by the pond. She had walked almost round the house, shivering in the cold air, and was about to return inside when she'd spotted a figure by the pond, a good quarter mile away. She had shaded her eyes, squinting into the sun, but for the life of her she couldn't tell if it was Tom or not. The man was picking his way among the tufts of soggy grass, his head down, his back turned.

She waved one hand furiously and hallooed to catch his attention, but he did not look up. She felt like a fool shouting across that distance. What were you supposed to yell? Halloo? Hey you? Yoo hoo?

"Goddamn it to hell!" Then she had made her way across the pasture to the pond, her high heels sinking into the god-damn grass, her stockings sure to be ruined by burrs and her shoes by cow pies.

Meanwhile Carolyn was on the alert to speak out at the first sign of Angus dropping an ice cube down Buffie's ample breasts or lifting his soup bowl in both troglodyte paws to pour hot mush down his lumberjack throat. Those were the sort of jokes Angus thought funny when he got stewed.

But Angus was on his best behavior.

"Damnedest seating I've ever seen," he said pleasantly to Buffie Jackson, who was sitting beside him and on Dutton's right. "Why are you the guest of honor?" To forestall more comments, Carolyn and Dutton, by those telepathic sema-phores common to couples long married, moved us to the next stage. As the soup was cleared, Dut *plinked* his knife against his glass.

"There is so much business to take up today," he said, "that, though we'd thought to put it off till coffee, I think we should begin. It's after two o'clock."

There was a shifting and murmuring of assent.

"Now, as you all know, we're here to discuss the founding of a school. We're in serious trouble here, and what with the present moves the government is making, we're going to be in a hell of a lot more."

"It's the destruction of our way of life," put in Billy Tyler. She was not alone in her real anguish.

"It's incompetence," said Cougar Roen loudly across the table. "Just common everyday ignorance on the part of the feds."

"No, I disagree," said the former ambassador, and everyone paused to listen to one who knew. "It's not incompetence. It's a well-meaning move undoubtedly. It's just *stupid.*" He looked around the table with a slow grin that set everyone laughing.

"It's a matter of principle, really. The first principle is that power corrupts." He nodded significantly. "And the federal government has grown more and more powerful since the War. That's all it has to do, just sit there and grow fat on our money, our taxes. . . . People sit up there in Washington. They're removed from the real world totally, and what happens is they get a little power-mad, that's all. Then a bit of demagoguery to stir up the colored, and the point is just power, pure and simple."

"Yes, but it's also a matter of States' Rights," Billy called.

"You hit it. Because what they're trying to do is take away our inalienable rights, the individual rights of the people to determine our own lives."

"We're supposed to be a republic. A federation of equal states."

"Oh, for goodness' sake! It hasn't been that since Roosevelt!" The table broke up laughing.

"What is the issue?" Tom whispered to my wife, Margaret, who whispered back:

"Schools. It's about having the same schools."

"As what?"

At this moment Elizabeth walked in, hot and flushed. She shot an angry glance around the table, sparks flying. She could be as haughty as her mother.

"Excuse me, don't trouble about me." She sat.

"Why don't we wait for just a moment," Carolyn commanded. "I'll ring for Bermuda to pass the lamb. Are you all right, dear?"

"I'm just fine." Lizzie's voice curled with anger. "Don't let me disturb you. I was just out looking for . . . someone."

When she entered, I saw Tom lift his head with a broad, open smile, as if delighted to see her, but she turned pointedly to talk to Charlie "Cougar" Roen.

Bermuda passed the lamb, and Mary served the carrots and butter beans and sauces. Everyone was quiet until the two servants departed again. Then Ambassador Bradley Schley spoke up.

"The matter is plain as the nose on your face. With this Supreme Court decision," he said, meaning *Brown* v. *Board of Education*, "they're trying to destroy purposely and maliciously our way of life. I don't think there's a man or woman who would want his daughter to marry a Negro, and I don't think we need to say that that's exactly what all this is about. It's planned homogenization—"

"Genocide," murmured Mikey Jackson sweetly.

"I disagree." The Cougar spoke. "I've seen genocide, but miscegenation . . ."

"I'd call it genocide! We can call a spade a spade!" the Ambassador shot back, and someone laughed.

"Gentlemen." Dutton cut off the impending quarrel. "The question concerns the founding of a school. We have here at this table an extraordinary group. Bradley Schley"—lifting his glass to the Ambassador—"is a renowned lawyer. We have a real estate expert." He nodded at Angus, still surprisingly on his good behavior. "We have an educator in the person of Cassandra Roen, who was the assistant dean of a girl's private seminary before my old friend Charlie was fortunate enough to cross her path."

"Well, my work in education was some time ago," she demurred.

"Still, you have an expertise. We have financial experts, including my colleagues in this community and myself, sound, investment-oriented men. I am on the board of the Bank of Naughton, as is John Woods. And we have a gentleman of the press."

"And you have a minister," Elizabeth drawled.

Dut smiled, a little perplexed, as if he could not remember why Tom had been included in the group.

"The Church gives it all legitimacy." She leaned across to me, all high spirits. "The Church's blessing on the project."

"Aren't you in favor of this?" I asked, surprised.

"I really don't have any opinion. Angus is all gung ho. But look, we don't have children in the public schools. I don't know what business it is of ours."

"What we have gathered here at this table," Dutton continued, "is the germ of a school. Now, we all live here, and it is not pleasant for any of us to see the National Guard forcing Negro children into our schools."

All this time Tom sat with his eyes fixed on his plate, and only the hunch of his shoulders giving any indication of his tension. I cursed myself for my stupidity: that no one on the vestry had thought to ask his views on race! I tried to catch his eye, but he was concentrating on his food.

"Well, it's just impossible to believe," Buffie was saying. Dut was so moved that he began to stammer.

"I never thought I'd live to see the day—I never thought— Angus, this is your baby. Do you want to tell about the school?"

Angus rose at his place and smiled happily round the table, enjoying the limelight. "What we want to do, what many of us think *needs* to be done, needs to be done," he repeated, "is to establish the Naughton School for Exceptional Children. It's to be a haven for the brightest kids, for kids with a love of learning and the . . . the values that—and so forth," he finished lamely. "So after lunch, Tony Reischetz is coming over. He's the head of the chamber of commerce and he can answer any questions. But we need financial help. We can all think of it as a contribution to the differences between men, to the glory of distinctiveness and of Jeffersonian libertarianism," he con-cluded grandly, overturning with one enthusiastic gesture his wineglass.

Buffie leapt to her feet to avoid the wine spilling down the table onto her dress, and Angus, apologizing profusely, was rubbing at her skirts with his napkin and then her waist and then her shoulders and breasts, until it was suddenly clear that he was creating the mayhem. She burst out laughing, flattered.

"Now, stop that!"

Carolyn rang her little silver bell for the maid, while Angus and Buffie, stifling their laughter, poured an entire salt cellar over the wine spill on the placemats.

"It takes the stain completely out," laughed Buffie. "Hand me that one down there, John."

"I'm sure it will be all right," said Carolyn stiffly. "Don't give it a thought."

Eventually the table quieted down, and the fund-raising began. It was a poker game, a potlatch. The smoke hung heavy in the room. Billy Tyler pledged $25,000 to the school outright. The bank, two of whose directors were present, committed itself to a six-figure loan, and Cissie Roen agreed to form a search committee for a suitable head of the school. That left only real estate, which Angus' firm was checking out. He named two possible sites, one being the old Foster estate. Computing his commission, I suddenly understood his interest in States' Rights.

"Why don't you use the church?" Elizabeth spoke up.

A stunned silence followed. Tom lifted his eyes slowly, in surprise, to hers, which met him in open challenge.

"Why, that's a fabulous idea!" Billy Tyler broke the pause. "There you are with all this space just going to waste—halls and extra rooms. It's never used."

"Well, I never—"

"Elizabeth, sometimes you have the best—"

Everyone was talking at once. Angus' face had turned a bright beet red. He'd swallowed an egg. Tom turned from one to another, listening contemplatively. A curious little smile danced on his lips, and I realized I had no idea if it was a smile of agreement or dissent. I had the uncomfortable idea he was smiling at something we could not see, as if he understood at a level we did not comprehend.

"It would even help the contributions," said Ambassador Schley.

"Well, maybe the Reverend doesn't like the idea." Angus pushed back his chair.

"We'd have to take it up in the vestry," I intervened. "I'm not sure this is a question the rector can decide alone."

"Oh, no, no." Elizabeth laughed. "I wouldn't want the rector to decide anything alone. Oh, my goodness, no."

"Gracious, Lizzie, what's got into you?"

"Nothing." She put one fragile hand to her throat, her wide eyes as round as innocence. "I just thought the authority of the Church might be useful to your venture," she added with a laugh of such utter and enchanting warmth that we joined in relief. "It could give all kinds of things. Property. Propriety. Don't you think, Mr. Buckford? Not only classrooms, but a kind of . . . *respectability*."

His eyes sparkled with their own malicious delight. He lifted his wineglass to her. "If we're doing our job," he said, "we're anything but respectable."

We all laughed as if he'd made a joke. I can't imagine why I didn't see the warning in those words, but we'd had so much to drink that our laughter rose graciously around the table, and then the doorbell announced Tony Reischetz. With a scraping of chairs and satisfied chatter the table adjourned, to the silver pot of coffee in the living room.

Look, I know how our talk about segregation sounds today, thirty years later about. Laurie's taken me to task enough. Daughters. I won't apologize. We were biased and afraid, but we were doing the best we could. It's curious how fast our values change. It's only been some thirty years. It's not so long. I look back on my life-span of three-quarters of a century . . .

and it's gone so fast. I feel like a young man inside, thirty years old, forty, yet I can't even move into the living room without kicking up the arthritis in my knee.

Our values were under attack. This is not an apology. It's an explanation. Like everyone, we were closer to our past than to our future. Why don't people see this? Look what we had gone through in only fifty years: reared on our parents' memories of Reconstruction and living through first a World War, then the Depression, then another World War. The South was *poor* in those days. We were working just to keep our heads afloat, and maintain standards, and educate our youngsters, because we knew you couldn't do anything without an education. Every one of us was being assaulted, under siege by people telling us our ways were wrong. Newspapers. Government. Liberal Northern idealists who didn't think it worth their while to look in their own backyards, but came driving down to Mississippi and Alabama to tell perfect strangers how to live. As if we hadn't loved our Negroes. It makes me mad to think of it even now. We grew up with Negroes, played with them as children, rested in our mammies' arms, and these *children* come telling us what to think.

A lot has happened since then: Martin Luther King and marches and the assassinations of presidents and demagogues. Men have walked on the moon since then. And the scientific achievements. I think that's what changes values more than any moral ideas. The end of polio, measles, smallpox. Television. Computers. Lasers. Hell, *air-conditioning*! That's what brought the South to its feet. Seventy million Americans moved to the South since the 1950s, the greatest migration in history—and you think *that* didn't make a change?

Because, in those days, we sweltered in the heat, and we

accommodated to it: we moved slow, talked slow, didn't let ourselves get heatstroke in the rush to hurry or to change. We took naps in midday on a summer afternoon. Or went swimming. Not all this running around. Today we have Movements. Artists' Rights. Women's Rights. Civil Rights, Human Rights, Prisoners' Rights, Animal Rights, Rights to Life, Rights of Choice, Children's Rights, Homosexual Rights. Rights to Freedom. Rights of Expression. In those days we had responsibilities, not rights; and we still believed in the difference between liberty and license!

There.

I've said it. I didn't know I'd get so mad. My hands are shaking. It's Laurie who does it to me. I can imagine her reading this account, God forbid, and tossing her black mane at me with that arrogant sneer. She doesn't know that hers is a prejudice, too, or that, born earlier, she would have used that sneer down at the Club, just like Carolyn, to snub Reischetz too.

Rye Shits. Ambassador Schley had been the first to drop the name on him. He walked in now, dressed in a checked suit and white buck shoes, his wife, Angie, trailing behind. A rustle ran through the room, a subtle ripple of movement. Mikey cast his eyes down to his tasseled loafers, then up at the ceiling, as he stood at the mantel with Bradley Schley, who thrust his hands deep in his pockets and leaned back at the waist, jiggling his coins. The Cougar remained impassive, but Cissie, his wife, shifted ever so slightly to Billy Tyler, and the result was a sort of closing together in tête-à-tête. Even worse, Carolyn turned her back.

I was mortified. Any ass could see the guy felt out of place.

His wife hung back, one hand tacked shyly to his arm. Her blond hair had been done fresh for the occasion, and she teetered on heels uncomfortably high and fashionable.

"Excuse me." I dove for Angus. "Introduce me to your guests," I said, propelling him to the door, and I prayed that that moment of discourtesy had passed unnoticed. Tony wasn't one of us and you wouldn't have him in to dinner, but that didn't excuse rudeness to the man.

"I'm John Woods. So glad you could come."

Angus hung back, heavy and red-eyed. His grin slithered across his face.

"And you must be Mrs. Reischetz." I elbowed Angus out of the way.

"Angie," she whispered.

"Would you like a cup of coffee? Tony, coffee? You'll be glad to hear we've had an interesting discussion already about the school. Raised some money for you too."

"You want a drink?" Angus asked, remembering what he could of manners.

I led Angie to the table for coffee, her husband following. She lifted her eyes, awed at the gleaming, beeswaxed antiques, the needlepoint-cushioned room. Tony, on the other hand, seemed to swell. It made me wince to see him with his demitasse balanced on his palm and one hand driven deep in his pocket, rattling his silver like the Ambassador. I wanted to shake the man. These airs were not for him.

Suddenly Dut's two black Labradors burst in, their tails whipping furiously at the chair legs and their noses sniffing up each guest's hands and shoes. Carolyn shouted gaily:

"Oh, the dogs! Get them out! Out!"

The men laughed and thumped the canine ribs gladly. The two animals circled the room till they both came up to Tom, who was sitting on a stool.

"Hey, hey." He grabbed his coffee cup to save it from their whiplash tails.

Dut took one by the collar and shooed him outside, but the other lay down beside Tom and rested her head on his leg. Tom pulled her silky ears and rubbed her throat and chest.

"She's a fine dog," he said; and next to his admiration for the harness brasses inside the bar, nothing could have pleased Dut more. He was so touched that a moment later he peeled Elizabeth away to ask if she'd go entertain the priest.

"Oh, Daddy." She tossed her head and gave a down-turned grimace of a smile. But she went.

"You seem to have a way with dogs." She threw herself into a chair beside him. He looked up, openly pleased to have her there, and that had its own effect. She noticed with a kind of stab his blue-green eyes.

"It's true," he was saying. "It always happens. A cat, a dog, a little child—if one comes into the room, it will always come to me."

Elizabeth speaks in her diary of a wave of warmth that swept over her. She fell into his eyes, hearing his voice as if from inside a seashell or from some great distance. *Yes,* she was thinking, *if I were a cat, a child, I'd come to him.* Suddenly all she wanted to do was to crawl on to his lap and rest her head on his shoulder. Shocked, she took protection in scorn that he would degrade his gift—this warmth—with such an easy boast. She almost said as much, lashing out contemptuously, but held her tongue. In a moment she answered.

"Well, that shows the child or animal likes you. It doesn't

necessarily mean you love—that you like it." She stumbled on the words.

"Oh, you'd have to," he answered easily. "It only comes in response to that."

"What? Do you mean the dog comes over *because* you love her?"

Still he stroked the black Lab's ears. "It wouldn't come because of hate." He could have said more, for he didn't feel loving just then, but confused and resentful of the situation he found himself in and of the people in that room. So why would the dog come to him? He didn't know. He only knew how grateful he felt for the bitch's presence.

"Animals don't have logic or analytical faculties," he said, "but I think in some ways they're smarter than us. Animals know things, they *feel* when a person's angry or suffering."

"But those have nothing to do with love," Elizabeth pressed him.

"No?" He didn't argue. "Well, you may be right."

What was happening to her? She felt a vast contentment in his presence. Yet, what was he doing but sitting there petting the dog with an occasional sidelong glance at her, his long, square-tipped fingers absently moving across the animal's soft hair. The dog's brown eyes drooped shut, and her mouth parted, exposing her white teeth.

"So, what do you think of the school?" Elizabeth asked defiantly, rising to her feet. She had to pull herself together.

"What do you mean?"

"I mean, what do you think of the idea? Will you sponsor it?" she pushed aggressively.

He stroked the dog a moment more, then gave a final pat.

"You know, I'm new here. I know almost nothing at all yet. In fact, I figure it will take me a year before I'm familiar enough with the people in the parish and with the . . . conditions that govern it so that I'm able to do a decent job. At this point I'm just watching."

She sat down again, surprised. Everyone she knew had definite opinions about almost every subject on earth, and, if they had no knowledge in particular, it never hindered the expression of a point of view. Was he so passive?

"Certainly I'm in favor of education," he continued. "That's not a problem. But it will take me a little while to understand the motivations behind this school and whether the church should be—"

"It's simple what's motivating it," she broke in angrily. "It's the integration decision. Why should integration be forced down our throats? It's a free country!" she continued, spouting all the words that she had heard since childhood. "We don't want people telling us how to raise our children. Soon it will get right down to book burning! They'll start telling us what we can read and what we can't."

"Do so many people tell you what to do?"

"Well, not *me* perhaps," she said. "But yes, people are always telling us what to do. And now here is one more layer of *oughts*, as if we don't all know right from wrong." She tried to control her voice, realizing how tremulous it sounded in her passion.

"I used to think I knew that too. But I don't anymore."

"Don't know right from wrong?"

"I used to think I knew, but as I get older it all seems so much more complicated. I so approve of the diversity of things."

Elizabeth, who had been reared to believe that everything

in the world can be divided into good/bad, right/wrong, proper/ improper, moral/immoral, was startled.

"But are you saying, then, there's no such thing as good and bad?"

"No, but often rules are made up by society, aren't they? They're social rules, or conditioning to make families or governments function without friction. That's why society imposes rules of right and wrong. But often what's wrong is actually right and we'd certainly be impoverished if we had no criminals, don't you think? They do us all a service." He smiled at her.

"Whatever do you mean?"

"For one thing, criminals make us feel virtuous—they satisfy our righteous indignation. Then, too, we can hear of murders by hatchet or strangulation or gunshot, or robberies or other crimes—and we are vicariously titillated, since some part of us might like to do the same."

"But surely you aren't saying the world is a better place because of crime! Why, you're a minister!"

"And then, thirdly," he continued, "right from wrong is so unclear, isn't it? You do one thing that everyone says is right, and it turns out to do much harm; and you do another act that everyone says is wrong and—"

"Well, Hitler—"

"Oh, well, Hitler." He waved one hand. "I won't argue that. We could argue the school-desegregation issue, if you wish. Or following your conscience. But this is not the time or place. Anyway, all I'm saying is it's unclear to me. Everything's unclear. I don't know anything anymore. As for being a minister, I'm probably the worst person you could pick to minister to your wounds, I have so many of my own."

Elizabeth stared at him. She had never known anyone who publicly admitted being vulnerable or hurt.

"Finally, I'm not sure it isn't all part of the same gigantic Plan. Light. Dark. Right. Wrong. You can't have one without the other, so they must need each other. Without the shadow, you can't see the light. Without wrong, you don't even know what's right. But it changes every moment. And then of course"—He looked over at her, and shrugged lightly—"it gives us the chance to choose, doesn't it? That's our Free Will. This minute, right now, will I choose good or bad? Light or dark? I get to choose over and over, but always blindly, since I don't know the Grand Scheme. That's what it means to be a human."

They were both silent.

"There are some theologians who say we don't even have Free Will: the choice is up to God, too, or fate. Or our past deeds. Did you know that the word *sin* only means 'to miss the mark'? Like an arrow in the target. You missed. It's about that important." And he took his hands away from the dog and laughed outright in her eyes. "If I were a brilliant philosopher, I'd write it all down and be famous."

"Or crucified," she laughed.

Meanwhile Ambassador Bradley Schley had fallen into conversation with Tony and Angus. I joined in.

"Your school's looking good," he said. "Damned fine idea. You heard we're making it part of the church?"

"The church?" asked Tony, surprised.

"Well, that's not settled yet." Angus leaned in heavily. A fine beading of sweat covered his brow.

"What church?"

"Why, Trinity. The Episcopal church. It's a splendid idea.

It'll save one hell of a lot of money to use the classrooms in the parish hall."

"It's not settled." Angus' voice rose anxiously. "We'll have to think about it. There are a lot of things against it. You don't want a religious school." He turned to Tony pleadingly. "Do you? Have the Church giving instruction to the kids?"

Now it was the Ambassador's turn for surprise. "What do you mean? The Church wouldn't instruct. And if it did, what better learning can you get? It's all decided—"

"Who decided on the Episcopal church? When was this decided?" Tony asked.

I started to explain, but Angus was shouting. "I think it's a lousy idea! I don't know what you think you're doing. I've found a perfect piece of property up in the Foster place. I can get it. With just a couple hundred thousand it'll make a terrific school. And now you—"

"Hell, this'll save money."

"You don't know that! You don't know that! Tony, don't let them do this. You all don't want a church school. What about separation of Church and State? It's misceg—it's seg—miscegregation," he finished confusedly.

"I don't know who decided this," said Tony, "but if we're going with a church, why not Our Lady of Mercy?"

"Catholic?"

"Or Baptist. Or Methodist!" Tony's voice lifted angrily. "Naughton has a bigger Baptist population than—"

"He's right," said Angus. "You all don't want to send your kids to an Episcopalian—"

"Look." Bradley was getting hot. "You come to us for money. You ask us to pledge thousands of dollars, and when we come up with a way to solve a problem, you ought to listen.

Trinity has a large plant. It's underutilized. It would be good for the Church and good for—"

"Now, if it were interdenominational . . ."

"The Foster place is—" Angus sputtered in his distress. "You can't come in. You all can't come in like this and push people around—" He shoved the Ambassador. Bradley reeled, caught himself on a table.

"You goddamn drunk." He grabbed Angus, and suddenly the two were wrestling, grappling clumsily at clothes and hair.

Cassandra screamed. Carolyn rose in panic, calling, "Elizabeth! Do something. Elizabeth!" For it was Angus who was fighting. "Stop it!" Carolyn shouted. "John, stop them."

Both Tony and I were clawing at the two men, trying to separate them. A chair crashed over, then the antique end table, sending its priceless China bowl shattering to the floor.

"Angus!" Dut was shouting, and Cissie Roen, dancing nearby, was whispering under her breath to her husband, "Charlie? Charlie?" though the noise level was too high for the Cougar to hear. Elizabeth had run to the fray, where her mother grabbed her arm, scolding:

"This is your fault, Elizabeth. If you can't make him behave—"

Elizabeth broke away. "Angus." She was pulling at him too. "Stop it, stop it. What are you doing?"

He landed a blow to Bradley's jaw, sending the Ambassador spinning to the floor.

Angus wrenched free from Elizabeth's grasp. "None of this would have happened"—he turned on her—"if it weren't for you!" He surveyed the guests, head lowered, a bull at bay, his face flushed. "I know. You all think I'm such a fool. Well, everything was going fine till—"

"Angus, I—"

"Elizabeth, you get Angus out of here." Carolyn was talking almost as loudly as Angus, and Elizabeth literally jumped.

"Come on, Angus. I'll go home with you."

"I don't need you!" He flung himself through the living room door.

"Are you all right, Ambassador?" Dut was asking. "I can't apologize enough."

"Bradley," said Carolyn. "He didn't hurt you, did he?"

"Angus," I called after him. "Wait!"

"No, go ahead, you all with your project." He was struggling into his coat. "You all know so much about it, all of you. I found the Foster—I was the one—" He glared wildly round the hall. His coat on one shoulder, he wrenched the front door open. "Goddamn it all." He slammed the door behind him.

"Lizzie." Carolyn was at her elbow again. "It's all your fault! How you could let him embarrass us in that way. . . ."

"No!" She clapped both hands over her ears. "Leave me alone."

"It's all right, Lizzie." I put one arm around her shoulder. My cousin. My goddaughter.

"Oh, John." She was trembling.

I led her to a chair. "It's not your fault. Don't listen to your mother."

"John." Dut called me back to Bradley Schley and Reischetz. Everyone was talking at once, pressing around Bradley, who was loudly defending his actions and protesting that he didn't know what had gotten into the boy. I noticed Tom standing to one side, his mouth screwed up painfully, and Tony and Angie likewise stood apart, but everyone else was babbling incoherently, questioning each other on what each had seen or done about the fight: Carolyn and Margaret were picking up the shards of the vase that had been a gift from the Empress of China to one of our great-uncles in the last century. It was irreplaceable. For the next few moments I was busy soothing hurt feelings and trying to explain to Bradley that nothing had been decided about the church, that it was merely an idea, that it would need to be voted on by the vestry and the congregation before it could be done. Everyone was upset. The Ambassador left almost immediately, and the others took his lead. From out in the hall came the voices of departing guests. Angie Reischetz stood near the doorway trying to belong to the circle of women who, with endearing farewells to one another, had turned their backs on her. She bravely fought back tears.

When I looked up next, I saw Elizabeth with Tom. They sat on the sofa side by side. Between Tom's knees was the black Labrador. He was stroking its throat and chest, and she stared in fascination as Tom's long fingers wove around the dog's ears and down her neck. They said nothing. But soon Elizabeth bent over the dog as well. Her hand, too, caressed the animal's back and ribs in long, slow massage, down one foreleg and up again to the back and ribs, until the dog with a soft groan lay back, lifting her belly in ecstasy to their touch.

Gradually Elizabeth's chills began to calm. Her hands were moving in unison with Tom's over the dog, and now an extraordinary thing occurred. She felt wave after wave of warmth wash over her, like breakers, curling at the edges and passing on away, waves . . . of light. She wanted to cry. Her head dropped to the dog. Soon her trembling stopped, and she succumbed to a quiet peace, to subtle waves of warmth as their hands caressed the dog.

———

But Carolyn did not forget that Tom had preferred the kitchen help to the society of her guests and made lunch so late that Angus had gotten drunk, hit the Ambassador, and ruined her party. What was worse, Tom never had a clue of the enemy he'd made.

4

AFTER THAT THE REST UNFOLDED AS NATURALLY AS A LEAF IN spring. Stop things? You might as well have dammed a stream with mud. We got the school, and by the end of November Elizabeth had joined the board as a special liaison to Tom. In a way it tickled me, the atheist and the minister. We saw it happening right before our eyes. What we didn't know was the spiritual dimension of this strange and curious story—God, sex, waves of light.

I have their journals and diaries before me on the desk. Tom wrote business notations, or else philosophical observations, thoughts to be dropped into a sermon, and later his exquisite spiritual pain. But Elizabeth's diaries are full of anguish, passion. They are the runnels of a heart deprived.

"I am imprisoned," she wrote that fall. "I have no one to talk to. Is everyone so isolated and alone?"

She would wake up in bed early in the morning, Angus asleep beside her, and, lying curled in the warm hollow of her covers, careful not to touch and wake him, she would drift in half-sleep. And then the images would come, a jewel exploding at the edge of her mind: Tom's face lifted in an open smile

across the table toward her—a sudden flash and gone! Or the
shape of his fingers kneading the black dog's neck.

Startled awake, she would clamp the memory down with
disciplined control. She would drop her feet to the cold floor,
snapping out of dreams and purposeful to the duties of her day.
There was breakfast to make and her horse to feed, and tromp-
ing downstairs in her old red bathrobe (the cat scuttling between
her feet), picking up the newspaper, putting coffee on the stove,
she would scold herself for . . . for . . . she didn't know for what.
No matter. *It* knew, that demon part of her, *it* knew what it was
being scolded for. Angrily she'd beat the iron frying pan on the
burner, whip the pancake batter with aggressive energy.

Still she could not forget the man. It annoyed her. Neither
did she see him again. That annoyed her too.

Twice she drove past the rectory, hating herself for the act.
Once, she rode her horse round the church grounds, like a dog
sniffing at a tree. Oh, she knew what she was doing and held
herself in contempt!

Weeks passed. She began to imagine what would happen if
they met. It would be at a large cocktail party perhaps. They
would shake hands, speak a few words, and she would turn away
in boredom. "Excuse me," she would say with a brilliant smile,
and edge away. That's what would happen. Nothing. But no
one invited her to a party with Tom, and gradually she forgot
about him and the waves of warmth and light.

Then one night she saw him at the movies. She and Angus,
and their best friends, Fran and Squeaky Hamilton, had a regular date on Friday nights for dinner and the movies at the
Community Center—which was the local bijou for a few months
after the regular theatre burned down.

He was standing at the card table in the lobby set up to
take tickets. She could see only the line of his cheek, the back
of his head, but she felt her heart opening, a silly smile spreading over her face, and, to hide it, turned to Fran.

"Do you know anything about the movie?"

Her voice, too loud, rang across the lobby. Would he turn
to see her? But no, he took his wife's arm, guiding her into the
auditorium as Angus and Squeaky approached the card table.
Elizabeth looked with curiosity after the woman he had chosen
as his wife, her straight back, her thick black bun, her heavy
tweed suit with its tight cinched waist.

"Say hi to Bitsy and Frank," Angus said, waving to other
friends across the room.

"I think it's so funny," said Fran, "coming to the Community Center for a movie. Doesn't it feel odd?"

Elizabeth, moving into the auditorium, cast a quick glance
round for Mrs. Buckford's face. She took Fran's arm.

"I'm in just the mood for a good movie."

"You are!" Fran laughed. "You feel so excited, you'd think
it was your first film."

"Well, they say it's very good. Alec Guiness."

"Come on, girls. I see four seats." Angus dodged down the
aisle, sucking the two women up in his wake. They settled on
the metal folding chairs.

"Just don't move. That's the secret."

"No necking allowed." Angus reached across Elizabeth to
cuff Squeaky on the arm.

Elizabeth took the opportunity to stand again. "I have to
see who's here," she explained.

Tom was on the far side of the room, his head cocked,
listening to his wife. She had a long nose. Her hair was beau-

tiful. Tom was turning, surveying the audience himself—and quickly, before he could spot her, Elizabeth sat.

"Oh, my coat."

"Good heavens, Lizzie, watch what you're doing."

She was fumbling with her coat and gloves to resettle in her chair. She didn't know if he had seen her. The lights went out. She turned her attention to the screen, the whistled theme of *Bridge on the River Kwai*, and the men slomping through the jungle, but, even while watching the film, she was aware of the wave of happiness that swept over her—a great fondness for Fran and silly Squeaky, for her dear Angus, for all the people in this makeshift theatre, including the child who suddenly cried, "That's mine!" outraged; or another whose foot clattered unexpectedly against the metal chair.

And then she was absorbed by the film, the dynamite, the prison, the last bold, brave, doomed Burmese attempt to escape.

In no time the movie was over, and all four friends were blinking in the yellow overheads with pleased accord.

"Well, that was really good."

"Was that a true story, Squeaks?"

"I'm still weepy."

She hunched her coat over her shoulders, smiling to the others, making her own distant murmuring and wondering if anyone could see this thing that had happened to her—such happiness. She looked across the room.

Their eyes met.

His face lit up, and she tore her eyes away in confusion. She did not dare look over at him again.

She reached forward to Angus. "Give me a paw," she laughed, then gave him a quick kiss on the cheek.

"If you don't go faster," he pushed her from behind, "we'll
have to greet the minister."

But Elizabeth was graciously giving way. "You want to go
ahead?" She permitted an elderly woman to creep into the
aisle.

"Thank you, dear."

She ignored Angus' impatience, and by the planned coin-
cidence that lovers consider miracles, the two met, crushed
together in the crowd.

"Did you enjoy the film?" His voice was almost at her ear.
She did not dare look up.

"It was very nice." Her shoulder brushed his arm. Paralyzed, head down, she could think of nothing more to say.
Her eyes flashed to his face. He was taller than she'd remembered.

"I like seeing movies in the Community Center." He
grinned. "Have you been coming here long?"

"Depuis toujours." With her wide, expressive smile, she re-
sorted to French in a flippant attempt to cover up her feelings.
She was bursting. *Depuis toujours* I have been coming to the
movies. *Depuis toujours* I have seen films here since the old
movie house burned down. *Depuis toujours* I have been waiting
for you. "We come every week." She didn't know if he understood French. He put out his hand to Angus.

"Angus." And then, gracefully: "I'd like to introduce you
to my wife. Priscilla, this is Angus and Elizabeth McEwen. . . ."

"Fran and Squeaky Hamilton," she completed the introduction. "This is Dr. Buckford."

"Mister," he said. "I don't have the higher degree. Anyway, you're to call me Tom." Elizabeth watched Fran smile at
him. She turned to Priscilla.

"When did you arrive in town?" (Stupid small talk.) Priscilla's lips stretched with a chilly formality against her teeth, and Elizabeth, previously radiant with love for all the world, went cold.

"Two weeks ago," she answered. "Thomas came down first."

"I haven't seen you in church." Tom directed the statement to Elizabeth.

"No, we don't go to church," Angus intervened.

"We almost never go," she added. "I don't know when I've been last."

"I'm so sorry." He was smiling down at her. "I'd like to see you there sometime."

Then they were outside under the black, starry night. The cold air hit her nostrils. He was gone.

She shook her elbow free of Angus' grip, then, instantly contrite, tucked her hand under his arm.

"That's more comfortable," she explained.

"Who did you say that was?" asked Fran.

"He's the new minister at Trinity," said Angus.

"Oh, he was dressed like an ordinary man."

"Oh, come on," Elizabeth said stiffly as Angus covered her words:

"He is just an ordinary man. Probably acts like one too!" He slapped Fran's rump playfully. She jumped aside and batted at his hand.

"Now you stop that, Angus McEwen."

Elizabeth took deep gulps of the black night air. Never had the stars seemed so beautiful. She was hungry for stars. They hung like lanterns, glittering in the black.

"Imagine his commenting on our not going to church. God damn!"

"Well, that's his job," Squeaky said. "You gotta expect that."

"Yessirree bob!" said Angus. "Well, he can keep his God-business."

Elizabeth drifted apart from the other three.

"He's just saying he's taken note of us sinners who ain't there." Angus laughed again. "How 'bout that, Fran? I think I'll take note you're here." He nibbled at her shoulder as she squirmed away with a shriek. Elizabeth stared up at the stars and wondered why she wanted to cry.

Those weeks I saw a lot of Tom.

We met mostly over church business, at first, while I showed him the ropes, told him who was who in the community, how the books were kept, what we expected and what we didn't like. We inspected the premises together, noted the need for a new roof, checked the furnace and the antique plumbing system. He listened with a quiet reserve that I respected. His questions were direct and to the point. He was intelligent. But all throughout I also felt a distance in him.

In his good moods he liked to play and joke, but at other times he would fall into brief black moods, destructive and self-lacerating. These were hardly distinct from the vague longing, the dissatisfaction that stirred through him like a wind, when, tormented, he would spend hours alone, prowling the hills as if he could run away from himself or his parish duties. If the mood fell on him at night, he listened to music—mostly romantic: Beethoven, Gluck, Brahms, but also lesser-known composers, like Max Bruch; and then, too, he wanted to be left alone.

One evening after he'd already put in a full day's work, I

found him in the abandoned flowerbed at the rectory, hacking at buried tree roots with an axe and prying them up, big as logs, with a six-foot crowbar. The sweat was seeping down his back, staining his shirt. His face was black.

"What are you doing?" I asked.

"Attacking memories," he responded.

I laughed. I understood that one. But he didn't care to tell me which he was destroying, so I stood stuffing my pipe, looking at the sunset spreading itself across our lambent skies, and then invited him and Pris up to the house for coffee and dessert later, as Margaret had sent me to do. When I left, he returned to his labors as if cold autumn nights were not falling on us then.

One day we drove together in his Plymouth on some errand, I forget what. He sprawled in the seat, one hand on the steering wheel, driving easily. He was in a good mood on that afternoon and began to talk about his childhood.

It sounded so idyllic I tended not to believe it all, since in my experience parents are never as loving as he portrayed. But it was what he remembered, or chose to deny. He told me one thing that day—a moment only.

He had been a little boy, he said, and one early morning when his parents were still asleep he had crawled out his window and slid, in boyhood joy, down the dogwood tree to greet the day. The birds had been whistling and calling in the pearly dawn, and he had lifted his arms and cried with the birds, running and trying to fly, and then for a moment something happened. He didn't know quite what. But he was filled with such joy that he remembered that liquid moment ever since.

"Did it ever come back?"

"Nope. But I remember it. For one moment I knew I was

perfect and the world was perfect and everything was *fine*. I wish I felt it now. I think that moment had something to do with my decision to go into the ministry."

"What happened then?"

"Nothing. I went inside and ate breakfast and never said a word to anyone. Then I grew up and went to school and had the bejesus beaten out of me the way we all do. Hated school. Thought I'd be a vet, but disliked the studies. I like animals, but. . . . And then I opted for the ministry. Maybe it was a bad decision."

"Did you have a calling?" I asked, curious, for I've always wondered about these men who go into the ministry, called by God. Did they hear a voice?

He laughed. "I thought I did. A nudge anyway." And he gave a grimace of distaste, for himself or seminary I wasn't sure.

His mother died of cancer while he was in seminary, and his father in a car accident within the year. "I've always thought that accident happened because he was so lonely once she'd gone," said Tom. "I don't mean that he committed suicide, but that he was just distracted by grief, not careful. And I was too. I missed my mother. Those were hard times for me." It was in seminary that he had met Priscilla, the determined daughter of one of the professors. She had taken him under her wing, and before he knew quite what had happened, he found himself engaged. "And I've been toeing the mark ever since," he said, but his laugh had an edge to it. "My perfect wife."

I noted a certain innocence and even passivity to his behavior, but I know a lot of men who've let the women lead them to the altar. I was more interested in his wild-oats days, when his mother was alive, when he had dreamed of heroically running away to the Spanish Civil War and, instead, had dutifully finished college and become an agnostic for two years under the influence of intellectual thought and a particular girl he'd fallen for. She had run off with someone else, though, to his dismay and hurt. Later he entered seminary and met Pris and so on. Later still, he served in the Second World War, in Europe, as a chaplain, and I know only that he was aghast and hurt by what he saw in those brief months. He'd led a sheltered life.

But he had me laughing that afternoon. Tom had a way about him. He had charm. He genuinely liked people, despite his need for solitude, and he could laugh at himself.

If he had business with Carolyn or General Shriver, all prickles and defensive aggression, he'd wink and clap one hand over his mouth: "The closed mouth gathers no feet!" he'd say.

I enjoyed his company. Being with him made me feel good, though I never felt for him the open adoration of some, like Natalie Williams, his secretary, who later, in the midst of the controversy, claimed to have come on him praying in the church one evening and seen light flaming off his hair and hands, Saint Elmo's fire, flaring in the dusky church.

Of course we took it with a grain of salt. We'd all known Natalie for a long time.

Only later did I learn how isolated he felt. He never talked about it. Instead he threw himself into church business, especially finances, which were in an abysmal state. It was money that made his third and last enemy in the triumvirate.

General G. Scully Shriver was in his fifties. His forehead curved back to his balding crown. He was a hawk with that downturned sneer clamped over his cigar. He had burning eyes. I could not meet his eyes. I found myself, dog-like, turning aside rather than checking his glance. Shriver, born a Catholic, had converted to Episcopalian as a wedding present to his bride. She'd been appalled. She never wanted it, but Butch prided himself on quickness of decision—once done, never regretted. A two-star general by the end of the war and a widower (translation: eligible bachelor), he had retired to the Valley to raise cattle. On his arrival he built an A-bomb shelter, which he stocked with food, cots, blankets, clothing, books, a hi-fi, and exercise equipment. He hooked it into its own well and fashioned a primitive sewage-disposal system. Then he armed it against the neighbors who would surely flock there in a holocaust.

He was treasurer at Trinity Church.

The week after Tom arrived, Butch had dropped five thousand dollars in his lap, to spend, he said, on a scholarship for some deserving kid in school.

Tom's mind reeled. He was humbled by that generosity and by shame at his earlier dislike of the man. He had watched with fascination as the General's pen scrawled strong black lines across the check.

"Here you are," said Butch, smiling on his cigar.

"I'll find you someone." Tom spoke warmly. "I'll find the best child in this parish to give the money to. My God! It's an entire college education."

I think that's why he was so angry when Butch later accosted him in the parish hall.

He ushered the General into his cluttered office.

Butch threw himself onto the cracked black-leather couch. "I've been thinking about that donation I gave you."

"So have I." Tom laughed. "I haven't found the candidate yet, but—"

"I've been thinking," Shriver interrupted, "that I know who should get it."

"Oh?"

"My boy." He pulled out a cigar and ran it through his fingers tenderly, a gesture that irritated Tom. "He wants to go to Princeton."

"Your son?"

"Graduates this spring from the military academy. He's a perfect applicant for this scholarship."

"Princeton."

"It's perfect," explained Butch, lighting up. "The money goes straight from you to the school. It's yours to spend. And when you do that, I'll give you half as much again for the church roof."

For a moment Tom could not move. Then he was on his feet.

"Get out."

"What?"

"I won't have you launder your money through the church!" His voice was shaky. "You want to use Trinity for a tax-deductible contribution to pay your son's tuition—"

"Tom, everybody wins."

"A charitable contribution."

"You don't have to say who—"

"Listen, I don't know who's going to get the money, but it is not some rich man's son who can afford Princeton or Yale. There are people living in this parish who support themselves on several hundred dollars a year, General."

"Well, of course if you're going to count Negroes!" shouted Shriver. "Or tenant farmers. I am not donating this money to be given away to Negroes."

"I am speaking of living, breathing human beings."

"If you think I gave that money to go to—"

"It's mine," snapped Tom. "It's in my bank account, to be spent at my discretion, as you pointed out. You may rest assured it will not go to waste."

"I can cancel the check."

"It's cleared." He spoke between his teeth. "And I have no intention of giving it back. It was freely donated to the church. You gave the money to God's work." He stopped before Butch. "Everyone in Naughton knows about it now. I've heard people talking about it over at the nursing home, praising your generosity. And I was first among them. Oh, yes, I was undone by your offer," he continued, striding up and down his office. "I suggest that you leave," he said angrily. "We will never speak of this again. What happened today will rest between you and me and your God."

"I won't have it," cried Shriver. "Do you know what you're doing?"

"You've given it away," said Tom, and made his third enemy with those words.

When Tom closed the door on Shriver that afternoon, he was so angry he smashed his fist onto his desk and then against the wall. He recoiled. His hand throbbed; he was so angry, he hardly noticed. He closed the office and hiked up behind the parish hall along the hill, walking out his frustration and rage. Almost running, breathing hard. He hated Naughton. Hated the people. Hated his wife for bringing him here. Hated himself for hating—or worse, for having caved in to Pris's imprecations, when he knew he didn't belong. . . .

He walked up past the old stone hay barn, which had been

a fort in the French and Indian wars, one large room, with walls three feet thick and little gun-slits for windows.

He knew he was taking out his dissatisfaction on his wife, and it only made him dislike himself the more. He hurt. He hurt. It was the dryness. Dry prayers. A scratching, scraping heart.

"Help me, God, help me," he repeated as he slipped through a post-and-rail fence and strode on, over the pastures. He was Heathcliff on the moors, fighting his soul. His pleas to God were hollow because he wasn't sure where he stood with God, or whether he believed in God. He felt no connection anymore with God, and maybe that hurt worst of all. There was a time (and not too long ago) when he could pray wherever he was standing and feel a kind of light spread through him—or, if not light, then a lightening of his burdens, a sense of relief or release—pure knowledge that everything would be all right. Now nothing happened either when he prayed or when he conducted a service. He felt empty. A fraud.

It was even worse because he had once felt that juice, as he called it, of a compassionate universe.

"I'm dead," he muttered to himself, striding over the scrubby hillside. "Like them."

Being the man he was, and hard on himself, he took the blame for his dryness. "God can't leave me. But I can leave Him. And if I don't feel the presence of God anymore, it's because I don't practice." Practice the Presence of God, he meant, as in the little book by Brother Lawrence. But in truth he didn't want to practice the Presence of God; he was angry, and God could jolly well come to him for a change.

" 'Nell mezzo del camin di nostra vita,' " he quoted to himself from the opening lines of Dante's *Inferno*. He didn't know any more than this by heart. But he felt exactly that. "In the middle of the journey of my life, I found myself in a dark and savage wilderness . . . the very memory of which revives my fear . . ." Only, Dante had gotten out, and Tom was right there in the middle of the terror, working in pretty Naughton.

By then he had reached the top of the little mountain—a big hill, really—above the parish hall, and the valley spread out placid and sweet below him, its streambeds marked by the trees and brush hanging over the banks. He could see the light traffic on the Joppa Road below and, across the way, a lone car chugging up Big Top, the mountain he had come rattling down only a few weeks earlier, into the valley of serpents.

"I should have taken his offer," he thought, "and made him give me double for the church, and gotten us out of debt. Fool that I am." And he began to wonder if he could go back to Shriver, but the thought of the man grinning at him over his cigar, triumphant, having reduced Tom to that level, was too much. "I'd be his dog," he thought.

"Help me, God," he prayed again, dry thoughts. "Get me out of this. Or else, be with me—show me what to do. Let me love again." That was the problem. He couldn't love. That was hell itself.

The night before, he had been in his study. He wanted only to be left alone to brood. Priscilla had an uncanny way of sniffing out his moods, and sure enough she'd come in right then to settle in the Turkish chair with her sewing, pursing her lips and waiting to talk. It was all he could do to keep his temper. He couldn't bring himself to say out loud that he wanted her to leave. "Coward," he spoke to himself, for this was nothing new, this scene they were playing out. His reluctance stemmed

in part from courtesy: *I'd like you to go away; I want to be alone.*
How could he say that to his wife? Partly it stemmed from
knowledge of Priscilla, who, in the face of such an assertion,
would stubbornly dig in to thrash things out. *Why not? Why do
you want to be alone? What are you trying to tell me?* She'd want
to *talk*, when all he wanted was his solitude. So, he had given
restless gestures with his hands, leapt to his feet, walked to the
door and back to her chair and back to the door again as if to
lead her out on the leash of his emotions. She sat, calmly mend-
ing the white linen in her lap and smiling encouragingly at him
every now and again, until he'd felt torn apart by rage and guilt,
and when he'd seen the book, facedown and open on the desk,
he had unexpectedly exploded:

"For Christ's sake! Must Philip break the spine of every
book in the house?"

He threw himself on the wet earth, then came to his feet
again, swearing at the dirt on his trousers. Mud. It was just one
more sign of how wrong his decision to come to Naughton had
been.

"Oh, God, help me," he called to the clear October air.
"Let me feel you. I'm so alone. Give me love again."

He did not return home until clear evening had fallen with the
moon coming up and glowing golden in the night. He had
reached a decision, and he set about it with malicious delight.

He was covered with mud, his shoes a sight. Priscilla
clucked and worried over him, asking repeatedly where he'd
been and whyever anyone would go off like that without telling
a soul. He had missed a number of calls. He told her he'd be
ready for dinner in fifteen minutes.

Closed in his study, he telephoned Shriver.

"I've been thinking over your proposal," he said, and he could almost hear the satisfaction as the General let out his breath.

He took a self-destructive pleasure in pushing on: "I've decided to take it up with the Board."

"What?"

"It's not a decision I should make alone, to give the money to your son. If the Board agrees—"

"No, no. We don't need the Board."

"—I'll give the scholarship to him. In return we'll accept your offer of a new roof."

"Goddamn you. What is this, blackmail?"

"Well, I can't give that money in good conscience to—"

"Then keep it," said Shriver, and Tom smiled grimly to himself. But as he put down the phone, he knew he'd crossed a line: he and Shriver were at war.

The effect of their mutual hatred rumbled through the vestry meetings, earth tremors growling underfoot as we prepared to sponsor or reject the proposal for a school.

Tom opposed it. "Integration is the law of the land," he said quietly. "Even if we disagree with the law, we must abide by it." He rubbed his palms together, his eyes riveted on the table. He knew he'd lose.

No sooner did Shriver understand Tom's position than he rammed the school motion through. Within a month a search committee was interviewing for a permanent headmistress, Cissy Roen acting in the interim as head. Teachers were being hired and furniture ordered by the Board; and it was a strange decision, since we still hadn't resolved the matter of money for the church roof.

————

As for Elizabeth, she threw herself into being Angus' wife with increased devotion. She cut flowers for their little house (the gatehouse to her parents' thousand-acre place). She cooked delicious meals. Each evening she bathed and dressed for dinner in a long skirt. She took pains to ask Angus about business, and she refused to listen to her nagging doubts that she was merely compensating for her guilt.

But what good did it do? It should not be difficult, she told her diary, to live dutifully on the side of right. Her mother told her constantly how she should feel or behave. The trouble was that she did not feel the things she should. One morning she looked in the mirror and saw two lines draw down her mouth and crow's feet at her eyes.

I'm getting old, she thought. *And I don't even know what it's all about.*

She did not know why she would suddenly start to cry. Riding her horse, sitting at the kitchen table in the morning sun writing in her diary, going to the country store for eggs, even doing things she enjoyed, she'd start to weep.

Yet she loved Angus tenderly. He needed her. He was having troubles now, so of course his temper was short. He was right to blame her for what happened with the school. She blamed herself. They had lost ten thousand dollars in commissions. He had gotten smashed at her mother's party, but she'd done worse. No wonder he'd stalked out, shouting at her in his hurt and fear. She understood that.

Elizabeth knew how sweet he was. She remembered the weekend she took him to her grandmother's, at Nacirema, when Angus had behaved so badly. She remembered her surge of tenderness toward him. He had seemed so vulnerable and helpless. She may have been one of the few people in the Valley

who understood his sense of gallantry. He should have lived
a hundred years ago, she thought, when brave young officers
could ride out to the Civil War and die for an honorable and
hopeless cause. She loved him for his romantic sense of justice,
his well-meaning, blundering, sweet, stupid goodness in the face
of life. And his persistent struggling against the odds. He embarrassed her. He was clumsy, and these days drinking too much.
But she was afraid too: ten thousand dollars in commissions
lost. They had no money.

If she were a better wife, she thought, she would be able to
eliminate his pain. Isn't that what her mother had always said?
A wife should always sacrifice, ease her husband's way. She
wasn't doing her job. And this was another reason why she
hated herself for thinking of Tom.

Elizabeth was not her mother's daughter for nothing.
She knew how to bully herself into submission, to apply a ruth-
less check on her needs. To her, rebellion did not imply origi-
nality, an expression of the creative life-force surging up in her.
No, just embarrassment.

One cold November day she took out her horse. Above her
the bare branches swayed like seaweed in a running tide; the
wind sounded hollow, roaring through the trees. She could see
the tangled limbs like fingers tearing at the violent clouds, yet
here below, sheltered by thick trunks, no wind blew.

She came to the place where they always galloped, and
even before she drew in the reins, her horse had broken into
his full stride, heaving up the hill with as much pleasure in the
movement as she took on his back. She stood in the stirrups,
urging him faster, "Come on, boy," she shouted in his ear, and
the big hunter stretched out, full tilt, belly to the ground, his

hot breathing filling her ears together with the saddle leather's creak. And then they had breasted the hill and were racing out of the woods into the open, yellow, winter-blasted field.

"Whoa, whoa." She pulled him to a trot. He leapt as the icy wind hit under his tail. The clouds were piling thunderously against each other in a roiling sky. Did they come together with the crunch of icebergs? If you were sensitive enough, could you hear their groans? She could have howled against the wind. She was the wind, whipping at the trees and running down the edges of chaotic time. She wanted to snag the branches of great solid oaks and bend them to the hollow roaring of her chest. What was wrong with her? If she'd had no body, she would have flown into the air, raging in the tumult of the wind. She stood in the stirrups and howled. She roared in the open windy field as her horse danced under her.

She thought that she was going mad.

One day Fran Hamilton dropped by. They had been at boarding school together and later been roommates when they worked in Washington as secretaries. Fran had worked with the Pentagon and Elizabeth at the Corcoran Gallery of Art. It seemed little short of miraculous when in the end they both married Naughton boys and returned to the Valley.

They sat at the kitchen table over coffee. Elizabeth stared into her cup, listening to Fran's happy chatter.

"Do you ever wonder what it's all about?" she blurted out.

"What what's about?"

"I don't know. Life. What are we doing? I mean, of course it's just a stupid question, isn't it?" Tears stabbed her eyes. "We're just here, and that's what it's about. But—"

"Lizzie." Fran's voice went soft in concern.

"The other day I got up and looked in the mirror." She could feel her voice rising with tension. "I was brushing my hair and I was just overcome with the thought, 'Is this all?' "

"Oh, Lizzie."

"It sounds so stupid, I know, even to ask the question, but I keep coming back to it: why are we here? To what possible purpose? I remember when I was younger. You were already married at the time, and Angus had just proposed—and I kept thinking all the time, 'Who am I? Who AM I?' I'd wake up in the middle of the night with this idea circling round me like a bat." She gave a strangled laugh. "Or I was in the center of the black pool of that question, swimming to get out."

"Lizzie."

"Just that thought: *Who am I?* I probably spent half a year worrying over that single stupid question. I remember once writing out all the combinations of answers I could think of. It was after I was married and before I got pregnant with Dunks. I wrote, 'I am the daughter of Carolyn and Dutton Page of Walnut Grove.' I wrote, 'I am a girl,' and scratched it out. 'I am a woman,' I wrote, and then, 'I am a lady,' because that was what we've always been taught, isn't it?" They laughed, their eyes meeting with shared, pained intimacy. "Finally I got the wording: 'I am female.' Which settled gender at least."

"Then I worked out all the combinations of my name. Mrs. Angus McEwen, Elizabeth Tyler Page McEwen. I wrote all the things I could think of that made me ME, and when I finished, I read over all the list, and Fran, there was no one there."

"Why, Lizzie, that's the silliest thing I've ever heard."

"No, listen, Fran. Please don't do that to me, don't deny it. My mother does that all the time. If I feel angry and resentful or whatever, she tells me it's silly to feel that way. But it's how I feel, and it doesn't go away."

"But you *know* you're someone." Fran was puzzled. She reached out to clasp her hand. "You're you. You're my friend. You're a beautiful, gentle, caring person. That's who you are."

"That's just it. I know all the faces I put on. I belong to this club or that school. I'm a product of my class and live in this town where I was raised. I do certain things. I ride my horse. I visit Dun—" She choked on her son's name.

"Anyway," she continued with a valiant smile, "I'll get a grip on myself in a moment. What I was going to say is that eight or nine years have passed since then, and I still don't know who I am. I remember one day I was so depressed, I wrote on a pad, 'My name is Elizabeth McEwen. I live in the gate-house to Walnut Grove. I am crying. Therefore I am alive.' That took all afternoon. That's what I did on that day."

In an earlier age she would have eaten clay. Or wandered to a witch-woman to turn her mermaid tail to feet. In a later decade she would have gone to a psychiatrist. But Protestants of her upbringing in Naughton did not turn to emotional phle-botomy. Breeding and grit were supposed to suffice.

"Have you told Angus how you feel?" asked Fran.

She shook her head. "He's going through his own bad times with the investment firm. What could he do anyway? I mean, the problem is in me. There's nothing wrong! My life is perfect. That's why this is so insane, Fran. It's just narcissistic self-indulgence! I hate myself for this. Look at me. I have every-thing—a loving husband. Food. Shelter. There are people in the world who are *starving*! And I have the audacity to—it's eleven o'clock in the beautiful morning, and I dare to cry about my life."

"Well, something's wrong, isn't it?"

"I'm thirty-four years old. I ride my horse and take care of Angus and visit my mother and go to stupid parties where we see the same people that we saw when we were children. It's so stupid. I keep thinking there's something more. Only there isn't."

"I think," Fran said slowly, "that you need a job. You need to get your mind off yourself.

"And make some money too." Elizabeth smiled faintly. "I'd like that. God knows, we don't have two pennies to rub together. We can't even afford the Club dues. Do you know my mother pays those?" Fran shook her head. "Angus isn't making any money, and Duncan takes up every cent. I only keep the horse because the stabling is free. I balance the bank account, and I'm a wreck all day. I mean, we're getting by," she said apologetically. "Don't think Angus isn't doing well. But things are so expensive." She laughed brightly, lying. "See how silly I've become, worrying about heat and food? Idle worry. Quite unnecessary."

That was how Elizabeth came to work for the school. In hindsight she saw more to it than chance.

Fran suggested the position. "The only thing, the pay is low," she said. "But you'll be working with an important committee. I'd love to have your help."

"Would you?"

"The only problem is you'd have to work with Tom Buckford. I know you don't like him."

"No, no, I wouldn't mind." Elizabeth ducked her head.

"You're so sweet," Fran laughed. "We all know how you feel about religion. But you just keep in mind you're helping a school and the children and Naughton, that's all, not the Church."

They toured the facilities the next day, made lists, and all the while Lizzie was watching out for Tom, who did not return until they were walking to Fran's car.

"Would you like a cup of coffee?" He shook hands with them both.

"Aren't you nice? I have to run," said Fran, as Elizabeth said:

"I'd love one." All three laughed. "We better not, then," said Elizabeth, "because, Fran, you have to give me a lift home."

"I'm driving out your way later," said Tom. "I could drop you off. Stop in a moment, won't you?"

"Well . . ."

"Then you two can finish the list," Fran added brightly, pushing the papers into Elizabeth's hands. "That's wonderful, I'll call you tomorrow then."

So Fran bounced to the car at her usual brisk clip, leaving the two alone.

He made coffee for her on the little hot plate in Natalie's office. Tom directed his attention to measuring one spoon of instant coffee into each cup, and Elizabeth admired the deliberation of his movements: no waste, no jerky lack of ease.

"Cream?"

"Do you have milk?"

"Milk!" He opened the refrigerator. "Sugar too?"

"No, thank you."

Those in love make love with common words, and commonplaces take on special depths. He handed her the cup. She

took it and sank into the scarred black-leather couch. Tom
hooked one foot through the rung of a straight-backed chair,
pulled it toward her and sat down.

"There." They sipped their coffee and for a moment were
content.

Tom broke the silence. "How have you been? I haven't
seen you in a while." As if he'd known her for years. Indeed
she felt he had. "I'm glad you're working with the school committee."

"Are you?" she said.

"Oh, I am. At least that's one nice thing the school will
bring."

"What?"

"The chance to see you."

She was amazed at his openness and glanced up in surprise,
though she felt the same.

"You didn't come to church. I kept looking for you."

"Oh, no, I don't," she said seriously. "I don't believe."

"You could have come anyway. I doubt if most of the congregation are real believers." He laughed, lighthearted.

"That must be a joy to you. 'O ye hypocrites,' " she quoted.

He sighed and shrugged. "What can I say? It's a job."

Their conversation lifted them on a tide, for it was not the
language of words that stirred them but that of the eyes. Elizabeth turned the warm cup in her hands. As for Tom, he ached
to push aside the curl that fell over her forehead, but recogniz-
ing the impossibility of so intimate an act, he drove his offending right hand into his coat pocket with a grimace, followed by
a smile, the very smile indeed, lifting the left-hand corner of
his lips, that served to ruffle her heart.

"But do you like it here?" she asked. "Are you happy?"

"Oh, well." He shrugged and smiled again.

"You don't." She jumped in.

He took a slow turn round the room. "You know, every geographical location has its own rhythm, its own inner tempo. Naughton has a different rhythm from up north. I don't mean it's bad. It's just that I don't fit in yet. It will take me a while. My body is moving at a different pace."

She frowned in concentration, not comprehending, and seeing this, he added with his quick smile, "I liked Schenectady. I had friends there. You hate to leave friends. I think it's harder to make a friend as you get older. Or perhaps as you get older, you value them more. A friend is a special gift, isn't it? A rare gift."

"It sounds like you're just lonely," she said, blunt as Carolyn.

His first reaction was to deny it, but her words hit with such force that he was seized by an ache he had not recognized before.

"Yes, well. I chose to come here. My wife wanted it. It's good for the children, I suppose. I have a daughter, Daphne. Fifteen. She's been given a scholarship at Miss Eugenia's."

"I went there. Miss E's, we called it. Get it? Miss-ease? And sometimes Miss Eu's."

"Misuse?"

They laughed together.

"I hope she likes it. I didn't much, but I've heard it's changed a lot since then."

"We'll see." He finished his coffee in one gulp. "Priscilla feels it's important for her to be brought up in the right circles."

"Is she your only child?"

"I have a boy too. Philip. He's thirteen. In the public school."

"And will you move him to Trinity when it's ready?"

"I don't approve of that!" His voice was harsh.

"You don't approve?"

"The vote went against me in the vestry. I'm not in favor of our backing a protective—"

"Why, this is a turnabout." She laughed. "The last time we talked, you didn't know right from wrong."

"Well, now I'm sure the motives are wrong. It's true. I'm weak." He smiled at her. "I vacillate. My wife accuses me of that often enough, so I expect she's correct. I don't know right from wrong in an ultimate sense."

"Then how do you know whether you approve or not?"

"When I say I don't know right from wrong, I'm talking about the results of an act. I see this all the time, and the more I see, the more I marvel at the ways of God. We were talking about this at your mother's lunch. A man does horrible things— the unforgivable—and out of it, flowers bloom. We are given such opportunities for heroism and love that you wonder if that's not the purpose of all life. Or you see the reverse, which I find equally incomprehensible. A person acts from his finest core—and the result is destruction and damage. How do I know what's good or bad?"

"That may be," said Elizabeth with a toss of her head. "But it doesn't mean you don't know how to *act*. Or right from wrong. Wrong does harm."

"I've never met a man yet," he laughed, "who didn't believe that whatever he was doing at the time was right. Anyone could name a thousand good, solid reasons why he should be doing just what he wanted to do, and just what he intended to do anyway. Let me try again. I believe that people are basically good. We try. We blunder along doing the best we can, often bungling the job, but we can never know if what we do will have a good or a bad result. Okay? We only know our intention. But the action merely *is*, a neutral fact containing within it the possibility of producing both happy and unhappy results, which we name 'good' or 'bad,' according to our values. No one knows, in committing the act, what the true outcome will be. All we can know is whether we act from purity of intent, in generosity, with innocence and simplicity. Do you understand? We are responsible for our intentions but not for the consequences of our acts, or how others use them, or whether they have good or bad results.''

"Well, I don't see," she interrupted so quickly she did not hear the last words, "why you'd oppose the school? It can as easily have a good effect as bad.''

"Exactly!" He threw himself back into his chair. "It's just that the motives for establishing it, from what I can see, are wrong.''

"Aha! So you do use those words!''

"Of course I use those words. You think a minister can avoid the use of *right* and *wrong*?" He laughed again. "The wrong in the motive," he continued seriously, "is to keep outsiders out. But what goes round comes round. And the result will be to shut ourselves off from our experience, to imprison ourselves in shallowness. We build protective walls and behind these walls of white superiority protect ourselves from knowledge of ourselves. . . .''

"Oh, I thought it was to protect our values!" she shot back.

"If these values have value, why do we keep them from others? And won't they last independent of protection?''

"But that's nonsense. You always have to protect the things of highest value. I'm not talking about possessions," she said passionately. "But ideals. Abstractions. Freedom of speech. States' Rights."

"And individual rights? Rights to happiness? Education?"

"Yes, of course, individual rights too. Yes," she answered urgently.

"And the rights of all people equally to these things?"

"Of course."

"Then why deny them by color? Or to outsiders? Or to poor people? Or the dispossessed?"

"Look, I have nothing against Negroes." She bristled. "I grew up with colored people. In the South we can't make the distinction. It's—"

"I know, it's deep tribal behavior," he said. "Ducks will peck an intruder duck to death if it tries to enter the flock. It's instinctual. The intruder smells different. But we're not ducks, Elizabeth. We have a higher possibility. I'm not going to argue. We've got this all-white school, and I will work to make it a success." He leaned back and closed his eyes wearily. "I won't say anything to offend the community. I'm here to serve the congregation, not to alienate it. But I do not approve of the motives for its establishment, and I don't want my boy to go there. That's the only thing I can do."

They were silent.

"It's indiscreet of me to talk like this. I'd appreciate it if you didn't spread my views around. I don't know why I'm telling you."

"Because I'm your friend," she said staunchly.

"You are. Yes."

Now it was her turn to prowl the office. To cover her confusion, she picked up a cheap glass paperweight from his desk, creating a snowstorm over the Eiffel Tower inside.

"I didn't know a clergyman's life was so hard."

"It has its compensations."

"So am I doing wrong by working for the school?"

"Ah."

"That means yes?"

"That means . . . I don't know. Answering on another level, I'd say no. There's some reason why this school is being formed, God knows why. But time will make it clear."

"Why, then," she said, "you really do believe there's a God directing things?"

"The Guiding Hand? Does that make you uneasy?" Without waiting for an answer, he leaned toward her. "Just don't work for the school out of hatred, do you understand? Or out of fear. Work for it because you want to build it into a fine, great school."

"Oh."

"Anyway, I'm glad for myself you're doing it," he said simply.

"Why?"

"So I can see you." For a moment she was lost in his eyes.

Priscilla, meanwhile, was counting linens at the large chest of drawers in the back room of the church. Some were stained with the antique marks of communion wine, and others were foxed with yellow blight. She pursed her lips, for it offended her that the linens should not be sparkling white and kept in perfect order for Our Lord. Moreover they should fit properly, with the lace edge dropping a good six inches below the edge of the table and falling into graceful folds. Our Lord would like the look of that. One of these cloths, she found, seemed a castoff from some other table, for it didn't fit at all.

She laid it to one side.

Whatever did the ladies of the Altar Guild do? she thought with undisguised contempt. It was the responsibility of the ladies of the church to maintain the vestments, to sew embroidery on the minister's stole, to wash and darn the linens. Not that Priscilla had ever known a church where things went smoothly without her supervision. She realized discretion was required. She would be firm with the ladies, but kindly, as she pointed out their errors and mismanagement. She would be tolerant. This was a small church, after all, and what could be expected, when only two or three ladies did most of the work? It was the Altar Guild that set up the church for services, provided the flower arrangements, and marked the books, though this job, too, Priscilla took onto herself. She knew that Thomas came right behind her and checked before the service began to ensure that the readings would be correct. Some large churches had people to help—associates and seminarians—and not only a part-time secretary, like Natalie Williams, but full-time office help, with assistants and supporting staff as well. They would have a large Altar Guild and perhaps one or two people in charge of the flowers full-time, and none of this scrounging for an acolyte, the humiliation of which must have been what provoked Thomas recently to suggest (she shuddered to remember it) that girls should be allowed to serve.

In the third and fourth drawers of the chest Priscilla found clergy vestments: black cassocks, surplices of plain white linen, tippets, maniples, and the preaching stoles in red, white, and purple. In cleaner's bags in the closet were further clothing. She had already gone through these, making her inventory, and even found, to her delight, a white alb, the long garment worn in High Church for the celebration of the Eucharist. How magnificent it was to see the service performed with style. Sometimes Priscilla wished that the church Tom worked in could be High Church. She had always felt happy at the few favored times she had had the privilege of attending High services: the swinging of the incense, the many priests in alb and chasuble, the chanting of "Holy, Holy, Holy"—actually singing the words instead of the staid and restrained recitation that characterized Low Church style. Angels and Archangels would sing, she was sure. "Therefore with Angels and Archangels and with all the company of heaven . . ." "Holy, Holy, Holy, Lord God of Hosts . . ." she sang to herself, as she continued to examine and refold the table linens.

From there she moved to a large wardrobe. She felt calm as she worked. Caring for the vestments was work that always soothed and healed her. It was the proper place for women in the Church. There were some libertarian feminists whom she had met (one, to be exact, but where there was one, others lurked: the plural was not to be despised for literal accuracy), who believed that women should be ordained. Priscilla hoped she would never live to see the day when a woman celebrated Holy Communion or read from the Gospels or preached a sermon in her church. But women (and yes, she humbly acknowledged that she could be included in this term) were the pillars of the church, without whose work in cooking parish suppers once a month, organizing the Christmas bazaar, assisting in the services with the dressing of the church—the Christmas greens, the Easter lilies—the church could not survive. Who but women could do such things? And standing here in the bare back wardrobes of this lovely country church, she felt her life was utterly sanctified. She could open the linen closet of Saint Paul's in Schenectady or this chest here and feel herself transported merely by looking on the sparkling-white holy linen cloths. Sometimes when working on church vestments, she felt that in another life (if Christians believed in such pagan concepts, which she did not, but just imagining for a moment) she might have been one of the women to serve the Christ. Perhaps she had prepared His body for burial (because someone must have done so, though no mention is made of exactly who) and wrapped him in a clean white-linen shroud (Egyptian, perhaps, of the finest, most expensive weave). Or perhaps she had made the garment He wore when the woman in the crowd touched His hem and He had turned, feeling His powers flow into her, and had questioned her. Priscilla felt that she herself would have washed and cared for His garments, too, because they must have gotten dusty with all His walking. She was sure He would have liked them clean.

It was ritual and liturgy that pleased Priscilla most about the Church. It was in this area that she felt she could make her contribution. She loved to figure on the calendar the movable feasts and holy days. She delighted in reckoning that Septuagesima Sunday is nine weeks before Easter, that Quadragesima Sunday is six weeks before Easter, that Rogation Sunday is five weeks after Easter. She took great pleasure in looking through the prayer book to learn and mark the lessons. It pleased her to read the rules, to know the fixity of form. There was something mathematically satisfying about precision. This Sunday before Advent, morning prayer, Psalms 15, 85, 112, 113. First lesson, Ruth 1:1–17; second lesson, Col. 3:5–11. It was the sort of thing Thomas took little interest in. He chafed under such details, so that it was her pleasure to

help him out, and of course her duty too. It was her pleasure
also to suggest the hymns.

Moreover it made sense for Priscilla to make the selections,
because she had found that Tom did not have her feel for liturgy and ritual. He liked people, and she sometimes felt if he
had his way, he would probably forget the services entirely,
losing himself in simply talking to the congregation. But she
was there to keep him in line and ensure that things went
properly.

As for Trinity, Priscilla was certain she would like it here.
Already she felt it was a good choice. How else could Daphne
have gotten into Miss Eugenia's? And that was going to be a
great asset to the child. There were girls in that school from
the richest, most patrician families in the country. "The best
friends you will ever have," went the maxim, "are those you
make in boarding school."

The girls at Miss Eugenia's would have brothers and would
invite Daphne to their coming-out parties, and who could say
what fortunate alliances might be made?

Priscilla could not doubt that the call to Trinity had come
at the direct intervention of Our Lord, and for purposes she
may not understand entirely (for who can truly understand the
ways of God?), but of which she certainly approved.

Shutting the wardrobe doors behind her, turning off the
lights, she moved out into the darkened church. Dusk was falling. At the front door, she genuflected a little guiltily, for she
was certain that no one in Trinity genuflected or crossed herself—both gestures of devotion that came easily to Priscilla.
Sometime she would sit in the very back of the church (instead
of in her favorite right-hand front pew) and watch to see if
anyone genuflected. If others did (especially the gentry), then

perhaps it would not be out of place for the minister's wife to do so too. She promised herself she would sit at the back at next Sunday morning's prayers. How annoying that Trinity was such a small parish. Thomas often had to open the parish hall himself, turn on the heat, and start the coffee in the morning. But what could be expected? One hundred and fifty families attending Trinity. Nine hundred individuals. Sixty-eight pledging units. One hundred and three communicants. The collection plate brought in $2,485 last year; pledges to Endowment, $30,709; and "other" sources, meaning wills and testaments, another $151. How could Thomas afford staff help?

She closed the church door behind her. Across the way she could see the light in her husband's office. She would speak to him, she thought, taking the shortcut through the graveyard to the rectory—yes, she would speak to him about asking the ladies of the parish to help him out. If he could not afford more than one part-time secretary, there was no reason why he could not ask for volunteers to answer the telephone, and if they could type a little, all the better. That way he would not have to work so hard. Tonight, for example, after dinner she was sure that he would retire to his own little study in the rectory and continue to work, ignoring Philip and herself. Yes, she would certainly suggest that he ask among the neighbors for some volunteers.

I pause, sitting here at my rolltop desk, dizzy with disbelief. I am astonished at what flowed from my fingertips, as if it wrote itself. How did I know all that about Priscilla?

True, Margaret told me the background. Margaret was Priscilla's only friend in Naughton, and many times they folded linens in the church and placed flowers on the altar or took off the dead and dying ones. Margaret told me about Priscilla's reverence. She told me, at the time, of Pris's disdain for the ladies of the Altar Guild and how she secretly genuflected to the altar if no one was looking, and her feelings on girl acolytes and women in the Church. And yet . . . I didn't know the scene until just now. I am surprised at its . . . *truth*.

Margaret filled me in on Pris, but it's Elizabeth I know most about, what she did and thought and dreamed, and reading these private diaries, I know also what Angus or Carolyn or Tom and a lot of others said to her. Now I wonder if she'll run away with my pen too, as Priscilla did.

Outside, evening is falling. Margaret has gone to Sally Grubb's cocktail party, a pleasure I willingly declined. I've seen enough of Sally Grubb and her foolish husband, Peter, in his green golf pants and striped ties and his silly grin. All he can talk about is the stock market. It's the past that interests me now, and Elizabeth leaving the parish hall that autumn night, her coat thrown over her shoulders, not even feeling the cold as she hurried to her car, while Priscilla thought her husband alone in his office all that time working stubbornly on a sermon.

5

That night on leaving Tom, Elizabeth was floating. In all her life no one had ever used words like *purity* and *simplicity* or *innocence of intent*. No one had ever given her the impression that what she thought or felt might be correct—that she herself was pure. Pure what? Ninety-nine-one-hundredths percent pure crap. But she could feel herself trembling inside with a kind of opening of spirit. Pure *essence*. Was it just an ordinary thing that happens when one falls in love?

Angus noticed it. She glowed, and the way she stepped forth, the turn of her head, arrested him with its high, proud grace.

"You look beautiful," he said.

"Do I?" She moved beyond the reach of his encircling arm. She couldn't bear to feel his touch tonight. "Well, I feel good," she added briskly. "And you? Did you have a good day?"

"Oh, yes. It was fine. I—"

"Do you want a drink?" she interrupted. "I'll get one for you." Before he knew what had happened, she had bolted for the kitchen.

"On the rocks?" she called lightly behind her.

"I don't want a drink." He followed her into the dining room, on through the kitchen.

"No, no, stay and sit. I'll bring it to you."

Usually she did not like to see him drink. Tonight she pressed it on him, and poured one for herself to keep him company. She sat in the chair on the far side of the fireplace, keeping up a constant prattle of news and commentary.

"You're so jumpy." He patted the cushions of the couch. "C'mere."

She laughed, ignoring the invitation. "I am jumpy. You're right. Want some music? I'll put on a record."

"For God's sake, jes *set*."

"You don't have to yell. Don't tell me what to do."

"I'm not telling you what to do. You jes make me nervous, jittering about like that. You're like a Mexican jumping bean. Look at you. Your foot's jiggling. Your fingers are drumming."

"I'm sorry." She forced herself to sit still, counting one, two, three, four . . . how long would it be before she would explode? She wanted to sing, to dance. She wanted to strip and walk naked under the stars, with the black air on her bare breasts, and her naked skin and back and shoulders gleaming in the night. Instead she sat rigid by the fire, concentrating on not moving lest she trigger Angus' reproof.

"Fran and I went up to Trinity today to figure out equipment for the school," she said, trying to make conversation. "It's going to be great fun. I mean, a lot of work, but—"

"I wish to hell the Church had never got involved. It makes me sick to think about it."

Instantly she was contrite. "I'm sorry, Angus. You know I

never thought anyone would take it seriously. I just said it without thinking."

"You've got to learn to think, Elizabeth. How the hell can we keep our heads above water with you undermining me?" He had risen and was pacing before her. "Have you seen the bills this month? Wait till you see the oil bill. I need another drink."

"I'll get it." She fled to the kitchen with his glass. He followed, aching for himself, his fallen plans, for her, and wondering if he should tell her his terrific idea for Elk Creek. His eyes followed her as she dropped two ice cubes in his glass, turned on her petite swivel hips to replace the ice tray in the freezer, and, graceful as a dancer, balanced on her toes to pour a drink. She looked so beautiful tonight with color in her cheeks, eyes sparkling. He wanted to cup her buttocks in both hands and twist her body against his own. What if he just grabbed her right this minute and kissed her breathless? He'd pull down her blouse and suck her breasts.

"What's the matter?" She interrupted his dream.

"Nothing."

"You had such a funny look on your face," she said, "with your mouth all twisted to one side."

He turned his back, lest she read his thought. "I was feeling a tooth with my tongue," he lied. Because she wouldn't stand for his thoughts, he knew that.

When they were first married, he used to come in from work sometimes, and she'd be painting a room maybe or starting dinner or maybe rising naked out of the bath after an afternoon's workout with her horse. God, she was beautiful. Sometimes right then they would tumble, wherever they were—on the living room floor or in the bathroom, up against the sink. She liked it as much as he did. But now he'd reach out his hand, waiting for her to put her own in his. Maybe after a minute she'd take his hand, and then he'd draw her to him, but more often than not she'd push him away, saying it wasn't the right time. Once, he remembered, he had come in and she'd looked so yummy, he'd grabbed both her boobs. "Want a roll in the hay?" he'd laughed invitingly, raising both eyebrows with a Groucho smirk.

"Really, Angus." She'd stalked out of the room. Okay, so it was awkward. What was he to do? He wanted her. He wanted any woman. One of these days he'd be unfaithful and go find himself a broad.

Since then he had learned to control his desire. He didn't let on what he wished he could do to her. She handed him his drink and pointed to the kitchen chair.

"I have to finish dinner." She smiled, surprising him with her sweet tone. "Sit and talk with me, won't you?"

He put one arm around her neck. "We don't have to eat dinner yet." He breathed in her sweet fragrance.

"Come on, Angus. I've got things to do. Sit down and tell me about your day. What's new?" It was very courteous and polite—but firm. He took a deep, long gulp of his drink, feeling the fiery golden fluid on his tongue.

"God, that's good stuff," he said. "Your father gave us that?"

"For your birthday."

By dessert she was afraid. The evening was taking a difficult turn. After two drinks Angus grew surly. Yet without a drink he followed her around the house, tugging at her emotionally until her nerves were on edge. He clung to her in some subtle psychic way. The problem was that she cared for him, yet recently she found it horrible to be with him. She did not understand it: One day everything would be all right, and the next they would be in the middle of one of those interminable all-night sessions, in which he would pace the bedroom floor, waking her up to answer his demands.

She never knew when his moods would begin, sometimes after dinner, sometimes as she moved to go to bed. Now, as she was cleaning up after dinner, one part of her mind was already worrying about what would happen later. Angus was telling her about his idea for developing Elk Creek farm, the last of his inheritance. The idea had come to him explosively earlier in the day.

"You can get a hell of a lot of houses on that land. Get it zoned in quarter-acre lots. It's a hundred and twenty acres, so that would be four hundred eighty houses at, say, thirty thousand dollars average—there's two million bucks. 'Course you wouldn't get probably that much, and there'd be expenses, and anyway we don't need that kind of money. I want to build a great community, Elizabeth. A service to all people. So we can forego some of the profit, right?"

"It sounds wonderful."

"Let's say you put up three kinds of housing: expensive and really first-rate construction, then a kind of medium-level house, and finally some low-income worker-type houses, so the whole place would be a single community, see? You'd have the people to service the big houses living right nearby." He raised one palm, intercepting her question. "I know what you're going to say. I don't mean right in their backyards. 'Course not. But there's all that land down by the creek in the lower pasture, and you could put in maybe twenty-five little-bitty houses down in there, and that could be your servants' quarters. For the domestics and the yardmen.

"Cuz, see, this is the way I see things now. The economy is such right now that people are having a harder and harder time getting servants, aren't they? Your mother talks about that all the time. And we have Elsie, who comes in once a week, but, hell, she's beginning to cost a hell of a lot. And it's just going to get worse. You gotta ask why? Why do servants cost so much these days? And the answer is because they can get better jobs in the city, and the houses they have out here in these areas are old and run-down, like Lillian and Elsie, living in that shack up in the woods, with an outhouse falling down and a barrel under the gutter spout to catch rainwater for their wash. Now, I know they'd love a nice little house in Elk Creek."

When he talked like this, she remembered what she loved about him: his idealism. "It's a wonderful idea," she said. "But could they afford it?"

"Well, we'd see they could. I don't mean a big house. I don't mean an expensive redwood ranch house. I mean a nice little place, maybe two rooms down and two up—that's what they have now, isn't it? With a decent kitchen and indoor plumbing. Hell, it'd be a palace to them. And they can get a bank mortgage and pay out ten or fifteen dollars a week. Or maybe I'll take back a mortgage so they can afford it. There'd be plenty of work for them. They'd make money. What do they get now, fifteen dollars a week?"

Elizabeth nodded.

"Well, they'll be in more demand, see, in my development." Angus was getting excited. "With all these upward-striving new people coming in to live in these fine old country manor houses. Why, I bet they could charge twenty dollars a week to clean house and get away with it."

"But, Angus." Elizabeth toyed with the pages of the book in her lap. "I don't understand. Who's going to buy the big houses way out here?"

"Jesus, Lizzie, you get me so mad. You don't have any faith in me. You'd like to undermine—"

"No, no. Angus, darling, really. I'm not undermining anything. I think it's a wonderful idea. I'm just asking a question, that's all."

"Elizabeth, listen. They're building that highway to Washington, and we're smack on the main drag. People are on the move all over this great country of ours, and people are richer than they've ever been in their lives, and people want real houses, not city apartments anymore, but four separate walls with lawns and a garden in back. All around New York you see this now. Hell, remember when we were up in Baltimore and you could see the building going on? All over the place. Richmond. Washington. There's not a city in the whole East Coast that isn't expanding, and it's into the suburbs they're going. . . ."

"Ye-es," said Elizabeth.

"You don't think I'll make it work. You think it's just one more pipe dream, don't you? Well, let me tell you something, little lady. I wasn't born yesterday. I can see the future coming as well as anybody. Naughton is going to be built up in ten, fifteen years. You mark my words. Elk Creek is right on the main road. There will be factories here, corporate headquarters, and people moving out of congested places like Washington and Richmond to get good country air. So you go build your little school, cuz I'm going to be the first in Naughton to start real developing, and when I'm finished, you're going to have one hell of a lot of people knocking at those doors to get their kids in that school. I'm going to change the face of this community. I'm going to make it into a real business town, not just some sleepy Southern village, snoozing in its post–Civil War backwater 1958 ooze. Nosirree! I, Angus McEwen, will wake this place up, and I don't want any sombitch telling me I can't do it, either, so you jes keep your tongue still, woman." He laughed to indicate a joke.

Elizabeth sprang to her feet. "I'm going to bed." It was beginning. Already she could feel her heart squeezed in her chest. "I think it's a wonderful idea, darling. And it's bound to succeed." As she leaned down to kiss his cheek, Angus grabbed one breast in his fingers and pulled.

"Ow!"

"You like that." He leered up at her. He had one hand tucked up around her neck, so that she could not straighten.

"Don't, Angus." She gave a quick, light laugh, as if to defuse his anger with gaiety. But he twisted his arm and flipped her into his lap. Then his lips were on hers. She held her breath, trying not to inhale his boozy breath. She had to submit; there was no question. Her arms lay rigid against his chest, both holding him off and holding on to him, and when he released her lips, she squirmed to stand. He held her down. He nibbled at her ear. One hand was feeling up her blouse, and the other, wrapped round her waist, held her tight to his lap.

"You look so beautiful," he murmured. His legs shifted suggestively under her. "I don't know when I've seen you look so good."

"Oh, Angus." She wanted to run.

"You don't know what you do to me."

"Don't, Angus," she murmured. "I don't feel like it tonight."

"Well, let's see if you get to feel like it." His hands were crawling over her everywhere, unbuttoning buttons, groping at her flesh. She forced a stern control over herself and kissed him back, holding her breath. If she hurried, she could get this over quickly. She pulled at his tie, unbuttoned the collar of his shirt . . . then rose.

"Come upstairs," she said. At least she could ensure no foreplay. Quick and dirty, and maybe he would fall asleep. Maybe it would not be one of those evenings when he woke up and drank and shouted at her for her selfishness, for abandoning him in his misery, when he needed her, for not easing his pain, as a proper wife should, but for contributing to it. Mother of his son—deformed. He would sometimes pace the room all night and finally throw himself on the bed at three or four A.M. in a stupor of sleep. By then Elizabeth would be sobbing with remorse and helplessness.

In the morning all would be forgotten. He would smile his cheerful boyish grin and stretch and say what a sweetheart of a wife he had; he remembered nothing. And she in her confusion would hardly know what to remember either. He loved her, that was all.

Moreover she had no one to turn to for help. Her mother? Carolyn could not support her. Carolyn believed a wife's duty was to her husband, and Elizabeth had made her choice of her own free will. Elizabeth had spoken her vows before God, to love, honor, and cherish this man, to take him in sickness and in health. . . . Anyway, a mother should not interfere in her daughter's marriage: Carolyn had always believed that. She wanted to hear nothing about Elizabeth's distress. Marriage, she would say, is always hard.

Carolyn would not have believed that Angus hurt her anyway, just as Elizabeth was not sure he did. He did not beat her. He gave her all his money to bank and share. He petted her, cared for her, adored her. How could she imagine there were faults? One part of her loved Angus tenderly, as a mother loves a child, wanting to protect and keep him; and at the same time another part of her was afraid of him, he had such power to hurt.

She undressed quickly and tumbled into bed. *Life is not meant to be easy.* Her mother's words. Everyone has a tough time in life, and one does not puke and cry, particularly if one is a Page. "Problems are given us," Carolyn used to say, "in order to test us, and it is not the test itself but how we answer to it that's the point."

Angus pulled her on top of him and pushed her legs apart with his. He was panting with excitement now. One huge arm encircled her waist, holding her on top of him. He pushed his pelvis against hers. "Help me," he muttered. She felt awkward. They were all elbows and knees and joints, working against each other. She twisted on top of him, easing him inside. Her eyes were closed. Silent. She forced her mind to drift away. Who would she like this man beneath her now to be? Instantly the answer came, and she felt a welling up, a softening run through her, her body relaxing into his. She turned her face aside, to avoid the hot scent of bourbon, and lifting, let her breast tremble at the tip of Angus' lips. He took it in his mouth, sucking at her, and she drifted further into her dream. A moment later Angus turned her over roughly, and then he was pumping, pumping, holding her buttocks between his hands, his body jerking against hers. He was growling as he worked her over, one hand now slapping her breasts and the other against her thighs. There was no way she could hold on to the dream. But she knew what she should do. Her breath came in quick gasps at his ear. "Oh, Angus," she whispered, "yes, yes, yes." And he was over the edge, ramming her so hard that her head was slapped against the headboard of the bed. Then he was finished. He lay on top of her, muscles collapsing into hers. She lay stiff beneath him, stroking his back, and stared at the white ceiling. She felt cold and empty. Angus rolled over. "Whew-ey! You are something else!"

"Am I?" In a moment he would release her entirely, and she could go into the bathroom and wash. She lay patiently, waiting for her signal, but he rolled back on top of her instead, and kissed her hard. "Delicious," he murmured. "Such a honey roll." She turned her head aside, looking toward the bare branches at the dark window.

"Was that good for you?" he asked in gentle concern. "Did I get you?"

Gently, she stroked his bare shoulder, then kissed it lightly.

"There's something wrong," he said. "Didn't I get you? Wasn't it any good?"

"No, I'm just feeling quiet." She smiled up at him. He was so dear sometimes. "It was . . . lovely," she said. "Lie still. It was nice."

"Do you want to try again?" he asked urgently. "I mean, if it wasn't enough. If you give me a minute, I'll be okay in a minute. I can—"

"Hush, hush," she murmured, pulling him down on top of her. "I just want to lie here and hold you. It was fine."

"Fine." He chuckled with contentment. "That's one hell of an understatement. You blew me through the roof." In another moment he was asleep. Elizabeth lay under his weight. She could feel the semen leaking down her legs. She felt dirty.

Silently, so that he would not wake, she let her tears fall, too, all the soft liquids leaking from her openings. She had never felt so lonely in her life.

It is time to speak of Angus, who plays a part in this. The story from his side takes on new tones.

I used to hunt with Angus for a time, after all these events were over, and sitting in the black blind as dawn began to tinge the sky, toes freezing in our rubber boots and us drinking hot coffee or (me) rum from a thermos, whispering in the dark, he used to confide in me, as people do who sit or sleep in the dark together, when their eyes can't meet. I've noticed it on long drives, too, how just being enclosed together in a car for a long time, facing forward and watching the hypnotic road run toward you, under your tires, draws out confidences. The same thing happens in the duck blind as the night lightens to a luminous pearl. This is before the sky streaks golden, and it is still dark and quiet. The ducks have not yet wakened on the dark water, although you hear an occasional *quack* and a ruffle of feathers followed by more sleepy silence, as if one had bumped into another and said, " 'Scuse me." In another half hour, they'll come awake and take to the air, and then the shooting will begin, so deafening you'd think you were on the Maginot Line, with the cannon in your ears and the sharp smell of gunpowder, the metal barrel of your shotgun hot under your mittened hand, and shells exploding from the chambers and new ones locked in fast, and the ducks calling in terror, and the dog quivering between your legs and whining in anticipation of his turn to dive into the cold water and retrieve a duck. Then it's all excitement and balance and that search for the perfect shot.

But in the predawn dark, sipping coffee and shivering from cold, in those fragmented whispered confidences, Angus told me his whole story. He was a first-rate storyteller, too, a Virginian through and through, so let Angus take the stage. I'll add one thing: I don't shoot anymore. One day I went duck hunting and everything changed, I don't know why. I just didn't care to go out and murder ducks, and though my guns are still lined up in the rack in the hall closet, oiled and in order, I haven't touched them since.

Angus. Thirty-six years old. He padded up and down his office, a jungle cat restless in his cage—except he was a brawny, overweight jaguar now. Three steps to the window, four to the door. The blue nap of the rug had worn to bare gray threads. The paint was peeling near the door, and everything showed the decay in his fortunes. He straightened the Scottish clansman on the wall. Precisely foursquare, that's what he liked things to be. And life prevented it.

Angus tried to position himself squarely in the room, foursquare and solid. The question was how? The door did not sit centered in the wall. A wave of annoyance passed over him. Who would build a room with an off-center door? How stupid! If he were a builder, he would never have made a mistake like that. Moreover the floor slanted.

He was so upset, he wanted a drink. He opened the file cabinet for the bourbon.

Not even a secretary to share it with. He poured a finger's width into the bathroom glass and sat behind his desk. It was only four P.M., too early to go home yet; and the school commission was lost, and no one else around to buy the Foster place. Had he sold it, people wouldn't have snickered at him.

Patronized him, pretending—pretending what? He could not remember. He poured another inch into the glass.

But things were serious. Elizabeth had no idea. There wasn't any work. Or money coming in. He looked with envy at his classmates who had gone into financing. They had it easy, working for a company, drawing regular pay.

It was hard when you were on your own. Now the truth was hard and tough, and Angus McEwen could face the truth— it was starvation down the road, and humiliation leering in his face with an evil grin. What the hell was a man to do?

If it weren't for Elizabeth, he could leave. He could go to South America. There was plenty of land in South America, and with a few dollars you could live like a king. He would buy a coffee plantation or a cattle ranch. Labor was cheap. You could still make money in South America. But not here in Virginia, with taxes eating you alive like red army ants—no, white maggots—gnawing you to dirt.

He had married too young.

That had been his mistake. And a mental retard for a kid. He was being wiped out by the institution bills. Well, Angus didn't feel sorry for the boy. He himself was in an institution of sorts, right here behind his desk, trapped in the need to make money to keep the kid in another kind of institution. That was what the world was about: people trapping other people in cages, and all of us prowling our cages, knowing there's no way out.

Elizabeth had no idea, he thought. She went along, gay and cheerful, keeping up a constant stream of chatter about what Fran or Nickie or someone else had done. She rode her horse and sewed her clothes and every couple months assuaged her conscience with a trip to visit Dunks. Oh, how easy was a woman's life! She had no idea how badly off they were.

His life now was a far cry from those halcyon college days. He lifted one fist in a two-inch punch. God! He had been beautiful! The football hero with a loose athletic frame, broad shoulders, and girls, girls. Elizabeth had been only one among many, and not even the most interesting in those days, when the Pack would pile into a convertible, girls and boys all tangled together, arms and legs and hands and breasts, and they would tool down the long, straight, easy highway, swinging in the orbit of a lantern moon. Or they'd run down to Richmond in a night and back at dawn, with the cool mists rising in streams off the road, clouding the car, and the smell of grass off the fields as the car rushed through the exciting cool, dark dawn. God! What days and nights those were, and he, Angus, was the hero of the Pack, the one who could raise most holy hell.

It was right at the end of the war. He had quit school to get commissioned in the air force. He had a dream about himself swaggering in a leather flight jacket. But he had a heart murmur, they said. Then, just as he had thumbed a ride to Norfolk to try the navy, they'd ended the war. And he had spent a horrible weekend moving from one crowded sailors' joint to the next, before he hitched back home, for there was no sense getting kicked out his senior year if he couldn't fight a war. But he had never forgiven God for pulling that one on him, just when he'd got to the point of lying about his health.

He'd gone to UVA. Senior year both his parents were killed in a car crash, and he inherited what seemed a fortune at the time.

Angus squinted at the peeling paint. There was something

leprous about that bare yellow patch beneath the blue. Tomorrow he'd take a little blue paint and cover the spot. His eyes moved slowly round the room. Dingy. He'd given up a secretary eight months ago, when he'd moved to this second floor above the Naughton *Horse Chronicle.*

He sipped his drink and turned over the papers on his desk. In the last ten years, Angus had tried his hand at insurance, investment banking, and real estate, and each time he had lost more than he'd made. He couldn't understand why. He wasn't dumb. A lot of stupid people in the world had a Midas touch— like Rye Shits. All you had to do was look at him and you knew it would be Rolls-Royces and stables one day for him. Crystal chandeliers in the horse stalls. And who was he? Nobody.

Angus remembered when he had first seen Elizabeth at her grandmother's house, Nacirema, which is *American* spelt backwards. Joe Foots had taken him there to a dance, and they had driven up the mountain to this pile of gray Gothic rocks looming in the dark night air. Every window was lit. Music poured outside, and they had entered this . . . castle, was what it was, with a suit of armor in the hall and a stained-glass window in the library. He had clapped his buddy on the back:

"Now, if the little heiress is pretty, too, this is going to be my night to howl."

"Nu-uh, she's mine." Joe had laughed. "*You* go hunt your own."

Elizabeth was pretty. But so were a lot of the girls at the dance, and Angus had had his pick. God, what fun he'd had. Days of play and nights of no responsibility.

Joe and Elizabeth had broken up, and the Pack had dissolved at the end of college, scattering to law school or Making a Living. Only Angus had still been crazy enough to continue to play. He had money on his hands. He and Elizabeth took up with each other, naturally drifting together. She had a little apartment with Fran Oliver in Georgetown and some kind of job as secretary-typist in a museum. He had "rescued" her.

Or was it the other way round?

One evening Angus had come to dinner at Nacirema. They weren't engaged yet, though Angus often proposed. Elizabeth stalled. She wasn't sure. Also she wouldn't put out for him. Oh, they'd clutch and grapple in the backseat of the convertible, or lie together on the uncomfortable couch in her apartment, so short his legs hung dangling from the edge, and in those prepill years you couldn't blame a girl for being careful. He respected her for that.

Also her ignorance amused him. It made him protective. He remembered one night when they had been snuggling on that horrible couch and he had finally gotten her skirt up, and his own flaring parts rigid against her little nylon undies.

"What if I get pregnant?!" She pushed him away in panic.

"But you can't get pregnant."

"Why not? How do you know?"

And murmuring in her ear, stroking her hair, and still squirming against her beautiful warm body—that delicious firm little bottom just inviting him inside—he had whispered soothingly the facts of life: that he could come right up against her panties if he wanted and she'd be safe. He'd have to be inside before she'd get pregnant, and even that was a one-in-a-thousand chance. He'd been touched by her trust, and she relaxed again, trembling, in his arms. She wanted him, too, he could tell.

He'd left that night at two in the morning, half relieved and aching for more. He could envision those adorable breasts poking up, the perfect fit to the palm of his hand, just asking to be squeezed.

When he asked her to stroke him with her hand, she complied, but modestly and shrinking back. He was never sure if she liked it.

By the time she took him to Nacirema, he had proposed twice and twice she'd turned him down. But this visit was to introduce him to her grandmother, so he knew it was a test.

He'd fortified himself with a light drink before he arrived, a protective double, because Carolyn and Dut weren't so fond of him, he knew. They gave him a drink, which made his second. He was feeling a little sick to his stomach and thought the bourbon would help settle it. The family had invited him for dinner at seven o'clock, but the other guests did not arrive till nearly eight. So that made a third.

He talked gruff, masculine conversation with Lizzie's father about football and The University, about his plans as an investment banker, his intentions of handling his own money and how he expected that with any luck at all he could bring in a 6 percent return on his investments, 4 percent at the least. To Carolyn he talked Family, answering her questions about his relations in Staunton and the Tidewater branch, until she had satisfied herself exactly through whom in the Moffatt branch the families were connected. To show her own goodwill, she had pointed out the Treaty of Ghent table, on which Madison had signed the treaty that ended the War of 1812, and she told how amused she was one day to discover that her cousin Lydia thought her own dining room table was the Treaty of Ghent table, but then Lydia had married into the family and couldn't be expected to know. The real piece was right here. Angus looked it over, nodding graciously. He was feeling really sick.

By the time the Andersons arrived, his forehead had broken out in sweat.

"Are you all right?" Elizabeth murmured as they rose for dinner.

"I'm fine." He waved her away. "I'll be just fine."

The Andersons had come down from Washington. He was a congressman. Angus was surprised to find them in black tie. The couples made their way into the dining room, and Angus discovered himself at the huge table—the very one that now graced Walnut Grove. It could seat twenty-four with all the leaves installed. The dining room was panelled in a beautiful soft tea-brown walnut, and with all the doors closed every entry vanished into the carved wood.

Maids entered, serving soup and crackers. The candles cast shadows on the panelling. The conversation was properly removed from any serious topics—a little politics, a little sports, the grace of Nacirema, courteous questions about Lizzie's grandmother, the dowager, now bedridden upstairs with a stroke. Angus would meet her in the morning.

Angus could hardly concentrate. His stomach turned. He wondered if he was going to make it through dinner.

Now he knew he was coming down with something.

Soup removed. Laughter. The maid passing a platter of rolled veal birds stuffed with sausage and heavy cream, surrounded by green beans and broiled tomatoes.

"Perfection, Carolyn," said Mrs. Anderson.

These were followed by glazed carrots and baby potatoes, by servings of butter rolls, and by everything coming round again before the plates were cleared for salad.

The conversation, now on the congressman's career, swirled

round him. Angus felt like a dunce with his eyes riveted to his plate and his attention on his dancing stomach.

Two wines were served, one red, one white.

"You're very quiet, Mr. McEwen," said Congressman Anderson. "And what is your opinion of rounding up the Communists?"

He muttered something—hell, he didn't follow politics— and watched the plates removed, and then with horror saw the maid was coming round with fingerbowls. Would the dinner never end?

"Save room for dessert." He heard the voice through a darkening distance. "You haven't lived until you've tasted Bessie's pie."

He rose from his chair, wobbly, his eyes searching desperately for the door. Where was the door? Closed around him was walnut panelling, without so much as a knob to mark the door. He tried fuzzily to remember from which direction the maid had entered.

"Are you all right, Angus?"

He could not answer. He dove for a panel. There! It had to be the door. His hand flapping up and down the wall, searching for the secret spring. . . .

He was sick all over the panelling, all over the floor. He had turned his stomach inside out, again and again, unable to control himself. Choking. Retching. Behind him rose a stony wall of silence. Around him floated the putrid smell of vomit. Futilely he tried to wipe it off the wall with his damask napkin, then realized the linen was also valuable.

"Here, come with me." He felt someone take his arm, pulling him away, and then Dut was leading him upstairs to a bedroom and bath. He was told to wash up.

"Lie down if you like. We'll come see how you are in a bit. What you need is sleep."

He washed. He swallowed a mouthful of water. He threw himself, humiliated, across the four-poster bed, his heart aching at the loss of Elizabeth. He had made a fool of himself. It had been his test, and he had failed.

The room was spinning violently. He could only hold it still by putting one foot on the floor and opening his eyes periodically. If he closed his eyes, he began to whirl.

The next morning he awoke in the dark, curtained room to utter silence and a splitting headache. At first he was disoriented. He hadn't a clue where he was! Then he remembered, and that was worse. He had slept all night in his rumpled trousers, lying on top of the bed. Someone had taken off his shoes and thrown a cover over him. Otherwise he had been left alone.

He crawled on his hands and knees to the edge of the bed and paused to still the throbbing in his head. Now he would have to straighten himself and go down to breakfast, if he could find the dining room. He would have to face his hosts, apologize to Elizabeth, and never see any of them again. He felt sorry for himself.

He splashed some water on his unshaven face, changed his shirt (imagine sleeping in his knotted tie all night!) and stole out of his room. The house was silent. It was creepy as he tiptoed down the thick carpet of the long corridor. Was there anyone about? Down the stairs, past the suit of armor. He looked in the cavernous living room—empty. The Renaissance furniture, heavy and carved, looked gloomy in the daylight.

The dining room showed no sign of his having been sick. On the sideboard in silver hot dishes lay sausage, ham, biscuits, scrambled eggs, and grits; also coffee in a tall silver pot, tea in a round one.

One place was set at the table. Obviously everyone else had finished.

He helped himself to coffee and a biscuit and sat humbly in his place, eating stoically. He had just poured a second cup of coffee when Elizabeth came in, fresh and clean.

"Oh, you're up." She plunked herself into a nearby chair. "Well, you certainly created a stir last night. Tennis?"

As if nothing had happened. "Sure." He grinned shakily. "Look—" He started to apologize.

"I'll see you on the court, then. I'm going to hit some balls. It's a beautiful day. Come on out."

She was gone, and he was again alone in this hideous panelled room. He went upstairs to change.

On the court he played badly. His only excuse was to murmur that he still wasn't feeling well, which was perfectly true.

After two sets (hers: 6–4, 6–3) he threw himself despondently on the grass. She sat beside him, blinking in the sun, the edges of her mouth flickering with smiles. She plucked a stem of long, sweet grass and peeled it to the vein.

"So, when do we get married?"

"What?"

"Don't you want to still?"

"Well, of course. Only—"

"Then, let's."

"Hey, now, Lizzie! But that's wond—" He reached up to pull her to him, and she flopped clumsily to the grass beside him, ruffling his hair and giving him kisses. But why? He never figured it out. Why did she accept his proposal after seeing him sick in her grandmother's dining room? Why, when she had refused him every other time?

"Oh, well, I have my reasons." She had laughed. That was the best he could get out of her. Or, "Ask me no questions and I'll tell you no lies," she teased. And: "The heart has reasons reason never knows."

He didn't care. She had everything a man could want. He even approved of her determined chastity, which showed the sense of virtue that he wanted in a wife. "I don't see why we need a big wedding," she said. "Why don't we just go do it. Tomorrow. Drive to Elkton."

"Elkton? Maryland?"

"Why not?" Her eyes were sparkling with the adventure. Why not indeed! He wished he had thought of it. In Elkton, you just drove into town, stopped at a justice of the peace, and had a few mumbo-jumbo words read over you—and bingo, you were married.

"Why not?" he agreed.

Two days later they eloped.

They spent their wedding night in a motel. It was not entirely satisfactory. Elizabeth seemed more scared than Angus would have liked. But he'd done the business right.

"How was it?" he asked. "Was it okay for you?"

"Yes, yes." She stroked his shoulder softly. "It was fine." Then she had gotten up and gone to the bathroom for a long time, which is what women did. Later they'd been remarried in a church, and then they'd gone on a honeymoon.

All of this had taken place eight years before. Carolyn and Dut had swallowed their pride and put a good face on things. Angus knew they boasted in public about Elizabeth's "catch." He was handsome. He had property. He had enough gumption to refuse to live at Nacirema, but to rent a little place in the valley, and he had set to work handling his investment business.

That all happened before Nacirema burned down.

Their love life picked up. Lots of times Lizzie was the one to suggest some fun. It was only in recent years, he didn't know why, that she'd withdrawn. But when his bad spell was over, she would be ready for good times again.

Right now he was hounded by bad luck. He and Elizabeth rented the gatehouse of Walnut Grove for a nominal sum, and he was grateful that no one was crude enough to ask more rent. Elk Creek was all that remained of his inheritance. One hundred twenty acres of scrub farmland, which did not produce enough to cover costs.

On his desk was an article and reports on land development. He had read them many times. He tipped the last of the bourbon from the bottle into his water glass and swirled the golden nectar. He had a feeling this was IT. A fortune lay there in land development—apartments, houses, schools, shopping centers crawling over open land. He tasted the tart, hot liquid on his tongue. Perfect. If he had ever seen a 120-acre site suitable for development, it was Elk Creek. And the figures! In one swoop he could recoup the losses of the past ten years. He could make millions.

The question was whether to undertake the development himself or to sell out to a middleman who would build.

The problem with going it alone was that Angus didn't know one hell of a lot about how to build a development, though it didn't appear so hard. The problem with selling to a middleman was he'd give up the profit to someone else; and that's where the big bucks lay—in construction.

What he needed was advice. He'd need to get zoning changed. Rye Shits would help. Angus slugged down the last of his drinks and rose. He made a fist and jabbed the air with a strong right hook. Oh, but life was Good-O now. He wasn't finished yet, not ol' Angus McE., the leader of the Pack. Stick with me, you'll fart through silk.

He switched off the light and reached for his coat. He could just see the houses packed tight over Elk Creek land. Angus would be in like Flynn.

He glanced at his watch. It wasn't too early to drop by the Club and see if he could pick up some advice.

Margaret just came in to look over my shoulder. She kneaded the back of my neck fondly, and I stretched my muscles under her touch, but I know when curiosity's killing the cat.

"Now, really. Tell me what you're writing."

Everyone asks what I'm writing. "My autobiography," I'd told my daughter, Laurie, who didn't wait to listen anyway before she was already walking out of the room. "Notes," I told Margaret earlier, but she's seen the pages piling up.

This time I admitted it. "I'm writing down Tom's story. Trying to make sense of it."

"Well!" She plumped into a chair and laughed. "That should keep you busy for the rest of your retirement."

I shot her an ugly look.

"Those were wonderful times, though, weren't they? What good times we had. We were all so young!"

"Middle-aged," I answered. But she made me stop and think. She'd surprised me. Here I'd been remembering all the suffering, each person caught in a private pain, and each pain carrying the fire of hell's poker. But touch any one of us, and we would have said we were happy.

"That was the year we put sheep on the farm, remember? We were going to raise sheep." Another failed experiment. But I was suddenly swept by a vivid memory of walking the farm with the surveyor, and my pleasure in that first shipment of three prize merinos coming off the truck.

"That was before he came, though."

"Yes, in the spring. And then Beverly Harris got married that year," said Margaret with satisfaction, checking the events off on her fingers like personal triumphs. She bent each finger backwards with each count. "And Barnacle won the Gold Cup—imagine, a Naughton horse. And I started the rock garden around then. What year did I start the rock garden, John? It was when Johnnie was still in school, wasn't it? We got them from the quarry. Remember hauling those rocks with a forklift? Oh, those were lovely times."

She patted her thighs and came to her feet, smiling. "Well, I'll start some lunch. Soup?"

"That would be fine," I said, but my mind was already floating backwards in time and musing over how differently different people remember. Or how different are the things important to us each.

We were happy. The sun came up golden in the autumn dawns, and the light streamed down through the scarlet leaves. The pumpkins were ripening, and the autumn mums bloomed pink and white and rust against the rusting shrubs. The nights were chilly as the cold air came off the mountains with the hint of winter snow. The fox hunting had started, and sometimes (Tuesday, Thursday, Saturday) you could hear the horn from far away, as you still can today. People gave parties and played tennis and laughed and drank together, and if you'd asked any one of us—Elizabeth or Angus or Shriver or Emily, Tom even— if we were happy, we would each have answered yes—why not? In my moments of deepest despair, I've always felt a little thread of hope. It's what keeps us from suicide, that optimism, the knowledge that everything passes, the memory that yesterday we felt bold and glorious and tomorrow we'll be up again. So, maybe I'm doing a disservice telling all the anguish without the joy and hope. We were middle-aged, too, in our forties and fifties, though looking back now, that seems pretty young to me. We'd hit our strides, as it were. We felt our power and strength, paid our dues, and were taking the dare of life.

Maybe we didn't know how happy we were. At least I could wake up in the mornings and stretch my body and feel fit and ready. Not like the creaks and aches of now.

"I always felt he was an innocent, you know?" Margaret said suddenly over her tomato soup, and I didn't have to ask whom she was referring to. "He was like a child, almost, in many ways."

"Oh, I don't know about that."

"You never trusted him."

"I did. That's not true."

"You always thought he had some cunning in him, but I believe he really had the simplicity of—of—well, I've never met anyone else that I could say had it. I'd have to cast back to Saint Francis or some medieval monk—"

"That's nonsense," I shot back, "because if you've read your history, the monks were keeping their women in the monasteries and buying indulgences and plotting intrigue and murder. Read Abelard."

"Well, Saint Francis, I said—"

"—first castrated for sleeping with a woman, hell, for marrying her—and then when he becomes the abbot of a monastery, he's so hated, the very monks he's in charge of try to poison him with the Communion wine. What innocents?"

"I said Saint Francis!" cried Margaret. "I don't know about those others."

"Well, you should. If you're going to bring up the saintliness of monks, at least you ought to know what you're talking about."

"I don't know what's gotten into you, John Woods," she snapped, picking up the soup bowls. "Whatever're you so prickly about? All I'm saying—no, don't interrupt—is that he was one of the few people I've ever met who tried—who—where the inner and the outer person," she stumbled, "were in conformity. And that he dealt with us from some deeply spiritual level. What you saw was what was going on."

"No duplicity? No lies?"

She waved one hand. "Say what you will, he was looking for God, you can't deny that, and he touched a lot of people with his vision. So, is it the sin you're concentrating on in your book or what he was telling us?" She squinted at me for a moment before turning: "Oh, you make me so mad."

She stamped out to the pantry, and I could hear her cleaning and scraping and banging the soup pot on the stove while she talked to herself.

I went back to my study. I wasn't going to give her the satisfaction of an answer. It's my book. Let her write her own, but I know what was most important. He was my friend, after all, and I know a hell of a lot more about Tom than she ever thought of asking.

Oh, Tom was far from a Saint Francis. He could be mean, and he didn't do so well with his wife and family, for one.

Here's one incident I witnessed myself: Tom and I were in the kitchen of the rectory when Philip wandered in, hangdog and drooping. I can't remember what we were talking about now, but I remember we both stopped and looked at the boy, with his dark hair falling over his forehead and his mouth twisted to one side. He threw himself in a kitchen chair and began to fiddle intently with his shoelaces. Now, anyone could see that the child wanted something.

"Isn't it time for bed?" Tom asked.

Philip said, yeah, without lifting his head or stopping his examination of his shoes.

"Come give me a kiss, then," said Tom, and held out his hand. He was watching the boy with a curious mixture of concern and distaste, which was not surprising given the unprepossessing nature of this child.

Philip said nothing for a moment, didn't move, and neither did Tom. A frozen tableau. Then Philip got to his feet.

"Good night," he said in his lackluster monotone.

"Are you all right?" Tom asked, giving him a hug as he passed, but his voice was cool. As the boy shrugged—"Sure"—and passed out the door, Tom turned back to me and to whatever parish matter we were discussing without another thought to him.

That's a picture I hold in my mind.

I won't have Margaret tell me he was just an innocent.

6

Now Tom and Elizabeth saw each other all the time. The church vestments moved, to Priscilla's satisfaction, from the red of Pentecost to the purple of Advent, the seasons of the Church proclaimed and praised by the colors of the altar and the robes. Soon it was time for Christmas greens and the smell of pine. The church bazaar made $129.36, which Emily Carter thought decent, given how little the rector contributed to the event. She wrote an anonymous letter to the Bishop, so informing him. It was one of several anonymous letters she sent that fall concerning Tom's faults.

Elizabeth, in addition to working with the school committee, was helping with Tom's typing on Tuesday afternoons (Priscilla's suggestion), for which she received a meager salary. Tom did not disguise his delight. On Tuesday mornings he found himself running up the last few steps to the parish hall and greeting Natalie with a glance that sent her own heart rocking. When Lizzie arrived just after lunch, he would break into such a smile that she would sometimes turn away.

Tom knew he was in love. He had no intention of having an affair. Was he stupid or merely naive? Did he really think he could work with her and not give way to lust?

I have raked through Lizzie's journals, and she, too, was under the impression that this was a Higher Love, though sex lay grinning all around them.

"So, now do you know what I do?" he teased one day, when the phone had not stopped ringing.

"All these people wanting help?"

"I don't always give it either," he said quietly, and told a story that Lizzie passed on to me. "I remember when I was very young, an assistant rector, there was one woman who used to come to every service, morning and evening prayer. She was quite pretty, so I noticed her."

"Oh, you notice pretty women?"

"You think I shouldn't?" She laughed and tossed her head.

"But this woman," he continued, "was extremely emotional and intense. When she took the Eucharist, she wept."

Elizabeth snorted skeptically.

"We never spoke, except to shake hands after the service, and then she would drop her eyes and say 'thank you,' or 'nice sermon,' or some such thing. Then one day she telephoned."

"Did you know who she was?"

"Of course I knew her name, but we hadn't any real contact. On the phone, though, she was in tears, crying that she had to see me right away. I thought she was about to commit suicide. I was scared, so I raced out to see her. She'd given me directions—confused, crazy, all the streets mixed up, but I managed to find her house. I pulled into the driveway and ran up to the house—literally ran. I could just imagine her in the kitchen with the knives and blood, my image the more intense, you see, because only a few days before another of my parishioners had shot himself. I thought maybe this girl had heard about that suicide and picked up the idea. People do that. It's

as if an action seeds itself in everyone's consciousness, demanding imitation. You get one suicide, you get three. That's what
I was thinking."

"What happened?"

"I rang the bell. I could hear footsteps on the other side of
the door. Then the door opened, and—" he gave an embarrassed laugh—"she stood there, stark naked. The only thing she
wore was lipstick."

"What did you do?"

"I ran."

"You ran away?"

"I couldn't take it."

"Tom."

"For one thing, she was . . . lovely."

"Oh, was that it?"

"No, it was . . . all of it. What the hell was I supposed to
do? Go in? Sit primly on the sofa and say, 'Lovely weather,
Miss Weaver.' "

"No, but . . . Oh, poor girl. What happened to her?" Elizabeth was caught between laughter and sympathy.

"I don't know. She never came back to the church. I never
heard of her again."

"Goodness, didn't you try to find out?"

"Well, I asked a few people, but no one knew anything,
and I let it drop. I'm the first to admit I handled it badly. I told
my superior, but I didn't tell Priscilla about it." He laughed
again. "The vicissitudes of a vicar."

"What would you do now?" Pushing him, teasing. "If it
happened tomorrow in Naughton? How would you handle it,
you being older and wiser?"

"It would depend on who it was," he grinned.

I imagine their eyes meeting, laughing. "Someone beautiful," she said. "Someone young and lovely who weeps at the
Communion service. What would you do?" For some reason
she felt excited, wild.

"Maybe I'd go in," he smiled. "Do you think that's what
I should do?" But she only shook her head and looked away.

That's what their relationship was like, tantalizing each
other. One day he invited her to drive down to Madisonville
with him on business.

"We'll be back by five," he promised.

Before Dr. Ellis left, the vestry had agreed to put up several
signs directing strangers to Trinity Church. For some reason,
we'd gotten arrogant and decided that because other commu-
nities had signs to their Episcopal church, we should, too,
though God knows few enough strangers came through town
questioning the gas station attendants and restaurant managers
for directions to the church. But the signs had been bought—
they were handsome Episcopal shields, blue and red on a white
field—and it was Shriver's duty to find the crossroads to put
them on and get the owners' permission and hire a couple Negroes to dig some holes and put them up.

Months went by and he hadn't done it.

Then Tom arrived, and almost immediately he and Tom
were at each other's throats, and when Butch discovered Tom
was in favor of the signs, he stalled some more, so weeks passed,
and the signs became a central issue between the two, a kind
of symbol of their mutual distrust.

At the last meeting Tom had burst out in his frustration:

"Goddamn it, I'll do it myself. Where are they? I'll take
the matter off your hands."

"I can do it," said Shriver huffily. "You don't have to do my business."

"It's not your business anymore," he answered.

"Well, you can't have them," said the General. "They're at my brother-in-law's in Madisonville. He's away. I'll get them when he's back."

There was a good deal more discussion, which I'll skip, but it was to pick up these five church signs that Tom and Lizzie were driving to Madisonville.

She was ready the next morning at ten-thirty, wearing a beige suit that he commented on as he let her in the car.

"I didn't know what to wear. I suppose you're taking me on a hike?"

"Not in those shoes," he countered.

"So, where are we going?"

"You are curious. I'll tell you, but first I'll tell you what happened to me yesterday."

"You were phoned by a naked lady?"

"Almost as good. No, it was an old woman. Do you know a Mrs. Edna Stubbs?" Elizabeth shook her head. He described the third-floor walk-up in a railroad flat, the smells of urine and garbage as he climbed the rotting stairs. He knocked at the thin door, and first came a frightened cry for confirmation of his name and then the clank and snap of locks unlatched, one by one, until the door opened a crack, still chained, to reveal a wary eye. Cautiously, she let Tom in. The apartment consisted of a bed-sitting room and a cubicle for a kitchen. It was stuffed with things: chairs, tables, books, magazines, bric-a-brac, and boxes. Mrs. Stubbs explained in a high whine that her daughter had recently died, and ever since, she'd been seeing spirits in her rooms.

" 'I'm very psychic,' she told me. 'See, I have these marks on my palm, right here. This cross shows how psychic I am.' " He laughed with Elizabeth and continued his story, recounting how she said the broom kept filling up with water. She would pick up the broom to sweep the floor and as much as a cup of water would pour onto the broken linoleum.

"There's a leak in the broom closet," said Elizabeth.

"That's what I thought. But I looked. There weren't any pipes nearby and no signs of water leaking from behind the walls."

Elizabeth was uncomfortable with the idea. "Then she's putting the water there herself. What did you do?"

"I prayed with her for the soul of her daughter," Tom said. "That she be at peace, protected by the Hand of God. I wanted to tell Mrs. Stubbs to forget the psychic phenomena. I didn't have the courage."

"You're awfully hard on yourself."

"Not hard enough."

"Why not think about the psychic? It's obviously on her mind."

"It may be a product of her mind."

"What? The water in the broom?"

"Yes. The mind is an extraordinary instrument. It can make anything happen. Here she is unhappy and confused, living all alone, hardly sees anyone. She hobbles on a cane to the market on the corner, and that's her day."

"So, you're saying the ghost is a manifestation of some unconscious thought? Not that she imagined it, but that by the power of her mind she's making something appear?"

"I don't have any idea." he shrugged. "Maybe it really is the spirit of her dead daughter, for all I know. Or maybe she's creating a drama for her own amusement."

"Oh my, Tom," teased Elizabeth, shifting comfortably in the car. "This does bring up possibilities. If you don't believe in spirits, does that hold for the Holy Ghost as well?"

So they were back to God. They talked about it all the time: Christ, original sin, the existence of evil in a supposedly benevolent scheme.

"Go ahead, tell me there's a God," Elizabeth challenged him. "What does he look like? Old man? White beard? If you tell me that, I'll kick you."

"Then I certainly won't." He smiled.

"Isn't that church doctrine? That man is made in the image of God? So, obviously you think that God's a man. It's so arrogant. As if God thought better of humanity than . . . than trees! Trees are just as important as mankind—maybe more so, and it's our pitiful defensiveness that insists a Creator made pathetic little man so special—in His own image. Well, say something."

He was smiling as he drove. "It's the soul they mean, Elizabeth. Our soul is the image of God. Or is God, is composed of Godness, as trees are too."

But Elizabeth went on, not listening. "And God so loved the world, He gave His only begotten Son to be sacrificed—as a true and living sacrifice. How can you say such things in church? Aren't you ashamed? 'For us and for our salvation.' It's such nonsense. If you love something, you don't nail it to a cross, a sacrifice. I love my son. I can't bear the sacrifice he has to make."

"What if those words are just a way of saying thank you for a gift He made?"

"What gift?"

"The gift of mercy."

"I just can't hold with it. Christ came down to save us sinners. If we're such sinners, why would God love us? And if we're not, we don't need a Christ. It's church doctrine, that's all, to suck people in and build a bureaucracy. Imagine! God looks down at the earth and sees all these people living in ignorance and sin. 'I know, I'll make my own Son, born without a father, the personification of Myself, and I'll send him to earth to preach, and then when He's killed for telling people to be nice to each other, I'll forgive them all their sins for all future time.' Good grief! Does that make sense? Died for our salvation! I'll tell you what it is. It's the weakness in humans that makes us long for a God. As we get older, we try to make meaning out of life," she said, quoting Angus now. "But there isn't any. And, terrified to look at that truth, we make up God. Deny it if you can!"

She stopped. The silence lengthened between them. "Well?" It came out as a plea.

"You bring up so many points that all I hear is your . . ."

"My what?"

"Your pain."

She stared out the window. "I wish I understood," she said.

"Understood what?"

"All of it." She swept the world with the arc of her arm. "The whole business." Tears pricked her eyes. "I understand nothing. Nothing."

"Well, join the crowd." He laughed. "I think you wish you could be convinced there's God."

"Oh, I do. I'd like to see God. I'd give him a piece of my mind. Tell me how you reconcile a loving God with all the

pain in life." Then she told him about her son and Briarose,
the institution where he'd been placed.

The main building of Briarose stands on a knoll, a massive
red-brick structure completed before the Civil War. When she
visited Duncan, Elizabeth told me, she kept her eyes on the
pavement so that she wouldn't read the inscription chiselled
over the doorway: HOME FOR THE INCURABLES. The nineteenth
century called a spade a spade.

Yet this private institution was one of the good ones, nothing to compare with the free state institutions, the snake pits.
She had read newspaper investigations of the State Home for
the Feebleminded, which had a capacity of 1,000 people and a
population swollen to 3,300 just last year; a plantation system
it was, in which the inmates were made to work for their keep
on the institution farms, raising their own food; or on the director's domestic staff, or in the shops making shoes and mend-
ing and sewing. They were not paid, for there was no place for
them to spend their money anyway. She had read of the abysmal overcrowding, where the children had to walk across the
beds of other patients to get to their own. Disease ran rampant—TB, syphilis, pneumonia. If one inmate got sick, the others were sure to follow. Cleanliness was impossible. The children
lay on bare mattresses on the floor. On summer days they were
pushed outside and in winter into cement showers to be hosed
down naked—that removed the feces.

At least Duncan was not in one of these places. But Tom
wouldn't talk of a benevolent deity if he had a child like hers.
Where was the God who would treat a child like that?

It was Carolyn who had decided Duncan should be "put
away." ("Now, Lizzie, there's no sense in closing your eyes to
reality," she'd said.) Carolyn had found the institution and

made the necessary arrangements, and Elizabeth had to admit that, yes, she did not have the facilities at home or knowledge to care for the boy, then two years old, though it was horrible to leave him among strangers in that noise and stench.

"Since he can't hear, the noise will be of no concern to him," her mother had answered firmly. "You are speaking out of guilt, that's all. You have a husband to care for. You'll have other children someday."

Angus had agreed one hundred percent. He said he didn't want to live with a deformed child. It wasn't healthy. All he had to do was look at his son, with that top-heavy head, too big for his underdeveloped body, and he felt awful. He didn't want him around, a reminder of . . . he didn't know what. He told Elizabeth she didn't want it either.

But once inside, how could you agree? The elevator had quilted walls. Was that to protect the patients if they fell against the metal? Or to protect the elevator from a madman's fist?

Once, she had accidentally gotten off at the geriatric floor, where aged patients in wheelchairs stared vacantly at the empty walls. They drooped against the arms of their chairs; the metal cut their flesh, which crumbled inward on its own gravity. One woman had reached out a claw, a little bird claw. "Miss, Miss." She could not escape the intrusion of that hand, of bones held in by the thin webbing of blue-veined skin. She had pushed the elevator button again and again in her impatience to get away, dizzy at the limp, deformed, and helpless limbs. How could there be so many weak, disfigured people in the world? Incurables, as the home proclaimed. *And weren't we all incurables?* she'd thought. *I am an incurable pretending to be alive. I maintain the pretense of living in a healthy body and protect myself from contact with the contagion of living death.*

Duncan's ward was for boys, some very small—like Dunks, who was now only five—and some as old as twelve. When she visited, she always saw one child with a bulking body, disproportionate to his age of eight, beating his skull against the wall. That's what he did all day. He had beaten the hair off the top of his head and built up a scab on his forehead. The nurses continually tore the skull beater from the wall; each time he fought like an animal. A few mildly retarded and physically healthy boys also lived on this hall. They raced madly round, pushing the wheelchair of one child or hooting at each other with startling concentration. They should not have been here at all, but had no other place to go.

The ward left the impression of noise, two lines of beds, children sprawling on the floor, twisted bodies, rocking and crooning. There was one boy with thickened lips and bulging eyes whom she now recognized, and another thin, tall boy (about eleven or twelve years old), his corkscrew body twisted in his wheelchair, chewing on a sock.

And then there was Duncan with limp blond hair and unnaturally white skin lying in unearthly stillness on the bed. He stared at the ceiling, unaware. Was it bad for him, shielded by the silence in which he lived? Did he feel the tragedy? Or did he move with the stolid, mute contentment of a dog? Perhaps her poignant yearning existed only because she understood the options. Did he hear sounds inside that little skull? Did dreams explode into light or fractured noise? He did not even shift his head to look at her. If she tried for eye contact, his eyes slithered away, disinterested, and off.

"So tell me there's a God," she said passionately.

Tom had listened in silence. When she finished, he said nothing for a moment, then:

"That's hard on you."

She felt a tightening in her throat and the stabbing of tears.

"I think you've really suffered," he said.

She gulped, and suddenly she was crying right there in the car, no, bawling uncontrollably, with great gasps of air, mouth twisted, and her shoulders shaking. Tom pulled over to the side of the road. She threw herself in his arms.

"There, there." He pulled her head to his chest and patted her back. "There, there." He stroked her hair until she quieted, and I am sure he kissed her hairline and temple and felt her body against his, though he never moved to kiss her lips. She rummaged in her purse for a handkerchief.

"I've ruined your shirt."

"It's good to let it out. You've held it in too long."

"I'm so ashamed. I don't usually cry."

"I know. It's all right, you know?"

But she kept apologizing. "I don't know why I'm crying. I never cry. I hate to cry in front of anyone."

Tom looked at her. "It's the appropriate expression of grief."

"Oh, Tom, what am I supposed to do?"

"Pray," he answered simply. "I'll pray for Duncan, too."

For some reason she was moved.

"Yes, I'd like that. Even if I don't believe."

"I pray for you anyway."

"You do?"

"Don't you want to know what I pray for?"

"What?"

"That you'll be happy. That you will be blessed."

She stared out the window, taken aback. "Tell me where

we're going." She changed the subject nervously. "I mean physically, not metaphorically."

"All right. There's a thermos of coffee in the back. Pour me a cup and I'll tell you." He watched as she found the thermos.

It began to rain, large drops were slashing at the windows. The rain turned to flat wet snow that melted as soon as it hit the ground. The wooded hills gave way to farms, cut by steep-banked creeks and marked by wooden fencing or barbed wire and in places by the old snake fences of good chestnut logs one hundred years old but strong enough still to hold a cow or pig. The grass was a parched, blanched buff, the winter tans and browns. The sleet drove against the windshield, and they listened to the scrape of the wipers and the heater hissing. They rode content in each other's company, enclosed in their cocoon.

7

ANGUS, RETURNING FROM ELK CREEK, SLIPPED INTO TOWN JUST as the snowstorm began. He was feeling good. A Porsche was a fantastic car, and this new gray Porsche-S (Porschesse, he called her fondly) hugged the road on a turn, hunkering down on two wheels and sliding round her own center of gravity like a ballerina. He'd bought the car the week before. Spur of the moment. Good-O.

There he'd been in Washington, D.C., trying to pull off a loan at the bank, and suddenly he'd had a breakthrough. Light bulb over his head: to get money, you spend money. That was a Law. Nothing attracts money like money. Act like you have it, and it will come to you. So he had trotted right down to the dealer's and bought this sweet feminine tool with its soft, curving fenders bulging outward and its motor so fine-tuned you could think it was a leopard purring in your ear. His Christmas present to himself. Then he'd gone to meet his banker, George Hoppleman, at the Metropolitan Club (courtesy of Dutton's membership), and his only regret was the car was parked in a garage. No matter. He'd managed to drop a word:

"You want a lift home? My Porsche is in the garage. I can run you out in a jiff."

George had declined, but Angus had seen how his eyebrows lifted toward his receding hairline with appreciation.

"A Porsche."

"Well, things have been going pretty well," he'd said modestly.

On the second drink he had turned the conversation to money. He had explained to George the possibilities of this property. He and George had known each other since The University. He'd always thought George a bit of a jerk, but he had to admit the guy had brains. They were talking big bucks. George asked all the right questions. The zoning rights. The height restrictions. County sewer and water laws. Development costs. Depreciation. Tax structures. God! It was terrific, and they were bandying about figures in the half-million-dollar range, then the one- and two-million-dollar range, as if they were talking about a five-dollar meal.

"Of course I can't promise anything. Among other problems, it's investment outside the city."

Angus had picked up the tab and signed Dut's name (with his own beneath, so everything was on the up and up).

"So you'll send me the figures," George had said. They stood on H Street under the maroon awning of the Metropolitan Club. "I'll be glad to take it up with the Board."

"Sure you don't want a lift?"

It had all been so businesslike, Angus could hardly contain himself. And that night he'd come home swaggering and boasting to Elizabeth of his prowess; he was the hunter returned from the woods, the great provider back from a successful raid: a throwback to a thousand generations of men returning home, hands full, to stomp around the campfire and slap their glistening bare chests, then pause listening to the rippling laughter of admiring women, pouring over each man's head in praise. Angus stood in the kitchen, feet planted and head thrown back, describing to Elizabeth his triumphant afternoon and his initial victory over banks and loans.

When he got to the part about the Porsche, she had stopped whipping egg yolks and stared at him, beater dripping over the side of the bowl. Her eyes blazed.

"A Porsche!"

"It's a great car. Look—" He'd tried to lead her to the window. He tried to tell her it could do circus tricks around the trucks, a bullet, one of the finest racing engines man had ever made. He'd always wanted a car like that. It was essential to have a good car, what with all the driving that he did.

"Don't touch me! How *could* you do a thing like that!" And then, in a tight, strained voice, between her teeth: "Where are we going to get the money, have you thought of that?"

Have you thought of that? Of course he'd thought of that! Elk Creek was going to be developed, and there'd be wheelbarrows of money. Didn't she understand? This car was an investment, and all she saw was debt.

"Your parents can loan it to us, until Elk Creek comes in."

"My parents!"

"They've got money. You're going to inherit someday. What's the difference if they give it to you now? It's an investment against the future, and we'll pay them back within the year."

"I'm not asking my parents for a penny. They support us now." She threw it in his face.

It made him fume to think of it. Her selfishness! She understood nothing about how hard it was to be a man.

He skidded on the ice and deftly brought the car back into

balance. He enjoyed the play of the wheels on ice. As he passed Ash Street, he suddenly thought (because his ideas were really flowing now, the old gray cells working with the clockwork of this sweet car) that Reischetz should be in on this deal. Reischetz was instrumental in the city government, and if Angus cut him in on Elk Creek, he could smooth the passage of the thing. Zoning laws and legal restrictions could be plopped into Angus' pocket just by offering old Rye Shits a percentage of the take. He wondered how much he should offer. One percent perhaps, no more. Or maybe the offer should be as an investor, with shares of stock.

Now Angus' head was buzzing, for it had not occurred to him before to sell stock in this development, but actually that was as good a way to raise money as a loan. Probably better. Only he would need to get himself incorporated. Damn! Why hadn't he thought of that before? He wished he had not seen George so soon. He should have done a little more homework before going to the bank. He glanced at his watch. It was three-fifteen. He left the car parked on Lee Street and raced up the steps of the eighteenth-century brick house where Tony had his office. A shiny brass plaque pronounced, ANTHONY REISCHETZ, ATTORNEY-AT-LAW. And that was a laugh, because everyone knew Tony had more irons in the fire than just law. He was into money.

"Is Tony in?" He stuck his head inside.

The secretary took in Agnus' neat dark suit, his striped Brooks Brothers tie. "No, he's gone over to the mayor's office," she smiled. "He's going straight home after that," she added. "The weather's turning sticky. We're closing up early. It's supposed to snow a couple of inches."

"I'll catch him later, then," he said, as if he could not care less. He noticed the office decorated with greens and tiny Christmas balls. "Happy Christmas."

He slid behind the wheel of the Porsche again. Now what? It was still early. Maybe he ought to catch old Rye Shits at his home.

Tony's house was in the lower town, a simple frame structure with fake stone paper covering it. Angus parked arrogantly in the driveway, blocking the garage, and pulled himself heavily from the car. God! What a pretty machine. It made him feel good just to look at it. Already the sleet was slanting down heavily, its stinging white rays sticking to the gray waxed surface of the Porsche and the stiff, short grass of the front yard. He almost fell on the slippery wooden steps, recovered, reached the safety of the covered porch, and, blowing on his hands against the cold, pushed the doorbell. If Tony were home, he'd probably offer him a drink. Maybe hot rum or bourbon on a day like this. . . .

The door opened to reveal Angie, a baby astride one hip.

"Oh, Mr. McEwen." She shifted the baby higher on her hip.

"Is your good husband in?" he asked, swearing silently at his own pomposity. He had not noticed before what a pretty girl she was.

"No, I don't expect him for a while." Behind her came a splintering crash of glass, followed by the crack of wood on wood and instantly a wail. Angie flew inside, leaving him at the open door. He stepped inside. The house was bigger than he'd expected and sparsely furnished. There was a grass mat in the living room, a sofa and one chair. The rooms were almost bare, and this he observed with nonjudgmental surprise, since most of the houses he knew were darkly stuffed with tables, rugs, chairs, sideboards, chests, *objets d'art*, and rows of paintings on the walls. He liked the emptiness. The smell of stew filled his nostrils, and his ears were assaulted by the spasmodic crying of the baby, sobbing and catching its breath in quick, indrawn, choking gulps. He shut the door behind him and walked back toward the sound. Poor woman, taking care of two little children all alone.

She was sitting on the kitchen floor when he entered, one baby in her arms, soothing its sputtering sobs, the other crawling on her lap in helpless concern, looking up at its mother.

"Is he all right?" Angus picked up the overturned highchair and set it on its feet. The floor was covered with the broken china of the baby's plate. "That was my fault," he said, "calling you to the door just when you were feeding him."

"I don't know how it could have happened."

"Here, I'll help you clean up. Maybe Tony'll be back by then."

Together they mopped the cereal off the floor. Then he stayed to watch her feed the baby.

"Would you like a cup of coffee?" she asked.

"I'd love one," he said, and was pleased to watch her swing to the stove to heat it up for him. She was a little nervous at his presence in the house and also flattered, he imagined, from the way she was behaving. She settled him at the kitchen table, chattering a mile a minute about the twin boys, two years old, Tonio and Paul, and how much trouble they were, but she wouldn't give them up for the world, and how terrible it was to have him come to the house when it was such a mess, which was natural on a day like today, what with the rain and snow, so she couldn't get outside. A two-year-old was a lot of work, and two of them! She laughed. He nodded, admiring her ample

bosom that strained her blouse, admiring even the messy cer-
tainty with which she pushed back a straying blond hair. (Well,
dark at the roots.) She had cereal on her cheek, and she spread
it into her hair with a generous swipe of one hand. This wasn't
usually feeding time, she told him animatedly, but today the
babies had gone off schedule, and she'd been trying to sew some
living room curtains, and that's why the accident had happened, because accidents always happen when you're tired. She
moved with a suggestive sway of the hips, and her feet slapped
the floor, flat and steady as boards, quite unlike that tiptoed
grace with which Elizabeth moved. *Slap-slap.* Angie moved like
a bear with a swaying broad bottom. He didn't remember those
wide gestures when she came up to Walnut Grove. But then,
he didn't really remember much about that lunch.

"Boy, was I nervous up there." She giggled at the memory.
"I didn't know how to act."

He thought that was endearing, her confessing uncertainty
to him. After a time he felt comfortable enough to ask for a
drink. She didn't seem to mind. He poured himself a liberal
scotch and settled down to wait for Tony, who was sure to be
back any minute, what with the weather socking in.

Meantime he took her to the window to point out his
Porsche. "It's a princess of a car."

"It's sweet. It looks like a turtle," she said. He had never
thought of that before. It did look like a turtle, with its short,
stubby body and soft, curving forms.

"Do you like it?"

"I love it."

"I'll drive you out to Elk Creek sometime," he offered generously. "You'll be impressed. I grew up there. It's beautiful."

He was enjoying himself, watching her humming at her

sewing machine. He liked the way she didn't let him disturb her afternoon. That was because she came from up north, New York City, and hadn't learned the Southern way in which, whenever a guest arrived, at whatever time of day, you had to put aside all work and just set, directing all attention to the guest.

Once, when he went to the bathroom, he sneaked a refill drink, careful to enclose the highball glass in one big hand and shield its contents from her view. He was dissolving into a golden glow. He told all his favorite stories, like hunting rabbits up a tree.

"Rabbits don't climb trees."

"Well, let me tell you. See, you've got pine woods all through that area, flat as a plate on the Eastern Shore. You ever been to the Eastern Shore?"

She shook her head.

"Wonderful country. Now, rabbits always run in a circle. Did you know that? So you send out the dogs to raise the rabbit, and you listen to the baying and try to get in line with the rabbit when he circles back, then blammo! You'll get him.

"So this time, we're all in these deep woods, and suddenly the dogs stop. We can hear them baying and singing up over yonder aways, and we know right away the rabbit's gone to cover. Dropped in a hole. We go over where the dogs are, and sure enough the dogs are pawing about around the roots of this big pine tree.

"Jerry Earnshaw, he goes over to a tree, pulls out a pocket knife, and cuts himself a nice, long, straight stick. Then he strips all the leaves and pokes it down the rabbit hole. Brings it back out"—Angus acted out the motions—"and spies the end, looking for rabbit fur. Nothing there."

Angie had stopped sewing and was listening intently. Angus swelled to his audience. "So this time he pokes it up the tree."

"What do you mean, up?"

"The tree's hollow, see? So he turns the stick right up the inside of the trunk of the tree, pokes about, brings out the stick, and there are a few little brown bunny hairs on the end of the stick. So now he reaches in his coat. You know how a countryman's always got on a big ol' jacket, nothing but pockets. He pulls out a little short-handled axe.

"Then with four perfect little snaps of his axe, chop-chop, he cuts a hole in the side of the tree, pulls out the rabbit by the ears and—"

"I don't believe it!"

"Swear to God. The rabbit'd climbed up the inside of the hollow tree."

"That's incredible! Rabbits don't climb trees!"

At that moment Tony opened the door.

"Rye Shits!" Angus shouted exuberantly, lifting his glass as if he were the host. "Here he is!" He did not notice Tony's scowl or the black look he cast his wife.

"I was wondering whose car that was," he said stiffly.

"Listen to my proposition and you'll have one too. Wait'll you hear what I have for you!"

"A business proposition?"

"It's terrific. I went to your office," Angus blurted happily, "but you weren't there. The secretary said you were on your way home, so I came by. Your beautiful wife's been entertaining me," he continued.

"I'll get some coffee," said Angie, who had folded up her

material and straightened up the sewing machine. "You look tired, Tony. Is it snowing hard?"

"Yes." His eyes were hard. "Well, what's the deal?" No small talk. Angus tried to pull his thoughts together. He hardly knew where to begin. The whole mood had changed with Tony's entrance, and the room, which before had seemed open, light, and airy, looked suddenly bare, the smell of stew oppressive. He wished Angie would come back in.

Tony was staring at him.

"What are you drinking?"

"I stole a bit of your scotch," he said. "Hope you don't mind."

"So, what's the deal," Tony pushed, "that can't wait until the office?"

"Gee, I hope you don't mind," he said earnestly. "I was just driving along in my new Porsche. They said at your office you wouldn't be back."

Angela brought in coffee, then left.

In the 1950s you stood to make a lot of money in real estate development. Even in Naughton, which was somewhat out of the way, we had a glue factory and lumber mills, and businesses were coming down from the North to take advantage of cheap labor. We had a Union Carbide office and a tire company out on Route 5.

Today you'd go bust developing. Today you take fifty acres and talk of fifty houses on one-acre lots, and you'd have an investment of five million dollars with annual carrying costs at over a million dollars, interest rates at 12 to 20 percent. You'd need a million dollars a year until you got your sales moving. But in those days Angus wasn't wrong.

He needed $10,000 an acre to cover his zoning and access roads, electric and phone lines, wells, and septic tanks or cesspools. He figured on building four houses at a time, and if the houses cost him $12,000 each to build, or less, say $40,000 in all, and if he sold them at $30,000 each, he'd roughly triple his money: $120,000 gross, he thought. Interest rates were only about 6 percent in those days, sometimes less. He wasn't talking about much more than a $72,000 investment a year at 5 percent. He stood to make a killing.

It wasn't Angus' idea that was wrong. The problem was he didn't know how to execute it.

Tony, meanwhile, was computing his own profit. Fifty acres at $10,000 an acre was $500,000. . . .

"Well, it sounds interesting," he said when Angus finished. "Suppose you write up those figures for me and send them to the office. Let me have a chance to study them at leisure and think about them some. I'll want to look at the property." He clapped Angus on the back as he led him to the door.

"Listen, tell your wife good-bye for me," said Angus politely. "It was nice to meet her. You know what the lightning bug said when he backed into the lawn mower?"

"What?"

"De-lighted!" Angus laughed. He clapped Tony's arm in a friendly punch and stepped through the door.

The sound of the Porsche had disappeared up the hill when Tony moved into the kitchen to find Angela.

"All right." His anger slashed out like barbed wire. "You seeing that man?"

"What do you mean?" Angela looked up surprised. "Sure I'm seeing him. You seen him in the house. I got eyes, I see him."

"Don't play innocent with me."

"Tony, he's your business friend. What do I got to do with him?"

He grabbed her hair. "That's what I'd like to know." She screamed. "You playing around with that crowd now? I take you to one party in one gentry house and next I know they're coming over to my house."

"Tony, I never saw the guy before. Stop it!" She was screaming with pain. She tore free from his grip. "Jeezus. What d'you think I am? He's your professional acquaintance. He comes to the door and says he's here to see you. He says you're on your way home. What do you want me to do? Shut the door in his face? I do that and you'll tear out my hair for losing you money—" Her voice had lifted.

"I see you with him anymore, I'll . . ." The threat was left hanging.

"There," she shouted. "Now you've gone and woken up the kids. See what you've done."

8

THEY SPENT LONGER THAN THEY INTENDED ON THEIR ERRANDS, dawdling over lunch, laughing, and looking in each other's eyes.

By the time they were ready to leave, the snow was coming down hard. It was already dark. Elizabeth tried to call her husband at the office and got no answer. Tom telephoned the rectory and said that he'd be late. He asked Natalie to pass the message on to his wife.

Then they ran for the car, Tom with one arm around her. They were floating—high.

They drove a little more than an hour, and the snow was falling hard, swirling in the headlights of the car.

"I can't stop smiling," he said. "I have this silly grin." She was bubbling with laughter. Ice kept forming on the windshield wiper, smearing visibility. He stopped the car. "For safety. I can't drive."

Elizabeth got out, too, to help chip off the ice.

Tom was surprised to see how much snow had fallen. It was drifting and in places topped his shoes. As he moved to her side of the car, he put one arm around Elizabeth.

"Your feet will be soaked. Shall I carry you?"

She leaned into him, curling to his embrace. "No, no, I'm fine." She lifted her face toward his, her breath warm against his cheek, but even as she spoke, he twisted and picked her off the ground.

"Oh." Her arms crept round his neck, and for one sweet moment she dipped her head, burying her lips in the warm pocket of his neck. For one moment Tom's knees went weak, but he was hardly conscious of her weight. At the car he shifted her skillfully, propping her against one knee as he reached for the handle of the door.

"Shall I get it?" Her voice was music to him, the particular questioning lilt at the ends of her phrases.

"Don't move." He set her feet on the running board. She teetered on the step, caught her balance, leaning into him, breathless, laughing in his eyes.

The kiss surprised them both. Long, rapturous mouths reaching, searching, drinking in the other's lips, tongues, their bodies pressed hungrily, they embraced; for a timeless moment they were entwined in one another's arms and lost in the dark of the snowy night. When Tom swam to the surface of consciousness and released her, he was weak with longing.

"Elizabeth."

Eventually he became aware of the cold, his feet wet, her dark hair frosted white with snow. He stood at the door and she, laughing, brushed snow off his eyebrows, his shoulders, his gray hair. He came to his senses then and forced himself round to the driver's seat, threw himself in the car, and then, overcome by withdrawal, grabbed her hand. He kissed the palm, his tongue licking her skin, sending shivers through them both.

"We have to go," she whispered. Her eyes were closed, her head back against the seat.

He started the car. They held hands.

"Stop the car," she said. "I want to kiss you again." Which he did joyously. "My dearest Elizabeth . . ." His lips grazed her neck. "My dearest, darling love . . ."

They staggered toward home, the car frequently stopping to permit them to gaze into each other's eyes, to let Tom trace the line of her cheek with his hand, enfold her in his embrace, and nuzzle the soft skin at her throat. He pulled her to him, and they drove nestled in each other's arms. Her finger drew the outline of his lips, and his mouth playfully moved to capture and suck her fingertip. Once he stopped the car to get a blanket from the back and wrap it round her knees. Anyone seeing the car might have thought its occupants were lost, or drunk perhaps, from the way the vehicle reeled from side to side on the road, disrespectful of the center line. It bucketed along, sometimes swift and directed along its course, then suddenly slowing to a creep that staggered, halted, then lunged on awkwardly. Inside the warm car the occupants were cozy. In the language of all love, they compared their love.

"When did you first notice me?" she asked.

"I saw you standing at the mantel talking to Roen," he answered. "I knew right away you were special."

"Our eyes met across the room." She smiled.

"Then you came over and attacked me. I thought you were wonderful," he laughed. "Until you opened your mouth."

"I know, I know." She buried her face in his shoulder. "What was I thinking of? I was so ashamed. I knew you wouldn't look at me again."

"I couldn't keep my eyes off you, and of course you were

right. You make me think. You see, I need someone to do that, to make me think.''

"I think you should stop the car and think about kissing me," she said.

No sooner said than done, and now the vehicle drifted to a halt at the side of the road. The motor died. They did not care. Only when Tom pulled back, laughing, to start the ignition, and the motor turned and turned, growling fruitlessly, did they fall silent, listening.

He turned off the lights, and still it would not start.

For the first time both became aware of the night around them, the snow flying even heavier than before.

Surreptitiously, Tom glanced at his watch.

"What time is it?"

He ignored her question, but he, too, was concerned.

"Tom, what time is it?" she insisted.

"It's eight."

"Eight o'clock."

The car coughed once and died.

"The battery's dead." He was stricken with remorse. "I knew it was weak." He drummed his fingers lightly on the wheel.

"What are we going to do?"

"Poor Elizabeth, what have I gotten you into? It's getting cold."

She nodded, pulling the blanket over her. "Do you want some?" she asked generously. Without the heater they could feel the wind blowing through the cracks.

"Do you realize we haven't passed a car in miles?" said Elizabeth. "Or seen a house."

"There are two choices." He took her hands and rubbed them lightly between his own, blowing on them. "I could walk ahead and find a house, or we could stay here shivering through the night."

"There's a third." She gave him a quick kiss. "I could walk with you to the house."

"You don't have proper shoes."

"I don't want to be left alone."

"Dear Elizabeth."

"We could freeze to death if we stay in the car," she said.

"We could freeze looking for a house."

"There has to be a house in a mile or so. Virginia's not that remote. I'd have to come."

"But I could send help back for you."

"No, I'll come with you."

That decided, they were reluctant to move. They huddled under the blanket, snuggling, holding each other and telling of their love, of what each found special in the other, and their hearts lifted to encompass the night. Finally they ventured forth, the blanket wrapped round their shoulders, and Tom's arm around her waist. Elizabeth leaned into him, ostensibly for support.

Her feet burned with cold. Soon she could not feel them, empty stumps, but each step in the white drifts brought a stab of pain.

"Let's sing. 'I'm dreaming of a white Christmas. . . .' " Her voice lifted beside him, and he joined happily. She sang work songs, folk songs, Negro spirituals, one after another. Tom did not know the moisture on her cheeks came from tears, not snow.

Earlier that night, back in the rectory, Priscilla had dinner ready by seven P.M., meticulous to the minute. Philip had washed and changed his clothes, as Priscilla thought proper for the family meal. Only Thomas was missing, and he, too, was usually punctilious in his regard for her dedication to such form. He had called the parish hall to say he would be late.

"I wonder where your father is," she said brightly. Philip shot her a blank look and returned to his homework, his head on his hand, concentrating on his math. Priscilla shook two pots on the stove, glanced out the window to see if she could spy a light up at the parish hall, and seeing nothing, decided Thomas must be on his way. Tonight the Adult Education met.

"It's snowing so hard," she commented. "You may have no school tomorrow." Philip ignored her. "Won't that be nice? And a white Christmas, imagine."

The clock hands crawled silently from seven to eight, drooped in slow decline to eight-thirty, and still Tom did not appear. At eight-thirty Priscilla called me, her voice bright as a penny.

"I was just wondering if you know where Thomas is." I could hear her smile right through the phone, but I knew nothing, and she only knew what Natalie had said—that he'd be late.

Philip and Priscilla went ahead and ate. They sat across from each other at the dining room table, Philip taking his father's place as head of the family. The candles burned a cool offering to their gracious living. They ate quietly, for not even Priscilla's nerves could stand the strain of Philip's resentful grunts to her bright questions on his day.

Outside, the blizzard slashed against the house.

At nine-thirty she called the police. The AE meeting had been cancelled due to the storm. The Naughton teenagers ran outside, building bonfires against the snow and sledding in the crisp white night, while a single police car patrolled the Joppa Road, flashing its spotlights into deep caves of white-coated timber in search of the clergyman's car. No one knew where he was or why he didn't phone.

Later still, Priscilla sat in her nightgown at the bedroom window. The blizzard had stopped, and a dusky moon sculled through the clouds, casting a ghostly pearl across the snow, the shadows of her dreams.

Rigid she sat, her chin high and suffering gladly this hurt that Thomas had instilled. Hurt was something that Priscilla understood. In pain she was brought closer to the Christ, and in sacrifice, in ascetic self-abasement, she felt purified—and righteous.

Righteously she looked in on Philip, asleep. His tousled hair curled over his forehead and around the tips of his elfish ears. She pulled the sheets and blanket to his chin and smoothed them, wrinkle-free, as she did every night at this hour, as she had done for both children almost from the time they were born. She caught his hands firmly in her grip, like catching goldfish in a pond. For an instant he struggled against her, then relaxed as she forced his hands, palms up, at his ears and again tucked in the covers so tightly that his hands were pinioned at the pillow, safe from inflicting self-abuse. Sometimes, doing this, Priscilla had to tear his hand away from his personal anatomy—which only confirmed her spiritual concern. For a moment she contemplated her son, asleep on his straight, narrow bed. He moved restlessly, murmured, pulled his hand under the sheet again.

For a second only he tugged against her, then again relaxed, and again she settled his hand beside his ear, the two hands

appearing like twin fans to frame his angelic face. At least that
was in control.

By the time Elizabeth saw the flicker of a light ahead, each step
was a stab of pain, and she was leaning hard on Tom's arm.
She was so relieved, she felt a surge of strength. "Look." His
kiss encouraged her even more. The house, a Negro shanty with
a sagging wooden porch, was set back ten yards from the road,
along a frozen rutted path. In back a dog was barking violently
and running on its chain, frenzied by their approach.

"Maybe they'll have a telephone," Tom said, as they
climbed the rotting steps. Elizabeth glanced at him in surprise,
for she had no illusions of what the house would have—two
rooms up, two down, the upstairs floorboards serving as the
ceiling to the room below. Still she was grateful for the haven
from the storm. She opened the torn screen door, its rusty
hinges squealing, and knocked with the flat of her hand.

"Hello?"

From inside came a hurried confabulation of low voices and
hollow steps. The door opened. They were looking into the
golden spill of a kerosene lamp. A strong black man stood before them and, twined between his legs, a gaggle of children
from small to halfway grown, peeping out so cute and curious
that Elizabeth could not restrain her smile. "Hello," she said.
Their mother stood at the rocking chair, from which she had
just risen.

"Our car broke down." She took it on herself to explain.
"May we—?" But the man had already stood aside, opening the
door.

"It's a minister," he said over his shoulder. "Do come in,"

His wife approached. "Come in, come in. This ain no night to be outside."

Do you know the unpainted, weathered, plain board shacks of that period? Elizabeth knew them well, having as a girl at Nacirema trotted down the hill to play with the farmer's boys. She was familiar with the galvanized bucket that stood on a shelf in the kitchen, providing water, a dipper hanging on a nail beside it; she had sat many times at a rough-hewn kitchen table just like this, picking at the splinters on its edge and letting her eyes wander over family treasures: a kewpie doll from the volunteer fire-department fair, the color calendar and magazine covers and sometimes a real picture tacked on the wall. Tom shook hands with the Negro as he entered.

"What you lookin' like that for?" The woman cuffed one of the older children away. "Don jes sit there. Stir up the fire in the stove. I'll git some water," she said to Elizabeth, "for to soak your feets."

"Thank you." Elizabeth settled at the kitchen table and slipped off her shoes. Even to touch her feet hurt. The woman sent one child scurrying for a pan of cold water.

"It has to be near cold," she explained. "Warm'd burn your feets, cold as they is."

Tom, meantime, asked innocently for a phone.

"No, we ain got no phone. Onliest place you can git a phone is up by Middleman, in the gas station there. But you're a preacher," the man continued. "You'n your wife can sleep upstairs. Come mawnin' we can git y'all back to Naughton."

Tom said nothing. He did not deny their relationship, and Elizabeth took that moment to focus her attention totally on her feet.

"I'm Storey Lunt. Tha's my wife, Eleanor. 'N the chil'ren."

Tom listened to the biblical nomenclature, committing each to memory with a gravity that Elizabeth found endearing. Ivery, Sarah, Zachary, Eustis, Isaac. The baby, Essie, buried her face in her mother's skirt.

"Mebbe a glass of something." Storey took a small jug from an exposed beam. A glass of white liquor appeared at Elizabeth's hand. It was a hot whip in her throat. Her head was swimming; she took another sip.

"Lord, you like to froze," said Eleanor. By now the wood stove was heating up, a pot of water coming to a boil. As Elizabeth's feet thawed, the temperature of the cold water was raised, first to warm, then to hot. Tom took one of her feet in his hands, rubbing it gently. The room began to warm them both, and they told about the dead battery, talked weather and the storm that had unexpectedly come tearing across the mountain, and how Eleanor's bad knee had been acting up all yesterday so they all knew beforehand how sumpin' was on the way. They told how Storey did some farming and picked up money as a handyman for several Valley families. Tom asked where the children went to school and heard how Zach, at the age of eight, had already read every book in his class. He was ready for the next grade level and school wasn't hardly begun for the year.

"So, he'll move ahead?"

"No, he cain do that. But his teacher, he loans him books. This boy, he's gonna be a educated man. Go git your book, Zach, and show how you kin read." The boy darted upstairs, returning a moment later with a book.

"What is it?"

"*Swiss Family Robinson.*" He held it out.

"Loaned by the teacher." Eleanor stood proudly behind her

son as he sat himself at the table and opened the book. Tom
listened, a smile playing at the corners of his mouth. Both his
hands enfolded Elizabeth's foot. He felt so humble and so happy,
he thought he could touch her foot to his lips, or embrace this
solemn child who was explaining the story.

"They's shipwrecked, see. I just come to how . . ."

After his son finished, Storey turned to his guests. "Now,
y'all kin take our bed tonight. My wife and me will sleep down
here."

"Oh, no." Elizabeth shook her head. "I wouldn't dream of
putting you all out. We can stay down here."

Tom joined in. "We wouldn't think of it."

"Ain no trouble," said Eleanor. "The little ones kin sleep
in their own room all together for a change—"

"I couldn't have a minister of the Lord here and not give
him my bed," said Storey with grave dignity. "It would be an
honor."

"I'll go git my things outta the room," Eleanor said. "It's
a blessing ackshully. Now I won't have to pull the stairs but
onct."

Elizabeth flashed Tom a look, but his eyes were lowered to
the floor. She could not bring herself to speak the truth. Had
she said at the outset that they weren't married, it might have
been all right, but now it was inconceivable to confess. These
beautiful people expected her to be the minister's wife, and if
she denied it, she could well imagine the scrabbling for beds
that would upset everyone, for surely Eleanor and Storey would
turn the children out of bed for her. Everyone in the family
would be cold all night in sacrifice to prudish modesty.

"But will you be all right?" Elizabeth took Eleanor's hand.

"I'm fine." Eleanor smiled, patting hers in return. "Don'

you be worry 'bout us. We sleeps down here jes as comfy as can be."

Storey gave a fine, deep laugh. "It's not ever night we have a preacher in our house. Tha's a blessin in itself."

Elizabeth felt sick at her duplicity. Her eyes met Tom's in a hollow exchange.

"Why don't you go up," he said. "You look tired."

"I am." She smiled weakly. "Yes, I'll get in bed." Behind her, Tom shook hands solemnly with his host.

"God bless you, Storey, and all those in this house."

Never a word did either say that night about their relationship. Never a word did either voice to indicate they were not man and wife. No, instead Tom looked at Elizabeth: "Why don't you go on up? You look tired," he said; and she, answering like one-half of a settled married couple: "Yes, I'll get in bed."

I'll wait in bed for you, she thought, climbing the bare board stairs. *I'll be undressed in bed for you.* She wasn't concerned for a moment with her responsibility, that here was a minister in charge of parish souls, come crawling adulterously to a married woman, himself married and breaking his vows to God. She wondered only if he wanted her.

The bed itself was an iron cot, double-sized, but with springs that almost touched the floor. It creaked at every move. The sheets had been fresh-changed by Eleanor in respect for a man of the cloth. But the mattress, the very room, smelled of the sweat of fieldwork and childbirthing and cooking and canning and preserving and all the years of sickness and servitude that go to make up poverty and family life. Elizabeth's wedding trip had been spent with Angus in the Virgin Islands, where they lay on sparkling white beaches by day and sparkling white sheets by night, the air perfumed by flowers and toiletries, their bonding marked by a privacy that remains the privilege of wealth. Her first night with Tom was spent in a Negro farmer's shack down the road from Middleman, where each shift of their weight was recorded in the squeaking of uncoiled springs. At first the noises came as tentatively as a cricket's chirp, with long, shy silences between the strains, but this turned then into a restless, rapid jiggling of the springs, and then to a steady *squeak-squeak-squeak*, together with the beating of the bed against the unlevel floor, where one leg slapped the boards in counterrhythm to the squeaking of the springs. *Squeak-squeak clunk; squeak-squeak clunk.* No one could misinterpret what was going on. In the other room the children listened, some with interest and others slack with sleep to a noise they'd heard on other nights. *Squeak-squeak clunk* and *thunk* and *thunk.* On the floor below in the warm kitchen, Storey and Eleanor laughed, low and guttural, pleased that the handsome minister should minister to his pretty wife, and both felt honored that it should be in their bed, as if a blessing of the Lord were being rained on them.

To make it worse, they both got off scot-free. Tom dropped Elizabeth off at her house the next morning. It was a brilliant day. The sun poured out of a clear blue sky; ice glistened on the tree branches, and the white snow piled in drifts, crystals glittering in the cold air. She went inside, her heart singing. She had no idea what explanation for her absence she would give.

She opened the door to a sour smell, and when she saw the dried vomit on the carpet and clinging to the banister rail, she knew Angus had other things on his mind than just his wife.

"Angus?"

"In the kitchen," he replied. So she was safe. She quickly moved upstairs and in the bathroom came across his trousers, socks, his leather shoes, his shirt and tie, all tumbled in a soggy mess in the shower. Her surge of anger dashed against her joy and fell, transformed in guilt.

She changed into jeans and a green Shetland sweater and went to find him. He sat at the kitchen table staring into a cup of coffee. She saw his forehead wrinkle up to indicate his pain.

"How are you?" She couldn't look at him. Busying herself with the coffeepot: "Have you had breakfast?"

"I'm not hungry," he answered. "I don't feel well."

"I'm so sorry." She turned to the sink, her back to him. She seemed to find a hundred things to do—feed the cat, put the garbage at the door, pour herself some coffee, and comment on the day in a running commentary that left no time for thought, and all the while no explanation of her night away came forth.

Angus, meanwhile, could remember nothing of the night before. He'd had blackouts before. He remembered seeing Tony and Angie, but after that he drew a blank. He had woken up this morning sprawled on the staircase and covered in his own upchuck. He had removed his clothes in the shower and come downstairs for coffee. Now Elizabeth had come in, presumably from an early-morning ride, and with no comment or reproach. It made him uneasy.

"Did you have a nice ride?" He congratulated himself on the innocuous question.

"Oh, yes . . . Thank you." They were both confused by guilt. "I was just going to feed him now." Even to herself she sounded forced. "Be back in a minute." She bounded out the back door into the glittering clear white air. With an axe she broke the ice in the horse trough; the cold handle bit into her ungloved hands. She opened the stall door for her horse, who stepped gingerly into the new white world and blew at the snow at his hooves in wonderment and pleased surprise. She swung into the tack room for feed, dumped a tin of grain into his manger and tossed the can back in the bin. Then to the loft for hay.

By the time she returned to the kitchen, Angus had left for work. Their separate nights would not be mentioned again. She scraped the vomit off the carpet, cleaned the spot with water and ammonia, and curiously she hummed as she worked. Once she broke into song. Which was more than Priscilla did for Tom.

"Where were you last night?" Priscilla asked, her voice aggrieved. It was dinnertime before Tom got back to the rectory, for he had the excuse of going to the parish hall to work, and he spent the day in a frenzy of calls and bills to pay and dashing about the snowy countryside, content to avoid the confrontation he deserved. His love for Elizabeth was locked away in a separate box, except when he telephoned her later in the afternoon. He tried to compartmentalize his guilt.

"Where were you last night?" Priscilla's voice was taut. "I called the police. I was worried about you."

"I'm sorry I worried you," he answered.

"That may be, but you could have telephoned."

"I had to go to Madisonville," he explained, explaining nothing. "The car died in the storm. I told you this morning when I called."

"But why not call last night? Just to pick up the phone!"

"I couldn't. I spent the night with a farm family up the

mountain. There was no phone. The car battery's dead. We need a new battery."

"Oh, Thomas."

I've thought a lot about the way he handled this. If people said he was a saint, this gave the lie to that. There was a certain cunning in his move—or possibly even malice, I don't know. First, he did not lie, but neither did he tell the truth, and second, he jerked his wife on the leash of impecunity. As a clergyman's wife she was accustomed to skirting the ice of poverty, for providing for a family of four on a salary of some $3,500 a year came hard. Priscilla took the bait.

"Can't the church pay for it? You were on church business. It's not as if we have the money to subsidize church affairs."

So he, too, got off scot-free.

9

THE NEXT MONTH FLEW PAST. CHRISTMAS CAME, AND TOM WAS busy not only with the ceremonies but with Daphne, home from school. He was delighted to have her home, but it was pleasure mixed with pain. He had sent away a loving child (he thought) and what he got back was an unrecognizable adolescent, a porcupine, all bristling quills at anyone's approach. True, she still baked cookies (smells of ginger and nutmeg trailing through the house), but she had new, smart gestures that puzzled him. The way she pushed her hair from her face with the back of one vague hand. The way she pulled away when he tried to give her a hug. "Oh, Daddy!" He respected her need for distance, but he felt helpless in the face of her hostility. He tried to talk.

"Tell me about school, Daf."

The shrug of her shoulders: "What do you want to know?"

"Do you like it? Is it fun?"

She put one finger to her lips and crossed her eyes. "A-duh."

He was stung.

"What's that?"

"What's what?"

"A-duh. Is that the way to speak to your father? I'm only asking because I care."

"It's just a joke," she said. "Can't you take a joke? We do that at school."

He watched her carefully.

"I just don't feel like talking about it, okay? It's fine. It's great. Neat people." Her voice had a whine in it he had not heard before, but when he mentioned his concern to Pris, she turned on him as well.

"Don't be silly. Daphne is fine. She's having a wonderful time. At least she tells *me* things. I don't think there's anything to worry about. It's her age. The teenage years are difficult."

Tom was told it was normal for a teenager to spend time in her room, not to worry that most all she did was sleep. She still fought with Philip, as they had always done. He decided he was being oversensitive. Meanwhile there were extra services at church and last-minute presents to buy, and stolen laughing moments with Elizabeth (a look, the touch of her hand), and the tree, the stockings, and packages for the poor, and the round of parties that Christmas brings.

Priscilla sent out Christmas cards, but neither she nor Tom thought to ask what would be appropriate, and the card, instead of being the modest black-and-white drawing of Trinity (which we could count on the former rector sending out, year after year for nearly fifteen years), showed a Holy Family. It had a lot of gold on it. In fairness, I have to add that Tom didn't choose it, didn't even like it much; but he had delegated the task to Pris, asked for her help, and he wasn't going to interfere with her decision. Carolyn and Butch Shriver ridiculed it, though, as being ostentatious. Emily Carter joined them. Moreover Tom included no personal note to individual members of

the parish. We couldn't help comparing the sterility of those
Christmas greetings to those of our former rector, Dr. Ellis, who
used to enchant certain favorites by including with his Christmas notes a few hairs from Saint Peter, his favorite prize blood-
hound; or else a cute little stamp with the paw print of a dog.
The Valley, especially Emily, loved greetings from the dogs.
This year, in the Christmas spirit and in an effort to mend poor
relations, Emily Carter had cut a few golden hairs from the
chest of her favorite Shetland sheepdog and enclosed these in
her Christmas greeting. As it happened, Philip opened the card,
and the hairs dropped to the rug without even being noticed.
Her few lines about "these" being from Gregory (the dog) were
entirely overlooked (not understood), and neither Tom nor Pris
ever mentioned them: another slap in the face to Emily.

Now it was Emily's turn to show her spunk. Gathering all
her courage, she decided to broach the topic and took it up,
where most of her conversation with Tom occurred, at the coffee hour after church.

"Did you like the greetings from Gregory?" Her face was
already scrunched up in rejection as she forced the question
out.

"Gregory?"

"Gregory. My dog. We sent you some of his hairs as a
greeting in your Christmas card."

Tom laughed.

"It was a custom," she defended herself, and explained the
tradition. Tom rocked back on his heels, hands in his pockets
and laughing down at her, eyes sparkling. She felt herself go
hot with confusion, and suddenly the whole business of dog
hairs sounded fatuous and Tom too commanding, or too dis-

tant. Was he laughing at her? She hurried away, flustered, and told Margaret she really could not bear the man.

"Why? He's very nice."

"Oh, I don't know," answered Emily, pulling on her heavy wool gloves. "I just think he's stupid."

Tom never knew he'd offended Emily again. Just as he didn't even know by Christmas, almost three months after he'd arrived, that he'd offended Carolyn Page. He didn't give it a thought. He didn't like Carolyn, and he had never sent her a bread-and-butter note or flowers after her luncheon party back in October, nor even telephoned to thank her for inviting him, and Carolyn, who had been taught always to write the following morning, noticed these slights. Tom assumed that her coolness to him, shaking hands after church, was just her way: he didn't take it personally. Neither did he think about the fact that she and Dutton sometimes missed Sunday service entirely.

I think he could have disarmed Carolyn early on with little attentions or visits, or by asking and following her advice in different situations, but he was self-absorbed and angry in those first months. He had no energy left over for amenities; and the longer he refrained, the more firmly her position against him grew, until by Christmas she no longer remembered the original humiliation but only the fact of her dislike, which was confirmed when he rebuffed Emily's peace effort, the greetings from the dogs.

So Christmas came, with carolling and festivities and wassailing and glasses lifted in happy toasts as we gathered at each other's firesides; and with either laughter or righteous indignation about the Buckfords' hideous Christmas card and our memories of Christmases past. It's hard to believe people were mad at him for not putting dog hairs in their Christmas cards.

After that the New Year came and went. Tom had only a few moments for Elizabeth—a phone call to affirm his love, a visit snatched from the festivities. Even her duties at the school had fallen off until the holidays were over. Another week and Daphne returned to school. Tom plunged into parish affairs. The first two grades of Trinity School opened with Cassandra Roen as acting headmistress. One day the school was empty, the next, to his astonishment, the little children were climbing the parish hall steps, their plaid book bags knocking their knees, their sweet faces knotted with hope and concern. His heart twisted with pleasure and pride: they seemed so small.

For Tom everything was fine. He was in love and his love flowed out of him to all the world. He felt alive. He was such fun to be around that I found myself looking forward to the vestry meetings, and I made up excuses to swing round the church to put my feet up on the scarred coffee table, playing intellectual games or gossiping about the Valley. I wasn't the only person drawn to him. He swept us up like particles pulled into the tail of a passing comet.

There was Carey Hill, who came from South Carolina originally and boasted of fighting alligators (thence his nickname, Gater Hill), and Tolli Wilson, whose Boston family made its fortune in the China silk trade a hundred years ago and came down during Reconstruction to make another on the backs of us defeated Southerners (though Tolli was one of us by then, his father and grandfather having both married Valley girls and Tolli more Confederate than a true Southern boy). Mimi had always been on Tom's side, but now Esther Ratcliffe was softening, as well as Anne Adams, who had originally preferred the intellectual Wentworth. Anne fancied herself an art historian, and somewhat above our little Naughton set.

Church was full at the eleven-o'clock service, even deep into Epiphany, when, Christmas over, the congregation usually slacks off again. It was extraordinary who showed up. Billy Tyler, for example, began to drop in whenever she was home in the country. And Elizabeth McEwen came. People who had never darkened the doors of a church in their lives. Under the Reverend Thomas Buckford attendance at Trinity Church climbed to something like five hundred communicants. Surely the compelling force came from Tom, from his air of inspiring and transcendent—well, I don't know any other word for it— happiness. Transcendent love. There was a holiness he made you feel. A minister can read a prayer without praying, kneel without submission. I've seen ministers make the sign of the cross as if they were crossing out God. But Tom's prayers were different, and the change dated from the Christmas holidays and that trip to Madisonville with Elizabeth. Margaret put her finger on the change.

"I like Tom's new way of speaking the service, don't you?" Even as she spoke, I felt a thrill of recognition. It was true. He had dropped the stilted, mannered singsong we were all familiar with, that high Episcopal voice that flattens meaning.

O Lord, our heavenly Father, Almighty and everlasting God who has safely brought us to the beginning of this day; Defend us in the same with thy mighty power; and grant that this day we fall into no sin, neither run into any kind of danger; but that all our doings, being ordered by thy governance, may be righteous in thy sight; through Jesus Christ our Lord.

The next day I listened with attention. I felt I'd never heard the prayers before.

Oh God, who are the author of peace and lover of concord . . . Defend us, thy humble servants . . . that we, surely trusting in thy defense . . .

When he said those words, a chill ran down my back.

Almighty God, Father of all mercies, we thine unworthy servants do give thee most humble and hearty thanks for all thy goodness and loving-kindness to us and to all men.

His voice caressed the words. "Thy goodness and loving-kindness. . . ." How many days in my life had I come to church? Fifty weeks of the year, probably, for some fifty years, say, give or take, and I had never marked those words: "thy loving-kindness."

His happiness did not touch Emily Carter, though, or Butch Shriver, or Carolyn Page. In their eyes nothing he could do was right. I'll never forget Carolyn, one morning after church, standing with us on the brick walk outside the church, clutching her brown alligator purse firmly to her stomach. She was dressed to the nines, with her matching alligator shoes and a mink coat and a perky little mink hat.

"God save us," she announced, "from the meek inheriting the earth. All those Christian airs."

Butch laughed, and spread her witticism across the Valley. But Billy Tyler and Gater Hill and Tolli and my wife, Margaret, and Cissie Roen and Bumpsie Carew, and many more remarked on the devotion in his prayers.

Elizabeth motivated the change. He admired her so much he would have introduced sword swallowers if she'd said the service needed them.

"Why do you read the prayers like that?" she'd asked as they sat over coffee in his office one afternoon.

"Like what?"

"As if you were chanting them. As if they had no meaning at all."

"Well, I don't know. I'll have to think about it."

"I mean, you don't talk to me like that," she said.

"Oh, no," he laughed.

"You talk to me as if you mean every word you say, but here you are in church and you address God as if you're hiding. Adam and Eve in the garden, right?"

She gave him pointers on his speaking voice, on how to deliver a ringing declamation. She asked him questions that he struggled to answer.

"You know what I dislike about religion most?" she said. "It's the constant breast-beating. If you believe there is a God— and mind you I'm not saying that I do, but *you* do, and I respect that—if you believe in a God of love and mercy, then all through the service you're moaning about how awful you are."

"What do you mean?"

"Well, the communion service. You go through all this business about your manifold sins and wickedness. You confess your sins. 'We have erred and strayed like lost sheep. We have followed too much the devices and desires of our own hearts. . . . *There is no health in us.*' Listen to that! How can that be, if we're made by the hands of a loving God? If there were a loving God, it would be impossible for Him to create such vermin as you say we are!" She finished triumphantly. "It's all so negative."

"Well." Tom had no answers at hand.

"Then you go through this long litany of remorse and contrition and so many prayers for forgiveness and then . . . *then*," she continued, her voice rising in passion (for she was not an atheist for nothing), "*then*, when you're supposed to be cleansed, shriven, forgiven, ready for communion, you begin all over again: 'We are not worthy so much as to gather up the crumbs under thy Table,' you say as you crawl forward, cringing to feast on flesh and blood."

"Good heavens, Elizabeth."

"It's true. It's cannibalism. If I were God, I'd smite us all for arrogance. I suppose that's why I'm an atheist."

"There's no such thing as an atheist," he laughed, sitting beside her. "And especially you, for you are the very embodiment of love."

"I thought God was love."

"God *is* love."

"Oh, it's such a cliché," she said. "Love is love." Inevitably the conversation turned to themselves. They argued, teasing, admiring each other. But her words had an effect on Tom, as his on her. Listening to the service, he agreed (was it because he loved everything about her?) that, yes, there was a concentration on suffering and guilt. Yet, for the first time in his life, carrying on an affair with a married woman, himself married, he felt so happy he denied his sinfulness, his guilt.

Their love was a mutual self-discovery. They thought it

could go on forever. "I should flirt with you more," she teased. "Play hot and cold."

"Why would you do that?"

She was taken aback. "Why, so you don't get tired of me. Isn't that what women are taught to do with a man? Keep him on his toes, play him like a fish, run away until he catches you. Don't look like that." She burst out laughing. "That's how you keep a man's attention."

"I wouldn't be interested if you did that."

"Wouldn't you?"

"It's you I admire. It's not the game I'm looking for. I love you," he said. "Do you know that?"

"Yes. I know that."

One day it occurred to him that his prayer had been answered. He had asked God that day on the hillside for love, for the ability to love again, and here love came in the form of Elizabeth. Which shows how careful you must be about what you pray for, he thought with a little grimace. There's an Arab saying: *"Take what you want,"* said God, *"and pay for it."*

But Tom, as far as he was concerned, had nothing to pay for. It was all given to him free. "Praise this world to the angels!" he shouted from Rilke's *Duino Elegies*; and, "Let us give jubilant praise to assenting angels!"

He had found his connection to God again. He had been lost, and now he was found. He was in love. He thought he'd entered Paradise.

He could pray again.

His soul was no longer dry and bitter and hard with suffering.

"Deus caritas est!" he shouted at me one brilliant winter

morning: "God is love," he translated, romping over, or rather through, a snowdrift with clownish boots to beat me on the back in happiness. "I have been in hell and come out into the light."

"What are you talking about?" At the time I still didn't know about Elizabeth. I only knew he'd pulled out of his depression.

"Love is not an abstraction," he said, immediately launching into abstractions. "It's the very essence of a human being. I understand it for the first time, John! Here I am forty-four years old and I'm only beginning to catch on. Am I dense? We are made of—our very cells are composed of—guess? Love! Isn't that terrific? Made in the image of God. *Deus caritas est.* We are, at bottom, *au fond*, in our very essence, love, and what we perceive as love is only a sign of our substance!"

I laughed, infected by his joy.

"Beautiful day." He rubbed his hands and shot into the old Plymouth, waved good-bye, and began his rounds.

Two weeks later he woke up.

He opened his eyes one sparkling January morning and was struck by guilt. He could hardly rise from bed. His legs were weak. What had he been thinking of? He had betrayed his wife, his church, his marriage and ordination vows, and the thousands of people who had sacrificed themselves to make the ministry something of honesty and integrity. Not to mention the trouble he was bringing down on Elizabeth and on himself. He wanted to run, a fugitive, from his life, his parish, his God, his wife and children, run from Elizabeth, run from himself. That night he raced panting through the swamps of his dreams, followed by guilt. Twice he woke with a roar from his nightmares, sweat on his brow and hands. Priscilla was astonished.

All day in his office he spent in a torment of soul. He had thought the Dark Night terrible, that sense of loss of God. But this guilt, in which he knew he deserved the loss—this was worst of all. He fled to the quiet church to throw himself prostrate, yes, full-length before the altar of God. Impurity.

Now there was no question of not knowing right from wrong. It fell on him like a fist, and he suddenly saw himself making love to her lustfully on her couch or kissing her behind his office door. It was a nail in his throat.

Had he seduced Elizabeth? One moment he thought their affair was all her fault, the next he raged at himself, hating the body (his own) that had led him from his vows. Moreover, he saw her all the time. In a rush of energy he turned his office upside down and rearranged his schedule. He would go to the Episcopal Convention that week (originally declined); and Natalie was suddenly confronted with the need to make travel arrangements. She could hardly manage to make the proper calls, it was all so hurried, and Mr. Buckford so tense, he flustered her more.

His soul had turned to snakes. They wrapped around his throat. They choked his breathing. He felt as if a board lay on his shoulders, pressing down on him until he thought he'd cry aloud in pain.

"Are you all right?" Natalie stood before him, the reservations finally made.

He stared at her for an awful moment, unable to focus his attention.

"Mr. Buckford?" Her voice came from far away.

"I have a headache," he murmured. It was true. His head was pounding now.

"You should go home," she said. "You should lie down in a dark room and keep very quiet. I know. My sister gets migraines."

His groan was hidden in the ringing of the phone.

"Don't answer it."

"What?" She was astonished at his voice. He was shaking. Sweat broke out on his forehead. "Don't answer it," he said. "I'm not here to anyone."

"I'll say you're out."

He could not bear to go home to Priscilla. Her hard sympathy would rasp like sandpaper. "I'm not here," he murmured to himself, stepping out and up the hill on his favorite walk behind the church. "I'm not here to anyone because I'm not worthy of helping anyone. How could I . . . ? I'm not here to God. He's not here to me. . . . O Christ, O Lord God, help me in my suffering. . . ."

Isolated in self-hate, he attended his conference, then took two more days. He telephoned Natalie. "I won't be back till Monday," he said. Voice short. "Ask Dr. Thompson if he can fill in Sunday. Or send his assistant." We had arrangements with our neighboring parish. Tom went to Virginia Beach, took a room in a guesthouse, and walked the cold, wind-swept sand, staring at the icy sea. He walked and walked. His hands were red and raw from the wind, his ears burned, his face was scalded by cold. But that pain was easy compared to the one inside. If spoken to, he started, or sometimes he stared off as if he didn't even hear. The guesthouse owner, Mrs. Garth, continued the common courtesies of "Good morning," and "Brisk out, Mr.

Buckford." She peered at him suspiciously from behind the kitchen door. When he left, she was relieved.

But no sooner did he return home than he went to see Elizabeth—and realized that while he was away, he had thought all the time of holding her in his arms. They made love passionately, hungrily, until, depleted, lying in her embrace, he panicked again.

"You have to quit," he said.

"Quit?"

"We can't do this. I can't have you around all the time."

"You want me to quit the school?" she repeated dully.

"Leave me alone!" he cried.

"Of course! Yes! I will!" she shouted back. "It's not my fault. You're in *my* house, naked in *my* bed. *You* go, then. Get out."

And he was pulling on his undershirt and boxer shorts while she, back turned, dressed sullenly. She clenched her teeth to keep them from chattering. He looked at her with anguished eyes and bolted from the house.

But hardly had he reached the parish hall than he telephoned her again. They talked by phone in low voices.

Sometimes it was Elizabeth who split off from him.

"I can't stand it. Go away. Go or stay, but make a decision! This is intolerable."

And it went on. I still didn't know about it then.

The January thaw set in. The ground went soggy, dirty patches of snow curling under thickets. In the fields the horses snorted, bucked, kicking their heels in the pleasant sun; and we could all smell a promise of spring that lifted our hearts, even as we knew we had two more months of cold. We scraped the mud off our boots, laughing at the wet, and the farmers who came into the feed store sat by the stove and dreamed of the planting soon to begin. It was in those muddy days that I saw Butch Shriver riding Lizzie's horse.

It was at a meet. The hounds were still circling up with the Master, and the riders gathering. I walked up to Butch, my rubber boots sinking in the mud, and put one hand on the horse's neck.

"Isn't this Majority? Elizabeth McEwen's horse?" I asked.

The General thrust his boots out straight in his stirrups, leaning back proud as punch. "It is," he said. "Finally got him. I've been trying to buy him for a year."

"I didn't know she wanted to sell."

"The horse is too big for her," he explained. "He's a handful, I'll tell you. I can barely keep him in."

I clapped the hunter's shoulder. I was trying to remember him giving Lizzie any trouble. The hounds rippled like puddles across the blanched bleached field, all brown and white and red against dry grass; the horses knew it was time to begin, and they jiggled their reins and pawed their hooves. Nearby, one animal swung his rump around so fast he hit me in his excitement, but Elizabeth's Majority stood foursquare, planted, ears pricked in anticipation. He was a war-horse, as familiar with the hunt as any man.

The General threw away the stub of his cigar. "You see that Porsche they've bought?" He gave a laugh like the crack of a whip. "They're not hurting for money, anyway."

We separated as the hunt began. I meant to ask Elizabeth about her horse when I saw her next. The circumstances of our meeting drove it out of my mind.

I was in Tom's office, when Elizabeth came into the outer room. She darted to his open door, knocked twice, and without waiting for reply, entered, dancing on tiptoe.

"Can I come in? Hello, John."

It was their look I intercepted, their whole souls in their eyes. I stared dumbfounded. They were drinking each other in; their intimacy lay tangible between them.

He turned away. Elizabeth, who had flashed her wide, expressive smile at me—"Hello, John"—caught his look, and her smile crumbled like a drawing tossed into the flames.

I closed the door behind her as she left.

"Tom?" Perhaps reproof lay in my voice.

"Don't say anything," he said. "I know."

I polished my glasses on my shirt, a diversionary gesture, since I didn't know what I wanted to say. I was annoyed.

"Listen, there's nothing you can say to me that I haven't said already to myself. I betray everyone, don't I, by loving her, yet when I see her my heart leaps up against my will. I can't control it. I can't run. I'm caught on God's pin. I'm married. She's married. There are times I've thought castration is the answer."

"Tom. Tom." I dropped one hand on his shoulder, but I tell you I was glad to hear that he was suffering.

"You should hear me argue it out. I know people fall in love. I've been around. It's not a question of will. The heart has definitions of its own, lunging off with total disregard for wisdom. Christ, what am I doing? John, what am I to do? Should I resign?"

"Resign from Trinity? I wouldn't let you," I answered. Then suddenly my anger burst out: "But you goddamn well better get her out of here."

His face went blank. Did I question my motives? At the time I saw only the virtue of my stance.

"You don't have to be seen smooching, holding hands," I said distastefully. "You just let anyone catch you, as I just did, see you greet each other, and it's evident. The least you can do is to think of her good name."

His face was drained of color.

"Tom," I said. "I'm your friend. You know I'm on your side."

"What should I do?"

"Well, first you get her out of this office. Then you stop seeing her altogether. Get a grip on yourself. It will pass."

He nodded stiffly.

"If you want to explain the reasons to her," I continued, generous in the expression of my wisdom, "for God's sake don't put it in writing."

"No, no. I wouldn't do that."

"On the other hand I can tell you from experience it's twice as hard in person. I know." For a moment I remembered Flossie, and the knife of regret twisted so sharply that I flinched: after all those years! "All you do is cling harder to each other. So cut it quick and clean."

He walked me to my car. I was glad to see that she had left her desk. She had stepped down the hall, I guess. I was gone before she returned, and what happened then I know from her reports, and Tom's.

Looking back on it, I wonder how altruistic my motives were. I remember I went home that night and in bed I threw myself at Margaret. I took her. But I took no delight in it, and neither did she. I kept remembering that look exchanged by Tom and Elizabeth. There was none of the natural repression you might expect—as if all their circuits were on GO. They had no self-control, and when you saw them together it was goddamn embarrassing, that fire flashing between them. They were shot with light. So I was jealous, perhaps, who knows, of him, of them, or her intrusion on my friendship. I went home and tried to make love to my wife. And rolled off feeling worse.

Margaret and I were best friends. We'd met in college. She's a red-setter dog, long-legged and athletic, open, friendly, forthright. I am bound to her after all these years by ties of deep affection. But passion? I don't think we ever shared that. I was twenty-five when I married, and that was twenty-five years before this story began. Years later I'd had one rollicking affair with Flossie Ringman—even now I remember her pretty, tidy body tucked under mine, her rakish, wall-eyed tits. I remember the way she'd throw back her head at climax and send out peals of laughter, the trill of a mockingbird's song, a gush of laughs. How I treasured that sound!

She did things to me that Margaret had probably never heard of, and I did things to Flossie I would be ashamed to have Margaret know I liked. Margaret was too pure for that. To Flossie it was just fun. "Having fun," she called it. I've never met a woman in my life who enjoyed sex more. Once, she came all over my ankle, squirming on my foot. I squeezed her nipples and felt the sluice of her warmth flow out over my foot. She came just sucking me.

I once tried to make love to Margaret the way Flossie and I made love, and I remember my confusion when it didn't work. Sometimes, after one of our quick, purposeful sex acts, lying apart, holding hands, I wondered if Margaret had a lover on the side. Did he kiss her soft, vulnerable underparts, the navel or armpit? Did he suck her breasts or lick those parts so personal

I couldn't bring myself to name them? Did she come on his foot in ecstasy? Did she compare him to me?

It was pure lust. I told her so. But I could understand how Flossie wanted a husband and kids. She grew impatient with the very arrangement that had pleased her at first—the free, wild lover uncommitted. She began to chafe at weekends and holidays alone, time that I spent with my family. What could I do? We quarrelled and made up rapturously. The only surprising thing is how long it lasted. Four years, five. Later the tension hung in the air between us, a blanket of resentment barring the electricity of our touch. The relationship finished. Flossie moved to Richmond and married Jack Foxwell. The name was not lost on me.

Do you know, as I write this now, I miss her. Sometimes at night I wake up, hypnagogic and, catapulted back in time, I hear her laugh rippling down the stairwells of my ears, a musical scale, and even now, at my age, I am so vulnerable my heart will catch. I reach across the sheets to touch my love, my love, and then with a grunt I wake up. It's Margaret beside me. That's all right. I wouldn't have it any other way. I chose her. Twice.

I think Margaret knew. I never told her, but I think she guessed. She also knew my conflict. It wasn't right to break up a marriage just for love. You see it all the time. People split up a perfectly good relationship, and do they marry their True Love? No, they let go of that relationship too (the burden too heavy), and maybe they stay single for five or six years and then remarry, this time someone as ordinary as the one they left first time round. They marry out of convenience or loneliness. Passion and marriage don't mate. You'll call me cynical. I'm just practical. It's what I've seen. The second time around a man will marry a woman half his age, plus ten years.

I've had other women besides Flossie. One year at a Richmond ball, dancing with a woman I shall not name, my hand low on the swell of her flank, her body pressed to mine and our muscles mirror-movements to Cole Porter's beat, I felt pawed by lust.

"I want you," I whispered in her ear. She knew it anyway. She could feel my rut as we danced.

"When?" Oh, clever woman.

"Right now." I led her off the dance floor and out to the parking lot to my car. Now I am ashamed of this: to make love in the backseat of a car at the age of fifty-four—I'm not a teenager anymore—and she in her best ball gown, with her crinolines billowing in our faces and me struggling against the points of my white tie, the stiff shirt popping out and crackling against my skin, and the two of us groaning and groping and clutching through the layers of clothing across the cramped backseat. Panting and sweating. It was a miracle we managed what we did. We dressed again, each feeling high and simultaneously let down at the execution of the job. Her dress was torn. She disappeared into the ladies' room for the rest of the night, but I returned to the floor and danced till the party closed. I collected Margaret, and we drove home in the same car I'd just used. I could smell my semen in it.

Six or eight weeks later we took a hotel room together for an afternoon, this lady and I, and tried to make it up to each other. But the chemistry was lost.

What I'm trying to say is that I know the biological imperative. I give it credit, especially among high-spirited healthy folk. There was hardly a man or woman in the Valley who didn't have an affair at some time. Divorce was not unknown. There was even a game played down at the Club called the Key

Game, in which couples met for an evening and exchanged house keys and wives, as if they were playing with a deck of cards. But I also knew the level of hypocrisy of the place. What was permitted for ourselves was not allowed the minister of our consciences and our souls.

I went home that night and made distasteful love to Margaret, but I couldn't get Tom and Elizabeth out of my mind, and Flossie's image, too, came reeling up behind my eyes.

10

When Tom left me at the car and turned back to the parish hall, I saw him square his shoulders and pull himself together to go inside.

Elizabeth at her desk looked up, her heart leaping to meet him. Her vivid smile flashed out.

"No!" He strode angrily past her into his own office. The door closed. She was dumbfounded.

"Well, good morning to me," she said acidly. One hand shot out in annoyance, reaching for the stapler too quickly. She overturned her coffee on the letters she'd just typed.

"Goddamn!"

She jumped up, helplessly watching coffee spread across the desk, then came a scrabble to retrieve the papers before they were soaked. It took a few minutes to mop up the mess with paper towels, and when she finished, Tom walked back in.

By then he'd had time to regret his curtness with Elizabeth. He had seen her open, leaping look. He had seen her face fall. He knew he had hurt her. Sitting at his desk, therefore, his head in his hands, he reconsidered. At least he could be polite. The truth was that he wanted to stand beside her. He wanted those wide gray eyes to rest on him. Simply, he wanted to be near that air of enchanted happiness she emitted. And thinking about that, temptation overriding duty, he jumped up to undo what he had done and share a cup of coffee and the parish business and his thoughts, before he grasped the nettle and they separated . . . forever.

"Elizabeth—"

"Don't speak to me!" She turned on him angrily. "How dare you!" She held a roll of paper towels in one hand, and her eyes were flashing. "You come in here and give me things to do. What do you think I am, your *servant?*"

He stepped back. "No, I—"

"Well, I have enough to do. I don't need more right now."

Tom backed out, confused. He returned to the papers on his desk and absorbed himself in work, the palliative to mixed emotions and to what he knew he had to do anyway about Elizabeth. Her outburst made it easier on him. He did not try to contact her again.

That afternoon she quit her job. Tom had worked on his sermon for an hour, written letters, made calls, and was leaving the office when he paused to drop off letters to be typed. She did not look up. She stopped typing, eyes glued to the paper, fingers resting on the keys. On her desk lay a neat pile of letters newly typed.

"What are these?" he murmured in surprise, then seeing the addresses: "I thought they went out yesterday. Didn't I already sign them?"

"These are letters I am retyping," she said stiffly. "I spilled coffee on them. I'll have them for you by the end of the afternoon."

He shifted. He didn't know if her anger was directed at him

or at her work. "Well, if you can get to it, I'll add these to your burdens." He did not smile. "I won't be back till late."

When he left, still without meeting her eyes, she sat, her elbows on the typewriter and both hands covering her face in perfect duplication of his earlier pose. Later she typed her resignation.

Tom:

I cannot find time to work here any longer. I trust my absence will impose no inconvenience. A faster typist will easily be found.

I've finished the letters. I've not had time to do the new work.

E.P.McE.

She put the letters on his desk in a neat pile ready for his signature. She put her own note on top. To one side she placed the letters he wanted typed and her office key.

He read her note that evening. Then he went to the vestry meeting, where he savaged Butch Shriver.

"I can finally report that the signs are up. If someone had been doing his job, they'd have been up months ago."

Shriver's face went black at the insult. So the poison began to fall, drop by drop, filling up the flask.

That wasn't the end. Tom took Butch on openly—a sublimation for his own self-hate. That evening he decided to give Shriver's scholarship to Storey Lunt's boy, little Zachary Lunt, who already read the encyclopaedia for fun. To a Negro! The thought had come to him like a bolt from the blue as he was driving away from the vestry meeting. It shows how sly Tom could be, that he turned the idea over and over, plotting its execution. He knew precisely what he was doing, and precisely the effect on Butch, on Naughton—and then he planned the careful execution of his plot.

Meanwhile Angus was drinking two bottles a day, and his moods shifted from volcanic depression to manic high. You couldn't say that he was happy, but The Big Picture was largely optimistic (he told himself). Things were swinging round his way. First there was the immediate cash-flow problem, resolved with the sale of Lizzie's horse. That had been an unexpected windfall. For weeks Elizabeth had been preoccupied. Twice he had come upon her at her desk, tapping the checkbook with her pencil eraser; or flowering long columns of figures from underneath her moving pen.

"What's up?" he had asked. But she had simply shaken her head in concentration. He didn't want to know anyway, on the principle that what you don't know can't hurt you. He knew she had visited her father's accountant and later the Mercantile Bank in Washington, which held her Trust.

"I don't know how we'll manage," she told him. Then one day she sold her horse. She got the blues immediately, but Angus cheered her up. They really couldn't afford a horse, he said, and this one was too big for Elizabeth anyway, standing seventeen hands. He was a man's horse. She looked ridiculous perched on him, a flea on an elephant. Moreover, Shriver was willing to pay almost twice the value of the beast, and the saving in feed alone would be substantial, not to speak of hunt fees. His final argument had clinched the deal as far as he was concerned, when he pointed out how much time she spent just exercising the animal. Elizabeth gave a little gasp of what he took to be feigned hurt and defended herself that she had always had a horse, that she had had a horse before they were married, and that he had never said anything about it. But he pursued his argument relentlessly. It was of no concern to him, but for her own good he had pointed it out: her time could be spent more fruitfully. There were lots of people pretty badly off in the world, and she could be helping someone else if she weren't so self-absorbed.

"How dare you!" Her response had been downright mean. Her hands had curled into angry fists. "Goddamn you! I have no more patience with you." And she had run from the room in tears.

The money was spent the same day it was collected on payments for the Porsche and the mortgages on the Elk Creek property, though he had managed to swipe enough for the two cases of booze that he squirreled away in the office. He was still spiralling into debt, and that concerned him. No way had he imagined that developing this property would take so much capital. Already he was deep in loans to Tony, but that was to be expected with the financial picture of these years, and, anyway, with arrangements between friends as close as he and Tony, things were sure to work out well.

His blackouts had become common. He didn't think that anyone noticed, but they embarrassed him. It was hard trying to figure out what he'd done or said the night before.

He had one sustenance and comfort, and that was Tony and Angie. He made it a custom to drop round by Tony's house several times a week, at the end of the day, to have a drink, to admire his children and talk to Angie.

"You're lucky to have such beautiful kids," he told Tony mournfully one bell-clear night. "Two beautiful children and a lovely wife."

"Well, you have a good-looking wife." Tony shot him a glance.

"Yes, but she doesn't like me," Angus admitted, staring into his drink, and suddenly the sorrows of the world welled up in him. It seemed so sad—his life, his relationships, his mental-retardee idiot son, an inmate in an institution; and when he wrenched his thoughts away from that blot on the McEwen name, there was his own terrible loneliness.

"You have everything." He looked up at Tony. "A beautiful home. Two healthy kids. A beautiful wife. And she likes kids, and she's a good mother."

He took a deep gulp of his drink. "Elizabeth and I had one kid," he confessed, "but he didn't work out."

"For heaven's sake," said Tony. "What does that mean?"

"It was Elizabeth's fault." Angus nodded. "I don't mean intentionally, probably. But she was careless. She got rubella while she was pregnant and damaged the kid."

"Good God!" It was unclear whether Tony was shocked at the fact or at the expression of blame Angus attached to Elizabeth.

"He's in Briarose now. He's a mental defective. And deaf."

"I'm so sorry."

"Yeah, it's a—no one can know what it feels like to—" Tears of self-pity pricked his eyes. Angie, in the kitchen, was singing as she cooked, and he could hear her clear soprano voice lifting and winding among the smells of the cooking sausage and cabbage, the two senses intertwining so sinuously that in his fuzzy state both sounds and smells were song.

"What's she singing?" he asked. It sounded plaintive and sweet, just matching his mood.

"It's from *Rigoletto.*"

"*Rigoletto?*"

"The opera. Angie likes opera."

"Oh." Angus knew nothing about opera. His thoughts drifted on the poignant notes back to his troubles.

"The awful thing is that it was so unnecessary." He rose to pour himself another drink. He did not notice Tony's fingers drum the back of the couch. "It was a couple of years ago. Elizabeth's grandmother was dying up at Nacirema, the big place. Grandma was the center of the family, a kind of magnetic core for everyone. The house had been in the family for years. Hell, for generations. Nacirema is *American* spelled backwards. Elizabeth was to inherit it. We would have had a fortune. Her grandmother had left a will that divided the money and stocks between the boys, because they had all moved away, but Elizabeth and me were going to be the next Nacirema generation. And actually that was a smart thing to do because Elizabeth loves the Valley and I come from right nearby, and we like the life-style and know how to manage it. There wasn't a penny of mortgage on the place. The only thing we'd of had to pay was the taxes, and it was all zoned agricultural, so even that wasn't too bad either. The house was filled with paintings, antiques. I mean it was terrific! The Virginia Garden Club used to try to get it every year for their House and Garden Tour. I mean it was something else. The sideboards groaned with silver. They had two eighteenth-century bull's-eye mirrors in the dining room—a matched pair. The living room tables were covered with Ming pottery and a collection of Venetian paperweights.

The place was worth a fortune. You'd of loved it," he said generously.

"Well, it burned down, and that's when Elizabeth got rubella and my son was damaged. I mean, talk about bad luck. Elizabeth's grandmother was about ninety-five then, and she died. I mean, it wasn't any surprise. We'd all known she was going to die for years, we'd all been expecting it. So the family gathered, and there was this big funeral. People came from as far away as California. A real send-off. Well, Elizabeth was pregnant at the time. She'd already had one miscarriage. Later she had another. We couldn't move up to Nacirema right away, and Elizabeth's cousin, Flossie, came to stay in the house, to take care of it while there was no one there. It was just a temporary thing. Flossie needed a place to live, I think that was it. This was before she ran off and married so suddenly. Flossie was real crazy. I've known her for years, and that girl was just batty, you know what I mean?"

Tony nodded, watching.

"I mean she was a grown woman. But she was just screwball. I think she must of been having personal problems at the time. She was strung up tight as a highwire. I always felt she was right on the edge. I don't know what was wrong with her, but she wasn't in the best mental state, is all I mean. So she's living up at Nacirema all alone, which is what she insisted that she wanted to do and that she never felt lonely and she'd always loved the house and all that, and she'd love to stay and watch the place till we could get settled to move. Well, I mean it wasn't all that lonely for her. She was an attractive woman. She had friends, and I suppose they came to see her."

He glanced at his empty glass. "Do you mind if I have another?" he asked politely. "I got to be going in a minute."

"No, no," said Tony. "Here, let me get it for you. We're going to have dinner in a minute, so I'll have to ask you to leave then, but you can have another drink."

Angus' feelings were wounded at this abrupt discourtesy. He hovered, watching Tony fill his glass, a little worried, because he'd noticed that Tony wasn't overly generous when he poured and marveling also that Tony didn't ask him to stay for supper. Wasn't that what any Southern gentleman would do? Angus put this down to Tony's poor upbringing, his lack of education, and he tried to forgive him for the breach of manners; but he had to admit, it hurt.

"Go on with your story." Tony handed him the glass and refilled his own. "You gotta speed it up, though, or we won't have time to finish."

"There's nothing to it," Angus continued brusquely. In the kitchen Angie was still singing, her voice floating up and down:

"La ci darem la mano. . . ."

He wished she would come in and listen to his story.

"Flossie took sick. She had German measles, and she was all alone up there. None of us knew the first thing about it. Her fever rose, and she was wandering through these rooms by herself, like a wraith in her white nightdress, and her mind burning with fever, and then she had this idea that there were too many things in the house. We'd told her, see, to feel free to clean up the place. Grandma hadn't thrown anything away for years. I mean, there were noosepapers that went back ten years, just thrown in the basement, and old magazines, and old wedding invitations. I'd told Flossie, just laughing about it, you know, that if she felt like burning some junk to feel free. Cuz I knew it was one helluva job we were facing, Lizzie and me, to get that place cleaned up. But I sure as hell didn't think she'd go delirious. I mean it's really sad. There she was burning up, and her tongue hot and no one to help her, not a soul around, and she's so sick and doesn't even think of getting on the phone and calling anyone, I can't imagine why. She trails down to the basement and begins to throw all these magazines and noosepapers in the furnace. It was a big ol' coal-stoked furnace, and Flossie was busy there for hours, burning up old papers. When they were all finished, she found a barrel of letters. I mean, God! The fire's flaming up in her red face, burning her skin, which is already scalding hot. She's out of her fucking mind, and she begins to burn these letters, which were, as it happens, all the family letters from the Civil War. I mean, they were precious. There were letters from General Mumford and letters from Lee and Stonewall Jackson, and Colonel Mosby, letters from the women to their Northern cousins describing the war and letters from one Yankee ancestor written on brown paper bags, describing the Southern prison he was in, the starvation and disease. There were diaries of planters from the 1750s and notes of county judges. It was a gold mine. All gone. She burned the whole thing. And when that was finished, and she's still sweating and feverish, with the tears pouring down her face, she pulled the barrel apart with her hands—you can see how out of herself she was—with her bare hands, and began to throw the wood into the furnace. That was when sparks flew out and landed on the roof and started this conflagration. It smoldered in the roof for a time, licking along the attic under the eaves and spreading out, so that when the blaze finally burst out, the flames were everywhere, running through the house. Flossie ran out. She did manage to call the fire department. She had that much sense. And eventually someone called the family, and Elizabeth heard about it and raced up to the house, where she found Flossie wandering half-naked through the grounds and the flames leaping up a half mile in the night sky. The house burned to the ground with every stick of furniture in it. There went my fortune. And Elizabeth wrapped up Flossie in her coat, trundled her down to our house, and put her to bed and nursed her until she caught rubella, too, and there went my kid."

"When did this happen?" Tony's voice was expressionless.

"Five years ago, six. After Flossie recovered was when she moved to Richmond, and then she got married about six months later. I don't think she was happy anyway. I mean, she was always bright and smiling, but I think there was something bothering her. She married Jack Foxwell, who was already practically sixty. We don't see 'em anymore. She has two kids, and she was almost forty when she had them. But they're both fine. It was our son who turned out the mental defective."

Angie came out of the kitchen just then, but Tony rose at the same time and, with suitable slaps on the back, ushered Angus out of the house before he had a chance to properly say hello, almost.

When Angus reached his car at the curb, the little steel-gray Porsche sitting there as pretty as can be, he remembered he'd once asked Angie if she'd like a ride.

"Sombitch," he said happily, and turned back to the house under the cold stars, to remind her of his promise. He wanted to tell her that he'd fixed the car up with a Dixie horn.

His finger hit the doorbell before he heard the voices raised inside, bickering. The buzzer silenced them. In the awesome quiet Angus shifted. He wished he hadn't returned or at least that he'd not raced so enthusiastically up the steps to press the buzzer without listening. He thought to tiptoe back off the porch and down to the car, on the theory that the couple inside might think they'd made a mistake about the bell; but in that instant the door opened. Tony and Angie stood side by side. Tony's hand gripped his wife's wrist. Her eyes, fierce and black, shot from Angus to Tony and back again. Angus didn't know what the matter was, or how to read her wide-eyed look.

"You forgot your next drink, I suppose?" Tony had murder in his face.

"What?" Angus smiled courteously, looking down on them. "No, no." He laughed then, getting the joke. "That's good. Forgot my next drink."

"Well?" The threat in Tony's voice could not be ignored.

"No, I jes remembered I once offered Angie a ride in the Porsche," he said, his voice rising with his tension into a nasal country twang. "And damned if I ever give it to her. I come back to see if she wanted a sombitch ride sometime."

"No—" cried Angie.

"No, she doesn't." Tony's face was black. "Now, you better make your fuckin' way outta here, mister. You're treading on thin ice at this house, you get on home."

To Angus' surprise the door slammed shut in his face.

Aggrieved, he folded himself into the little car. What did Tony mean by hurting him that way? He makes a nice gesture to him, holds out his hand in friendship with an offer of a ride for his wife, and he gets the door slammed in his face. Angus turned on the ignition and listened with satisfaction to the engine roar. Well, fuck 'em. If she didn't want a ride in his steel bullet of a car, fuck her. A few moments later, sweeping round a bend, his mood shifted to one of forgiveness. Tony hadn't meant anything by it, Angus decided. Maybe he was hungry and tired, was all. Because no one could be a better friend than old Tony Rye Shits. Weren't they partners? Buddies. Didn't they trust each other enough to stand side by side in debt together on Elk Creek? At least Angus stood to lose. But that was the risk you took if you stood to gain. Tony had financed the construction, and he, Angus, had signed over the property as the bond for raising the development money. There was something nagging at the back of Angus' mind. He couldn't remember what. Something he had forgotten to do. Or something he was supposed to check again about this deal. Well, Tony had drawn up the papers, and Tony was a smart, tough kid. Tony'd take care of things. He hit the claxon, kicking off a Dixie, and, the matter out of his mind, concentrated on driving this fine, sweet tool of his. He poured on speed, and as he whipped past the truck stalled by the side of the road, his headlights spotlighted a colored man half under the hood, who straightened, wrench glimmering in the headlights, as Angus whipped past quick as running water. It was Storey Lunt, though Angus did not know him at the time or why he'd be important later on. Angus was already thinking how it was too bad Angie hadn't come and how he'd ask her again soon, and never would he have guessed that as Tony closed the door on Angus, Angie wrenched free of his grasp and ran to put the sofa between them, then skittered behind a chair as he grabbed at her.

"Tony, I didn't do nothing. Tony, listen to me, goddamn! You dumb bastard—"

"You been seein' him."

"I ha-ant been seeing nobody. He's your friend. He's a drunk nobody."

"So you admit it. He's a nobody and you been seeing nobody. Then you been seeing him."

"You're crazy." She was panting with fear. "Stay away from

me. Tony, don't look like that. Didn't I stay in the kitchen? Didn't I stay away? I never said one fuckin' word to him, you dumb—Tony, Tony, I love you. Goddamn it! Don't touch me!" She screamed. He grabbed her skirt and lunged across the back of the chair as she ran, holding the material, twisting her body around. The skirt ripped, and the sight of her bare thighs drove him to fury.

"You fuckin' broad, I turn my back . . ." His fists were pounding at her face. She rolled on the floor, trying to fend him off, screaming and kicking out at him, another minute curling into a ball on her stomach to protect her face and belly with her hands. He was smashing her with his fists, kicking her. "I warned you! I warned you!" he repeated again and again in time to the rhythm of fists and feet. "You fuckin' whore. You whore."

After a time he realized she was lying still. Straddling her back, he gave her one last swat to the side of the head, just to finish off. Her head snapped back with the blow. He was breathing hard. He sat on her hip, eyes narrowed, watching. She did not move. Blood was smeared over her cheek. Blood covered his own right hand. He looked at it in surprise, registering only the color red for a moment, before he realized what it was.

"Angie." His voice was hard. If she was going to just lie there, pretending to be hurt, he had no time for that.

With a grunt of discomfort he lifted himself from his knees, threw one leg over her supine body, and stood up.

"Angie, you can get up now." It annoyed him the way she lay there, crumbled in a heap. He could see her chest rising and falling. She was breathing. In a minute she'd probably get up and start yelling at him, and he swore that if she did, he'd knock her head off.

"Go on, get up," he snarled, rubbing his sore right hand. "I'm not going to hurt you." Now there was blood on both his hands, and upstairs one of the kids had begun to cry. "Shad-dup!" he yelled, as he moved to the kitchen to wash. She'd get up once he'd left the room. Her pride was hurt. He knew be-cause they'd gone through this before, though not so violently, he had to admit. Still, in a moment she would get up and come unhappily into the kitchen and they'd move grudgingly around each other for an hour and then make up. Sometimes after he hit her, they made love really well. Then she was putty in his hands. It was as if the fight made the making up the sweeter.

Tony washed his hands and checked the food on the stove, which was warm and ready to eat, the fire safely off.

"Dinner's ready," he called. He got down two plates and set the table in the kitchen for her, but there was no answer. "Angie," he called again, getting the two glasses down. "I told you, dinner's ready. You coming?"

When she still didn't answer, he returned to the living room, annoyed that she would make him come to her. Now she was going to sulk until he apologized. Upstairs he could hear the kid still crying in his crib.

In the living room Angie was lying as before on the floor. Now for the first time he noticed her torn skirt, the odd angle of her arm, her bruised and bloodied face against the white rug. Blood was dropping onto the rug.

"Angie?" He was scared. "Angie, honey, answer me. An-gie, you all right?" He turned her over. Her head lolled to one side. Her breathing came with a high whistle and a little gurgle in the throat.

He left her lying there and went upstairs to soothe the kids. Tonio was asleep and Paulie standing, sobbing, in his crib.

"Don't cry, honey." He lifted up the baby gently. "There, there." He breathed in the cool, sweet smell of that new skin. It always turned his head. "Daddy loves you. Don't cry. Don't cry." The child reared back in his arms, sobbing harder. Remembering Angie downstairs, he kissed the baby's head and returned him to the crib. "Go to sleep, tootkins." He wrapped him in the baby blanket and left the room. In the bathroom he wet a washcloth and returned to the living room downstairs. There he carefully and with much tenderness washed the blood off Angie's face and arms, her shoulder, her hands. Blood was everywhere. Every time he thought he'd got it all, he found another place. Her blouse was bloody too. She needed a doctor. She wasn't coming to. He was going to have to take her to the hospital, and even as he pleaded with her to wake up and come round, his darling, his honeysuckle love, that he hadn't meant to hurt her but just to give her a little scare; even as he explained (lifting her in his arms) that he'd only hit her 'cause he loved her so, and if he didn't love her, he wouldn't be jealous, that it was her own fault for making him jealous by looking so great with her platinum hair and her heavy breasts and that sensuous, fine shading of a mustache like a doubling of her lips; even as he murmured all this toward her dangling hand, he was trying to think of a good reason to tell the hospital why his wife could be in such condition.

An auto accident?

A burglary perhaps, or a rapist who had entered the house. That would do. For a moment he thought of pinning it on Angus, but rejected the idea. He'd gone out for cigarettes, or maybe some butter once Angus had left, and when he came back . . . In the car, driving frantically to the hospital, he began to think the story out. . . . First, as soon as he got her to the emergency room, he had to telephone Mrs. Andriochos next door, to go watch the kids until he came back. That would establish his story too. He had come home that evening to find his wife lying on the floor like that. He had rushed her to the hospital without even looking at the kids. No, better say he'd looked in on them. He had washed Angie up. Yes, because he'd left the washrag on the couch. He had checked the kids and seen they were both asleep. He had rushed his wife to the hospital, too distraught to think of getting a sitter for the kids.

In the emergency room he learned that Angie's broken rib had punctured a lung.

11

TOM MADE NO EFFORT TO CONTACT ELIZABETH. HE READ HER resignation note with numb anger, then carefully placed it in the upper-right-hand drawer of his desk. He could not throw it away, though it contained not a single personal word and, being typed, no curve of her own hand. He did not permit himself to think about her, but set immediately to the task of finding a replacement.

In the days that passed, he still smiled, white teeth flashing. He thrust his hands in his pockets and leaned back to squint at the sky in imitation of a farmer's stance. He performed his duties with exemplary dedication, but once, when he turned away from me, I saw his shoulders sag, and another time, when I came on him unawares, I couldn't help but note his heavy mood. As soon as he saw me, he came alert. He no longer whistled or broke unexpectedly into a fragment of song.

His work hours were shorter. He came home early and his mood matched the repression of his home. Weeks passed. He did not telephone Elizabeth, and she, each passing day more hurt at his withdrawal, made no move to contact him.

One day in late February they met unexpectedly on the

main street in Naughton. He came out of the bank, counting
his money, absorbed in thought, and almost bumped into her.
His body thrilled.

"Elizabeth!" He made no attempt to conceal his joy. "How
are you?"

"I'm fine," she answered, guarded.

"Are you?" He took one step toward her. For a moment
she thought he would sweep her in his arms. Then he stopped.
His face closed. She did not understand that he was holding
himself in check with rigid discipline.

"Never mind. Be seeing you," she said.

"Elizabeth!" It was a silent cry. She did not stop. He
watched her galoshes whop the sidewalk in straight, strong
strides, jump a snow bank in the gutter, cross the street. Without a backward glance she was gone. And he? He was so weak
he had to support himself for a moment on the brick building,
oblivious to the traffic whishing past or the mother pushing a
stroller who pressed by him, angling her load in some annoyance at his being in her way.

Later that night he wrote some lines in his journal so
exaggerated and self-pitying that I copy them here.

"I am a cave of skin. Inside, the walls are dripping with moisture. I am filled up and weeping like rain."

"Food," he writes on another day, "lies dry on my tongue. I
can hardly swallow. I am dying of thirst."

He writes: "To love one person is to love all things. To be
deprived of that delight is a death of the soul." Ultimately discreet,
he never mentions her name in his notebooks.

Some of his writings concern his aridity, the loss of faith.
Without love, he had lost God. "I am alone. The whole experience of God has been swept away."

He told me that he thought he was being punished for having loved one woman more than God.

He vowed to love her no more. That he could not manage it brought him further torment. He asked God to direct his love to Priscilla instead, but the prayer caught in his throat. He could not finish it. He lacerated himself for his hardness of heart, his inability to feel alive.

His dejection affected his services. Now, in contrast to his earlier joy, his sermons were markedly stark. He felt inadequate. He repeated platitudes on how God so loved the world that He gave His only begotten Son . . . while all throughout he was thinking if God did that to His most beloved Son, what horror did He have in mind for Tom? Better to keep your head down and hope God didn't notice you.

His days were spent in a frenzy of work, in committee meetings, board meetings, with people talking, talking (was anything decided?) about the school, or zoning plans, or the lower-town decay, about how to increase pledges for the church and what to do about the teenage zoot-suiters with their drake-tail cuts who hung out at the Dipsie Diner (jukeboxes at each booth) before rollicking restlessly to one of the pool halls or the pinball arcades in the two-block Greek quarter. Alcohol, poverty, decay, abuse. There was vandalism growing in the public schools and the need for more wheelchairs in the nursing home. Out-of-work colored men leaned on the lampposts at street corners, right under the signs that declared NO LOITERING.

Now his actions were forced. Tom attended these meetings in body, but his mind was fighting its own crusades on the hot red sands of his Jerusalem.

Once, in a meeting, he jerked alert and looked round the table to discover faces turned expectantly. They waited for his response. A flush rose to his cheeks. He cleared his throat and leaned forward, fingering the documents on the table before him. "I'm sorry. I was thinking of something else." His voice was hard.

So the winter passed.

As for Elizabeth, she was going through her own hell. She thought Tom despised her. Why not? Look at the shameless way she had thrown herself at him (she told herself). Of course he held her in contempt.

Her moods erupted like an angry ulcer. She snapped at her mother, burst into tears for no reason, shouted at Angus and the next moment threw her arms around him, contrite. It was all she could do to drag herself out of bed each morning; with her horse gone, she had nothing that she liked to do. No exercise. No child. No job at the church (though *that* was no loss! she told herself fiercely). She walked across icy fields. She watched her cold breath smoke out in the air. She stopped at frozen hoofmarks in the path, iced as thin as rime, the crystals forming around the edges of the circular print—and stomped on them, shattering them in rage!

"Get a grip on yourself, Elizabeth. I don't know what's eating you." That was her mother, Carolyn, speaking with amused tolerance. "You're working too hard. Why don't you go on vacation, you and Angus."

"Vacation!"

"Your father and I went on a nice vacation to Martinque this time last year. A little sun. Some swimming and golf. It'd be good for you."

Elizabeth bit her tongue. "Good for me," she wanted to shout. "I am on perpetual vacation. There is nothing I am supposed to do except cook and be a good wife and run the tractor. I don't even have money for my own house, much less a vacation in Martinique." The very idea of vacationing with Angus, moreover, made her shudder. His smell clung to her nostrils, his skin felt clammy to her touch. To listen to his jokes, or his quick, braying laugh, to watch him sneaking to the kitchen, making up excuses, to refill his glass was . . . horrible. That he drank she took on herself, as her fault. Adulteress! She could not forget that she had thought so little of herself as to sleep with Tom at the Negro Storey Lunt's. To kiss him in his office. To offer herself in her own marriage bed. No wonder he refused to talk to her.

She drove up to Briarose in the same dull rage with which she attacked the frozen earth. How she would like to tear it down! Flatten the buildings, beat them into stones and bury under the rubble each of these horrible, half-human, crippled spastics that they housed. She hated Duncan for bringing her here. She hated herself for bearing such a child, Caliban of the crooked limbs. Sitting in the car outside this heavy red-brick building, she wished that he would die. With all her heart and soul she wanted her son dead, and resting her head on her hands on the steering wheel, she let the sobs shake her. She felt so tired. There was no one to comfort her, no one to hold her. She alone was holding up the pillars of her life—her alcoholic husband, her controlling mother, her mentally retarded son. "Oh, God," she prayed, "if Tom says you are there, I'll believe you're there. Help me, God. I can't go on alone." After a few moments she took possession of herself, disgusted at succumbing to self-pity. Other people had real problems, she told herself. There were people without enough to eat, people right in her own country who went hungry at night, slept in the cold, while she had every comfort known. She must pull herself together. But, again, sitting in the car, she was swept by loss and grief. What made things worse was that for a few months she had felt, in her love for Tom, a surge of strength and vital joy. With that gone, was nothing left?

"Nonsense," she reproved herself. "Pity-party." She could at least go in and talk to Duncan. Tom said the child knew, even if he didn't respond, when his mother paid a call.

It was lunchtime when she arrived. The smell of food hung heavy in the corridors. A black man was pushing a wagon that stood higher than her head, laden with trays. Elizabeth had a long wait for the elevators, and once the wagon was on the elevator, there was no room for a passenger.

"Watch the cart," the man shouted. She quickly stepped back. She felt a wave of annoyance. Didn't he see she was a visitor? The parent of a child? Another cart was trundling down the hall. She decided to take the stairs and, climbing them, running, two at a time, she was glad to have the outlet for her energy.

At the fourth floor she stopped, winded, and slowly walked toward Duncan's ward, delaying her arrival, for it was no fun to push through that soundproofed door, to be confronted with the howls, the twisted faces, the odors of the kids, one of them her own. At the door she lifted her head in that characteristic gallant gesture, a sidewise tossing-off of care, squared her shoulders, and knocked.

After a moment the nurse opened the door.

"Good morning." Boldly she stepped inside. She was hit by the white, upturned faces. Contorted bodies lay collapsed in their wheelchairs or crawled on the floors or beds. She stood trembling, her back to the door. A hydrocephalic boy, his enormous head so heavy that she could not imagine his neck would have the muscles to support it, was lying on a bed next to her, moaning softly to himself. She stared at him. It did not matter, since his eyes, like those of most of the children, would not meet her own, but travelled aimlessly over the ceiling or the floor. If she touched him, he would not respond. There was a fascinating beauty to his head, his eyes so popped and soft, his skin so pearly smooth. She could not think of him as human but as some beautiful soft pulpy sea creature, dainty tentacles swaying in the tide. In the bed on her other side lay a twisted creature with bulbous lips—a common sign of mental debility. He hung across his bed, his muscles slack. As she watched, he threw his upper body forward to sprawl across his knees. He rested his monstrous lips right on his outstretched ankles. Elizabeth turned her head away. Two nurses behind the glass partition were laughing together. A larger boy pulled himself across the floor toward her, laughing. He was looking right at her, babbling, his mouth open exposing his crooked teeth, his lolling tongue. His eyes were crossed, and Elizabeth felt herself go weak: If he touched her, she would scream. It was a madhouse. The idea flashed through her mind as she herself began to laugh hysterically. It was only a momentary collapse. Then, clutching her leather handbag, she pushed past this creature on the floor and stepped toward Duncan's bed in the far corner. But when she got there, she didn't see him, no, but only more twisted and crippled bodies, gazing eyes and misshapen lips and foreheads, and young children with dank, dripping hair who appeared as old as aged men and other children lying diapered and dull. Her head was whirling. She could not see.

Duncan? She looked frantically about. Some of the patients

she recognized, and others she had never seen before. Quickly she moved to the nurse's window. The two women in white, starched uniforms had their backs to her. She rapped lightly on the glass. They turned. The taller one gave a quick smile and opened the door of the cubicle, which had been closed against the noise.

"I've got to go. Be back as soon as I can." She pushed past Elizabeth. "Excuse me, please"—and stepped toward the door. An astonished Elizabeth watched her leave. She was not even on duty, but came apparently from another ward.

The other nurse had thin blond hair tied back in a ponytail. She looked no older than twenty-one.

"I'm looking for my son," said Elizabeth. "Duncan Mc-Ewen. Has he been moved?"

The girl glanced up at her with a resentful look, then reached for her clipboard. "McEwen. He's here," she shrugged. "They're filed alphabetically. Did you look over there?"

"I was just there. I didn't see him." Elizabeth stepped back, appalled. Filed alphabetically? She turned back to the corner. The beds were so close that they almost touched. Since her last visit more children had been moved into the ward. The noise was intolerable.

"They've doubled our population," said the girl briskly. "We had to close down one ward for repairs, and we've moved a lot of patients here. You'll have to look around."

"But don't you know?"

"Look, I'm the only one on duty now. He's in his bed, so look over there."

When Elizabeth found him, she realized with a start that she had passed right over him before. She had not recognized him. She stood at the foot of the bed, numb, wondering what she felt. He lay on the bed, knees akimbo, his arms thrown out. His head was rocking from side to side. He was covered with his own filth, his hospital gown brown with dirt.

When had they put him in a hospital gown instead of pants? For the first time, she realized that all the children were wearing these coarse, unbleached gowns, open at the throat. Some had torn them off. One boy had draped his over one shoulder as a toga and was naked, chewing on the ends of the strings. Suddenly she was filled with rage! How dare they treat these children so? She returned to the small blond nurse isolated in her cage.

"My son is dirty." She hardly knew what she was saying. "He needs to be changed."

The girl looked up in surprise. At that moment the double doors opened with a crash, and the cart of trays rolled in. "Feeding time," called out the orderly. He turned and left.

"Did you hear me?" Elizabeth said, her voice high, breaking with tension. "I said my son is dirty. He needs to be changed."

The girl turned on her. "Look, lady. I don't know who you are," she said. "But if you have a child here, you don't like the way he's kept, go change him yourself. I have a roomful of people to feed. I'm here alone. You want something done, you do it, see?" She threw two diapers and a gown at Elizabeth, turned, and was gone. Shakily Elizabeth changed her baby. She wiped her angry tears with the back of her hand, resentful at being spoken to like that. That dreadful nurse. Poor, dear, lost Dunks. What kind of care did they give?

"You finished?" said the nurse. "Put down your purse. I need help. Take this." She thrust a tray in Elizabeth's hands.

"And here." She pushed a spoon at her. "Don't just stand there. Feed this boy."

She turned Elizabeth about to stand beside the nearest child. "Feed him. He can't control his arms to feed himself."

The girl grabbed a tray in each hand and carried them to those children who were well enough to feed themselves. She set a tray beside one boy, pushed the spoon in his hand. "Eat with the spoon," she said, shoving the utensil into the bowl of mushy stew. She was gone immediately, carrying trays, propping up bodies. She was a whirlwind. Elizabeth stood frozen.

She looked at the child on the bed. It was the boy with the heavy lips. She put her shoulderbag on the floor, set the tray on the edge of the bed, and lifted the child into a sitting position, straight enough to eat. He had hardly any arms at all, shrunken, withered stumps. "Here." It came out as a whisper, inaudible in the room. "Open your mouth." She pushed the spoon toward his lips. They opened, curled around the spoon, and hungrily licked the food off. She dipped the spoon again. What was this stuff? She leaned down to smell it, but could find no identifying odor.

"When you finish with him, there are more." The girl ran past. "You're doing fine." Her smile of encouragement and brisk, determined trot had their own effect on Elizabeth, who watched the deft way that the nurse manipulated trays, lifted patients, or moved beds or wheelchairs out of the way with a kick of her heel or hip.

"My name is Annie," she shouted as she passed next time.

It was bedlam. No sooner had one boy been fed, his dish wiped clean, than Annie had pressed another tray in her hand.

"I can't tell you what a help it is," she shouted. "Ellie's

coming back in a minute, but thank God you're here. I couldn't do it all alone."

After that they worked in unison. Elizabeth had shoved her purse under the counter in the nurse's cubicle and, without regard for her fine wool skirt or silk blouse, she lost herself in work. There was nothing but spoon, tray, mouth, spoon, tray, and children dumping the stuff all over themselves.

After the trays were collected, Elizabeth filled a bowl with water and, together with Annie, washed hands, faces, arms, even hair. "Sometimes they turn the bowl upside down in their hair and then have no food," Annie said. "They go hungry." They worked as a team, switching off when Annie went to get more water, leaving Elizabeth to clean alone.

"Will this just be repeated at dinnertime?"

"That shift's okay. It's just mine right today that's under-staffed. But, yes, we're always understaffed and overcrowded. What can you do?" She shut the cubicle door against the noise, and for a moment Elizabeth sank gratefully into the silence. She had not realized that the levels of moaning had risen again.

"We give medicine in a minute. That quiets down the worst. You should go on home."

"Don't you have volunteers to help?"

Annie shook her head.

"But I thought there were always volunteers! What about the women's auxiliaries and the Junior League and all that?"

Annie laughed.

"The Junior League! No one cares about these kids." Elizabeth was shocked, but what was most astonishing was that she felt wonderful.

"What happens tomorrow?" she asked.

"Want to come again and see?" Annie laughed. "We'll take all the volunteering you want to do."

"Shall I?"

"Wear something that won't matter."

"I'll wear blue jeans," she said. "If I can muck out stalls and tromp through the cow sheds, I can help feed the children." Then, seeing Annie's expression: "Well, you see," she explained, "it's okay to take care of horses and dogs. That's what I grew up doing. It's people I have no experience with. And you know what's amazing, for the first time I think of them as people, as children. I've been thinking they were monsters."

"They are, poor things. Little monster kids, and so sweet and dear, some of them. All they want to do is hug and kiss. There's one here I particularly like. For the life of me I can't think why. He's so . . . bad. And I just love him."

"It's nearly three. I have to go."

"See you tomorrow if you want to help. If you don't, I certainly can't blame you."

Why did she feel so good? She had worked nonstop for three hours, feeding, cleaning, washing. Her mother, brittle in her wit, said it was just a matter of getting enough exercise, but to Elizabeth it was a miracle. For the first time in weeks, she felt at peace.

The question remains, did it really happen? One day, Annie, this laughing angel-girl was gone. No one knew a thing, though one of the nurses said she'd had to leave to take care of her mother who was sick. Elizabeth could never find her: no forwarding address. It was as if she never existed. Some of us wondered if she did. Still, Lizzie insisted on her story. To us it smacked of romantic delirium, especially in light of the scandal

that came out two years later at Briarose: of children beaten
black and blue with hoses, placed "in leathers" in solitary con-
finement as punishment for yelling, or left without food so that
one at least is known to have died of malnutrition. TB, pneumonia, polio, hookworm ran rampant in the place.

We wondered if Elizabeth was hallucinating when she told
us about that day.

Yet, no matter what we thought, something had happened.
After that day she went twice a week to help at Briarose. She
began to organize a women's volunteer group. She found three
mothers at first. By the end of the summer she had thirteen or
fourteen who took turns helping out. A superhuman effort.
None of us could believe what she had done, for she had no
experience and no background in mental health. That she could
catalyze a group into action attested to her strength.

When Elizabeth got home from Briarose that night, she heard
about Angie. All of Naughton was on the phone. Carolyn had
heard the news when she stopped for gas and, remembering that
Angie was the same child who had teetered into her luncheon
the previous fall on her spike heels, she had hurried home to
call Elizabeth and warn her to keep her doors locked.

"But what happened?" Elizabeth said.

"No one knows. Angela was with the two babies. Her husband had gone to the store for some cigarettes. He says he
stayed out longer than expected, and when he came back home,
he found his wife lying in a pool of blood. Can you imagine?
The poor man. My heart goes out to him."

"Good God."

"But he's that friend of Angus', isn't he?" pursued
Carolyn.

"A business associate. I'm not sure they're friends."

"Well, even so."

At this moment Angus entered. Elizabeth, one hand covering the receiver, passed on the news. He took the phone.

"Who did it? What sonofabitch would do a thing like that?"

"We don't know," Carolyn replied. "Apparently the girl had her ribs stove in, a puncture in the lung. It's an absolutely meaningless attack."

"Great gods!"

"Now, Angus, I hope you're seeing to proper locks on the cottage. Have you done that? Dutton went to the hardware store this afternoon as soon as I told him, and he's bought some chain locks for our doors here. It just makes me sick. We're keeping a shotgun loaded in the rack. If you don't find locks, come up. I'll give you one of these."

"Christ, do you know I was just over there? Just last night? I just *saw* them!" It sent quivers down his spine.

"I'm going over there," he said when he hung up the phone. "Poor Tony. Good God! You ought to come with me."

"But I don't even know them."

"Good God, Elizabeth, the poor guy's just seen his wife raped and practically murdered. He finds her lying in a pool of blood in his own living room, and you won't even go over and help him out?"

"But I don't see how I would help," she defended herself. "I've hardly met the man. He'd feel as if I'd come to ogle at him, like a freak in the circus."

"I'll take him a bottle of bourbon," said Angus generously. "God knows, he'll need something."

"Oh, Angus."

"Are you sure you won't come?" He had already accepted

her refusal. "Well, listen, lock up after me. I have my key. But I don't want anything happening to you. Jesus H. Christ, what do you suppose is going on around here?"

Naughton was in a state of turmoil. We weren't accustomed to having so many exciting things to think about at once. Angus' development plans had come out, and that in itself would have sufficed for a month of discussion. Now his business partner's wife had been attacked, maybe raped, and beaten up. Angie would not say anything when questioned. She just shook her head. Tears seeped down her cheeks.

Tony had been the first person at the hospital when she woke up. He was sitting by her bed, and he leaned over her gently when she opened her eyes:

"Are you all right?" he asked. "You've been raped and beaten up, do you remember?"

"What?"

He rubbed her hand. "You're going to be okay. The kids are well. You'll be just fine," he explained again with care. "Someone came in the front door. I was out. We don't know who it was."

One of the doctors was in the room with them. Her eyes flew over to him, and that was when she turned her head and let the tears drop.

"She's upset," Tony explained. "I don't blame her. Can you leave her with me alone, Doctor?"

He nodded understandingly. Both he and Tony knew that the police chief would want to question Angie as soon as she felt better. "Don't stay more than five minutes," the doctor cautioned. "We don't want to wear her out."

Later: "Who was it, Mrs. Reischetz?" Teddy Schildhauer,

the police chief, sat in a chair beside her bed. On the other side Tony sat on the bed itself, holding her hand for comfort.

"Can you describe the man who attacked you?" the police chief asked.

Her eyes moved from the police chief to her husband and rested on his face in a long and serious look.

Tony squeezed her hand. "It's all right."

"Mrs. Reischetz, I'm sorry to do this to you, believe me. If you know the man, you should say something."

"She doesn't know who it is!" Tony burst out. "She'd say if she did. Anyway, who do we know who'd do a horrible thing like this? It's unforgivable."

"Mrs. Reischetz," he persisted. "If you don't know who your assailant was, can you describe the man?" He already had Angus under suspicion, Angus, who had boasted innocently to several witnesses how he'd been there that very night.

She turned her head away.

"You see," he continued gently, "it's possible you could save some other woman from attack. If you know anything, if you can remember any detail. . . ."

"Can I talk to you alone?" Her words were no more than a whisper.

"What?"

"She wants to be alone," Tony put in. "It's all right, honey. No one's ever gonna hurt you again. I promise you. Darling, Angie, I promise you. Never again. I swear it."

"Suppose I ask you a question." The police chief walked to the foot of the bed and turned to face her there. "Can you nod or shake your head if I just ask. You answer yes or no, okay?"

She nodded.

"Was it someone you know?" Again her eyes flew to Tony. Again she dropped her eyes.

"No," answered Tony.

"Was he tall?" She shook her head.

"Medium build?"

She nodded. "Medium," she whispered.

"Mrs. Reischetz, was he Negro? Was he white?"

She plucked the sheet with pitiful, helpless fingers.

"This is killing her," Tony interrupted fiercely. "Do you have to go through this?"

"Mrs. Reischetz, you saw the man. Won't you tell me anything?"

"Was he colored, Angie? He was a Negro, wasn't he? I can tell by her expression he was black." Tony's voice rose excitedly, laying emphasis on that insult. *Black* was a word as bad as *nigger* those days. Angela's fingers picked at the sheet.

"Was he a Negra?" asked the police chief, using the more polite and formal term.

"He was the blackest man I've ever seen." Each word she spat out clear. The police chief raised his eyebrows. With those words the field was narrowed to one of those shining, blue-black shades, a strong enough man to have kicked her ribs in, but moderate in height. It excluded Angus too.

"Can you give any indication of his age, Mrs. Reischetz?"

"Oh, for God's sake, let her alone," Tony cried.

"About like Tony's," she said.

The police chief laughed, embarrassed at her response. "About thirty-five," he jotted in his notebook.

"I think we should leave her." Tony rose. "Honey, no

one's ever going to hurt you again, and right now we aren't going to disturb you anymore."

"Mrs. Reischetz, thank you very much."

"Can I see you—?"

But Tony's voice came in loud: "No one's going to see you anymore. No more questions, honey. I'll protect you."

All of Naughton was talking about the attack. It brought others to mind. We remembered the axe-murder fifteen years earlier, when old Mrs. Tuttle, ninety-seven and bedridden in the big house on Tuttle Road, had her head smashed in with an axe, the blood all over the climbing roses on the wallpaper in her room, over the floor, her bedlinens soaked. That murderer was caught, a madman from the insane asylum, who'd crossed a river and two counties to find himself at Mrs. Tuttle's place, and was discovered afterwards cowering in the abandoned smokehouse, crying and shaking and flicking his hands as if he were a frightened two-year-old and not a six-foot maniac who'd just done in a helpless woman.

If we hadn't seen him carried off in a white straitjacket, arms behind his back, we'd have thought he had come back to attack poor Angie Reischetz. But he was a white boy anyhow, and we were looking for a darkie now.

We buttoned up against his penetration. Women, driving at night, took to locking their car doors. They slowed but did not stop for Stop signs. We put extra locks on our doors and windows, and all of us were looking at our neighbors suspiciously. We found ourselves searching the faces of Negroes we had grown up with, boys we'd played with behind the barns as children, our own friends. Was this the one? A cold wind blew over us, and we shivered at the touch.

As for the colored of the area, the whites' new wariness created a change in them as well. Our perception fashioned reality. They could not meet our eyes. Even a black man known to us all our livelong years, like William, the janitor at the church, an honest, simple country man, a deacon of his own Pentecostal Golden Temple Church, an important man among his own people—even a man like William seemed to shrink back, eyes dropping at the white man's approach. We looked at him askance. Was there a sullen look about his lips? A latent malice in the eye? The whole business was made more frightening because at the same time riots were breaking out farther south. You could see it on TV, the colored folk rising up in Atlanta and Alabama, and the KKK re-forming and screaming its own mottoes. *Civil Rights* was the code word. No one had heard of it before. We didn't know what to expect.

Angus got excited when he realized he'd probably seen the man who beat up Angela. "I saw him," he kept repeating to Tony. "It must of been him." He tried to describe the man— that brief glimpse in the dark—a Negro in coveralls, bending over the motor of his slat-backed pickup truck. The description could fit anyone around. Nonetheless an indignant Angus alerted the police, Tony being oddly reluctant to press charges. Angus thought Tony was probably too shaken by the incident to act responsibly. Angie simply seemed withdrawn.

"So, they're looking for him," Tony told her. He petted her hand. "We're never going to have anything happen to you again." She was to be released from the hospital in another few days.

"How're the kids?" she asked.

"They're fine," said Tony, relieved that she would speak at all. "They're just fine. They miss you. They really need you home. But we'll see that they're no trouble. I asked your mother about coming down to stay for a time, but she can't do it. I've arranged with Mrs. Andriochos to help out till you get well. I want everything to be just great. It'll be wonderful having you home again."

She turned her head away, but she, too, wanted to go home. She missed the kids. She told herself that Tony's battering was a single, isolated act. His attentions to her in the hospital demonstrated that. He brought her flowers. He showered her with gifts, including a lace bedjacket that was the nicest thing she'd ever seen. He told her he was sorry, that he adored her. She accepted his apology while at the same time wondering what it meant that he let the police go looking for an innocent man.

Eventually Storey Lunt was picked up. Angus identified the man. He worked occasionally, it turned out, for a family down the road from the Reischetzes. The police talked to Angie about the crime. She stared vaguely at the floor and shook her head. They couldn't get anything out of her. They talked to Storey, who denied he had a part, though he couldn't establish a good alibi. So they had one nonwitness (Angus) and one denial (Storey) and one victim (Angie), who wouldn't incriminate anyone. They dropped the charge, suspiciously.

Tom, of course, had nothing to do with all this. He was at a party at our house when he heard the story, and he shook his head.

"They don't have any idea who did it," said Bunny Randolph.

"Yes, they do. It's a Negra who lives up by Middleman. Shore or Stevedor, some name like that."

"Storey Lunt?" asked Tom.

"That's it."

"He wouldn't do it."

We looked at Tom in surprise. "Why, do you know him?"

"Very well," he said, jaw set.

Priscilla laughed with a fluttering brightness. "Well, you certainly do get around. Who don't you know?"

"Well, I don't know this man," said Carey Hill approvingly, "but I've great admiration for the Negra people, and I'd feel the same loyalty towards one I knew."

"Well," said Billy Tyler, "I've known lots of men, and slept in the same bed with them, and I'm amazed how often I'm mistaken about a man I know extremely well." She gave a raucous laugh.

Tom looked up at her and smiled painfully.

No one was going to argue, and the conversation turned to questions about Angie Reischetz.

"She was badly beaten up, but she's all right now. Her husband's been wonderful, I've heard." It was Bunny, who had all her information from Angus himself.

"Maybe I'll go see her," Tom said.

And he did too. He paid her a call one afternoon all the way over on the far side of town, though she had her own Catholic priest. I don't know what they talked about.

12

Now March came flooding in. The earth softened under the lengthening light and buds came out and fields were greening. People hungry for flowers were forcing grape hyacinth and forsythia in sunny windows. In spring we had more work too. Our feet tromped over the rough, bare boards of the feed store. The whole floor shook with the rumble of the metal four-wheeled trundle-wagon with its long tongue, carrying sacks of seeds and fertilizers to farm trucks. Mares had already dropped their foals, and these wide-eyed, long-legged, gangly colts were confronting the new world, tails twittering, all joy and wonderment and not a kick-of-the-heels care that Priscilla's mother fell on the Chicago ice, where March 3 was still dead winter, and broke her hip. Pris flew to Chicago to take care of her. She took Philip along, not trusting the boy to Tom. Margaret used to laugh about her overprotectiveness, though there was nothing funny about it: the woman was smothering him. Margaret was so concerned that she went up to the rectory one day and begged Pris to let us keep Philip for the week so he wouldn't skip school.

"No, no." Priscilla's smile could have cut butter. "He's better off with his mother. It's very nice of you, but no. I can tutor him. It's a mother's privilege." One hand strayed to the beautiful hair in the bun at the nape of her neck. She smiled and smiled, teeth bared. Tom, introspective anyway, was left entirely on his own.

I thought Tom would feel freer without his attachment to Elizabeth. The reverse occurred. Some spark had died in him. One day I came to his shabby church office I found so comfortable, with books everywhere and papers piled on every flat surface and tabletop. I came bursting in, confident and cheerful. It took about two minutes for me to be squirming in my seat. I knocked my pipe nervously in the ashtray, asking what he'd been doing with himself.

"Nothing much."

"No?" I laughed. "A clergyman doesn't have time for that."

"I've been meditating."

"Oh."

"You turn inward," he said, his eyes crawling like flies along the molding of the ceiling. "You let the mind go still."

"Stop thinking? Whatever for?"

"You're right," he answered, but his smile did not extend to his eyes, and I felt badly that I had contributed to his pain, for it was on my advice he'd broken off with Elizabeth.

I watched him seat himself at his desk and open the account books heavily.

"Well, to work," he said.

Priscilla's week in Chicago stretched into two, then three. Lent was upon us. Tom began to fast as well. Often he went into silence, isolating himself from everyone for an entire day.

Also, as he'd said, he'd started meditating. It was a Buddhist discipline—God knows where he learned it—that concentrated the attention on the breath. He watched his breathing, counting. In . . . out . . . It made no sense to me at all. He was so serious, however, that I was moved.

"I'm trying to *see*," he said passionately. "I'm listening."

I felt he had a secret for me, if only I could understand. He tried to explain how, when he meditated, he suddenly felt he *became* the universe. He understood that he had substance beyond his thoughts or physical body. He touched his soul.

"Who was it who said when you're praying you're talking to God," he said, "and when you're meditating you're listening to God speak to you? I'm still trying just to learn. The other night I tried something else," he confessed with a shy smile. "I lit a candle and just watched that. Concentrating on the flame."

"Staring?"

"I suppose."

I sucked my pipe, considering the information. "What happened?" He didn't answer at first, but examined his hands dangling between his knees and then began, gathering enthusiasm as he talked. "What I'm doing is watching how the mind operates. I've discovered only three things happen to me." He looked up with that tender smile, as if asking for approval. "There are only three things—stimulants—irritants—whatever you want to call them, and I'm reacting to one or another all the time. The first is a physical sensation, either pain or pleasure: prickling, tickling, throbbing, pressing, itching, hurting— whatever. Second, an emotion, like fear or grief or envy; and third, a thought. That's all I've discovered there is."

"Reality?" I asked. "There's external reality."

"Well, I don't know," he answered, to my surprise. "I'm not sure I understand what reality is. Maybe I make it up as I

go along. That's why I need to *see*, to *hear*. I want . . ." he
stopped. "Clarity. Was it Euripides who said it's not the event
that disturbs us but how we think about it?"

"Shakespeare," I said. " 'Nothing is good or bad but thinking makes it so.' "

I was prowling his office, reading the names of books I'd
never noticed before, by authors I'd never heard of: Aldous
Huxley and Christopher Isherwood and Henry Miller (I knew
him all right). There was Evelyn Underhill and Einstein and
Hermann Hesse and also the sayings of the Compassionate Bud-
dha. There was Krishnamurti and Gurdjieff, and a copy of the
Bhagavad-Gita. I ran one finger along the shelf, tracing all these
authors thrown together in no order at all, together with Bibles
and liturgical works and the *Imitation of Christ.* Thoreau, I knew,
and Emerson. Today I've learned who some of these unknown
authors are, because I inherited a lot of these books, but at the
time I'd never heard of Annie Besant or Madame Blavatsky,
and I didn't have any idea how they fit into Christian thought.

"So, there you have it," Tom was saying. "That's what
I've found composes a human being: a physical sensation, an
emotion, or a thought. We're always engaged in one or another
of those three. But *who's it happening to?* That's the question I
keep asking. *Who is watching all this? Who am I?*"

That's the way he was talking all that winter when he split
up with Elizabeth. I didn't know what to make of him. One
evening we were up at his house, listening to Beethoven's Em-
peror Concerto. He was lying on his back on the floor, a cush-
ion under his head, and his feet up on the couch, a position
Priscilla would never have allowed. As the second movement
ended, he said, "I'd like that to be playing when I die."

I looked over and damned if tears weren't standing in his

eyes. I was startled. Men don't cry. But he wiped his eyes without the slightest shame. "It's so goddamn beautiful," he said. Then, seeing my look, he laughed and rose and took me to the kitchen for a beer.

I wonder now if the meditating made him open up like that. To hear music to that degree.

We went for lunch once downtown at Doc's drugstore. My treat. I was concerned about his fasting. We sat in a wooden booth. I had a BLT, and Tom, a grilled cheese, and then he began to talk again.

"I think I've found it, John." He leaned forward excitedly, forgetting his sandwich. "A few days ago when I was meditating, I saw that I am a great empty sky. John, it was wonderful. I say *I*, but it would be the same for you or Margaret or anyone. All of us. I saw that we're a huge blue clear sky. Across it floats a cloud. This may be a thought or an emotion—annoyance, say, or happiness. The itch on my nose."

I nodded, listening.

"It comes along . . . and if you do absolutely nothing"— he looked up at me with his eyes dancing—"it floats away. The sky is clear again. After a moment there comes another emotion. Or another thought. And it floats off too. You watch it disappear and ask, 'Well, who is watching this? Who is *me*?' Is that thought me? No, because me-ness existed before the thought and it's still there when that thought has passed. Here comes a wave of loneliness. Or doubt. Or boredom." He laughed. "I have a lot of boredom, restlessness. Or desire for a cup of coffee. Or a book. Or a woman. Is that desire *me*? No, I'm the sky!"

"Are you all right?" I reached across the booth and put one hand on his forehead. It was just a joke, but he pulled

back, frowning. I withdrew, too, to take an embarrassed bite of
my BLT. Stupid me. I felt as gross as Angus or Carolyn. Still,
I couldn't stop pushing.

"I don't get it," I said. "To sit staring at your navel in the
dark when you could be out enjoying God's good world? You're
looking at yourself looking at yourself. Good heavens, Tom,
there are things to do out there. Why not just enjoy life?"

And when he didn't answer: "Aren't you worried that it's
narcissistic? You'll have more chance of finding who you are if
you get out and deal with other people."

"There's time for that." He looked away grimly. I remembered how we used to talk together, with Tom's face alight.
We'd had good times. To think he preferred to sit in an empty
room, examining the Great Void, rather than engaging in the
tumble of the strife—I tried to say that.

"The kingdom of God is within you," he murmured.

"Oh, well, if you're going to quote the Bible at me. . . ."
Then, still squirming inside: "Is that all you do?"

He laughed. Then he told me about his readings in Bud-
dhism and Hinduism, looking for the Cosmic Egg.

"But that's horrible!" I'd thought his meditating was some
esoteric Christian mystery. But Hindu gods: I had seen those
disgusting art works in an exhibition once in Cleveland. It had
been full of bronze gods dancing on one foot. They had six or
eight arms, like spiders, and snakes twined around their naked
bodies. The females were bountifully endowed with wide hips,
overflowing breasts, and more snakes crawling round their
necks. From the gaudy orange paintings male gods beamed dev-
ilish and blue, performing perverted sex acts with all eight hands
and feet. The colors hurt the eyes.

"It's not Christian!" I burst out in disbelief.

"No, it's not, is it?" He smiled at me nervously. "But it's not unchristian, John, to read or meditate. The Bible tells us to meditate. Mary went away from the Annunciation 'and meditated on these things.' "

"That's a different thing entirely."

"Is it? Christ meditated in the desert. Even recommended it. 'Be still and know that I am God.' "

I couldn't answer, but I felt a door close between us. He'd gone inside with those words. Shut me out. It was as if he had someone he was impatient to return to, who did not leave room for me. I paid the bill, and we stepped outside into the March wind. I zipped my jacket. Tom smiled his faint farewells, but he was already far away. I tried not to be hurt or take it personally, but I went away feeling cut. He didn't care.

I see now, reading this material again, how all March, all Lent, his writings became more passionate. Where formerly his notes were mainly business reminders, he'd begun to keep a spiritual journal of sorts, dreams and fragments of thoughts, not consistently, and not enough to give any picture of his inner life, except to see its torment.

He was reaping the results of his own righteous act. At least he was certain there *was* a God, so he was better off than when he'd arrived in Naughton last October. He had recovered faith in a sense. Just that God still eluded him. And you cannot say that he was happy either. He was gnawing at his own flesh, mortifying himself. Both of them were doing that: Elizabeth chewing over money, or Duncan, or her loveless marriage and the loss of her lover; and Tom feeling the hole at his heart, which is the existential loneliness that Sartre says marks the condition of humanity and which we all try to fill with children or danger or drugs or drink or work or sex or war or material goods—with *living*, in other words. Tom was trying to fill it with a skittish God.

It's curious, isn't it? They had both done the right thing, and they felt awful.

Margaret saw his despondency. "Come to dinner tonight," she offered. "I never see you anymore."

He refused. He curled into Lenten isolation.

We were not the only ones to reach out to Tom. "I'm reading a wonderful book," said Dutton Page, "*Mosby's Men*, about the War Between the States. I'll loan it to you. That's the kind of thing to take your mind off troubles."

But Tom refused all offers. Here, from his journal:

"This solitude is a gift," he wrote. "It is the very thing I am most afraid of. Is that why I've been given it? That I may come to terms with loneliness? Will I see that *alone* means all one? Oh, God! I hurt!"

You look at these jottings, his notebooks. Most of them weren't put into the record at the trial. Sometimes his notations are prayers, usually that single one to serve the will of God: "Show me what I am to do," and "Help me to hear you." He neglects to capitalize respectfully the pronouns for God, just as he calls God familiarly "you," as if speaking to an equal, not the proper "Thee" or "Thou." But apparently he suffers doubt, since here, after the end of February, he's bucking himself up with lines from Blake:

If the sun and moon should doubt
They'd immediately go out.

A month earlier his jottings were on love, loss, abandonment. In Lent they concentrated on pain. Despite his disciplines (fasting, praying, silence), or perhaps because of them, he hurts.

"My body is on fire," he writes, and: "March 11. The pain is so intense I cannot walk. My shoulders, my neck—I cannot bear it. Please, God, release me from this pain. . . ."

Or this, on the 13th: "I am crippled by pain. Is this my cross? Yesterday I saw Miss M. She said I am not looking well and asked if I was eating properly with Priscilla gone. I refused her invitation to dinner. I don't feel up to polite conversation, the social masks. But the pain! I know it is the physical manifestation of my emotional distress. How can I tend others when I'm sick myself?"

On the 14th he analyzes the purposes of pain. "For the biological organism it serves as a survival mechanism, warning of danger. When you put your hand in the fire, it hurts. The pain instructs you to remove it. Emotional or psychological pain must be a similar gift, given us to warn of something wrong. God does not intend for us to live in pain. I'm sure of that. But how do I pull my hand away? Oh, God, show me what—?"

He did not finish the sentence.

"If we are not intended to live in pain, then why does life consist of suffering?"

"War, starvation, disease, deprivation, loneliness, fear. Why do we suffer so?"

The next entry turns on himself: "*Why* is a stupid word. From now on I'll never use it."

And then March 17—I read it here—he gave in to acceptance, not in forlorn resignation or in quiet Buddhist nonattachment, a kind of not caring, but in a raging Christian surrender, a plunge into pain. He told me about it at the time. I'd forgotten. Reading it, I find myself marveling. I wonder if I've ever dared such surrender into hurt.

"Something happened today. I was walking up in the woods, suffering the most intense and agonizing pain. I walked doubled over, unable to stand up straight. My neck and shoulders were on fire. 'Was this what Christ felt hauling the cross to Calvary?' I suddenly thought. And then it occurred to me that Christ did not just die once, but dies again and again every minute of our mortal life. 'Then let me take Christ's cross one weary step for him,' I thought, 'relieve his precious pain.' Suddenly, instead of praying for release, as I have done all these weeks, I gave in. Where the idea came from, I don't know. It occurred to me that I am always willing to accept the love of God; all expressions of beneficence and grace, all goodnesses I gladly take. But not his pain. Yet pain, too, must be an expression of his love. It is his gift. 'Then give it to me,' I prayed. 'If this fire is the expression of your love, O Lord, I can take much more! Pile it on. I'll take it all. Give it to me! More! And let me have more of the fire of your love, this pain.'

"Instantly it was gone. I felt a wave of such warmth and love flow through me as I have never experienced. I felt the universe tilt with love; the light spring air was rippling with laughter, as if it were all a joke! A heavenly joke! And I've just broken the code."

From this moment he'd crossed a line. "I have nothing left," he writes. "No ideal. No knowledge. No expectation. No demands. I have no intellect. I am without resources," he wrote. "I am yours."

I remember this period, when he came out of his Lenten

depression, and you could see the green light return to his eyes. Sea eyes. It's all here in these cheap pages with their fading ink.

That Sunday he celebrated the Eucharist and found tears springing to his eyes. How beautiful were the words, the Christ, his parishioners. Delicately and with loving care, he put the wafer in each folded upturned palm along the altar rail. He smiled at some, and some he whispered to by name. It had been years since he had celebrated the Eucharist with such tenderness.

I should insert two prayers here that he especially marked in his surrender. One was the prayer of Saint Francis, and given the discord he sowed, it's ironic, his repeating it:

> Lord, make me a channel of thy peace—that where there is hatred, I may bring love—that where there is wrong, I may bring the spirit of forgiveness—that where there is discord, I may bring harmony—that where there is error, I may bring truth—that where there is doubt, I may bring faith—that where there is despair, I may bring hope—that where there are shadows, I may bring light—that where there is sadness, I may bring joy.
>
> Lord, grant that I may seek rather to comfort than to be comforted—to understand, than to be understood—to love, than to be loved. . . .

He meant it all. He prayed with a kind of concentrated longing of the heart.

Or this:

> O, Lord, so draw my heart to you, so guide my mind, so fill my imagination, so control my will, that I

may be wholly yours, utterly dedicated to you; and then
use me, I pray, as you will, but always to your glory and
the welfare of your people; through our Lord, Jesus
Christ. Amen.

Sometimes, though, he said both of them in shorthand:

Lord, I am yours. Use me this day, as you will.

It gives you pause, given what happened to him, to us all
in Naughton, in the months to come. Because, goddamn it,
that's my question. Was he serving God? Did God come down
and ordain what happened and use him? Didn't we have Free
Will? Will to choose chastity? Will to choose self-discipline?
Or were we just marionettes with God pulling at our strings?
That's what Tom would have me think.

March 27. It was Sunday after church. He drove up the
mountain to visit Storey and Eleanor Lunt. They had struck up
a curious friendship, the Yankee minister and the Negro tenant
farmer, whose woman was a midwife and probably half a witch,
whose son Tom wanted in his school. Tom had been able to
confess to them what he could not admit to most of us: his
sense of isolation, his search for God. From them he learned a
little of the rumblings of the Negro world, though neither Storey nor Eleanor had much truck with civil rights.

"Uncle Toms," Buckford teased.

"Just won't come to no good, tha's all," Lunt commented.
"They're going to stir up a mess of trouble, and then we'll git
us some lynchings. Leave things be, I say. You don't stick your
bare bottom in a beehive."

Nothing Tom said could change their minds. "You may have to choose that martyrdom to get what's yours." He told them about Gandhi. "Marching, protesting. Maybe it's the only way to make a change."

"Change!" Lunt snorted. "Won't nothin' change 'cept for the worse." Country folk are the ultimate conservatives. "Hell, just holding on to what you got is hard enough."

That was the afternoon Tom helped Storey repair a fence line.

Some of what happened came out during our long talks, Tom recounting it to me word for word with the clarity that marks intense crisis and feeling, and some I learned later when I, too, drove up the mountain and made a point of befriending the Storey Lunts to see what they could tell. Spring is our busiest season. I didn't spend all my days that spring tailing Tom, his Boswell, recording every word. One thing I'm sure of: Tom felt that visit had a lot to do with everything that happened next. The opening of his heart. The prayers.

"So what do you think life's about?" he asked as they worked on the fence.

"Ain't about nothing," replied Storey.

"No?"

"You jes keep on, tha's all. It's about jes keeping on keeping on."

"Lord, I hope it's for more than that." Tom smiled. "I was thinking driving up here of a whole new prayer I'm working on."

"What's that?"

"To have a sign. I was asking, 'Show me what it's all about. I understand nothing.'" He smiled, remembering that Elizabeth had used the same words on their drive to Madisonville.

Storey, leaning his weight onto the post, looked up with an appreciative grunt. "Well, tha's what it's 'bout. Nothin'. You got your sign already, loud and clear."

"There's one thing sure to understand," Eleanor put in. She was watching the two men work. "Tha's your heart. You got a heart. I got a heart. We has to use them, tha's all. A heart is BIG. You carry round the light of the Lord in your heart, sprinkling a little here, a little there, like stardust. You raise your chil'ren, you try to do to others. And all you got to do that with is heart. Your heart sails through Heaven for us all. It's the ship of God."

Tom laughed aloud in his delight. "Well, Eleanor, you do that. Of all people, you sure do." Perhaps she was right, he thought, and she had just expressed the whole meaning of life: to discover in the course of a lifetime how to use and trust your heart. We are all angels ministering to one another each moment of our time on earth, angels who reach out to touch each other with a call of encouragement. Courage. From the French *le coeur*, meaning "heart." No angels in Heaven, but just us mortal ones down here on earth, and Heaven centered in our hearts.

Is that it, Lord? he thought. Heaven held in the heave of a hammer, in the coffee he shared with these two friends, in the Eucharist celebrated this morning, Heaven in the sweet weak springtime sun pouring on his back. Nothing special. Only Paradise.

Eleanor said: "I'll say a special prayer for you, Tom, so you gits to unnerstan'." Her lower lip thrust out flat. He couldn't tell if she was laughing at him, scolding, or serious. "Tha's what you want, ain it?"

"Be nice," he said.

"I'd be careful, I was you," grunted Storey.

"Why?"

"Might git it. You have to be careful what you ax for. You likes to git it, only sometimes it come with a hook on the end." He hammered home a nail with four strong strokes. Each bang echoed against the greening mountain slope and slapped against their ears, a double-stroke. "God got his own sense of humor. He play rough."

"Lord, Storey, you too much," Eleanor snorted. "You 'fraid?" she teased Tom. "You wants to see it or not?"

"Yes," he decided, driving back to the rectory. "I do want to see it," though what "it" was he could not have said. "I want to understand," he sang out loud, "to *stand under* the shadow of God." He was smiling as he left, warmed by the goodness of his friends. Was that the sign? he wondered idly, for surely his heart felt light, and light his mind. Nothing mattered anymore. He was alive with such sweet, open reverence, he couldn't even remember his prior arid state. He blessed the earth as he drove. He blessed the birds skimming through a liquid sky, the tendrils of the early budding trees, the very air ringing with gratitude.

Until he passed Elizabeth's house and was smacked by her absence. It was all he could do to drive past.

He reached the rectory at six. Empty rooms. He lit a fire. The Sunday papers lay unread at his feet. As suddenly as his serene and joyous mood had come, it left. Sitting before the fire, he was caught by desire for Elizabeth. He could taste her. He could feel the touch of her skin. He trembled with desire—and then with the awfulness of separation—and then with the wrongfulness of his desire. Yet all he wanted was to hold her.

"Elizabeth," he said aloud. "Elizabeth!" He stared into the flames.

They shot round the logs. They played in reds and oranges against the wood, which had cracked into a lacework of black charcoal. It was her goodness that he loved, he thought, staring at the living flame. It was God he saw in her. His love for her enriched him. He loved her for the purity and sweetness of his own heart when he was with her.

There is something ridiculous in his innocence, his confusion of sex and God, of the spiritual and physical; and yet I find myself wistful writing this.

"Lord, help me," he prayed. "Let me see Elizabeth again. If it is good in your eyes." Then with a smile, remembering that every prayer is already answered even before its wings have spread: "Thank you, Lord, for giving me my prayer." He didn't consider the twist Storey had spoken of—every prayer answered with a whiplash at the end. Maybe he didn't believe it, or maybe he didn't remember. His heart was opening. He sat hypnotized by the crackling fire. He did not deny God for Elizabeth, but neither could he any longer deny her for God, or turn love on and off like a spigot, or direct it where he or society or his vows decided it should flow. Suddenly it occurred to him (how blind he'd been!) that love can never be wrong. It was not love that was wrong, but what one did with it—if passion, for example, should turn the lovers toward each other to the exclusion of others or of their responsibilities or their God.

In a moment he was at the telephone dialing her number.

Oh, he was stripped of pretense. Yes, he wanted his God. But he wanted Elizabeth too. Love was not wrong. Or sexual desire, which was another gift of God, by which we cleave and clasp one another in our souls' coarse efforts to unite. The wrong lay not in loving but in closing off the heart.

She did not answer. He put the phone down dully and returned to his chair. A log split and fell to the front of the andirons with a spray of sparks.

"Elizabeth!" I imagine him there. His fist drums each word angrily on the chair arm. "Elizabeth! Elizabeth!" What did it matter if he hurt? No one promised satisfaction. "Elizabeth!" It was the beat of drums, the heartbeat of the gods.

One devil part of him was laughing at his posturing earlier in the day, when he had sat on the mountain asking for a sign of God, when, oh, Christ, Elizabeth would do!

The doorbell startled him. By now he had been alone so long that he disbelieved his ears. It rang again. There was no one whom he cared to see. He rose heavily, weary of parishioners. He opened the door.

It was Elizabeth.

Monday dawned bright and crisp. Tom, waking to the sight of her head on the pillow beside him, felt a wave of happiness. He shifted enough to see her face, trusting as a child's in sleep. In a while he would get up and make her coffee and they would drink it in bed, he thought, and later have breakfast and return to bed.

He telephoned Natalie to say that he needed to be alone that day. Under no circumstances was he to be disturbed. And Natalie, who admired and stood in awe of his Lenten disciplines, agreed, leaving the two to their love.

"You are the husband of my heart," she said. "I don't understand it, I've tried to dismiss it, but my very soul is wrenched out of my body when we part."

"You've been given as a special gift to me," he answered. "When I am with you, I am made whole. I am in perfect peace and harmony."

"When we part," she said, still travelling over the stones of separation, "it's as if a piece of me is torn in half. Like a sheet of paper."

By afternoon they were talking of the divorce that each would get, of how much time they would have to wait before they could be married, of how long they had to wait before they could publicly declare their love.

"Why did you come last night?" he asked.

"I was home alone. Angus was out. He's out all the time now. Sometimes he doesn't come home at all. He's drinking more and more, and when I ask where he's been, he gets angry. Or else he sulks. I've stopped asking. But last night I couldn't get you out of my mind."

"I was calling you."

"I found myself pacing the living room. I'd pick up a book and throw it down. I couldn't concentrate. I tried to telephone Fran or Sally or other friends, and no one was home. I couldn't stop thinking about you."

"Or I you."

"I was so ashamed to come."

"I'm so glad you did."

"But I thought Priscilla would be here, you see. So it would be all right. I was going to talk to you about Angus. I mean, I know I could have phoned, but I was looking for an excuse."

They discussed how to get Angus help. Later they confessed their guilt and feelings. They kept no secrets. He told her of his efforts to turn his love for her onto Priscilla, and how it had failed.

"You don't choose by willpower the person you love," she said sententiously.

"Wise Elizabeth."

"That's why you so often see a man who loves the entirely wrong girl—the barroom stripper."

"But unconsciously she may be right."

"Or you see a woman—"

"You talk too much."

They laughed and kissed. "It's not that there is some quality I love in you," she said. "It's as if my feeling flows onto you for no reason. Just because you're there."

In the late afternoon she left. Tom was both exhausted and exhilarated. To calm himself, he meditated, spiralling up and down the stairwell of his soul. He felt centered and steady in the specific gravity of his own body, the earth pressing up against his feet, the air holding him in its embrace. He wanted to sit quietly and consider the blessings of the earth. At the same time he was exploding.

Elizabeth had been gone for an hour when he grabbed his lumber jacket and strode outdoors in the cold evening for a walk. Black clouds were piling in the West. He climbed the hill behind the church. By now all of Naughton would be preparing for dinner. He was alone in his empty fields and meadows, the great sky above cleft by two birds diving on unseen currents, aerial fish, each wingstroke a song of gratitude and praise. The light wind ruffled his hair.

"Oh, thank you, God," he said aloud.

Around him the grasses shone, and he was humbled by the beauty of the place: the hills and woods, the yellow-greening trees, the blue scilla spiking upward in the grass. The colors seemed more brilliant than he could absorb, the scenery so magnificent he knew God took a special joy in carving the valleys with His own hands, molding the hills and gullies to the shape of His palm; then creating flowing water, streams like silver thread, and flowers, grass, and grains.

He walked through the evening air. He picked a stem of grass and was ravished by its beauty. Holding it to his lips in the open window of his heart, he felt humbled by the miracle of this world. Dusk spread to dark. He went inside.

The next day was Tuesday. He moved through his parish duties, blessed. He floated. Others recognized his state of grace. Natalie spoke of his being "of the essence," and all day she found excuses to come into his office, to stand at his side, to have him talk to her.

For Tom everything came easily that day. He telephoned Elizabeth, and their exchange of love lifted him higher still. What an effect the woman had on him! But as the afternoon wore on, he began to feel a sense of urgency. There was something to be done, for which he had to allow an hour, a half hour. . . . He tried to snuff the anxiety down. It clapped him with both hands. Finally his urgency reached such a pitch that he sent Natalie home and closed the parish hall. It was almost four P.M. There was something he was supposed to—what? He didn't know the rest. To do? To see? He started to the rectory, but then, as if guided, turned abruptly and once again took the hillside path, the same one he had climbed the night before.

He was almost running, scrambling up the hill to get there in time. That was exactly what he felt: as if he had an appointment he could not miss.

At a certain place he stopped. He sat down on a rock.

Below him spread the valley. He marked the houses far below, the still serenity.

Then he felt a sound. It came as a hollow roaring in both ears, like the inside of a seashell. The silence of the wind, he thought, but there was no wind, no breath of moving air. And fearful, made uneasy by the sound, he rose and walked farther up the path, and stopped again to . . .

Like a thunderclap it came upon him. The light was so intense his knees gave way. His eyes were closed, yet he was surrounded by light.

Tears were coursing down his face, and he was immersed then in such sweetness as words could not signify. He could hear the singing of the planets, the low roar of the rocks. His mouth was filled with a taste so delicious that he thought he would expire, and he was bathed by wave after wave of light, a radiance that washed him up and down, through him, around him, over him.

In that light, in rapture, he saw the order of the universe, the dancing of atoms, spirit-lights that played across the planes of . . . plains of . . . but he had no language for what he saw.

His soul was whirling, his mind stumbling to catch up. His body was paralyzed.

In that moment he knew he had seen, not God (for that would blind him), not God, but the waving of the grasses at the passing of the Hem of His garments. He had seen to the edge of the unknowable.

Who knows how long it lasted? Gradually he began to come to himself. He felt the sweet etheric music fading on his tongue. For long minutes he remained, stretched out on the cold earth, tears running down his cheeks. He could not stop them. He was swept by rapture. It was the bursting of a dam of joy. Minutes passed. His shaking ceased. He sat up clumsily, mind reeling, opened his eyes—and instantly shut them again. He was blinded by the light.

More time passed. After a while he opened his eyes again. The sky was an iridescent pearl, a dull reflect. He stared then at his hands. Light was streaming from the palms of his hands, rivers of golden light. A blood vessel had burst on the back of his right hand, raising a blue bruise, and that, too, was astonishing, for he had felt nothing. But it was the radiance that filled him with wonder. He could see it on his hands. He could feel it like electricity pouring off his skin.

In ecstasy he staggered to his feet. Below him stood his church, nestled in a fold of earth, from which the valley spread on farther out. Never had it seemed so beautiful. The whole earth was shining in the evening air, the grasses shimmering with divine light, the steeple gleaming in the rays of a dying sun. He could hardly walk, but he started—staggered—toward his church. He wanted to open the door to let God's light stream in. The grass under his feet was still streaming with light, and at each footstep it scattered in the air around him. Not ordinary light, the sun's last rays, no, but the living fire of life, the earth's divinity.

At the church he stumbled in his hurry and fell on his knees at the door. He opened it, still weeping, then gasped to see the altar likewise gleaming in the dark.

Then came the madness, for he was running up the aisle, hardly aware of his own impulses.

He stumbled, caught himself on the altar cloth, pulling down the candlesticks, the vases with their flowers, all crashing to the floor, some rolling off the red rug, clinking on the bricks.

The brass cross fell, caught on the edge of the table, and held, askew. He never heard the sounds. His ears were filled with other songs. He grabbed one of the large silver platters under the credenza table and stumbled out again into God's clean world, where the leaves and grasses, the trees, the sky, the horns of cattle and the very horses pacing in the fields were flashing with fire; and, weeping still, sucking for sweet air, he was on his hands and knees, pulling up great tufts of light. He was filling the silver platter with light, with earth, with grass and sticks. They were streamers of light, and he was filling his plate with the singing of the planets, the gyre and sweep of stars. Above, in a darkening sky, a single planet shone, a drop of gold in azure clarity, while all around the clouds piled one upon the other, soaring to the heavens, and all tinted as a Tiepolo sunset. In that single open space, in that lustrous, luminescent blue, shone the Evening Star, a prick of light so quiet that his heart rocked with rapture.

Heavy in his hands he carried the platter to the church. Heavy was the silver bowl with the weight of God's own world. He lifted it toward the altar in two reverent hands, his offering, his worship of His Very Grace, the Blessing, the Suchness of it all.

Seeing with an inner eye, he took no notice of the table linen askew and trailing on the floor, the candlesticks, the silverware. It was the cross he wanted, and, overflowing with emotion, he reached out to right the cross on the table. The salver of his offering tipped on the rug. He was scraping it back into the bowl with both hands, and, humble before the Power just shown him, enraptured by the gift, the Grace, he was lifting handfuls of light in streamers to the tabletop, piling on the altar, light on top of light.

He buried his face in Grace and fell again to the floor, unable to stand, but with weak, fluttering gestures, as a bird with a broken wing strains back his breast, beats his pinions softly once or twice before falling still again, so he heaped his offering of God's own gifts at the foot of man's puny altar, this sorrowful attempt to build a structure worthy of God's praise. Oh! With what knowledge he understood all things. It was a mockery, a desecration of the name of God to give to Him, the All, the IT, our carved stones or brass or books, bits of inter-woven threads—pathetic offerings, when the miracle lay just here, in this which, holding in his hands, he pressed in adoration to his lips, his heart, and then to the cross itself, the sign of Christ, the Son.

He was weeping with gratitude. There was nothing but God. He was himself a piece and praise of God. He dissolved in waves of love, smearing love upon the cross.

It was at this moment that Emily Carter entered the church, gruff and abrupt at noting the side door open. In the dim light she did not at first comprehend what she saw—a man—it was the rector—lying at the communion rail, his head toward the altar steps. Was he sick? she thought, and waddled farther into the church, stepping up to him with Christian concern, her eyes slowly growing accustomed to the dark. She stood helpless at the sight of Buckford lying on the floor—"writhing" was what she thought. His mouth was covered with dirt. His shirt was smudged with dirt, and also the altar table, and in a huge plate she saw manure and dried grass lay heaped—the silver alms platter! Her eyes swept the devastation: the great brass cross, tipped over, and, strewn everywhere, the holy vessels of the church.

"Desecration!" She ran to the altar, echoing his very

thoughts aloud. He turned, saw her, saw the figure of Emily Carter, fat and fulsome, rocking towards him on her tiny feet— but what he knew was the beauty of her soul, the inner light that was streaming from her head and shoulders in the gloom, an aura of living light. With an incoherent cry he pulled himself toward her, on his knees, and fell in worship at her feet. In fear and horror she saw he was kissing her feet. He was kneeling before her, kissing her shoes, her shadow, the earth on which she stepped. His face was smeared, his hands brown, with manure.

With a cry she pulled from his grasp and ran.

13

THAT WAS THE STORY AS IT CAME OUT AT THE TRIAL.

Yet by that time, months later, the matter was far from clear. Not even the facts fell neatly into place, and when it ended, none of us knew for sure exactly what had happened, except that our minister had had an ecstatic vision. Or else gone mad.

Had he knocked over the cross or not? We didn't know.

According to one version he smeared the cross and holy vessels with dirt and manure, deliberately violating them, demonically possessed.

According to another, he never entered the church at all, but, caught in the fire and flame of revelation, was literally paralyzed—Saint Paul falling off his horse—and lay as if dead on the damp grass, either in the graveyard or just outside the lych-gate, where Emily found and roused him.

Soon it was impossible to determine truth; and Tom was no help. He remembered only his inner voyage, and even that he was helpless to transmit. Weeks after the vision the Bishop questioned Tom, especially on the desecration of the altar.

"Earth is no sacrilege to God." His voice was acrid with contempt. "I would make that offering anytime."

At the time we knew nothing about mysticism, visions. Not even Bishop Crowley. How were we to know? We knew nothing about spiritual quests or meditation, or even the love-ins and Flower Children of the sixties—all that came later. I'd never even heard of the word *mysticism*, or of the types of ecstatic experience spoken of by saints—absorption, rapture.

I've read a lot since then about these visions—Saint Francis seeing the Christ, and Jakob Böhme, who was caught by a ray of light reflected from the bowl of a spoon, one ray of light that changed his life. But Tom's vision was held against him.

Like a shock wave the news hit Naughton, and we trembled with delicious horror at the prospect of our pastor grovelling like a dog, like a hog, with bits of grass in his mouth where he had tried to eat ordure before falling in worship at the fat feet of Emily. But I'm ahead of myself. At first it had its comical side.

When Emily Carter left the church, she threw herself into her car, her heart pounding as much from the physical exertion of her dash as from the shock of the rector's acts. Driving down Laurel Hollow Road, she was so shaken that she pulled to the side and sat staring straight ahead, lips trembling. It was there that Carolyn Page found her. Carolyn was so concerned that she climbed into the passenger seat beside her.

"But Emily, whatever is wrong? Something's happened."

"I can't tell you."

"One of the dogs has been hurt?"

"No, no, nothing like that. Nothing."

"Then you've been hurt. Are you sick? You've just received bad news. Your mother? Of course you needn't tell me if you don't want to. I don't want to pry. It's your life, Emily. I just was thinking I could help."

"Carolyn." Emily turned to her. "I have just seen the worst sight in the world. It makes me faint to think of it."

"What?"

"I can't tell you. But if I did, you would understand."

"But that's nonsense, Emily. There's nothing in the world you couldn't tell me. Darling! We went to school together!"

"Promise you won't tell a single solitary soul."

"Why, of course."

"It was up at the church!" And Emily burst into tears. "Oh dear, I can't control myself."

"But what?"

"It was Mr. Buckford. Oh, Carolyn, no, I can't tell."

"Yes, you can. Now, you get a grip on yourself, Emily Carter, and tell me what has happened," said Carolyn firmly, "or I'll drive us both right up to the church and see."

"I couldn't do that. I couldn't," said Emily, and it flashed through her head to wonder, for the briefest second, if he would kiss her feet again! Or perhaps would not! Thus forced, her story poured out.

"But what could have gotten into him?" Carolyn kept repeating, to Emily's annoyance. "I mean, to kiss your feet. Whatever possessed the man?"

Carolyn then did just what she had threatened: She drove up to the church, leaving Emily to get herself home alone. Which was not as cruel as it might appear, Carolyn assured herself, since Emily had only a few miles to drive and a big car with automatic shift and power brakes. The danger, if any, was hers. As she got out of the car, she picked up a good-sized chunk of gneiss.

When she arrived at the church, the doors were locked. No one was about. In one way she was relieved and in another disappointed, though she did not drive down to the rectory to hunt the man down, and neither did she toss her stone out the window until she was well away. Back at her own house she telephoned me.

By the time I got to Tom's, it was late at night. He was standing at the kitchen steps, waiting.

"Hello, John." We shook hands and turned inside against the evening cold.

Tom was quiet in a way I hadn't met before. His eyes glowed. He seemed to be only partly listening, as if his concentration was centered elsewhere. I was awed. His quiet was so profound that I could only think that it was Emily or Carolyn who had gone mad.

On his desk lay a yellow legal pad, its pages covered with fine scrawl, and on top of it a fountain pen, beside the open ink.

"I was writing when I saw you driving up." He screwed the top on the ink and collected the pages.

"Saw me?" I said, surprised, for his study faces west, away from the road.

"*See* is the wrong word, perhaps. I knew."

"Oh." I flicked a piece of lint off the shoulder of my jacket, wondering what he meant. Then: "Carolyn Page called me. She's been talking to Emily Carter."

The pause lengthened between us, until I burst out: "Tom, aren't you going to tell me what happened?"

"John, if I told you what I've seen," he began, "you'd say I'm crazy. Perhaps I am. I have been given a gift beyond comprehension. It adds new meaning to the word *grace*."

His voice, rich and deep, seemed to fill the entire cavity of my chest, only it created not soothing peace but an intolerable ache.

"To tell you the truth," he continued, "I don't want to talk about it now. I've been shown something so precious, so sacred, I don't know what to do with it, except hold it to me for a time. I need time to think about it."

"But you have to say something. Emily—"

"I'm not sure I even have the words to do so. I have seen into the depths of the universe. I understood things beyond . . . it was a vision of God." His face was radiant. "It's like standing on a hill, John, on a stormy night, and all around you lies impenetrable blackness, and suddenly the sky is rent by lightning. For a few seconds everything is spread out before you. You can see the trees, the hills, the cloudy skies. The lightning ends, and you're again enclosed in black, but you remember. You don't forget what's there. That's what I feel like. But in that moment I knew . . . everything."

He stopped. I waited, until suddenly it dawned on me he wasn't going to tell me any more. One part of me respected his privacy and another resented his selfishness. My next words burst out at him aggressively:

"And what about this story of Emily's? What about the dirt on the altar and the platters knocked to the floor? And kissing her feet as if she's some goddamned saint? And what about—?"

"Be quiet." He held up one hand, and my mouth closed of its own accord. For a long moment he looked at me, and I felt ashamed, like a little boy caught out, and at the same time I felt what he had said: quiet.

"What did she say happened?"

I told him the story then as Carolyn had told me. He lis-
tened, his head resting on the back of his chair, eyes closed.
When I told about his crawling to Emily, he gave a quick laugh.
"That must have startled her."

At the description of the dirt on the altar, he grew serious,
but even then his face never lost that joy.

"Did it happen?"

"I remember other things," he hedged. "Come on, we'd
better go see." He didn't seem ashamed or guilty, just listening
to a problem to be solved.

We went up to the church together, walking in the new,
wet grass under a crescent moon. Tom threw one arm across
my shoulder. He was resonating. "Each blessed moment is a
gift of God. Each second, John, we by our free will are writing
out our lives, deciding, *choosing*, not necessarily what happens
to us but how we will receive it—whether we wish to be happy
or sad. We *choose* the attitude we bring to life. Did you know
that?"

I stumbled beside him in the dark. I could hardly keep up
with his long strides, though I was the taller one.

"We are like moles tunnelling in our blind night-alleys, not
knowing that all we have to do is stop and look. We can dig
out of the tunnel just by paddling one inch upward—a simple
ninety-degree turn, and we can dance in the silver moonlight
to the praise of God. We give Him thanks."

I didn't understand his words, but they flowed over me. I
wanted to be the first to whom he explained these things.

"I didn't see God," he continued. "I'm not strong enough
for that. But I saw the grasses waving in His praise. His Presence sets the earth aflame."

We got to the church, and here was another mystery. The

altar was all in place, the cross aright, the Bible on its stand,
and everything as it should be, except that one of the silver
platters was dented and on the lip of another clung two blades
of grass. The cross itself—heavy, burnished brass—stood in place
upright, but off-center, and, yes, its polish blurred by hand-
prints. Tom did not seem troubled by these details. We straightened things up, washed and dried the one plate, and while we
worked, he told me about the light he had seen pouring off his
hands and the light he'd seen in Emily—the light in all of us;
and, listening to him, I felt strangely excited and disturbed. He
did not tell me that before his vision he'd spent an adulterous
night with Elizabeth.

Margaret will tell you I hate conflict. She says I'm slow to
react. But it's caution. I like to get my facts straight and then
think about things until they get clear, and not go running off
half-cocked, making foolish decisions that only have to be undone. My whole effort in those first weeks was to keep people
calm.

The next day I visited Emily at her dog-feeding time, which
is one of the happier moments of her day. We went round the
kennels commenting on the conditions of the dogs, doling out
their portions of meat, filling their water bowls amidst a splendid frenzy of barking. The dogs raced up and down their runs
and leapt against the wire while she, waddling cautiously with
her pails, laughed and sang to them, sent kisses, and pointed
out to me with pride the good show qualities of this shepherd
or that.

Afterwards we sat over tea in her dark, dusty living room,
the screeching parrot hooded so that we could talk.

"I saw Tom last night," I said, at which she smoothed the

sleeve of her blouse with intense concentration. "He says he had a vision of God."

"Good gracious."

"Yes, that's what I say. And in the midst of the vision he indicated that he saw God in you. He saw a Divine Light, as he called it, and it was that which he was worshipping."

"Divine Light? In me?"

"I know it's hard to believe," I said—and could have cut off my tongue! "What I'm trying to say is that he did not mean to frighten you. He's a good man, Emily. He wanted to call and apologize himself for frightening you, but I said I'd speak to you first. The only thing is that great harm could be done if word got round. I hope it will never be mentioned again."

She looked snippy. "Well, I don't know if I should be quiet," she said. "I mean, he kissed my feet. He was on his knees before me. He worshipped at my feet. Surely that's not something usual." She blushed so red I had to cover my smile by relighting my pipe. One of the benefits of pipe smoking is all the puffing and cleaning and lighting to be done.

"I mean, he has to be held accountable, doesn't he?"

"I'm sure he won't deny it," I answered. "That's not quite the point."

"Well, I'm sure I won't be the one to talk. I told Carolyn only when she promised not to tell a soul. And just look what she did! Ran straight home and telephoned you. I'm sure half the people at the Club know it by now. And it wasn't my fault. I asked for her promise of secrecy."

"Well, I'll talk to her too. I'm going over there right now. I just wanted to tell you how much harm could be done by this. I know Tom's sorry he scared you. He lost his head."

"It could happen to any of us," she said.

"Now, that seems excessively generous," I laughed. "Perhaps not to any of us. But I trust this will go no further."

"I wouldn't want it to go *further*." It was her turn to laugh. "Kissing my feet is enough. I am so glad you dropped by, John. I enjoyed feeding the dogs with you. Tell Mr. Buckford that as far as I am concerned, the incident is closed."

Carolyn gave even more exuberant promises than Emily, but I had hardly reached my front door when Margaret greeted me with a detailed account of the incident, gathered from Mrs. Crabtree, the laundress who did church linens. Everyone was wondering what had happened.

The phone rang. It was Butch Shriver announcing he had called a special vestry meeting at his house that evening to discuss the incident. Angrily I retorted that it was my place as senior warden to call special meetings, if there were to be any, and that we did not use star-chamber proceedings at Trinity, secret from the rector. But things were already swinging out of control. Shriver said if I didn't attend, he'd run the meeting without me. Mutiny.

I didn't take the time to eat. I stalked out, with Margaret fluttering behind me, protesting that at least I could take a sandwich in the car; but my stomach was too nervous to hold down food.

At the meeting I tried to maintain calm.

"The man's insane," Butch shouted angrily. "Schizoid. It's been evident from the first moment he arrived."

Emily looked appealingly at me and said she felt sick and wasn't going to say anything, not a single word, but just wait and see what happened. Esther Ratcliffe, seated next to her, held Emily's hand and patted it encouragingly every now and again. Emily said it would all be made clear in time, a statement that amused me, being a direct quote from Tom.

So she sat through the discussion, lips pursed, and left Tom's defense (what there was of it) to me. I wanted an investigation, too, only a quiet one. "He's been under a lot of strain. I happen to know he's been fasting. He's working like a Trojan. His wife is away, his family unsettled. . . ."

"Fasting?" asked Mimi Foster, shaken. "What an extraordinary thing to do. You mean he doesn't eat anything?"

"Well, I don't know." I wished I'd never brought the matter up. "It's in the Bible."

She laughed. "No wonder he's seeing things."

"As for his vision," said Rod, the banker on our board, "the Virginia state mental hospitals are full of people with a direct line to God. I, for one, did not ask for a minister to come serve us at Trinity who talks to God. I, for one—"

"Look." I snapped. "It's not completely unheard of, even in the Church. Moses, Joan of Arc, Saint Paul—"

"Good God!" said Julian. "Are you suggesting that Tom Buckford is a saint, because—?"

"No, no, of course—"

"And if we had Joan of Arc as a minister here—"

"I don't see what Moses and—"

"I'd put her to the stake too. God does not appear to people who—"

The meeting was falling into sniping and quarrelling. Emily looked more and more unnerved. I made an impassioned speech about how none of us knew what had happened. I spoke about generosity and caution and about the importance of avoiding scandal or witch-hunting. We had just come through the Mc-Carthy trials, and whatever we wanted, it was not to repeat in

microcosm that national hysteria. Moreover to fly off the handle, as we were doing, to talk it up would attract the press, the
wolves come down like Assyrians in the night, and nothing
would be left us—Naughton, our reputations, our church.

In the end the vestry voted to demand an apology and an
investigation. Mimi suggested that we cable Priscilla to return
home, for Pris had a dampening influence on Tom—beneficial,
she felt, in light of his emotional temperament. We decided to
ask Margaret, who knew her best, to write, without giving anything away, urging her to come home.

It was after midnight when the meeting broke up.

The auto-da-fé, I thought, turning in my drive. It was
my job to ask Tom to apologize, and next morning I drove up
to the parish hall. He listened with that steady inner quiet,
saying nothing, then:

"Why should I apologize?" he asked. "I have nothing to
apologize for. For seeing what is around us? For having my eyes
opened? I have no intention of apologizing."

How could I say the apology was for embarrassing us, for
that damned offering on a silver salver, for behaving like a fool
with Emily, and humiliating us with his extravagance? And
maybe for desecrating the cross in his enthusiasm. He must
have known.

"Sacrilege," I murmured. "Propriety."

"I committed no sacrilege," he said. "I won't even mention your social rules. But I'll be glad to tell what happened.
Yes, I'd love to do that. Come to church on Sunday, those of
you who can hear, listen to the Good News!"

Instantly I changed my mind.

"No, Tom, leave it alone. We can still hush this matter

up," I said. "Don't apologize, then. A simple explanation will be fine. I'll help you write it."

But Tom laughed, flirting with the danger.

"Don't you understand what you're doing to us?" I said angrily.

"Yes, I know exactly what I'm doing to you," he said. "It hurts, doesn't it? It hurts me too. I think in a bit it may hurt even more."

That Sunday the church was almost full. Some people came who had not been to church in years. It's no good trying to keep a secret in Naughton. Margaret and I nodded to Carolyn and Dut Page as we proceeded to our pew, to Emily Carter and the others of the vestry. Elizabeth was there, with Angus in tow. He sat stiffly erect, his fedora in his lap, looking annoyed. After I sat down and while I was still leaning forward in the reluctant crouch that passes for acceptable prayer in the Episcopal church, my forehead on my fist, our grudging bow to an authoritarian deity—while I was murmuring my introductory prayers of thanks and pleas, I heard the bag-woman enter.

The bag-woman came to services once or twice a month, usually late. The prayers might be half over before she came slapping down the aisle in her bedroom slippers—*flop-flap, flop-flap*. Dirty, unkempt, she carried two shopping bags filled with papers, and she preferred to sit up front beside someone else, though there were always empty pews. She would cross right into yours with a cheery " 'Scuse me," *flap-flapping* above the minister's prayers. She'd settle in her seat with a loud "There!" only to start rummaging in her bags, talking to herself. Glasses, books, whatever she was looking for she never found; but the rustle of papers would continue until she suddenly would stop, then sit in quiet until the need began again.

Tom and I had often laughed about her. Once he'd stopped the service, waiting for her to settle down, and the entire church had been suspended, quivering, as she wrestled with her bags. Suddenly she'd become aware of silence. She stopped, looked up. In the silence Tom began the prayers again, and when he'd started, his voice lifting and falling above the murmur of the congregation, she had set to work once more, digging with rabbit concentration in her hutch. She always left noisily before the service ended. We never had a chance to question her.

She took Communion too. Once I found myself at the rail beside her and was ashamed to discover my reluctance to put my lips against the silver chalice after hers, even though Tom wiped and turned the cup. For the only time in my life I dipped the wafer instead of taking a swallow of wine.

Had the bag-woman, too, heard something about today's service? She shuffled up the aisle, her bags *whap*ping against her bandaged legs, and called out " 'Scuse me!" loudly as she squeezed into the pew past Dutton Page. " 'Scuse again. I like the wall," she explained, pushing past Carolyn—Carolyn Page, of all the people to pick out.

The congregation exchanged mute, flickering smiles, the ladies' hats fluttering like flowers in a breeze.

Of the seven seasons of the church calendar, none is so grim as Lent, with its general concentration on sin and the subjugation of the body to fasting and flagellation. The readings are all about casting out devils, about sin, fornication, adultery, whoremongering, covetousness, the lust of concupiscence, uncleanness of body and spirit. It is the season when we hear that whoever looks at a woman with desire has committed adultery

in his heart, that whoever divorces his wife (except for fornication) causes her to commit adultery, and that whoever mar-
ries the divorced commits that sin. This is the time of Jesus'
temptation in the wilderness, and the time when Saint Paul
really lets it rip with his remembrances of his own afflictions,
stripes, imprisonments, tumults, and labors. It's a cold, flinty
period, unrelieved until the last two weeks, when we catch
brief, brilliant glimpses of charity and hope and breathe with
relief as the miracles begin again—feeding the multitudes or
healing the vile Canaanite woman's devil-ridden daughter (a
miracle performed grudgingly enough, we admit, with our Christ
muttering about casting God's bread to the dogs and the woman
whining that the lowest dogs are allowed to lick the crumbs
under their master's table). Tom laughed when I told him my
feelings about Lent, and explained again the purpose of spiritual
exercise—to develop your inner life—but I doubt if many of the
people in church that morning looked at Lent as more than a
time to give up sweets.

The organ gave a blast, and the congregation came rustling
to its feet as our six-person choir entered from the back, their
voices urgent in the effort to belt out the hymn. Merry Mere-
dith carried the brass cross. Tom, resplendent in his purple
robes, brought up the rear.

> Rend your heart and not your garments, and turn
> unto the Lord your God: for he is gracious and merciful,
> slow to anger and of great kindness. . . .

Back then we didn't have a lot of the innovations they
have in church these days. We didn't have lay readers and
young acolytes bobbing up and down and generally making a

fuss at the altar. We had one priest and the choir and the congregation. So it was Tom who led the prayers.

"Let us humbly confess our sins unto Almighty God." His voice had taken on new timbre.

"Almighty and most merciful Father; we have erred and strayed from thy ways like lost sheep. We have followed too much the devices and desires of our own hearts. . . ."

The bag-lady bustled and rustled a few seats ahead of me, lifting her voice in querulous song; we ignored her, as polite people should, though certainly I was sinning right through the confession in my desire to strangle the bitch.

The readings! In any Episcopal service there are two Lessons, an Old Testament and a New Testament reading. The minister has wide latitude in choosing which reading to give, but on this particular Sunday (I'd looked it up) the Epistle was an obscure letter to the Galatians, a metaphor on slaves and freed women; but the Gospel reading from Saint John is a favorite of everyone: Christ feeding the multitudes with five loaves and two small fish—a rousing, well-told story, direct and simple. It names who said what and gets right down to the disciples' panic in the face of the mob—just what any of us would feel looking out over a sea of five thousand hungry faces. You can feel their fear when Christ says casually, "Where can we buy some bread for everyone?" And Philip's response: "Good grief! Two hundred dollars wouldn't be enough to buy bread for all these people and give everyone a slice." At which point Jesus sits them down and does his stuff. It's a great story and comes, moreover, with a special relief after the rigidity and

self-flagellation of the readings of the previous weeks. All week
I'd had a foreboding about what Tom was going to do. It was
so intense I'd actually asked what the Lessons were, if you can
imagine, and even made some suggestions on his sermon and
the telling of the story of the fishes.

Then he was reading from the Lesson, and it wasn't the
fishes story at all.

> Don't you know that you are the temple of God
> and that the Spirit of God dwells in you? If any man
> defile the temple of God, him shall God destroy; for the
> temple of God is holy, which temple you are.

It took me a moment to realize Tom was casting it into
modern language.

> Then they asked him, "What shall we do to work
> the will of God?" Jesus answered, "This is the work of
> God—that you believe in him whom He has sent."
> They said, "What sign are you showing, then, that
> we may see and believe you? What work do you do?"

Margaret leaned over and touched me with one white-
gloved hand.

"Are you all right?"

I waved her off. Margaret left her hand on my knee, giving
me a comforting pat every now and then, but I was scrabbling
frantically through the prayer book for the passage he'd just
read. I couldn't find it. When I looked up again, we had finished the *Jubilate Deo* and the creed and were concluding prayers
for the President. I stumbled to catch up and put in my special

intercessions for Tom, for us, for comfort, for Divine Intervention to prevent (my foreboding) disaster.

I could have saved my breath.

He came to the pulpit, eyes shining. He stood a moment, surveying the congregation, and even the bag-lady grew quiet. Right through the closed windows we could hear a mockingbird singing its pretty heart out.

"My dear friends," he began. A shiver ran through the crowd, a restless wind. There was a pause. It drew out for one sickening minute, then two, and then he took a big breath.

"I had a sermon drawn up for today, a perfect eight-minute oration, just as we were taught in seminary. I am not going to give it. Instead I want to talk to you, just talk. Talk to you from my heart." He had our total attention.

He began to speak faster now, impassioned. "Oh, my dear brothers, my sisters—for isn't that what you are? Aren't you made of my flesh and I composed of your very spirit? We are one and the same." And now he moved down from the pulpit into the aisle; to stand at the first pew, right in our midst almost.

There was an uncomfortable shifting in the church, an exchange of looks at this Fundamentalist Billy-Graham-type talk. We were *never* brethren and sisters, the idea being as tacky as it was offensive. And as for calling us "dear"—!

"Many of you have heard by now that this week I had an epiphany, a revelation. I don't know if it was a vision from God. Maybe it was just a stroke," he laughed around at us, self-deprecatingly. "I'm waiting to see, just as you all are, because if that ecstasy was real, if it came from God, then the truth will be shown in its aftereffects. Its grace will be demonstrated. But if it was false, then that too will come out in time. I was shown things, though. I saw things. I understood things for which we have no words. Listen, our language is only a hundred thousand years old, and its words and structure serve us for this physical plane on which we live. English, especially, is full of good strong nouns. *Pew.*" He struck the edge of the pew with his hand. "*Floor, brick, roof* . . . but we have no words for the language of the spirit. Even Christ could find no words to express what he'd seen. He had to speak in parables. I feel the same. But I'll tell one thing that I saw.

"I understood the miracle of this life, the munificence of the gifts we are given: plants to eat and herbs for medicines. And water. I saw the stream behind the churchyard there, but it wasn't just water. It was a silver ribbon cascading through the grass, licking the earth—this precious substance given for our sustenance; and animals—I understand that these, too, are gifts to us. But also they *are* us! We have a responsibility to love and care for them, to see they're kept from harm. Because we are all one single unit on this earth. You are that water, the air, the grass, the horses eating it."

(We liked the idea of being the horses.)

"I saw the earth shining, pulsating with light.

"I saw—that we are made of light and that these particles of light infuse not only the physical universe of trees and earth and animals and humans, but also dimensions beyond our comprehension. These particles are dancing in constant praise to God, held together by a shining juice—invisible—the same way that gravity is invisible, immeasurable, but still palpable. What is the magnetic force that holds it together?" He paused a long moment. "I say it is an active energy and that we call it *love*; and it is this love that we call God and that we are experiencing every moment of our lives.

"Unless we block it out! And that's what I want to talk to you about."

We were still as death. Not even the bag-lady moved.

"We have only one thing to do. Christ said it. It's so simple. We think there's a trick. We come to church once a week to get it. But it's not found here in church! You don't need church! You're not going to learn it here at all! Not giving one hour a week to a social duty! It's so simple. Don't you know what it is?"

He looked around at us, and we looked back, startled that he would be talking that way about church, missing his intention totally. His voice grew very soft.

"It's to love ourselves. That is absolutely all." He pointed to the Bible on the eagle stand. "That's the whole message right there, in all those hundreds of pages of prophets and histories. Love ourselves. Love one another. Love our very own souls.

"Listen, we are composed of love. The very atoms of our bodies are love. And when you are loving, you touch your very essence. In loving you achieve integrity. And this is the gift, do you see? We are permitted—do you understand?—by grace to engage in loving.

"And for that, what are we supposed to do? We're supposed to touch one another, yes, even physically. Touch with the gentleness of our souls, brushing like the kisses of moths against each other's bodies and souls."

"Is he advocating free love?" Margaret whispered to me, but I had no time to answer before he went on.

"Why should we love each other? Why bother?

"Because when you love, with all your heart and soul and mind and strength, when love is pouring out of you, then—it's

what Christ was trying to tell us—the Forces of the Universe
are able to spill their abundance onto you. It's a law. Like
gravity. Like the sun coming up. Whatever you think about is
what you'll get. If you allow your thoughts to dwell on worry,
fear, doubt, despair, loneliness, then *that* is what you will get.
So loving is this spiritual Principle, so *giving*, so willing to give
us whatever we desire, that it will give us everything—even fear
and unhappiness, if that is what our minds project.

"That's why the Bible tells us to have faith. To give praise
and sing thanks. Because then we automatically get out of our
own way to allow the Force of the Universe—this energy of
love—God, if you wish—to give us our heart's desire. It's a
spiritual law."

"Amen!" cried the bag-lady, whom we were being admon-
ished to love as the image of God.

Tom went on. He was jumping from subject to subject.
Some people were deeply moved, and some suspicious, but all
of us held spellbound—until he committed the unforgivable
and started naming names.

"Look, we are taught in our society that to love yourself is
vanity, pride. We are told to have a healthy self-esteem, or self-
respect. But self-esteem is not the same as love."

He turned and moved down the steps into the aisle. "Carolyn." His eyes reached over Dutton's shoulder to rest on her.
Her back stiffened; her chin flew up. She stared straight ahead,
ignoring him with all the self-command at her possession. "Carolyn, don't be so hard on yourself. Let go, let go. . . ." He
turned to a man nearby. "Ned, when you muff a golf shot, can
you still feel kindly toward yourself? I am talking of the greatest
power of the universe, love. It is the glue that holds it all
together. It is the matrix, underlying all, our right, our gift; it

is given to us to hook into as a source of power and replenish-
ment. Edgar"—His hand shot out to touch another in the congregation. "You don't have to treat your mother with such
contempt!" You could hear the congregation gasp. "It's yourself
you wrong. Because *you are her!*"

Oh, God, I don't remember all that he did and said. He
was pacing up and down the aisle, pointing to one person after
another, calling each of us by name to give up his venom, or
fear, or anger, while the rest of us craned to see whom he had
picked out and how that man dropped his neck into his shoulders or how this woman pretended to control her trembling
chin. Did he know what he was doing to us? Christ! He went
right to his own enemies, talking with no control or sense.

"Esther," he said tenderly, pointing to elderly Esther Wis-
ter, "when you go home after church, you will make dinner
and share it with your sister; and in that sharing you are expanding the energy of the universe, you are expressing the nature of love."

"Amen!" shouted the bag-lady.

"Except that halfway through dinner you and she will start
to quarrel, as you do every week, until she walks out of your
house, leaving you in tears. Esther"—his voice grew soft—
"when you are loving, you become the energy of the universe.
You become God. But when you are criticizing, don't you see,
it's because you're afraid. You want comfort and call your criticism love. 'I'm only doing it for your good,' you say. It's not
love, Esther. It's controlling, neediness. Turn to God and beg
to be relieved of your neediness so that you may love. And
then give thanks that it is done."

He was pacing up and down. One or two couples had discreetly tip-toed out, and the only one who seemed enamored

of his speech was the bag-woman, who lifted her arms and interjected a loud "Amen" every few sentences. "Amen," she shouted, her hands held high above her head. Dutton reached across Carolyn to try to pull her down; and the man behind also grabbed at her, his lips tight with choked reproof. And Tom? Feeling our resistance, he pressed harder, trying to make us hear.

All this time I was unable to see Elizabeth, sitting with Angus in a pew at the far back of the church. Now Tom stopped, and I turned around in my seat to see him, as did most of the congregation. He was standing still, eyes beaming at Elizabeth, who looked back at him, appalled. Her eyes were wide, startled as a spooky mare's. And he broke into an open grin, his gladness apparent throughout the church. He walked toward her. She was shaking her head, appealing to him, and Angus, looking from one to the other, was confused. Some people in the congregation came to their feet. We all knew something was about to happen. But when he reached her, he put one hand on the edge of her pew, resting beside her own, and turned back to the congregation. A sigh ran through her.

"It is said that man is made in the image of God, and I can affirm that it is not that God has two legs, two arms, a nose, two eyes. No, but a thousand thousand eyes, and forms too varied for us to know, God in all forms, playing, hiding, finding Himself again and again in a constant game of hide-and-seek throughout the universe. More powerful than can be expressed, more gentle and compassionate, more loving. You see, it is not that we are made in the image of God," he continued. "We *are* God. God lies in us. You . . . *are* . . . God. The Godness is in you, as also in the stars and trees, the grass shimmering with light, the horses whinnying in the stables of the air. We are composed of, our atoms are, the light of God. We are God! With all the power of God."

I was stunned.

"Listen to the Apochryphal Acts of John:

A lamp am I to you that perceive me
A mirror am I to you that know me.

"What is he saying? That when we see Christ—God—the Infinite, we see Him as a light illuminating the landscape. But when we *know* God, when we touch God, then"—his voice dropped; you could hardly hear him—"you are looking into the mirror of your soul: you see your Self. You are God, because you are made of Godness."

Suddenly he started and looked around with astonished eyes. As if he'd just woken up. It was Keats writing on first opening Chapman's Homer, where all his men looked at each other with a wild surmise, Silent, upon a peak in Darien.

"Look at you!" he cried in horror. "Look, you're sitting here like posts! Embrace each other. Touch one another. Wouldn't you touch the living God? It is through touch that we pass this love back and forth. The energy replenishes us, like a battery we are restored. It's no good for me to say these things. You have to experience it! Touch each other. . . ." He turned round in anguish, for no one moved. "Get up! On your feet!" he shouted, his voice as stern as a drill sergeant, and immediately we stood to attention, at his authority. "Now shake each other's hands!" He ran up and down the aisle again, his anger flaring. "If you can't embrace openly, if you are so afraid to love, at least shake hands and wish each other God's joy and blessings for this day. 'God's love be with you,' you must say. Say it, Edgar! Mimi, Esther, say it to him. Don't you understand? You do it to bless your*selves*!"

It was hopeless. The congregation stood muttering or sat down, in confusion. Only the bag-lady had exuberantly thrown her arms around Carolyn, crying, "Amen, Amen," and then had proceeded to do the same for anyone within her reach. Carolyn was aghast, and Tom, seeing the bag-woman, galloped toward the front again, delighted that someone there had understood, even a stranger and a mental cripple too. "Carolyn, embrace her," he pushed Carolyn Page toward the dirty woman. "That's it, you understand!"

Carolyn shot him a look of such pure and baleful hatred as would have stopped a mule, and for a moment Tom looked confused. His face fell. His shoulders sagged, and hurriedly he turned to the altar, hands outstretched in the universal blessing: "Let us pray," he whispered.

It was a disaster. Afterwards the congregation fled the church, many from the side door so that they would not have to shake Tom's hand; and others edged their way into the aisle, whispering among themselves with meaningful glances and pursed lips. In the reception line at the front door Carolyn Page gave Tom a glare like a sword thrust, twisted her chin upward, and in her carrying voice declared:

"You're not thanked for that performance! You ought to be ashamed!"

His heart curled. Betsy Griffin, the gentle young wife of one of the choristers, who usually greeted him with an ingratiating smile, this morning sidled past and fled rather than touch his outstretched hand; and Edgar Whitehouse, whom Tom had singled out, stamped up the aisle, blowing through his nostrils and venting his anger in staccato tattoo to anyone around. When he reached Tom in the receiving line, he gathered himself— and spat!

Tom jumped. Behind him he heard a gasp. His hand lifted in reflex to his burning cheek.

The congregation continued past (the next person mumbling incoherent regrets: "Please, I'm so sorry, please—"). Some greeted him with warmth, and others appeared frightened or reserved or embarrassed. To make matters worse, he could hear the babble of voices outside the door as the congregation burst to liberty.

When everyone had gone, Tom moved slowly to the sacristy, removed his stole and chasuble, and hung them in the wardrobe. Then he sat, despondent, on the slipper chair in the dusty, empty room, his face hidden in his hands. His emotions flickered in him like tongues of flame: despair, anxiety, and rage. For a moment he wondered if they were right and he was crazy. Surely that was possible, for to him the world was shining—

The world is charged with the grandeur of God.
It will flame out, like shining from shook foil;

Gerard Manley Hopkins saw it.

It gathers to a greatness, like the ooze of oil
Crushed. . . .

That was all he wanted to tell these people: to wake up! To see how beautiful the world was, how rich and full! He rubbed his face, swiping at the dry spittle.

"I can't tell them. They don't want to hear."

Later that afternoon he sat at his desk doodling circles in-side circles on a pad, and each represented one gyration of his thought, from Elizabeth to Priscilla, to the question of whether he should resign, his conflict at every turn. Every now and again his heart leapt up at his newfound sense of holiness, then circled back to what had happened that morning in the church. He had been angry at being spat upon (anger circling blackly on the page), followed by regret, an overwhelming sorrow and sense of failure. Surely had he spoken better, they would have understood. *Oh, God, I'm not strong enough,* he thought. His hands were trembling. *Don't ask it of me, please.*

14

Meanwhile many of us had gathered for lunch at the Pages'. Elizabeth and Angus were there, Mikey and Buffie Jackson, and, in place of the Ambassador, Dutton had invited General Shriver. Billy Tyler came, too, since Carolyn was always trying to match her with the widowed General. The subject was Tom.

"You shall not speak to me about it," said Carolyn. "I have never been so humiliated in all my life. Mr. Buckford may be a very fine man, but if spiritual endeavors lead you to that, I have no intention, you may be sure, of pursuing *my* spiritual development."

Butch grinned triumphantly. "You didn't like it?"

She joined in his laugh.

"You don't think you're God, then?" Mikey Jackson bounced over. "Don't you like that idea? I must say, it makes things simple, doesn't it? I'd like to be God."

"Can you imagine!" Carolyn snorted. "And he saw God in Emily Carter," she continued angrily. "If you can see God in Emily Carter"—her voice lifted—"you could see God in . . . in . . . one of her *dogs*."

"She thinks you can."

"Well, I know, and in fact I shouldn't say anything because she's coming to lunch in a minute, but *really*. Do you suppose there's something he wants from Emily, Butch?"

"Money for the church?"

"He could have picked someone richer." They both laughed. "Anyway she's leaving all her money to the dogs, haven't you heard?"

"Poor man. He'll be so disappointed."

Elizabeth stood to one side, nursing her drink thoughtfully. Angus leapt into the conversation with both feet.

"I liked it," he said.

"Oh, Angus!"

"Well, if I'm an artist," he said seriously, "and make a picture, isn't there something of myself in that picture? So if God is busy making people right and left, wouldn't there be a touch of Him in each creation?"

"In which case, why would there be the crippled and deformed?"

"Ah, that's the question," said Mikey, lifting his drink. " 'And did the potter's hand then shake?' "

"What?" asked Angus, who had never read *The Rubáiyát*.

"How does a Perfect Being create an imperfect something?" Mikey explained.

"Never mind, Angus." Carolyn patted his arm. "Don't stretch your mind. Anyway, I thought the whole thing was in very poor taste. I wonder if he did it as a joke. You know the man, Elizabeth. Was it a joke?"

"I doubt it very much," she said quietly. "He believes . . . it."

"Well, I don't," said her mother with a vicious glance. "Love, love. It's just sickening. Christ didn't mean all that when he talked about love. He meant *respect*, pure and simple. Respect for one's fellow man, black or white, and of whatever class. That's quite enough. Christ understood life on a lot more levels than our young minister," she continued, and now her anger was darting out more forcibly than she probably wanted. "Christ understood about authority, Dut will tell you. Render unto Caesar what is Caesar's. He didn't go around hugging filthy beggars. He *healed* them, maybe . . . but he did not ask anyone else to consort beneath his social level." She gave a quick laugh, concerned at having revealed too much. "Well, I'd better go see about lunch, or our social inferiors will serve us nothing at all. And I, for one, am hungry." We broke into pleasantries of agreement, sipping our whiskeys and separating into groups.

"You know the one about the golfer who picks up this girl hitchhiking?" said Angus. "A real knockout. Wow! So on the floor of the car there's one of the tees that's fallen out of his bag, and she says, 'What's this?' 'Oh, that's what I put my balls on when I'm driving.' 'Ask a stupid question. . . .' "

We laughed politely. It was then that I learned about Angus' development plans for Elk Creek.

"It's going to be spectacular." His enthusiasm erupted in a lurching hand-wave that slopped his drink over his tie and shirt. He mopped at his front with a cocktail napkin as he explained how he and Tony Reischetz had founded the Elk Creek Development Corporation, with Tony as director and Angus as president. Angus took 80 percent of the stock and gave Tony 20 percent, and he was wondering if he hadn't shortchanged his partner, since it was Tony who had all the contacts with lending institutions, county agents, and zoning boards; it was Tony who was running the corporation; and it was Tony who had suggested what Angus thought was a brilliant move: the land had not been transferred to the corporation but *loaned* to it. Angus still stood as owner, and therefore as president of the corporation, he held the mortgage personally.

"Well, I hope you're watching over it."

"We stand to make millions."

I sucked my pipe, considering.

"It's financial leverage does it," he continued, and before he could launch into a discourse explaining all that he had recently learned about economics, I said:

"The reverse is equally true. Aren't you personally liable if anything goes wrong? You could lose your shirt."

He punched my shoulder good-naturedly. "We could." He winked. "But we won't."

"Isn't Tony Reischetz the man whose wife got raped a couple months ago?" Buffie interrupted.

"Yes, it was awful. And do you know she's never been the same. I go over there now and she cringes away from me. 'Cause I'm a man. She hides in the kitchen. If Tony isn't there, she won't open the door at all. It's tragic. You can hear her inside prowling like a cat in a cage, and she doesn't dare open the door. Even to me, a friend."

"My goodness."

"I just go away. I wouldn't hurt her for the world, and just to see a strange man—well, I'm not a stranger, but any man, you know what I mean, sets her off."

"She needs help."

"You mean a psychiatrist? Well, Tony's old-fashioned that way. He wouldn't let her. I agree. I think that's a lot of self-indulgent bunk. You ought to be able to solve your problems for yourself, don't you think? A little willpower?"

At lunch the conversation returned to Tom.

"You know perfectly well," said Mikey, "that he was talking about himself. Anyone who knows a thing about psychology knows that. If he's saying there's God in a person, he most certainly means himself."

"You know, you're right," said Dutton. "Remember his reading about Christ saying, 'I am the bread that came down from Heaven'? And the Jews didn't understand? It's a perfect parallel. He thinks he's Christ."

"What do you think, Emily?" said Butch. "You were there."

But Emily, at the far end of the table, only shook her head.

"Well, I think," said Butch, "there's a lot more going on there than we'll ever know. We should write the Bishop."

"I don't care what anyone says," Carolyn interjected. "It was outrageous what he did today. Don't look at me like that, Elizabeth. The next thing you know we'll have evangelists crawling out of the woodwork. Those ghastly radio ministers preaching." The table burst out laughing.

"Or healing services," said Billy Tyler. "Laying hands on all the crippled and poor in the state, pretending to do miracles."

I was laughing in spite of myself.

Elizabeth, head down, concentrated on her plate. She hardly spoke at all. As we rose for coffee, she caught my hand.

"Come in the library a minute." She closed the door behind us and leaned her back against it, then pushed past me, hands clasped to her breast—quite literally wringing her hands.

"John." Her eyes shot to me in appeal. "John, what's going to happen?" She fell in my arms and burst into tears. "Oh, John, I love him so!" I rocked her gently.

"Elizabeth." Understand, I'd watched this girl grow up. I had stood as her godfather (myself no more than fifteen), bandaged her skinned knees when I was in my twenties, and later hired her to baby-sit my own two children. I attended her wedding, and together we feasted the holidays of our lives—cousins at the family gatherings. Now I stroked her hair until she quieted down.

"John, I'm so scared. I don't understand what's happening."

We sat together on the couch, Elizabeth half turned toward me, her foot tucked under her.

"You don't mind my telling you this, do you? Oh, John, please help me." She described how, earlier in the week, Tom had told her about his revelation. "But, John, he *did* see something. He's different."

"He's lost his caution," I said.

"He's found something." She spoke at the same time. "There's something he knows."

She stood up suddenly. "Oh, damn his God. Oh, damn!" Tears welled up in her eyes, and she threw herself beside me on the couch again and leaned on my chest, one hand curled about my neck—the gesture of my baby, Annie, when she was one or two.

Suddenly she broke free and said fiercely: "Listen, John, I didn't bring you in here to talk like this. Margaret will be looking for you. You must promise me something."

She paused, watching me.

"Promise!" she repeated.

I laughed. "First, what am I promising?"

"It's nothing wrong. John, promise me—" She took my hand, lifted it to her cheek, then kissed it. "Promise me you'll protect him. Promise."

"Protect him?"

"You must help us, John. Help me. Do it for me if you can't for him. I'm family. Please."

"I didn't say I wouldn't do it for him."

"Oh, John!" Her face brightened. "Then say, 'I promise to protect Tom and care for him in his troubles.' Just say that."

"I promise to protect Tom and care for him in his troubles."

"Thank you." She rose to her feet. "Thank you, John. You know he'll need it."

"And how about you?" I stood beside her. "Are you all right?"

"I'll be all right. Somehow."

"Come see me, Lizzie. Call anytime. You'll need a friend."

"I shall. We're allies now. Oh, John, thank you." She pulled my head down to hers and planted a kiss straight on my lips. "John, don't tell anyone about Tom and me. Please, not even Margaret. We're trying to do what's right."

I didn't say I'd already told Margaret months ago. "I won't," I said.

"Do I look awful? Anyone can see I've been crying."

As we left the library, Margaret and Carolyn stood talking in the hall.

"Oh, there you are."

"John, we were looking for you."

"It's time to go," said Margaret in a voice as crisp as laundry.

I suppose it was roughly about the same time that Natalie found Tom sitting at his desk drafting a letter.

"Are you all right?"

"I don't know." He rose to his feet.

"You're sick."

"Natalie, tell me, it was awful today in church, wasn't it? What I did was terrible, I don't know what got into me. I didn't mean to do that."

She wanted to reach out and touch him. "Don't be silly. It was funny—the bag-lady, Mrs. Page, the whole thing."

"I'm writing to the Bishop to replace me."

"Oh, Mr. Buckford, no." The words burst out.

"You've always been my ally," he said.

"Give yourself some time. There's no hurry."

"I'm not going to be able to help these people. I—"

"You were wonderful, Mr. Buckford. Wonderful! You were filled with the spirit of the Lord! Your voice . . . it was wonderful. We all felt it."

He groaned.

"Don't resign."

So he decided to wait. He needed time to think. To pray and ask God's will.

But that evening, alone at his desk, he wrote a letter to Priscilla. It took four drafts.

My dear Priscilla:

This letter comes as a result of months of thinking about our marriage and what we give to one another now, after twenty-one years of living together. I would like to request that you remain in Chicago with your mother. . . .

He went on to detail what monthly provision he could give when they divorced. He said he did not wish to deprive her of her children. On the other hand he wanted Philip to live half of the time with him. He concluded with an expression of his regard. He wanted her to feel no guilt; any fault was his.

But the next day Priscilla returned with Philip. Tom put the unmailed letter in a drawer.

Now everything came together at once: God, sex, hate, heresy. All of Naughton was on the phone to Bishop Crowley, and he in turn to us. At the same time the anonymous letters began. Crowley opened his mail one day and read:

What the BuckFuck's UP
At Trinity?

He had received two or three anonymous letters way back in the fall, when Emily's feelings were hurt. They were pathetic, cautious notes on heavy blue stationery. I have only one. "I am a friend of Trinity Parish and am very concerned about the new minister, Mr. Thomas Buckford. He doesn't show proper respect for antiques and other valuable possessions. I thought you should know. Sign me 'A Friend of Trinity Parish.' "

The Bishop had thrown them away (all but this one, apparently misfiled). The new letters, though, carried malice, and Crowley, disturbed by the messages, collected them in a manila envelope.

One, clipped out of newsprint, was pasted, letter by letter, to a cardboard shirt board:

Frere Thomas and Frere Tommee
Worship God and Satan's pee
Ding, dong, dung

Then more news hit: Word had it that Tom had awarded Shriver's scholarship—to a Negro boy! Months earlier Tom had had young Zachary Lunt tested privately. The boy touched genius; he blew us off the charts. Submitting the boy's name to the school board, Tom had cunningly neglected to mention color, and the board had accepted Zachary with delight. He stood as a credit, they said, to the Trinity School for Exceptional Children—by which they meant white. By the time they learned his color, the appointment had been publicly announced.

Into this storm Priscilla returned, sweeping into the house with the retribution of a vengeful angel, cleaning, laundering, shaking her dust cloths out the window and her head at the dust. She clicked her tongue with satisfied dismay. When she had finished with the house, she turned her attention to her beloved church—and instantly found the altar cloth, still smudged with grass and dirt. Holding it up, she felt her heart twist, for it was the very one that she had trimmed by hand with lace.

"What happened to this?" She held it in both hands outspread before Miss Myder and Mrs. Compton, two members of the Altar Guild. They exchanged quick guilty looks.

"Oh, that."

"Here, I'll take it," said Mrs. Compton, removing the material from Priscilla's hands. She proceeded to refold it with smooth gestures. "It got dirty, and the stains haven't come out, that's all."

"Got dirty! But those are brown stains! Whatever were you doing, picnicking with it?" And when no one answered: "I demand to know what happened." She held the wardrobe door dramatically, barring Mrs. Compton's way. "Don't look at each other that way. I know you know. I shall report this to my husband." There is something about being accused that makes you shut up. Neither woman confessed.

Pris took the matter up with Tom, who listened, strangely unconcerned.

"It's been taken care of. Don't trouble yourself."

"Don't trouble myself!" The very idea offended her further. "Honestly, Thomas, sometimes you haven't the brains God gave a goose. The altar cloth is absolutely ruined, and you don't even care. You won't investigate. If you did, you wouldn't pun-ish anyone. You haven't any backbone, and I suppose you don't care that we shall have to buy another cloth. Who did it, that's what I'd like to know!"

Tom came to his feet. "I did it." His voice was firm. "Now, please be quiet."

Never had Tom spoken to Priscilla like that. She turned without a word and left, but she was not finished. Lips tight, she questioned the laundress, then drove down to see Margaret, and over a cup of coffee in our wide kitchen she picked at her till she pieced together a story that left her in shock.

"Sacrilege." Once spoken, the word kept ringing in her mind. That it was her husband's blasphemy made it worse. To have visions, to befoul the altar, and finally to change radically his behavior toward her . . . He was distant with her, as if she had no power anymore to touch him. He listened when she scolded, not unsympathetically, but frequently not answering at all on the level she engaged.

"How dare you," she confronted him, "give General Shri-ver's scholarship to a Negro boy?"

"Why? Are you afraid?"

She felt he saw her secret thoughts. She wondered if he'd

gone stark mad. She walked around him gingerly, avoiding him and keeping Philip from his father's path. For the first time in years she wished she had a friend in whom to confide her fears, then realized that such troubles could never be told to anyone. What could you say? *I think my husband has gone mad.* They were words no dutiful wife could speak.

She took refuge in the quiet of the church, whispering her misery and shame to the cross. Yet even this comfort was denied her, for as word of Tom's vision spread, the tourists drove in, jarring her prayers. In the weeks after Easter, people crowded to the services, some from as far away as Madison. Others dropped in, just for an afternoon, to gawk at the church and graveyard, and some pried splinters off the weathered back door as souvenirs. She was horrified.

As for Tom, he was not oblivious, but he retreated from the gathering storm. It was at this period that he could read only spiritual books; nothing else satisfied him. Newspapers, biographies, novels, even the classics, seemed as superficial as stones skipped on the surface of a pond. He found his attention wandering. Instead he consumed William James's *Varieties of Religious Experience* and Evelyn Underhill's *Mysticism*, with their long, rapturous quotations from Meister Eckhart and Saint Theresa and Ruysbroeck, Fox, Böhme, and Saint John of the Cross.

He marked the margins, "Yes." Or, "I, too, have seen that."

I have these books before me now, the pages crisscrossed with his enthusiasm.

He marked with double lines Saint Theresa's words on the spiritual storm that initiates one into "heavenly secrets" but leaves, by its violence, mental disorder behind.

That he had an effect on people is unmistakable; none of us was immune. He had no inhibitions about throwing an arm around me. "Ah, John," he said one day. "I am so blessed. Look at you, for instance."

"Me?"

"You're a gift, given specially to me."

I hardly knew how to react. No one had ever thought of me as a gift before.

It is hard for me to talk of the changes that took place in Tom. Each week brought some new phase, and anyway I only know bits and pieces. Sometimes joy rushed over him like music. Or he would wake up in the morning, body pulsating with light, so that he wondered how Priscilla, beside him in bed, could not see the radiance pouring out of him—as if the Lover were working with white heat to cleanse his sins.

As the weeks passed, however, he noted his high energy draining out of him. He was swept by a sense of his own smallness, a dreadful awareness of the worm of himself, awkward and helpless in the withdrawal of his God.

"Don't leave me," he cried out one night, and woke from his dream in a trembling sweat, ashamed and mumbling, to stagger downstairs and out the door to check on the stars reeling in the cold night wind. Then he turned back to visit Philip, sprawled, drunk with sleep, across his childish cot, so open and vulnerable that the father feasted on the features of his son, straightened the covers over him, and caressed the tough, straight hair.

The first of many meetings with Bishop Richard Crowley took place at this time. Dick, the diocesan bishop, with almost thirty years' experience in the Church, had started life as a banker and entered the ministry at the age of thirty-five. Today, at seventy-two, he had a staff of fifteen, including a secretary-treasurer, two assistants, the dean of seven Episcopal schools, and various floating staff. In Alexandria the suffragan bishop and two retired bishops assisted him with the 168 parishes in his command and the 307 clergy (including those retired and in secular employment). Either the diocesan or suffragan bishop visited each parish once a year for confirmation services. Crowley did not know Tom. But he believed in miracles and in the mystery of Christ.

Nonetheless he felt uncomfortable with visions. The word curled on his tongue. True, Saint Paul had his epiphany on the road to Damascus—fell off his horse, blinded by the light in a scene that the Bishop always associated with the beautiful Caravaggio painting: the centurion stretched, armored, on his back, light-struck, beneath the piebald belly of his horse. And true, the Bible was full of communications to and from the Lord. But it made Dick Crowley nervous in the twentieth century, when we know something about science and psychology, to hear Tom describe what had happened to him. Tom leaned forward, elbows on his knees, shyly rubbing his palms together in his characteristic way.

"I know the Church distrusts visions."

"Especially the Church," said Crowley, and deliberately he placed his pen before his inkstand, careful to line it up against the stand's straight edge—and picked it up again. It was a gesture he repeated throughout the interview: set down the pen, align its edges straight, and pick it up.

And Tom? He tried to explain what he had seen—the living earth afire—and felt again confused by his inability to transmit anything except the fire of his feelings, so weak are words.

"The New Jerusalem," murmured Crowley.

"I made a mistake," said Tom, "in trying to tell the congregation. It was a disaster. I made a fool of myself. Of it."

Crowley moved back to the desecration of the altar, which had caused such a storm with us.

Tom's head came up. "But earth," he snapped with contempt, "is no sacrilege to God. I would make that offering anytime."

"I don't like it, I can tell you that," the Bishop said.

"I started to write a letter of resignation," Tom said. "But I've changed my mind. I want to stay in Naughton."

The Bishop pursed his lips. In fact he was relieved, for his mind, whipping ahead to count the clergy at his disposal, found few replacements for Tom. Moreover the parish had been without a minister for nearly a year before Tom came. To inflict on Trinity another interim rector and another search was more than he liked to do.

"If it's a true vision from God," Crowley said wisely, "it will be made clear in time. The test is not in the outward ecstasy but in what happens afterwards through your own actions and their effect. Meanwhile I'll tell you what I want." Crowley picked up his pen one final time. "I want to hear nothing more—not one more word—from Naughton. About Naughton. By Naughton. Not one word about you. Just calm things down. Do you understand?"

Why are things the way they are and not as we imagine them to be? Why does God, who should be our friend, appear to be our enemy?

There was Tom surrendering to God, asking at every moment: What do you want me to do now? And now? And now? He was God's dog, he said.

We have an idea of justice. Certainly Tom did. He thought God was on his side, that when he surrendered perfectly and placed himself, like a child, a lover, in the hands of a compassionate deity, then this Creative Power (which was also inside him, you understand, inside, outside, indivisible) would take care of him, totally. "No one but a monster could pass by a naked, starving child in the snow," said Tom. "My God won't leave me. If something is good for me—and for everyone around—He'll give it to me."

He actually believed this.

He actually believed that a Force of Love lay all about, so inextricably intermingling that he had only to desire something, and if it was good for him, it would occur; and only the fact that he refused to cross the will of God (whatever that was!) gave him a logical out from this illogical view. He could desire anything and then not get it and still have proved his undemonstrable point. "We always get what we need," he said.

But where is this justice of God? It makes me, for one, agree with the ancient Greeks—the idea of a Zeus despising his own creation, sending evils to punish it. Or maybe a blind fool of a Hindu god, laughing in mad play. I keep bringing up Laurie's Hindu concepts. Here's another: that God is a child playing in the sand who, hearing his mother's voice, runs off and steps heedlessly on the sand castle he's just made.

So what's God's justice? How could things have happened as they did to Tom, whose only failing was to love? Or was the failing that he forgot Christ's admonition to his disciples that they must also be as sharp as serpents?

———

Elizabeth made me her confidant. I watched her shed God-knows-how-many tears, while she and Tom worked out the effect of his revelation on their love. His vision had clouded everything.

"It's not our love that's wrong," Tom said stubbornly. "It's what we do with it."

Yet the revelation had an effect on Elizabeth. One part of her loathed his God, contemptuous of make-believe; another part was jealous.

But there was a progression, a movement in their arguments. Take that first week after his revelation, when suddenly for Tom everything was thrown into new sharp focus, and Elizabeth felt him distancing himself, holding back.

"Don't worry," he told her. "If we are meant to be together, nothing will keep us apart."

"But I don't believe it," she told me. "I have none of his faith that Other Hands are taking care of matters competently. I'm supposed to take responsibility. What's happening to me, John?" She looked at me with tears in her eyes. "I haven't even seen him in days."

"Call him," I said.

"I can't. He knows where I am. If he wants to see me, he can call," she said, her teeth clenched, fists tight. "I don't want to invade his space if he needs privacy. But"—she gave me a look that broke my heart—"it hurts."

He didn't call. Finally she broke down.

"I'd like to see you," she accosted him. Hadn't she the right? Hadn't she put her reputation on the line? She was still aware of his being her social inferior, as if she'd given herself away.

"Of course," he said. "Do you want to come up here?" She felt a wave of irritation. Was he protecting himself from her, barricaded in his sanctuary?

"No, let's go for a walk. I want to see you alone."

"That's a good idea." He agreed with such alacrity that she was taken aback. They met at five o'clock on the hill above the church, and her mind was whirling with her attempts to analyze her situation. Had he just not thought of seeing her for days?

So, when he met her on the path and reached for her hand, she turned, eyes flashing.

"Well, what are you doing?" she snapped. "I don't understand."

"What do you mean?"

"I mean about me," she said, pulling back her hand, setting off again. "I mean, what's the matter? One moment you make passionate love to me and you're throwing yourself almost literally at my feet, telling me that through me you have seen into . . . I don't know what. Other dimensions. God. One moment you say you're determined to get divorced, to marry me. I thought you were serious. I took it seriously, and all the while you were—what were you doing? Seducing me? Do men still seduce women these days?" She gave a bitter laugh. "Well, it certainly didn't take much to get me!" she continued. "Crook your finger and I come, I just believe it all!"

He didn't answer. He walked beside her, letting her hurt and anger pour over him. "I suppose you were too busy to telephone," she said. "I suppose you'll tell me you forgot."

"No, I won't tell you that," he said. By now they were halfway up the hillside and had come out of the trees to the edge of the meadow, with the valley stretched below. In the distance she could see the various colors of the trees in bud, each wood reminiscent of the shade its leaves would turn in fall, the reds or browns or brilliant yellows of maples, oaks, and poplar.

He drew her to him. She rested her head on his shoulder, quivering under his touch, as he stroked her hair gently, gently. Gradually her anguish eased. Still he did not speak.

"I miss you," she said. "I don't see you. I don't know what's happening."

"So you doubt?" He pulled away.

"No, never when I'm with you. But when I'm not, I do, yes." They walked on, skirting the meadow and back into the woods. The path climbed steeply here. They had to pull themselves up the rocks, and Elizabeth's attention was divided, her confusion increased.

"Well, aren't you going to say anything?" she demanded.

"There's nothing to say."

"What do you mean?" She flared up again. "Has the vision made a difference? Are you going to tell Priscilla about me? About us?"

"Not yet," he answered after a long moment. He still held her hand. Now he looked at it as if it belonged to someone else. "I need time to think. We're been married twenty-one years." Each word was a cold knife through her.

"Then you don't love me."

"I do love you." His voice was hard. "I also desire you. I can't get rid of the desire. It comes sweeping over me and I'm taken by surprise. Then after we've made love—"

"You're ashamed," she finished for him.

"No. Not that. Ever. But don't you see, Elizabeth. I've seen this other thing. When I was having my . . . revelation and it was passing away, I could feel the light draining out of me and the darkness closing in. It was like a door closing. I could feel it going, this glory—glory!—and I tell you I would have given my soul for it. And then I realized I didn't have to. I'd just been given my soul."

So what's that got to do with me? she wanted to ask.

"You're trying to say you don't want me anymore," she said instead.

"I want *that*," he answered fiercely. "But no, we don't have to give each other up. That's what's so wonderful, don't you see? You are this light. It is the God-ness in me that loves the God-ness in you."

She didn't understand. All she wanted was for him to pull her into his arms and kiss her, make love right there on the cold, damp, new spring ground, and here he was *talking*!

"Listen," he went on. "In my whole life I've never known anyone like you. I've made love before. Before Priscilla, I mean." He gave a lusty laugh. "And it was like eating a delicious peach. I took them. But with you, it's an act of worship."

It's amazing what awful lines can make a woman happy. Elizabeth liked the act-of-worship part, totally ignoring the peach. And it was only as he blundered on that she wanted to scream at him again.

"But right now, I also want . . . to be pure. And that's why I've—"

"Been avoiding me," she finished for him. He said nothing. "The God-ness in you doesn't want to worship at the God in me? And what about Priscilla?"

"I'm not sure what to do about that. The situation's intolerable. I cannot live as I am now. I don't know what's right. I search my soul. I pray. I'm not married to Priscilla; I live with her. It's you I'm married to, but I don't want to hurt her."

Elizabeth sprang to her feet. "Then don't," she said. "You don't have to hurt her. I have no claims on you. You have none on me. Don't worry about it. Just go off in search of your God. It has nothing to do with me."

Before he could move, she had run down the steep hillside, slipping and skittering down the rocky incline, out of sight. He had not managed to explain.

How could he? He didn't understand it himself.

As for Elizabeth, she got as far as the Chantilly crossroads in her car before she changed her mind. She was annoyed at his weakness, contemptuous of her own, yet she knew she couldn't leave him.

All right, she thought, he didn't have to leave Priscilla. She would not ask him to do something so much against his nature that he would only end up hating her. Let him stay with Priscilla. Whether she left Angus was another matter. The thought hit her with such force that she stopped the car to think. What she did with her life was independent of Tom.

It would take weeks before she acted on her decision, but from that moment her divorce was never again in question.

The weeks passed, and she and Tom continued to talk. She went back to him—"crawling back," as she put it to me, with undisguised self-hate. But merely being with him was having an effect.

One day she asked him if seeing IT were available to everyone.

"Of course," he said. "Everyone has those liquid moments

when you break through into another sphere and know that it's all perfect. You've had that, haven't you?"

She nodded. But he'd had a more powerful experience than just that twinge.

"So, yes," he continued. "Anyone can have it. Mine was just a common garden-variety mystical experience. But you have to stop doubting and you have to ask to see."

"Ask! That's like telling me to stop thinking!"

"That too," he laughed. "It can't be reached by mental effort. But when you are truly desperate, brought to your knees, open, holding nothing back, willing to take whatever comes— then it will be given to you. But you can't demand the form it takes either. No expectations."

"I couldn't do that," she said. "I couldn't beg."

"No, you're too proud. But it's a change of attitude, that's all."

None of it made sense to her. Defiantly she faced him, tears pouring down her cheeks. "I don't understand your way. I don't like it."

He did not behave like ordinary men. She wanted him to sweep her into his arms, protest, or even kneel at her feet as he had to Emily. Instead he stood six feet away, head down, making no move to dissuade her. Did she mean nothing to him? "I don't have to go your way." She challenged him.

"No, of course. The mystic path—"

"Don't start lecturing me. I won't have it." She clapped both hands over her ears. "Anyway there's nothing odd about it. I know the earth is a living, breathing thing. I've lived here all my life. You think I don't feel that?" One arm swept the valley below them.

"Then come with me," he said.

"No, I don't know what to—"

She began to shake. Her teeth were chattering. The thought flashed through her that she was in hysteria. And then it happened, as easily as stepping over a stream. It came so swiftly, was over so fast, that when she recovered and found herself in his arms, her head on his chest and his voice a cello at her ear, she hardly knew what had happened. She believed.

"I can't explain it, John. I believe in God." We were on my front lawn, when she told me. I was trying out my new split-bamboo Orvis fly rod. "Will you stop and listen to me?" she said.

"No," I laughed. "So you believe in God."

She waited for me to reel in the line, and turn to her.

"I began to shake all over," she said. "It's not that he did anything, or *said* anything, and nothing really happened. It was so subtle. But one moment I was angry and the next I just *knew*. It was like a hand on my shoulder, not Tom's, I mean, but an invisible hand. . . . No, it was a breath, a wind. I'm not explaining it. One moment I was me, with all my anger and fears and doubts, and the next moment I *believed*."

"I'm glad for you." I didn't know what to say. I made a cast, watching the line spin out in a glorious curve, and thinking of the trout I'd have got on that one.

"Yes," she said exultantly. "Yes!" It made me uncomfortable, envious, annoyed.

After that Lizzie belonged to him even more, because it was Tom who had brought her to another, higher level, so they saw one another continually, and not always spiritually—oh, no—but physically, too, as Carolyn soon learned. There was that balmy day in May when Tom was standing with Elizabeth at her front door. Imagine, her head resting on his chest, his hand clasped in both of hers, while he murmured "Darling" in her ear. At that moment two black Labs came bounding round the corner followed by Carolyn. The lovers leapt apart.

"I'm going now." Tom bent to brush Elizabeth's cheek and took the steps in one long jump. "Mrs. Page, take care of your daughter. She needs you."

Carolyn stared after him.

"Well!" she said. "What was that about?"

"Nothing." By then Elizabeth had regained her self-possession.

"Nothing? My, my. That we should have so many nothings in our lives. Elizabeth, what's going on?"

"Nothing. He came out to talk about something."

Carolyn clamped her lips. She was determined to ask discreetly her next question.

"Are you two having an affair?" She had not wanted to blurt it out. Her heart had frozen at the sight of them, and it was not because her daughter could not fall in love. Carolyn had no illusions: such things happen. But with the minister, the white rat, her enemy! Nothing good could come of that.

"My, you are a romantic." Elizabeth laughed her off.

"I'm not romantic. I'm a tough old woman who has seen enough of the world to know what I'm talking about. And I don't trust you for a minute. You haven't a head on your shoulders. I remember when you were just a baby, first learning to walk, and you stood at the top of the stairs and thrust out your foot, thinking you could step downstairs. You couldn't even walk on flat ground yet. You're impulsive. You just dive in. You don't know anything about the man. He's a minister. He's married, and if that's not enough, he's crazy. He's perfectly horrible."

But Elizabeth turned away. "We're friends, that's all."

Carolyn closed her bitter lips. She loved her daughter in her way. If Lizzie refused to listen to reason or even to discuss the matter with her own mother, then Carolyn's only option was to get the rector out of Naughton. Time would heal any passion, she told herself. Time spent apart.

15

ONE BLACK NIGHT THE BUCKFORDS CAME TO THEIR FEET AT A
piercing scream. They rushed outside—man, wife, boy—to find
that someone had hung their cat by its tail in a tree; and Tom,
in cutting the rope (cat swinging, clawing the empty air) was
scratched till his face bled. No one knew who did it. Tom was
choked with rage.

He wondered if General Shriver could have done it, for
their enmity was open now.

Shriver had grown obsessive in his hatred. When he heard
how the minister had given his scholarship to a Negro, he took
it as a personal insult. He went to each school-board member,
only to find them as confounded as he. By then Tom had done
his politicking, pointing out the advantages of taking in Zach
Lunt. How better to obviate suspicion, Tom said, or to get the
feds off our backs, then to take in one first-grade Negro. The
child was brilliant. Then, too, Tom was paying full tuition for
the boy, which not even all the white parents could afford. In
other words the Lunt boy was picking up the tab for whites! To
Shriver it constituted theft, his son's college tuition bilked out
of him by raw deceit. He started keeping lists of Tom's offenses.
He lined them up on a single page with a line down the middle:

offenses against the Church and offenses against the Valley's
social rules. Then he organized them into groups and by degrees.

THE CHURCH	THE STATE
Sacrilege:	Stole my $5,000!!!
Desecrates altar	Insults white values:
Manure	Integrationist
Tears down cross, etc.	Eats with Negroes
Pagan rites:	Approves miscegenation
Elephant gods	Insulted Carolyn
Fasting Rituals	Insults vestry:
Hindu?	Signs
Heresy:	Sex?
Man is God	No sense right and wrong
Don't need church	Destroying Trinity School
No evil, no sin	
Visions, voices:	
Schizo?	
Where is God in vision?	
Christ?	
(I John 4:1)	
Screwball services/sermons	
Kisses E.C.'s feet	

His eyes flickered down the list. The fact that women
seemed drawn to Tom annoyed the General. Even Billy Tyler,
whom Butch considered his personal property (though he'd
never asked her to marry him), even she was seen talking with
too much enthusiasm to Tom.

He stared at his list, wondering how much political weight
he could swing. It's true that the congregation was taking sides,

but even some of the people most offended by that sermon
(Edgar, for example) found a certain pleasure in being talked
about. To Shriver's disgust they were softening, going over to
Tom. The old saw goes that if 15 percent of the congregation
are hostile, the priest should leave. The number of those against
Tom was not that high . . . yet. Moreover he had tenure, so he
could not be removed against his will. But there were rules.

If a rector does not agree to resign, the vestry can give
notice in writing to the Bishop, who shall settle the matter by
"his godly judgment," and such judgment shall be binding upon
both parties. It's all in Canon 22. If the rector, asked by his
Bishop to resign, refuses, the Bishop can suspend him.

Buckford would refuse, thought Butch, so all he had to do
was get the Bishop to demand a resignation.

He went over the list, beginning on the secular side. "Stole
my money" was the most damaging offense in Shriver's eyes,
but it could not be used. Butch left it on the list to goad his
rage. No less powerful, however, was overturning the cross of
God, or his signs of madness, if they could be proved.

Insulting Carolyn and Dutton Page appeared trivial, and
yet that was a strong charge. Without the Pages' annual contribution (and that of General Shriver himself) the church cof-
fers would be seriously depleted. It was an argument the Bishop
would understand.

"Insults white values, has no values, can't tell right from
wrong"—these were different aspects of the same crime, all arguments against a minister of God.

To have no sense of propriety meant an insensitivity to his
community's needs. To insult white values meant degrading all
it stood for.

If none of these charges stuck, Butch had the spiritual side,

insults to the Divine. His secret cultish practices of silence and
fasting—probably flagellation as well—God knows what acts—
were frowned upon in a conservative Protestant country parish.
Hearing voices, hallucinating, having visions, desecrating the
altar—could Butch get him dismissed as a lunatic? It would
depend on the Bishop, but if the Episcopal church accepted
visions, then Shriver could shift his attack to Christology.
Where was Christ in the rector's vision? Tom read Buddhist
and Hindu and other pagan tracts. The books were right on his
shelves in plain view. Shriver was pleased to have stumbled
accidentally across that quote from I John (a stroke of luck, for
the General did not know his Bible well enough to dig it up
himself):

> Beloved, believe not every spirit, but try the spirits
> whether they are of God: because many false prophets
> are gone out into the world. Hereby know ye the Spirit
> of God: every spirit that confesseth not that Jesus Christ
> is come in the flesh is not of God. . . .

That stood clear as day. But there was more, for here was
the minister trumpeting his outlandish ideas: *Man is God,* he
said, and *The path to God is found alone; don't rely on outside
authorities, even the Church. It's all inside you.* No bishop could
ignore the challenge to church authority. Butch was sure the
man was nuts.

Shriver planned his moves like a military campaign, and
Tom, innocent as a lamb, walked into the trap.

One evening Butch took Pris for a drink at the Club. It
was a courtesy no one had ever extended to the poor woman
before. He pumped her with Dubonnet and complimented her

on her care for Trinity, which had not gone unnoticed. Then he asked for her opinion. Could anyone withstand such flattery? Shriver was a domineering, handsome man.

"I need your advice," he said. They sat in the bar with its plaid carpeting and round oak tables set for parties of four to six. Men drifted through after their golf games, flushed and ready for a celebration drink. Other parties were congregating before dinner on that Friday night, ushering their long-skirted wives before them and greeting each other with boisterous Dixie yells. The women's voices lifted an octave in excitement as they called to one another across the room.

Priscilla sat straight in her chair, a flush from the wine spreading lightly on her cheeks.

"Anything I can do."

"It's about your husband."

"Oh."

The waiter brought baskets of potato chips to the table. "Thank you, Gray," the general said, then offered Priscilla a basket, watching in heavy sympathy as she picked out a chip and nibbled at it delicately.

"I know you share my concern." He leaned in toward her. "Our concern, I should say, for it's the whole vestry that's involved. Tell me, Priscilla, do you think he's having a breakdown?"

There! Words spoken aloud, her worst fears verified. She felt a flood of relief that someone finally cared. It seemed the answer to her prayers, and in another moment she was pouring out her story: how her husband had reared up, roaring at her that he had no interest in the altar cloth—and never to bother him with the altar cloth again.

"I care about the spotlessness of my soul," he had said, "as you should look to yours, not to a cloth with one spot of God's good earth. Who cares?"

Then the matter of integrating Trinity School concerned her—"inexcusable," murmured Butch; and add to that the question of their daughter, Daphne, whom he wanted to remove from Miss Eu's.

"He says it's undemocratic." Her voice cracked with strain. "He says he can't bear the way she's walking now—her carriage, the turn of her head. He says she's learning the wrong values. Oh, General Shriver—"

"Butch."

"Butch." She ducked her head over her wineglass, moved by his generosity. "I don't know what to do. It's a wonderful opportunity for her. Of course it's elitist; it's supposed to be. And it's hard on Daphne, I admit. She's not been happy there. She was homesick for a time, but she's got over that. She's made friends. He says all she talks about are her friends' vacations to Switzerland or the Caribbean. He's afraid she'll get ideas."

"Nonsense," murmured Shriver. "I've met your daughter. She's a lovely child." He actually could remember nothing about her, but that disturbed him not at all. Priscilla glowed with the compliment; then commented, still concerned:

"And Philip. I sometimes think"—her eyes narrowed—"he wants him just to run wild, undisciplined, make mistakes. I have to hold on tighter now," she said. "I'm the only one keeping any semblance of control.

"But worst," she continued warmly in a rush of confession long suppressed (and I think it was the wine at work), "are his statements about the Church."

"What does he say?"

"Oh, I don't think he means them." She played with her wineglass. "I sometimes think he says things just to shock me."

"Like what?"

"That the Church is less important than one's inner search."

Shriver knew that one; it came as no surprise.

"That he doesn't like the services."

His head came up. "What?"

"He told me only yesterday he wished he could rewrite the Communion service. Change the order of the prayers. He said the service distances us from God."

"Distances God?"

"I was shocked! And then he goes on about bureaucracies." She glanced at her companion with real anguish. "He says that they always corrupt the purpose for which they were established, and the Church is no exception. The older and richer the institution, he says, the more likely it is to have lost its sense of purpose. But it's not only the Church he's referring to. Any authority becomes corrupt.

"He goes on and on about people being *dead*. All they want is to be stroked and comforted and made dependent, he says, and taken care of. And that's right," she added. "That's what we're taught about God—that He will take care of us. I don't even know what to make of Tom saying that. He calls the Church a spiritual gas station and says it doesn't teach us how to worship God. He says someday woman priestesses will perform the services. Women at the altar of God! Can you imagine?"

Shriver shook his head, but inside he was smiling like a wolf.

"Do you know, he leaps out of bed in the morning smiling.

It's unnatural. No one gets out of bed that way, as if every moment is exciting. He says there aren't enough hours in the day for the praise and worship of just living. Does that seem odd to you?" Her relief at finally voicing her doubts was so intense she could hardly stop.

"How do you deal with this?" asked Butch, discreet as death.

"I? I do nothing. I stay out of his way," she said. "I pray for his soul. But really . . . I'm frightened of him," she whispered. "Sometimes I come on him in his study, writing, writing. What's he writing down, that's what I want to know? He used to pay attention to what I said and do what I said. Now he simply listens with an odd expression. I don't know what to think!"

Shriver was delighted, and when he got home, he added items to his list. *Frightens his wife.* That was in the physical column. On the spiritual side, he wrote, *Against Church: wants to rewrite liturgy.* And, most damaging: *a corrupt bureaucracy. Spiritual gas station.*

The final weapon fell so neatly into his hands that he almost would have agreed with Tom about a generous God scattering his abundance on those in need. Have I said that Butch was treasurer of the church? One Saturday he was at the parish hall when Storey Lunt drove up, looking for Tom. Lunt, in coveralls, climbed down from his slat-backed pickup truck that stank of pigs and corn, the interior torn, the stuffing coming out of the seats, the dashboard layered with dust, and the instrument panel not working anyway. It was a farmer's abused green work truck for hauling cattle, gear, and men.

"I'm lookin' for Doctah Buckford?" Storey said, pulling off his hat.

"He's not here. Can I help?"

"I come 'bout my boy in school?" said Storey, his Virginia accent rising like a question at the end of his sentences. "It's my Zach he's takin' into school next fall?" His pride shone.

The General's eyes flashed. It took only a few minutes to put Lunt at his ease, to ask how Tom had found the boy.

"Well, suh, I'se known him a long time now. Evah since before last Christmas, when he were caught in the storm, him and his pretty wife. They passed a night wif us."

"He and his wife?"

"Yessir, and they was so nice. Miz Buckford, she'd like to froze her feet walkin' in the snow."

"And when was this?" The General, smiling, smoothed one hand across his balding head, knowing he'd hit gold.

Priscilla was in the church.

"Have you ever seen the church?" Butch invited Lunt inside, where a nod toward Priscilla coming from the sacristy, a single question, confirmed that the darkie had never clapped eyes on this woman before.

Butch felt his excitement rise. He said he'd drive Lunt round to Mr. Buckford—no trouble at all, he had the time. He also took down the date of that wintry night as closely as he could ("It were after the cat died and before the chil'ren's holidays from school, so it must of been . . .") Shriver could check later by one quick look at the rector's calendar. He also noted Lunt's description of this small and pretty, dark-haired girl-of-the-frozen-feet, and further confirmation of the love they shared; and nice it was, he agreed, to see such devotion in a man of God.

So Butch drove Lunt out to the gatehouse at Walnut Grove, where Elizabeth was spreading lime on her lawn, a beautiful young woman in her work shirt and jeans, feet straddling a twenty-five-pound sack, lifting handfuls of white lime into the flowing wind. He hardly needed to hear Storey's, "Why, tha's Miz Buckford. . . ."

"Tom's car's not there." Shriver drove on past and back to the church. He was too smart to have them meet or let Lizzie know he'd found out her secret yet.

Then he came to me.

I was sitting in my office at the feed store, feet propped on my desk, chatting to one of the boys when the General graced us with his importance. Butch is the kind of man you slink away from, and that's about what Gary did:

"Back to work." He shied out the door. I pulled down my feet.

Shriver hooked one heel around a chair, pulled it over, and sat down. He set his hat on the surface of my desk with never a "May I?" and gave a grin that made me shudder.

"I've got him."

"Got who?"

"Your fucking minister. Your boy, Tom Buckford."

I blew up. "Goddamn it, Butch, you've had it in for Tom ever since he arrived. I won't tolerate it!"

"You don't have to tolerate anything at all. I can see you're protecting him. But I've got the goods on that bastard now, and I want him fucking out. O.U.T., out. I'm going to have him drummed out of the whole friggin' Episcopal church before I'm through. He's going to be defrocked—"

"What the hell are you talking about?"

"I'm goddamned if I'd let him loose in some other parish. The man's a menace. Sanctimonious. Holier than thou," he said, standing, pacing, heels clunking on the bare-board floor. "Accusing us—I won't stand for it. He thinks he's Christ. He has a goddamn shit-faced Christ complex."

I tried to laugh him back to balance. He turned on me.

"And you're what—his Saint Peter? Tagging along, supporting him."

"All right, Butch. Calm down." I rose to meet him eye to eye. "If you have something to say—"

"You bet I do, and the Bishop is going to hear it too. Buckford thinks he's above authority. Above the congregation and the wishes of his community. He goes around having visions like some goddamn Joan of Arc—and then dares to tell us how to live. We never asked for that. When we were looking for a minister, did anyone ask for a man with a pipeline to God? Jesus! Mark my words, John Woods, I'm going to run him right out of the fucking Church. I'm going to have a full-scale public trial before the Bishop. I'll see him ruined."

"A trial?" Carefully I dug the dottle from my pipe with my little pearl knife. "Butch, there hasn't been a trial in the Episcopal church for three hundred years. Who do you think you are? Torquemada?"

"Oh, yes, turn it into an *ad hominem* argument. It's what I'd expect of you." He gave me a sly, sidewise glance. "Anyway I have the cards. Don't worry."

"What?" I faced him straight on, across my desk. "That he gave away your scholarship money to a Negro boy?"

"He's not fit to be a priest."

"No?" Against my will my voice quavered. Suddenly I knew what he was going to say.

"You know he's having an affair with Elizabeth McEwen,

don't you?" His voice dropped low, sultry. "He probably screws her in his office on the leather couch. He likely fucks her in the church."

"Jesus Christ, Butch."

"I have an eyewitness. She spent the night with him in a Negro tenant farmer's shack up on the mountain. And you know whose?" He threw back his head triumphantly. "The family that stole my scholarship! That's fucking who! That kid is getting a payoff so the family will keep their mouth shut. As for Buckford, he's an adulterer, defiling a married woman. How goddamn long has he been doing that? Five months? Six? Fornication and adultery—and all the time he's playing saint. 'Act like God, I see God.' When all the time he's getting his dick into *women!*"

A thousand thoughts stampeded through my mind.

He straddled his chair, arms on the back. "I've got him on three counts." He flicked his forefinger out. "Sexual immorality. That's called conduct unbecoming to a priest."

He held out the second finger: "Blasphemies against church doctrine, against the Cross, against the *Book of Common Prayer.*"

He flicked out the third finger. "And the third he hasn't done yet, but he will. Defiance of Church Authority." He looked at me, swelling with pride. "All true. And the best of it is, I never frigging mention either my money or colored integration of our schools."

And all the while spring burst over us in waves. It hit us overnight. We woke up one day to a riot of color—bluebells and buttercups and tulips and azaleas; trees bursting into blossom and blowing in the breeze—pear, apple, peach, chains of wisteria, and my favorite Catharine crabapple with pale-pink double-centered buds. The dogwood were scattered in the woods like pearls. God, it's so beautiful! It goes on and on: April, May, June. In Virginia you can taste the colors on your tongue—blue, pink, white, yellow. They hit the eye like the smack of your palms, and the smells are rich in your throat and the hum of bees in your ear; and everywhere warmth, abundance, rebirth, the land surging forward in praise of the name of God.

Some evenings were so clear we sat outside, the women in sweaters on the porch steps. Our nostrils quivered with the light chill. The stars gleamed and everything promised the fulfillment of hope.

Meanwhile Tom lost one admirer, gained another, lost one, gained two, the church packed, and people gathering for his Wednesday-morning prayer group—but with each day the sentiment toward him swinging out of balance.

New people came to church. Some dressed a little "off." The women wore hats a shade too big and gaudy, or they put on eye makeup, this at a time when no respectable woman in Naughton wore any makeup besides a touch of color on the lips. Some were voyeurs, ogling the latest attraction in life's zoo. Some were waiting for him to go crazy again, froth at the mouth, I think, and fall epileptic to the floor, or maybe talk in tongues. And some were true worshippers, I admit it. He attracted these as well. It all made the inner circle of the Valley uneasy, as any change is viewed as bad.

Carolyn said they were waiting (the children's eyes like saucers) to see him smear the altar vestments and knock the holy vessels to the floor. Then we began to see the mountain folk, farmers and small-store owners, some as ignorant as Appalachian hillbillies, who shuffled into church in scuffed work boots,

their big rough, work-hardened hands dangling at the ends of
their arms and their eyes trailing off to the left in that shy
middle-distance gaze that marks the countryman. At their sides
would be wives who looked twice their age, and one step behind came big, hulking sons with broad grins across their teeth.
They would run their tongues between their lips as they surveyed the gentry already seated in the church; they tiptoed up
the brick aisles in a hopeless effort to lessen the clatter of their
steps. The farmers, mostly Baptists and Fundamentalists, sat at
the back of the church, and they were shy, careful not to belt
out the hymns as if they belonged. Still, their presence confronted us with a problem. We were glad to see the congregation growing, but to us, who had been coming to Trinity all
our lives, they were intruders as well. Moreover they accepted
Tom's statements without question. Simple, country folk, they
had no discrimination, but followed "like sheep" as Carolyn
put it, "just sheep." It was we, the educated, well-read, well-
travelled upper class who were offended by Tom's pronounce-
ments. These new people gulped the message down. Why not?
What did they have to lose? "Give yourself away," Tom proclaimed, "let God take care of everything." It smacked of tent
preaching, except that he did it without that fire-and-brimstone
revival style. And yet I know he didn't say anything that wasn't
in the Bible. It's in *Matthew*: "Seek ye first the kingdom of
God, and his righteousness; and all these things shall be added
unto you." You hear it in church, but you don't take it seriously. "Don't be afraid. Do nothing but worship. Let God provide."

Lord knows, everyone wants to believe in a loving God.
Tom liked to quote those lines about what man would give his
child a stone when he asked for a piece of bread, a snake when

he asked for a fish; and how much more would God the Father
do for us, not confusing slithery snakes and fishy bodies or hunks
of stone with bread. But who amongst us doesn't know fathers
who would do just that, give their kid the stone, either by
malice or by mistake? These farmers fawned on Tom, ready to
abdicate responsibility.

Dutton expressed our discontent one day down at the Club.
"You don't just swallow everything that comes your way," he
stated. "That's what the Germans did with Hitler, isn't it? They
accepted totally a man who insisted he was right. And look
what it got them. The intelligent man has doubts. He questions."

And all this time Tom's sexual energy poured out. Why
should we be surprised? Saint Theresa herself commented on
the confusion between sexual and spiritual love—how, as one's
spiritual powers grow, so does one's sexual force. It happened
with Tom, not like my son, Johnnie, as an itch of the crotch
for any passing skirt, and not like me, eyes slithering on the sly
toward a woman's ass or tits and away before it was observed
(hating women at times for what they made me feel), but rather
an open lovingness ripping out of him in tidal force.

One day he met Angie Reischetz by the barrettes and bobby
pins at our local five-and-ten. He stood, shoulders back, looking
down at her, all energy, admiring the two boys who tugged at
her dress. For a moment his eyes rested on the livid, blue-black
bruise she carried on her neck. He said not a word about that
(though she covered it with her hand), nor about the twitch
that jerked the corner of her mouth and that, later, in concern
he mentioned to me.

"I wish you'd come see me, Mrs. Reischetz," he said, and
lifted his hat good-bye.

At the register Angie counted out fifteen cents for bobby pins, mumbling in a strangled voice.

"I belong to Our Lady of Mercy! I'm a Catholic. He shouldn't look at me like that."

Just then Emily Carter waddled into line.

"Whatcha say?" The checkout girl shifted her wad of gum.

"I don't have anything to do with men."

"What?" asked Emily.

"The minister. Did you see his eyes?"

"Oh dear," said Emily, coming to her wits. "Has he kissed your feet?"

Angie jerked at the pin-thin arms of her two sons. "Hurry up. Move!"

But instead of doing so, she stood rooted to the bare wood floor of the five-and-dime, her shoulders shaking and great sobs tearing at her throat, while the two boys looked up, first dumb with shock, then bursting into tears themselves.

"Don't be concerned." Emily fluttered round her helpfully. "He kissed mine too. He didn't mean anything. It's just his way."

Curious, Emily defending Tom. It wasn't till the trial that we heard how Tom had gone to her place soon after the vision. He had stood at her door, bareheaded, and asked himself in, and then sitting stiffly in her dark living room, one hand on each knee, he had talked about what he'd seen.

Afterwards they had gone round to the kennels and shovelled food to the dogs that raced and leapt at their wire enclosures in an explosion of barking, he leaning down to tussle with one shepherd or turning to compliment Emily on another's looks.

———

What I see are moments—Tom standing right in the church aisle preaching; or Tom, later, shoulders hunched, cowed by the crowd yelling at him; or Tom, his face black, suddenly turning on Priscilla, his own wife, with anything but spiritual growth in mind.

The facts are these: In those days a priest divorcing was a terrible thing. The Episcopal minister could marry, but his vows were as sacred as the Catholic priest's vow of celibacy. His vows stood as a sign of his honor and integrity: ". . . forsaking all others . . . for better or for worse. . . . What God has joined together let no man put asunder."

I don't mean that people didn't get divorced. But a divorced woman was called a divorcée, remember? A sophisticated, racy taint clung to her name. Divorce happened, yes, but it was still so frowned upon that a divorced person had to wait a year to remarry in the Church, and required the Bishop's consent. It wasn't taken lightly, even by someone like Billy Tyler, twice married and divorced. For a priest of the Church the marriage vows were inviolable. And Tom twisted on his decision.

I understood. I've been there. Remember, it was Flossie whom I dreamt about. It was Flossie whose figure I would catch on my occasional trip to Richmond—the back of a woman, the grace note of a swirling plaid—but enough to make my heart jump and my legs leap forward, hurrying to catch up, until I faltered, awkwardly stopped by the wrong face.

Meanwhile Lizzie, too, said nothing to Angus. I remember talking to her about her pie-in-the-sky dreams of living with Tom.

"He won't leave her, you know." I threw it right in her face. "Men don't leave their wives."

"Don't you speak to me like that, John Woods." Her chin snapped up. "Good Lord, he's in enough trouble. Do you think for one minute I'd add to his cup? You act as if we don't even talk."

She went into her catalogue, then, of the circumstances that kept them apart: the backwash of Tom's vision, and their sudden recognition of matters ignored in the first confession of their love—where they would live, on what, whether Tom should leave the Church, and always his search for purity, the spiritual in their love. These were the reasons they weren't together, she assured me, not because he wouldn't leave his wife.

" 'Methinks the lady doth protest too much,' " I quoted.

"What's that supposed to mean?"

"He won't ever divorce her." It was cruel of me.

"I thought you were my friend."

"I am," I said, "but part of that friendship is to make you open your eyes. Christ left no doubt about his position on di-vorce. Or adultery, either, for that matter. Do you think a min-ister—?"

"We've talked of that," she answered, but I noticed her clenched fist. "Why do you care so much? What difference does it make to you what he does?" I didn't say anything. "Anyway I have another problem to think about."

"What's that?"

"Me. What I'm going to do about me. I've decided to go back to college. I want my degree. What do you think?"

"About what?"

"Getting my B.A. Can I do it?"

"Sure you can do it. Go for it!"

"I will." She tossed her chin. "You just wait and see. I may have to support myself, too, but by God I'm going to get my education. So you see," she said lightly, "some good's come out of Tom being here. Don't you think?" Her eyes were filled with tears.

"I think it's been terrific for you both."

"Tell me you like him. Tell me you think he's a wonderful man." I felt a wave of compassion; she was so vulnerable. "Tell me you think it's all right for me to leave Angus. What do you think?"

"Jesus Christ, Lizzie, I don't know what I think. Frankly I wish I didn't know anything about you and Tom."

Then one day Tom made up his mind. He told Lizzie he'd file for divorce—they both would leave their spouses and marry, God knows on what.

He drove to Richmond to see a lawyer. He came back shattered by the news. He learned that in Virginia a man could get a divorce for the following: committing an infamous crime, being in prison a year, deserting his wife, or being separated by agreement for several years. He could get a divorce for adultery, or if his wife is a prostitute. . . . The lawyer did not presume to advise him, but by the books in Virginia the courts could prohibit remarriage entirely if an adulterous affair were proved.

So Tom could not get divorced. Or even leave Priscilla, it seemed, for he would not drag Lizzie's name through charges of adultery nor smear his wife's honor with the same.

It was a blow. I know he was in conflict, fighting to accept his cup. He was a horse with too tight a curb in his mouth. He was a fish on a hook, angry and struggling not to cross the will of God but not liking the way it was coming out.

But I was telling about the General and his hunt.

That day, after Butch left, I called Elizabeth to my office.

She sat, tipping back in my office chair, bravely flashing her smile. I leaned on my rolltop desk, admiring her. Strength in adversity, I thought, wondering if it doesn't do every woman good to have a bit of misery, and then I threw the works at her.

"Butch knows about you and Tom."

"Oh, God," she said. "How?"

I told her what I knew. She listened nervously, biting her nail, then tossed her head with her old, defiant gesture. "All right," she said. "Well, let him come." She rose to her feet and began to pace nervously.

"Butch is a menace," she said. "Goddamn. I hate to lie. But I will. And I expect you to too, if necessary." She turned on me fiercely. "You promised."

"What, to lie?"

She gave a sudden laugh. "I don't think we'll have to," she said. "I'm smarter than Butch. Just watch me. And if you can't lie, lie low."

But matters hit her quicker than she guessed.

That afternoon, turning in her drive, she saw Angus standing on the porch. He stared at her as she came to a halt at the house, then walked down to open the car door for her. Guilty and surprised, she was uncertain how to read his gesture. Her eyes flew to his face.

"I hear you're laying the minister."

"What?"

"How could you! Murderer!"

"What are you talking about?" She stalked away—anything to gain a moment's time.

"I heard it at the Club. Plain gossip at the Club."

Elizabeth blanched.

"My wife. You bitch!" he shouted. "You've murdered my home." He was following her as she ran into the house. "Was it fun? Did he fuck you good? You slut. I've been waiting for this. I've always suspected it. Spreading your legs . . . how many—? You think I wasn't prepared. I've been waiting for this for years, but Christ, to give it to that fruit ball. I'm surprised he could get it up."

"Stop it!" She covered her ears with her hands like a child blotting out the sound. "Who said this?"

"Butch. Thank God we were the only people in the bar at the time. But now I understand your sudden interest in God. Dragging me to church, even, and I 'spose you sat there melting mentally in his arms."

"Angus."

"I'm working night and day to provide us with food and a fine house. I'm killing myself to take care of you, and what thanks do I get? To walk into the Club and hear—you, screwing that *woman* in his long black skirts." He twisted his mouth and mimicked, " 'O Lord, make us pure and happy. O God, give us women to screw.' "

"Shut up!"

"Do you know he approached me one day about AA? Can you imagine? I can't believe it. He accused me of being a drunk practically. And I *went!*"

"You went?"

"Once. But I'm no alcoholic. I like a drink every now and again, nothing wrong with that. When I think he sucked up to me, all smiles, and I was practically taken in. . . ."

She let his rage pour over her. She moved from room to room in the house as he followed, shouting. She couldn't think. She couldn't escape.

"To think you never told me."

"Tell you!" She rose to her own defense. "I haven't seen you in months." Then stopped, for anything she said would ricochet onto Tom. "You don't even ask if it's true." Cunning. At chess she'd learned attack is the best defense. But Angus didn't hear.

"I'm closing a big deal—millions of dollars. Working my fingers to the bone for you, for us. And you're giving out to— all right." He turned on her. "I suppose you two are getting married?"

"I don't know," she mumbled in shame, for how could she lie to her husband, her old friend?

His eyes shifted. "What do you mean, you don't know. Doesn't he want to marry you?"

She said nothing.

"He won't even make an honest woman out of you? Christ! It's smarmy." He watched her angrily. "Well, then, you'll just have to give him up, won't you?"

She stared back at him. Did he understand nothing? Had they really lived together all these years and he thought she felt no pain?

"I'll sleep in the guest room tonight," he said loftily. "You sleep alone and think what it means to be laughed at down at the Club. My own wife's name bandied at the bar. Does he call in here at the house when he wants some pussy? Do you do it in our bed? Who else is he servicing in Naughton, do you know?"

She slapped him in the face. "Goddamn you."

For a moment they stood frozen, a few feet apart, his cheek reddening.

In times of crisis it is trivia that burns into the mind. She was standing at the stove heating hot water for coffee and no-ticed his face was almost the same pink color as the hot burner on the electric stove. His heavy cheeks wobbled with his hurt.

"Oh, yes, hit me," he drawled. "You've already smashed me emotionally. It really helps to hit out physically. I'm going to get a drink." He turned to the glass bar built into the pantry. She poured water over the coffee grounds, watching the muddy liquid trickle into the hourglass base.

"It's begun," she thought. "I didn't do it right. We'll be crucified for this." She did not know what she had admitted or denied. A numbness settled on her mind. *I didn't want him hurt,* she thought, meaning Angus. She wondered if Tom's God would protect His minister or whether He was in actuality a vindictive creature angrily lashing out to punish sin. She took a mug down from the shelf above the stove, aware of the move-ment of her hands with exquisite intensity. It was as if she had never seen before how graceful was the human hand. She poured the coffee into her mug, holding up the filter paper full of grounds with strong square fingers, again observing the mir-acle of fingers, tendons, muscles, bone. She felt suspended in a liquid drop of time. And would it splatter in a moment and dash into a thousand tears? *Oh, God, help him,* she thought. *Help Angus and me and him, dear God, please help us all.*

Across the room Angus was staring at his shoes. "Elizabeth, I didn't mean all that. But how could you do this to me?" She turned at his choking voice. "What's happening to us?" His shoulders shook. "It started so well. Look at us. I'm a failure," he said, "my work . . . my marriage. . . ."

"Don't, Angus." She crossed to him.

"What are we to do?"

She held him as he wept. He would not hurt her, she knew,

not only because he cared for her but because of his code of
honor. He would protect his wife. She stood in the kitchen
holding her husband, yet all the while her mind was casting up
and down, searching out the problems they would face. It
seemed surprisingly clear now, looking at this mess.

Once the rumors began she could only lie for Tom. They
would have to fight cleverly and stay apart.

"We'll be drowned in lies," she whispered to Tom on the
phone. "One lie will lead to another until we're sucked down
by them. That's the impurity."

"Then we won't lie," he said.

Yet she would not agree to this. "What we'll do is lie low,"
she laughed, repeating her little joke.

"Lizzie, I promise this will all work out."

"Don't make promises you can't keep," she said. "Meanwhile I'm not admitting anything. It's no one's business at all.
Don't you admit a thing. We're friends, is all. Now we can't
see each other for a while. I love you. Lie." She hung up.

The next day Butch dragged me along on his inquisition. We
stopped first at the Lunt house, up the mountain road. Even I
was uncomfortable with the poverty, though it was nothing rare
to see a house without electricity or plumbing. And dirty children. I've seen worse. I've seen them weak from rickets and
worms, both colored and white. These children didn't look un-
healthy despite the rags for clothes and hand-me-down shoes
with no socks on their feet, and one boy barefoot in the warm
spring dirt.

Storey was away. I ran the band of my hat nervously through
my fingers, pushed my glasses up my nose, and introduced myself and General Shriver to Eleanor, who glared at me, mouth

of a grouper, sullen and suspicious. She barely tolerated us. We talked our way inside, where we cast an eye around the dark main room, the bare clapboard walls. There were some chairs, a table, a rough-hewn chest, but it was no room for a lady like Elizabeth. Butch raised one eyebrow in disdain.

"May I?" He lit his cigar, not waiting for her reply. He wanted to stifle the acrid smell of food and sweat. Then he explained our mission in flat, curt phrases, direct and to the point. Had they or hadn't they? That's what he wanted to know.

"There weren't no wrongdoing in this house!" Eleanor rose to her full height. "We got beds here. We got chairs. Them as got filthy minds will find filth," she said, thrusting out her lower lip at Butch. "But other folks don't have to waller in it."

Her fierce black face was shining, her eyes glittered. I was ashamed. I was reared by Negroes. My own nurse, Louetta, had cradled me, hugged me, spanked me, bawled me out. When she hollered at me, no one stood up against her, not my mother, not my father. Louetta could do no wrong. I felt myself a transgressor in this house.

"I'm so sorry, Miz Lunt," I said, "for disturbing you. It's a serious matter."

"It's not you, darlin'," she said to me. "It's that man there, who's come to do no good. Wuffo you hanging round the likes of him? You got no *pride*?"

The General had gone outside in the yard by then, out of earshot. I watched him through the open door. He was staring at the yellow hound that lurched back and forth on its chain, locked to a rubber tire that in turn was tied to a tree. The cur barked and barked, winding its chain until it nearly choked him, then unwinding it, snarling, growling, baring its teeth.

Shriver stepped forward, holding out his cigar; the dog attacked, snatched the lit cigar, then dropped it with a piercing yelp. He howled, his tail between his legs, and slunk to the farthest reaches of his chain. The General laughed. I moved on outside, feeling sick. Shriver ground the hot cigar under his heel and turned to Eleanor and me.

"Don't you believe nothing against that man," she charged me. "He's a saint. 'N that girl, like to froze she were. She be suitable for him, I'd say, but tha's in nobody's hand but that of the Lord. Judge not that ye be not judged. All I say, as far as what happened in this house, they behaved *correct.*"

Her mouth shut in one firm line, a slit across her broad face. The screen door slapped behind her. We had to find our own way through the yard.

I was relieved. "Let's get out of here. That's taken care of."

"I wouldn't be so sure," said Shriver.

We arrived at Lizzie's an hour later. She led us into the living room and sat down stiffly. She offered no refreshment. Again, it was Shriver who began the questioning. Elizabeth readily admitted she had been with Buckford on that day.

"I understand there was a storm and you stayed—"

"We walked to a house nearby. It belonged to a Negro family." She did not know how much Butch knew or what Tom might have told him. All her senses were alert.

"We've just been up there," I said, ignoring the look Butch shot me. I felt my face go red. I was aware of the morass I was sinking into. Here I was, trying to do the decent thing and remain true to the truth and also to Elizabeth, whom I loved, and Tom, whom I also loved, goddamn it, loved, and they were pulling me into their dirt! I wouldn't turn them in, but neither could she lean on me for help.

"We were wondering exactly where you slept that night," Butch said.

"I slept in that house." She rose from the sofa to face him from above.

"Yes, we know. But exactly where?"

She looked at him, her face a changing mirror. Surprise, fear, disgust, anger played like storms across her lips and eyes. Her nostrils flared.

"Where did I sleep?" Proud daughter of Carolyn! She took one step backwards, her lips curled in scorn. One hand was trailing the chintz back of the armchair, and I saw the fingers tighten on the cording as she passed. "Do you mean, did I sleep with the Negro farmer?"

Butch barked—a single laugh. That was not at all what he had in mind. He had no quarrel with Elizabeth. It was her lover he was after.

"Or are you saying I should not have taken shelter in the storm?" Elizabeth continued angrily. "General Shriver, I grew up in Naughton. My family have lived here for generations. I was raised by Negroes. I know you've only just moved here in the last ten years. Are you saying I did something wrong? Because if so, I'd like to know it. I slept in a Negro's place. I don't suppose you've ever done that, have you? Are you going to tell me that was wrong? A white girl doesn't do that?" She stood viperish before him, swaying gently from side to side. Her voice was mesmerizing in its cunning whine. "A pure white girl, you mean. Yet all we did was take shelter from the storm."

"No." He broke her spell. "That's not what I care about at all. It's whom you slept with. We have a right to know if you and Tom Buckford—"

"And how do you know I slept with anyone? Who says someone slept with me? How *dare* you come to my house and talk such rot to me? How *dare* you! And you, my own cousin, John. You stand there beside this bully and don't say a single word. Listen, it's no business of anyone whom I sleep with. Or whom I don't. Or if I sleep at all. You come here accusing me of staying overnight with a Negro family. It's true. I did. I did sleep there."

"It's not you, Elizabeth," I broke in. "It's not you we're concerned with."

"I have it on good authority," said Butch, "that Buckford slept with you."

"In the same house?"

"In the same bed."

"It's a lie."

"It's a lie?" Butch blinked. He had been so sure of himself, he was startled at her retort.

"He's lying. Did he say that of me? No, he didn't say any such thing, did he?" She was stalking the General, pushing him backwards in the room. "It's someone else accusing me. Smearing my good name. Is it you? Are you trying to slander me? I can sue you in court for that."

"Are you—?"

"So you've learned I stayed overnight with a poor Negro family. Of course I wasn't going to spread it around, now, was I? You can see why I wouldn't go boast about it, right?"

"Will you swear you've never made love to the rector?"

"I don't believe this! John, are you just going to stand there?"

I could feel the sweat breaking out on my brow. "We have to ask it," I said.

"Then, of course," she laughed. "I've slept with him dozens of times. I'm the cause of his epiphany, didn't you hear? The big O. I make love to any man around. Why not ask about the others too? You make me sick," she said. "You told my husband yesterday in the public bar at the Club that I was having an affair. Now I'll tell you something, Butch Shriver, and you listen close." Her eyes had changed color to a dark, smoldering charcoal. "I want you to apologize to him in my presence, you hear? And if you don't, I will cut your balls out and smear their blood on the gateposts of your house. I will see that your name is dirt in this town. You will be blackballed. People will turn their backs on you at the Club and on the hunting field. Shall I go on?"

Shriver's eyes were slits in his face. "You bitch," he whispered.

She grinned a malevolent sneer, her lips stretched tight on her lips. "What do you want me to say, Corporal?"

"Yes or no," he said bravely. "Have you slept with—are you carrying on with Buckford?"

"Then, no. My husband and I are splitting up. I expect rumors, but I don't expect this of you. Who are you hunting? Mr. Buckford? Is he the game? Well, you can find better ways than through me." She threw back her head, looking from one to the other of us there. "We've never, do you understand, never, done anything . . . even the least bit *wrong*. I was working up at the church. He invited me to go with him on his business trip. We were stranded by a storm. It's embarrassing enough, Butch. I don't have to have it spread around the Valley, thank you kindly.

"I don't know why I bother to explain. It's no business of yours. Go ask the minister"—she turned on Butch—"he's the one you're after. Ask him if he has sex with his parishioners. That's what you're looking for, isn't it? Only one thing: If he says he has ever so much as looked at me . . . I deny it. I swear to God."

Shriver was livid. He stormed out.

"Well, you're happy, I suppose," he snapped at me.

I said, "I am."

Later Butch went back alone to confront Storey. He was convinced he could still nail Tom. By then, however, Eleanor had warned her husband. It wasn't any of his business, and he wanted no part in whatever the man was cooking up.

"Oh, I didn't mean they slept together. No suh. They was nothin' wrong going on at all. My mistake was, I thought she was Miz Buckford, tha's all."

"Where did they sleep? In the same bed?"

Storey stopped. "I gotta feed the pigs," he mumbled. "You know, we don't have so many beds as we kin give 'em to people like what white folks can, what have guest rooms and extry rooms. We only got us a few chairs."

"You're lying to me." Shriver was shouting. The yellow dog barked and barked. "You know they slept together, and you're protecting him. Well, it won't do any good. He won't get away."

16

AND TOM? I'VE SAID HE CHANGED. HE HAD TAKEN ON A TANGIBLE power. You could see it in his eyes. Sometimes the light seemed to leap across the room at you, like a living spark. At other times you'd think his eyes were suffering pools, so silent and deep they held the secrets of the universe. At one moment they'd be so filled with compassion that you would almost cry aloud to think that someone recognized your pain, and at another they'd be dancing with laughter.

He was busier than ever, and to do any business, you had to catch him on the run—while driving to a board meeting or rushing to the hospital to pay a call. He seemed to have a hand in every venture in town: committees, services for shut-ins, a new program for ferrying the elderly to church. Only occasionally would he collapse. I saw him do this at the end of one long day. Natalie had left. It was after six, and he sank into his chair and for a moment he looked so tired—so *old*—I thought he was physically sick.

"Are you all right?" I said.

"I'm all right. I just need to stop and sit a moment."

"Do you want me to go away?"

"No, stay. But no business." He rocked back in his chair,

one foot propped on the desk, his hands clasped behind his head, and then leaned forward suddenly and stuck one finger right through the hole in the side of his shoe. He waggled the finger at me mischievously.

"I'm wearing them into sandals," he said. Then: "Well, tell me, John, I've been wondering. What do you think happened to Lazarus after he rose from the dead?"

"What?"

"I've been thinking about it. We don't know, do we? And it's *the* question! Whatever do you think the Gospel writers were dreaming about not to finish the story?" He laughed at my expression. "I mean, look, here's this guy, a friend of Jesus, the brother of Martha and Mary, and he's been dead not just for a couple hours, like the little girl, who might not have been dead anyway. This guy's been dead three days. Buried. He's stinking, as they so graphically point out. They hold their noses to open the tomb. So, Jesus, not wanting to do it at all, from what we can gather—'I'm doing this so you'll understand my Father's power,' he says. 'This isn't for me, and if I had my way, I wouldn't do it at all, but okay, here goes'—he raises Lazarus from the dead. The corpse stands up and walks out of the tomb into the hard white desert heat. 'Remove the napkin from his face,' says Christ.

"But then what? They don't say! The goddamn fools don't even know what's most important!"

"Isn't rising from the dead important?" I asked.

"No journalist today would stop the story there. Imagine, here's the only man on earth brought back to life, and you know they'd all rush in for his testimony, microphones to his mouth. 'How was it, Mr. Lazarus? How're you feeling? Can you tell us what it was like on the other side? Have you any words for the folks back home?' I mean that's big-time stuff."

We were both laughing.

" 'Well, actually I'm feeling a little nauseous.' " I picked up Tom's theme. " 'I haven't eaten in a while. Can I have something to drink?' "

"Or, 'Where am I?' " Tom shouted. " 'Why am I dressed in these sheets?' " He grew serious. "But wait. It's also a real question, isn't it? I'm not so sure it would've been terrific for Lazarus either. Maybe he was damned mad at being brought back to earth. He'd seen God! He was living in the Light. He was hearing the music of eternal silence and he's wrenched back into his physical body—but what a body. Three days it's been buried. Is he cured of that wet-rot? We aren't told."

"Oh, you'd have to assume he was," I said. "Christ wouldn't leave him in a worm-eaten body."

"Ah, then what about the mind? He goes home with his two sisters, who are hanging on him, hugging him, supporting him. They can't get enough of him, their beloved brother, whom they could not even permit the grace to die. Is he glad to be back? Maybe not. He's got to plow and plant and heave and strain his body again. He has to put up with his sisters quarrelling, and probably scolding him when he goes off of an evening to have a drink. Or nagging at him to take a wife, or complaining if he does get one. And neighbors squabbling and feuding, and countries going to war. . . ."

"But if he's alive, he'd like that too. That's life."

"Maybe, but there's worse to come. Imagine what happens at night. Darkness comes. Lamps are lit in the rooms. A little glow of light, but shadows in the corners of the room, and with the night comes the memory of the grave, the body's memory of rotting in the dark. Does he dream of the tomb? Does he feel the worms chewing on his flesh at night? Does he scream in his sleep and waken the whole town, fighting to step out of his body—as he had for those ecstatic and divine three days? No, now he's trapped inside it again, caged in his physical form.''

"I gather you don't think he'd be grateful to be alive."

"I don't know. What do you think? There's something the Gospel writers aren't telling us, isn't there? Why don't they say, 'lived happily ever after'? Why don't they say how long he lived, what he eventually died of? Where was he when Christ was crucified? Did Christ bring a babbling idiot back, alive but rambling through the thickets of his mind thereafter, constantly getting lost?

"Or maybe—" Tom's eyes traced the ceiling thoughtfully. "Maybe he came back healed in every way. Maybe he dove back into this physical dimension where everything operates in logic, form, and polarized duality—either/or . . . black/white . . . good/bad . . . yes/no. Back into man's petty perceptions of 'If this, then not that.' Maybe he was alive to life on another level, knowing by a rather dramatic experience that there is no death. 'Death, where is thy sting-a-ling-a-ling?' " he sang. "So, maybe he was alive with a quickening of the soul that most of us never know."

"Born again?" I teased.

"Well, *yes!* So few of us have that opportunity in such a literal way, do we? You know, I wonder if actually we aren't dead now."

"What?"

"In this life. Maybe we're not alive in these bodies, but are actually only born once we die. In which case, you see"—he raised his eyebrows—"ol' Mr. Lazarus been brought back *from* the life."

I was delighted. This was the old Tom back, talking the way he used to.

"*But!*" He raised one hand and rose to his feet, looming over me in the dusky room. "Let's say he's pleased to come back. Now he *knows* there is no death. He *knows* what will happen when he dies, and he's got no fear whatsoever of anything that can possibly happen to him on this earth. What could he possibly be afraid of ever again? Starvation? Disease? The death of his family? Pooh! He knows that death is the beginning of life. Suppose he is strong of body, young, surging with vitality. He would just go around, I suppose, laughing all day long and praising God: for eyes with which to absorb colors, shapes; for skin with which to feel the wind; for a nose to take in the odors of the world; and a glorious body with which to make love to his love—eyes to see her with, lips to kiss her with, tongue to taste her sweat, and ears with which to hear her voice, or the voice of his mother, or sisters, or friends. Such gifts. Arms to embrace each other with, to hold our children with, to feel and grab each object physically. Maybe he'd go round seeding the maidens of his village—all of them, just taking his joy when he could."

I was jolted. "Tom, stop it."

"Look how dark it's gotten." He paced to the door. "You sound as if there's something to fear." For a moment a chill ran down my back. Then he turned on the light, and my courage returned.

But when I looked, I saw his face was working. He threw himself in his chair, one hand covering his eyes. His shoulders were shaking.

"I've made so many enemies, haven't I?"

I said nothing.

"Butch is still circulating his letters. Oh, goddamn it!"

"He wants you out," I said softly.

I think it was that which brought him back into control.

"Well, I'm not getting out," he said savagely. "Why? Is the vestry asking me to resign?"

"We've discussed it. . . . You're . . . unorthodox."

"Oh. Well." I saw the muscle in his jaw working, his face twist, ravaged.

"You want to know how serious it is?"

He nodded.

"Butch doesn't want you to resign. He wants to run you out of the Church entirely. Defrock you."

He gave me a savage grin. "Oh, I love that man." Then, fiercely: "Listen, John. Naughton is mine. I belong here now. I have been shown my path and I will do the work of God right here, if He so wills it. And if He does not, then I shall go where He leads. But it will not be General Shriver who makes me leave." Now he came to his feet, knocking his fists together in a gesture reminiscent of Lizzie's determination. "Yes, I'll enjoy a fight with the General—a good, knock-down, drag-out fight. We'll see who wins."

"You don't know what you're talking about. You won't have a prayer."

"Well, a prayer, maybe." Was he teasing?

"You want to know the charges?"

"Ah, so there are charges?"

"He's preparing material for the Bishop. Some relate to your personal life. Adultery," I added, looking him in the eye. "He has witnesses."

"What witnesses?"

"A black man named Storey Lunt."

He flushed a deep rose hue, the rush of emotion flooding his face.

"What other charges?" His mouth was grim.

"You don't need any others. If he proves sexual misconduct, that's enough. You heard of that woman, Connie Ireland, over near Sutters Mill? She was excommunicated two years ago from the Episcopal church. For what? Adultery."

"Hmm."

"It's not even like your story. She wasn't anybody. She and her husband were already separated when she took up with another man. Her husband brought charges against her in church, because they were still legally married. She was excommunicated. Can you imagine what they'd do with you?"

"What other charges?" he asked.

"Your vision, voices. The filth on the altar, your behavior toward Emily . . . There are statements you've made about the authority of the Church and the liturgy. There's all this talk, Tibetan Books of the Dead. God knows what-all."

"Oh, for God's sake, John. You sound like one of them."

"One of who?"

"The Valley people. Troglodytes. Form-ridden, caste-conscious, materialistic. I don't mean people like Shriver—he's looking for a fight. I mean the ones who don't dare peek in their own pants for fear they'll find some dirt. You know my beliefs. There's one God. Call it Allah or God or Yahweh or the manifestations of Shiva. All of it's the same."

"Well, that too, goddamn it, Tom. You just walk into their traps. Look at what's happening. You invite everyone in. All these farmers coming in. Who are they? Baptists, Pentecostal Holy Rollers. You let them take Communion and they haven't even been confirmed."

He made a gesture of disgust.

"You'd let a Catholic in."

"I'll let a Muslim in. I'll let an atheist in. I'll let in anyone who wants to worship God, and I'll make him welcome. I'll say, yes, come worship God, give praise, give thanks to God. It is meet and right so to do. It is very meet and right and our bounden duty."

"But the Church, Tom. The Church. You don't have any adherence to *form*."

"None. None. I have none."

"You don't see that they're different?"

"Who?"

"These people. They don't belong in Trinity."

"Any person belongs in Trinity—black, white, green, red. Any person who can walk, or crawl, or creep is welcome in my church. Come with a pure heart to the worship of God, and you shall not be sent away."

"We're off the subject," I said. "Listen, even the rumors of sexual scandal can be worked through, if you're sensitive to our needs. We're all sinners. We'll give you the benefit of the doubt, if we can see that you're living a godly life, if you two aren't seeing each other anymore."

"I love her."

"Oh, for God's sake."

"I know."

"You know."

Then he told his innocent version of the story. I knew most of it from Elizabeth, but he filled in details—how they had struggled to stay apart and how an act of God had brought them to each other's arms.

"All lovers think it was *meant*," I said. "It's part of the litany."

But his eyes flashed, and suddenly I found myself confused. I was responding in the same fantastical language that he used: "How do you know she was given you?" I asked. "How do you know it wasn't your lust or the temptation of the Devil?"

"I pray to God, not the Devil," he said impatiently. "If I prayed to the Devil, I'd probably assume she was given by the Devil. But no Devil could have shown me such a vision of God's grace. Good heavens, why are we discussing this anyway?"

"It will be brought up in a trial, if there is one."

"Well, there won't be." Neither of us spoke.

Then he said, "I'm living lies. What can I do?" he asked. "If I deny my love for Elizabeth, I lie to my deepest self and to God—for God is the Lover. If He gives me Love, who am I to turn my back? Refuse my blessing? Say it comes from an unclean source?

"Therefore I do not deny I love Elizabeth. She knows my dilemma. If she doesn't like the situation, she is free to change it, though I shall not stop loving her.

"So, let's turn to deceiving Pris. You're right, that is a lie, but for the short term I don't see what else to do. She's sick. I firmly believe she's not healthy, perhaps incapable of recovering from a blow like this. When she's ready, I'll tell her. Divorce her. Provide for her. Some solution will be given us. In the meantime I love Elizabeth, yes; and no, I will not leave her; and no, I will not hurt Priscilla. That's my position."

We sat in silence, thinking.

"Elizabeth is just a red herring, isn't she?" he asked after a moment. "If there were no Elizabeth, Shriver would still be out for me. I hope we're fighting together, John."

"I'll do everything in my power to protect you."

For the second time I blurted out this rash promise, and why, I still don't know.

So spring moved into summer, with the rockers squeaking on the screened front porches, the tongues keeping time to fingers that flashed like knitting needles over gingham laps; and the fingers stripping round green peas into aluminum pans with a thunderous fall. The voices rippled over knives that slashed heads off stringbeans and slit their throats; the summer would pass in a haze of slicing peppers, cukes, corn, carrots; crushing red June strawberries, then raspberries, then peaches, apples, concord grapes; canning okra and tomatoes; and later making jelly, while the whispers travelled on, moving through the seasons from vegetable to fruit.

Angus and Elizabeth had separated, and Angus was living over the garage at Fran and Squeaky's place, in what had once been the chauffeur's lodge—one room and kitchenette. Lizzie had found a job at Martha's Dress Shop as a common shopgirl, if you can imagine, and what was worse, her mother had cut off the proceeds of her trust. Oh, plenty of the Valley folk thought Carolyn justified in that regard, while others wondered why Dutton didn't stand up for his daughter, but, henpecked, polished his brass medallions and stayed out of domestic fights.

I couldn't intervene. I was on the board of the Naughton Bank but not the bank that held Lizzie's trust. Moreover, Carolyn was a trustee. What chance did Lizzie have? Carolyn leaned on the bank trustees. She said her daughter did not deserve to withdraw any principal from her trust unless she changed her way of life. When asked what that meant, Carolyn grew silent and shut one eye, peering under the brim of her latest summer hat.

"She knows what I mean," said Carolyn. "Just tell her that."

In the end she relented some: she told Gough Warren, the vice president, just enough to arm him. Gough, thin and balding, leaned across the conference table opposite Elizabeth and, for the entire forty minutes of their interview, opened and closed the fingers of his hands, like flashing semaphores. He accused her of being unable to handle either her money or her life.

"You're divorcing your husband, aren't you?" he said.

"I am. I'll be going to Reno soon."

"I understand you've made him a generous settlement. You're giving him your money."

"I'm giving him some money."

"And your house."

"No, I have no house. It's rented from my parents," said Elizabeth. "I'm giving him the furniture, though."

"Everything?" Gough leaned forward, fascinated. "It's more than he's asked for. It's not necessary. It *proves* you have no concept of handling money. The trustees have power according to the will to withhold any money, income or principal, until you can prove your competence. . . ." And his fingers flashed.

The Valley buzzed with news.

One day Mrs. Clark came into Martha's Dress Shop, leaning on her cane, her chin thrust forward, sharp as a crab. Mrs. Clark was a friend of the Pages, and well into her seventies. She fingered the cashmere sweaters with two hooked fingers, gnarled and knuckled knots.

"What's this I hear about you and Angus getting divorced?" The question rang through the quiet store. It set the motes to dancing in the shafts of sunlight that streamed through the plate-glass window.

Elizabeth was startled. She took a step behind the counter for protection and absorbed herself in a flurry of activity, sorting and counting frail thin scarves.

"Is it true?" Mrs. Clark leaned with both hands on her cane, peering over the edge of the counter at the young woman, who then crouched on the floor, sorting through the drawers of sweaters, scarves, and shirts. "Well?" Two ladies at the dress rack exchanged a knowing smile and drifted to jewelry, where, backs turned, they could watch discreetly in a mirror on the wall. Mrs. Clark lowered her voice to a hissing whisper:

"Your mother's told me you're separated. You needn't deny it. I just hope it's not true."

"It is." Lizzie rose to her full height with a defiant toss of her head.

"Oh, my poor dear," said Mrs. Clark; and Elizabeth thought she preferred her malice to her dripping sympathy. She smiled with courteous chill:

"Is there something you wanted to see?"

"No, I came in to talk to you—to tell you you're making a mistake. I've lived longer than you. I've seen a lot of things, and I know it's a new world. Here you are working in a . . .

dress shop!'' She looked around as if it sold tarantulas. "I know all you modern girls want independence. Why you think you have to break free, I can't imagine. I suppose you want to claim your independence. Well, you have plenty of independence— Angus wasn't keeping you from that. He gave you every support it's possible for a man to give. You don't know what it is to live alone. I've been alone ever since my husband died. Eleven years ago this fall, and let me tell you, it's no fun. Angus is a fine young man. I knew his parents. Anyone can see he's devoted to you. If he's done something foolish, well, that's nothing new. It's the business of the wife to forgive and forget. I don't know what he's done. . . .'' Her voice trailed off expectantly.

"He's not done anything.'' Elizabeth rose to his defense. "We have decided to live separately, that's all.''

"Well, it certainly is queer. Whatever happened?''

Elizabeth returned her stare, cold as a queen. "Mrs. Clark, I'm at work. Is there something I can show you in the store?''

"I just came to warn you,'' she persisted. "Don't leave him too long. You'll find some young woman has snapped him up. He's a handsome man, mark my words. Don't do something you'll regret. I'm sure that minister would not approve. He's a special friend of yours, isn't he? You should talk to him before you make a decision. He'd tell you the same thing, mark my words.''

As she left, back straight, her left hip giving only the faintest hint of an arthritic limp, Elizabeth rolled her eyes at Martha. She pretended to shrug it off, but inside she seethed with anger. What did anyone know of her relationship with Tom?

Then the letters began:

Early Quakers seemed a lunatic fringe of Puritans.
They heard voices, insulted betters, and appeared naked in church. One of them, James Nayler, thought he
was Jesus Christ and entered the city of Bristol riding
on an ass, with his admirers singing, "Holy, holy, holy."
The authorities bored his tongue with a hot iron,
cut off his ears, and branded his forehead with the letter
B. for Blasphemer.

This was one of many anonymous notes circulated by
Shriver. Typed on plain white bond, with copies to both the
diocesan and suffragan bishops, they would appear on a table
at the Club or tacked to the drugstore bulletin board. Each
carried a reference to Tom.
The rockers squeaked. We were further titillated when the
poems began.

There was once an Episcopal rector
renowned among girls for his nectar;
for who could resist
if the chance should persist
to sup at his high priestly peckter?

Or this:

A clergyman marriage wrecker
Was known among all as a necker.
He couldn't resist
Fornication and kissed
Any cunt that would twist on his pecker.

It was scandalous. Delicious. Horrifying. Sad.

The rockers slapped porch boards and tongues *tsk*ed and laughter lifted to muted shrieks. We wanted to know who was writing these notes and whether they were true. A lot of people brought up (it had hardly just died down) Tom's madness last March, grass on his lips and horns of fire in his hair, and as if he himself were not wild enough, there was his family served to us on platters, in particular Daphne, like Salome, home from boarding school. Sixteen, and her pretty little ass tucked under her, and her breasts hanging down like clusters of fruit ready to be nibbled off their stems. She was a hot ticket. Some people laughed that the clergyman's daughter turned out like that, but others were sympathetic. I know Priscilla, at first sight of her, sat down, one hand fluttering at her throat—then scolded, voice taut as wire, following her daughter right to her room, right to the door that closed in her face. Daphne went up to the Thursday dances at the Club. That's where my son, Johnnie, met her. Like the other boys he took one look and set off panting in pursuit, and he was twenty-one. Daphne wore tight, white, little-bitty shorts, so high her bum stuck out; and she twirled her rump, rested her weight on one thrusting hip and one hand for accent on her waist. Sometimes she'd twist her shoulders restlessly, her mouth moving over her gum and her eyes straying over the boys. Her fingers would crawl up between her breasts, playing with the cross that dangled on a silver chain around her neck, and it was all you could do to keep your own hands from crawling in there after hers, snuggling underneath her blouse. The rockers slapped, *slappity-slap*; the tongues *click-clack*ed; and all predicted the predicament that later fell. When I learned it was Johnnie who had knocked her up, and when

he used Tom's very language to justify his act—"A little worship," he laughed, "at the fountains of the Lord"—I couldn't
speak. My throat choked tight. But now I'm ahead of my story
again.

Summer burned the countryside with its heat. The sky
glazed over, white and humid, and the grass scorched dry.

Meanwhile Angus drank steadily. His eyes had the hollow
look of drunks who've seen to the bottom of bottles. His skin
went white and pasty, and you could tell by smell alone when
he'd entered a room, the musky odor of muscle and fat trying
to throw its toxins out. Angus' blackouts became more fre-
quent, and his mental powers fuzzy even when awake. He was
obsessed with money. Money and Elk Creek. He talked of nothing else, unless, in his self-pitying whine, it was about women
and divorce. He thought the whole world was against him. He
sat in his shabby office, a drink at his hand. His dreams floated
in and out like waves. Out at Elk Creek the houses were beginning to go up, the foundations were poured, and wood frames
were rising above a lacerated landscape, the hills scraped raw
to the bleeding bronze earth, and the valleys made straight in
the desert a highway for thousands of dollars of concrete and
tons of steel, for well-digging equipment and cesspool liners.
Up in the woods an idle earth-mover lay pitched at an awkward
angle, waiting, its mandibles open wide.

When Angus walked his land, he saw stores and streets and
children roller-skating, men who mowed their lawns on Gravely
tractors and women who fed the dogs and filled the swimming
pools, and all of them would be paying their mortgage money
to him, Angus McEwen, feeding him for life. He had named
the streets already. There was McEwen Street, and Angus Lane,
and Duncan's Way. For Tony he had named one Angela Court,

and for Elizabeth's family, Front Page Road, the pun tickling
his funnybone. There were two low brick buildings for the low-
income group, and through it all wound Elk Creek, undammed,
the very sluice he'd played in as a child, lifting stones to catch
the scuttling crawfish in the swirling mud. Someday a whole
mess of kids would wade in his stream, submerged in the endless
hollow light that comes on summer evenings, the white dusk
giving way interminably to indigo, and then to fireflies gleaming in the black, just waiting to be caught and put in jars. Their
voices would ring out clear, carried on the still air, and their
mothers would call them in to bed, and then they'd hear the
slap of the screen doors and their parents' low voices rising from
the porch steps to the open bedroom windows, to the hot and
deadened air that hung in their childhood rooms.

He wafted on his dreams, but reality in the form of bills
poured over his desk, covering the sign saying PRESIDENT, which
he had bought to mark the day of incorporation of his firm.
None of the figures added up. Angus had asked Tony why they
were short $200,000 in supplies, but Tony had shrugged, hand-
ing back the papers. "Maybe you need an accountant," he had
said, and turned away—but not before Angus caught his look,
a grin like nothing he had ever seen before. Angus was left
wondering if he had dreamt that smirk.

The rockers squeaked, and heads nodded or shook reproof.

Tony had taken a leaf from Angus and set up his own development company, named the Angel Corp. after his wife—
separate from Elk Creek. Tony was building five or six houses
just across the county line, and for some reason he had plenty
of supplies. So why was Angus in trouble? And where was his
$200,000 in lumber and equipment? Elk Creek was stalled. The
suppliers claimed he owed them for materials received, and they

had signed receipts to prove it. Yet the construction boys were screaming for studs or lumber or miles of pipe, saying they'd never received their order. The bank refused to give Angus the next installment loan until the roofs were up, and the roofs could not be finished without lumber. The lumberyard claimed they'd delivered the material but had not been paid. They threatened him with a mechanics' lien. If Angus did not pay in ninety days, the bank would foreclose. But how could he pay without the bank loan, and how could he get the loan without having paid his debt?

Meanwhile Tony's houses were going up great guns. Angus came to me about it. I tried to suggest he look at his partner's books, but Angus wouldn't think of such a thing. Tony was perfect in his eyes.

One night Angus disappeared. He was found two days later in an alley up in Leesburg, covered in urine and vomit, unconscious or dead drunk. The wrecked Porsche lay in a ditch. The tongues clacked more, for Elizabeth, together with Tom Buckford, the Episcopal minister, drove him right up to Willowhill, our local drunk farm for the very rich. Some of us thought she did the right thing, and others thought she had no right to incarcerate her husband as she had her son. A child in one institution and a husband in another. . . .

But I can attest to her anguish driving Angus up to rehab at Willowhill. She held Tom's hand for comfort and struggled first with her conscience and then with her anxiety over where to find five hundred dollars a week to keep him there. When they arrived, Willowhill refused the patient.

"He's too sick," the nurse told her. "We don't have facilities for the likes of him. You'll have to dry him out. Take him to a facility in Washington." She wrote down a name. "Give him little swallows of booze. He could have convulsions. He could die. No," she said, "bring him back when he's sober."

So Tom and Elizabeth drove all the way to Washington, Angus rotting and stinking in the backseat, oblivious to the couple in the front. By the time they got him into detox and the papers signed, the black sky was clearing with first light. Elizabeth and Tom shared a cup of coffee, watching the sun come up, their eyes burning with exhaustion and fingers intertwined. Elizabeth never went to bed at all. Hours later she walked over the fields to Walnut Grove to catch her father at breakfast.

The two black dogs leapt up to greet her at the door. She absently noted the dining room in morning light, the waxed table, the gleaming silver, and the newspapers spread out—these were her childhood memories as well. She bent to kiss her father on the cheek.

"Good morning, Daddy."

"Well, to what do we owe this visit?" He put the paper down, tilting his bifocals to the tip of his nose in order to see his daughter over them. He was very pleased. "We haven't seen you in a long time."

Mary set a place for Elizabeth. "Good morning, Miss Lizzie."

"Good morning, Mary. How are you? Just toast and coffee, please."

"You don't want no egg?"

"No, thanks. I've had breakfast already." She waited till Mary disappeared into the kitchen. "Daddy," she began. "I need money." Midway through her story, enter Carolyn, fully dressed, who offered a cheek for her daughter's kiss and sat down, remarking on how nice it was to see her, that Elizabeth didn't come up as much as she used to, didn't care for her aging parents apparently, and had no time for them. Elizabeth regretted her mother's entrance. She had hoped to have her father to herself.

"Go on, go on," Carolyn said. "Don't let me interrupt. I won't say a word." She poured herself coffee, settling down to listen, until slow comprehension dawned on her. "You mean you want your inheritance now?"

"Well, some of it."

"Before we even die?"

Elizabeth turned red. "I won't deprive you!" She explained again about Angus and detox and Willowhill, and you can imagine how hard it was to come crawling home, asking for her inheritance in advance after what her mother had done with her trust.

"Well, I absolutely refuse. I remember Cousin Alice," said Carolyn, her voice trembling. She set down her buttered toast. "Her daughter, Nora, persuaded her to hand over all her money when she got old, her whole inheritance, and I happen to know that she promised Cousin Alice that she would stay forever at Beaulieu. Cousin Alice believed her. Why not? Her own daughter! Nora put her in a nursing home. She sold Beaulieu and put her own mother in a nursing home—"

"Oh, Mother."

"—and there was no reason to do a thing like that! There was plenty of money. She stole her mother's money! I went to see poor Cousin Alice once. She was in an old rag of a sweater with holes in it, and these horrible bedroom slippers, sluffing around this dirty place. It was ghastly. She was way up North, without a soul she knew around, no friends. Nora left her there to die, and there was nothing Cousin Alice could do about it.

She'd handed over all her rights. I swore right then and there I'd never be dependent on my children. No, you have plenty of money. You have your trust."

"I don't!" she cried, but Carolyn ran on:

"Angus has all of Elk Creek. Wait till we die. It won't be long now, I'm sure, though it may be too long for you. Meanwhile it's good for the young to have to struggle just a bit. Too much money isn't good for anyone."

Elizabeth shook with rage. "My trust!" she cried. "You've barred me from that too." She closed her mouth. She was incensed, but no less stubborn than her mother. She would not give in or show them what it meant.

Her father saw her to the door. "I'll think about it, Lizzie," he said softly, kissing her forehead. "Don't worry, I'll see if we can't do something. We have a lot of expenses just now. Your mother . . . well, you know her and money."

"It's shameful."

"I'll get back to you."

"Don't worry, Daddy. I'll manage. I don't need you two." She could hardly control her rage.

"Here, can I give you twenty dollars now?" He was digging in his pocket.

"No, I don't want twenty dollars. I need five hundred a week for Angus. Weren't you even listening?"

In the end he slipped her one thousand dollars—a bold act, not mentioned to his wife.

The irony was that Elizabeth was a rich woman. Yet she could not touch her funds, sitting in that inflexible ancestral trust, ransom first to the Law of the Propertied Class—*Never Touch Principal!*—and second to her mother's blackmail.

"All you have to do is give up this tainted relationship.

Promise you won't see him. I'll give you a loan at three percent
to cover Angus at Willowhill. It won't cost us," she said, oblivious to her daughter's hurt. "We can forgive the loan on our
taxes. You won't have to pay us back a cent. Elizabeth, it's so
simple. I'll even help pay for Duncan at Briarose."

"No." Extortion! She'd rather starve.

When Angus was released from the clinic, she drove him
up to Willowhill again. They held hands fondly all the way.

"Are you scared?" she asked.

"Sure I'm scared."

"Do you think it's the right thing?"

"God, I don't know." He was miserable.

"You'll make it," she said. "Don't worry. You're a strong
man. Just hang in."

"You do whatever you have to about the money," he said.
"I trust you." She went through the Elk Creek books. She
talked to the bank, to Tony, to the accountant. She filed for
bankruptcy in the courts.

She sold the wrecked Porsche first. Then she called Parke-
Bernet to take her few antiques, the good wedding presents.
Finally she held a yard sale. She advertised it in the local newspaper, and one scalding Saturday in July her little gatehouse
was crammed with buyers. All afternoon she sold. Her friend
Fran helped, taking money at a card table by the door and
counting receipts. Whatever anyone wanted Elizabeth sold—
except her bed, two chairs, the couch, the kitchen utensils, and
the cat. "I won't sell you." She shooed him upstairs. At one
point Carolyn poked her nose in to see what was going on and
quickly left. She was shocked by her daughter's display: people
on the lawn, in the house, carrying off the furnishings. The

impropriety of proclaiming poverty! She thought it reflected on herself.

When the day was over, Elizabeth stood alone in the house, exhausted and shaky from the excitement. Fran had left. The crowds were gone. Her house was a shell. Elk Creek was bankrupt, but the creditors would take the development alone—they had no claims on her. The only person to make money on Elk Creek was Tony Reischetz. Elizabeth knew he'd milked it of a couple hundred thousand, but not a shred of proof to take him into court!

She roamed the empty rooms of her house, which, yes, she would ask her father to give to her rent-free. He would not refuse her that. Suddenly she felt released. She wanted to dance. She had enough money for one brief month of life. She had two chairs. A couch. A bed. The sideboard was gone, the tables, lamps, the books. She twirled through the rooms and found herself singing, chanting, arms flung wide and spinning like a child: "All right, God!" she called out. "I'm yours, you hear?" She laughed and laughed hysterically. "I have nothing now. Take care of me, you hear?"

I think she went crazy, for that moment anyway. It's here in her journal, how, after the weeks of strain, after the sale, after she was left alone, she danced in the empty rooms, her hair smacking in her eyes with each heel thrust. She lifted her hands to the ceiling, threw them to the floor, stomping in her war dance: "All right, God! All right, God!" She'd take this challenge too. "All right, God! All right, God!" She sang until, exhausted, she collapsed, despairing, on the couch, angry tears wetting the cushions. She sobbed with fatigue and release.

Since meeting Tom she had lost her horse, her house, her

possessions, her husband. She had lost her way in life. She had
lost the respect of her mother and gained instead a certain
distrust of her, a lingering disdain, and anger that her mother
would treat her as she did. Carolyn's attempts to pry Tom from
her only hardened her resolve.

Later she cooked a soft-boiled egg and toast for her solitary
supper and crawled to bed, hugging her knees. Even if she had
lost her possessions, she had the world in Tom. She saw him
when she could and loved him the more for his courage in the
face of difficulties, for his integrity, and for his love for her. He
called her his wife, his love, his sister, his best friend. I think
he would have died for her, and Elizabeth knew it. Like Sleeping Beauty, she had come alive through her prince. She put all
thoughts of the future out of her mind—the poems, the divorce,
the drumbeat of the march of enemies. The fall would come,
but when they lay together, lips touching, when she felt the
warmth of their bodies mix, she was washed with radiance. She
took his hand and held it humbly to her cheek. She kissed it,
placed it on her breast. It was this running radiance she wanted.
Such sanctity. She could feel her own energy field, a magnetic
current captured, enlarged in him, and returning back to her
in a steady flow.

Meanwhile Priscilla, unclean, kept trying to purify herself. Tom
watched in misery, unable to help.

She washed her hands again and again, several times an
hour. She cleaned the house with obsessive intent, sometimes
scrubbing until midnight. Nothing helped. Moreover there was
the task of trying to keep the others clean as well. Daphne.
Philip. Tom. Her world was spinning out of control. One day
she found dog dung smeared on the mailbox, on the handle,

filling the inside of the box. She wanted to vomit. It was due to Tom! It was a sign of her own uncleanliness. She prayed to purify herself. No one knew the depths of her defilement. She lied. She held vile thoughts. She did not do her duty. She was not righteous in the sight of God. The dung could be cleaned off the metal mailbox, but it could not be removed from her heart, for she was filled with filth. The others, too, were seared by dirty thoughts. She saw darkness—great tangible blobs like hairballs in the house, in her closet, clinging to her own shoulders. They were black webs enshrouding her. She was no longer worthy to touch the linens of the church. She asked the Altar Guild to do the work, yet knowing that these women, too, were besmirched with unchaste, murderous, foul deeds, so that even to delegate her responsibility was wrong. *"And wears man's smudge."*

One day she found a poem in the mailbox. She opened the blank envelope. The paper that fell out almost scorched her. She burned it, the edges crinkling into black, but she knew the char in her soul could not so easily crumble to white ash.

17

GENERAL SHRIVER ENGINEERED A TWO-PRONGED MILITARY ATTACK. One was to spread his verses round the Valley, the other was to pressure our two bishops: Ben Cochrane, the suffragan bishop in Alexandria, and Dick Crowley, the diocesan bishop in Richmond. Butch dropped in on each. Tom Buckford's a son of a bitch, he said, in clear shorthand. He's emotionally ill. He has visions. He's screwing one of the parishioners. Had a formal charge of sexual misconduct been made, Dick Crowley would have demanded his collar instantly. But the Bishop would take action only when he had some proof—not rumors but a knowledgeable witness willing to face the priest, or else a confession of sin, possibly from the woman herself. No one came forth. And we waited.

Even at the time I wondered, Why didn't I accuse?

For me, that summer blurs into a succession of meetings, sweltering July nights cramped in the parish hall without air, or scorching, white-hot days. We fanned ourselves with newspapers and mopped our heads with handkerchiefs already damp with sweat. The windows were open in the parish hall, but not a breath of air would stir in the stifling room. Outside, the althaea were in full bloom. I could see the soft pink flowers,

each a tiny trumpet, and the bees humming and working furiously.

The limericks grew more pointed:

There once was a man of the cloth
Who swore a prodigious oath.
He saw his cock as an omen
Cried: "God is a woman,
The Sacrament union of both!"

We discussed them in the vestry meetings, and on the
streets, and rocking on front porches in black nights. Finally
one came that made reference to Lizzie Page McEwen.

Though the page of her name seems pure
                    (to you 'n' me)
And her mind seems clear and quick—
How to explain
When she strips in the rain
To leap on the minister's dick?

Carolyn blew. She accosted the General in the study of his
own house, waving the poem in her hand.

"Have you seen this?"

He was about to acknowledge grinning authorship when
she turned on him.

"That's my child! If I find the person who's writing these,
I'll ruin him."

Shriver swallowed his drink in one gulp. He had forgotten
about Carolyn. Shriver had lived in Naughton only ten years.
He may have been a SAC commander once with his own lim-

ousine, flags flying at its fenders, his military valet, and several
house staff and yardmen. He may have been given parades and
ribbons, but his social position in the Valley would never stand
against La Belle Dame Sans Merci.

"Mmrrmp," he mumbled.

She paced his study from the Munning racing print to the
oil portrait of his wife: a she-wolf snarling in her cub's defense.
The poems came in unmarked business envelopes. There was
no way to pin the work on Butch, but Carolyn was no dummy.

"I won't have my daughter's name dragged into this. I will
not have her hurt." She turned on him. "So, think. You're on
the vestry. Get that man out of Naughton." Her hands made
tight, swift, chopping motions emphasizing every word.

"I've tried. We had a meeting the other day, and he's still
got a majority. But there's hope. The vote was close.

"You have to understand," said Shriver, and Carolyn noticed a new tension in his voice, a kind of querulous whine,
"technically the vestry has no business quizzing its clergy. That
is the proper jurisdiction of a bishop. That's whom he's responsible to and where he gets authority. We're just stockholders of
the parish. We own the physical plant, raise money, spend it.
But the minister makes all the decisions relating to worship.
He has the keys to the Kingdom . . . and the building, too, as
it happens. Our hands are tied, Carolyn. He's supposed to help
our spiritual growth, whatever that means, and not to be questioned by the members of the vestry."

"So what do we do?" she asked.

He shrugged. "Damned if I know."

"I'll tell Dick Crowley I'm withdrawing my contributions
to the church. That's a sizable sum," said Carolyn.

"Maybe we should organize a boycott."

"Get the canons," she ordered. "There must be something there."

The only thing they could not use was the single weapon that would have finished Tom at once: his affair with Lizzie. Carolyn saw to that. But they had other ammunition.

According to the canons, if three communicants write the bishop citing their pastor's guilt for even just one act, he can be brought to trial. Better yet, Carolyn pointed out, the Bishop's Council could prefer the charges. They knew the Council did what the Bishop asked.

It was the end of July when Carolyn and Shriver dragged Emily to a meeting with Bishop Crowley in Richmond. They learned there was almost no way to get rid of Tom. We weren't Methodists, where the Bishop has the arbitrary power of a pope and can remove a priest at will—a penstroke and he's gone. Nor were we Baptists, where a ministry is founded on no more than a following, where any Baptist can set himself up as clergy and start a church by walking round the corner and plunking down rent. The Episcopal church, rich in history, fell somewhere between the two, explained the Bishop, forming diplomatic steeples of his hands. The Episcopal church was designed to protect the independence of the clergy, both from the vagaries of the congregants and from the spite of bishops.

"Now, if he's engaged in real wrongdoing . . ." Crowley said. "Embezzlement. Sexual misdemeanors. . . ."

"No!" cried Carolyn. "There's absolutely nothing of that." She shot a look at Shriver, another at the Bishop. "But how about defiling the altar? Having visions? Kissing the feet of his parishioners!" she concluded with a triumphant wave at Emily, who lifted her eyes for the first time in this unpleasant meeting and shook her head shyly, and withdrew again into unhappy silence. "Or giving these god-awful sermons. He's an embarrassment to us all."

"For God's sake, he smeared manure on the cross of God!" cried the General. "What do you need? He hears voices. He's a certifiable maniac. At least remove him for what he does to liturgy. What do you *need*, after all?"

But Crowley needed more than their distress. The Episcopal church, he stated once again, lining up his pens, then steepling his fingers, is noted for its liturgical freedom.

"You mean he can just drop prayers?" Shriver burst out angrily. "Shuffle the deck any which way?"

"Which prayers?"

"In the Communion service, in the Psalms. I have records. He does anything he likes: drops a section, adds a section, moves things around, rewrites."

"It's entirely optional," Bishop Crowley stated flatly. He felt irritated by these three. "Lots of priests move prayers around," he said, "sometimes leaving them out entirely. It's a violation if you skip the Lesson, but even that can be done occasionally."

He did not want to tell them that the priest cannot tamper with the Eucharist, the Communion service. He noted the accusation and kept still. He let them know it is practically impossible in the Episcopal church to hold an heretical doctrine. There's no such thing as heresy, since every priest interprets Scripture as he likes.

"Of course if he's celebrated no services for a month . . ." he said, "ignored his duties. . . . Has he done that?"

But there was no faulting Tom in this area.

"Then his statements that you don't find salvation in the Church?" asked Carolyn. "They don't mean *anything*?"

But the Right Reverend Bishop Richard Crowley interpreted this charge generously too. Clearly salvation occurred outside the Church. Hadn't Thomas Merton, the Catholic theologian, written that even Buddhists can be saved? Every diocese, he explained, has one or two priests a bishop would love to get rid of, especially, he laughed, the ones who stand up in conventions making picky motions for new rulings and sub-paragraphs to the text. In this case not even our vestry could organize itself to request our pastor's resignation, and the Bishop would not intervene.

"And the poems that are going around?" cried Shriver. "You don't care at all? He's stirring up a damned lot of trouble."

Crowley smiled blandly. "I will speak to him," he said.

Throughout the hour he rocked back in his chair, his fingers forming those judgmental steeples before his nose. Or he lined up his pens with immaculate precision, curbing his annoyance. He paced the resplendent purple rug between his visitors, stopped at the window to point out the dirty garlands and decaying Byzantine towers of the Jefferson Hotel across the street, then propped one hip against a corner of his desk and polished his glasses with his handkerchief, smothering their outrage with the blanket of his charm.

Nonetheless he had been listening, and the door had hardly closed behind his visitors before he was dialing Tom's number.

The whole business was out of hand. He couldn't force Tom to resign, but he could lean on him. He could offer him a year's sabbatical at the Virginia Seminary, or perhaps, now that Tom had visions of God, he'd like to work in a prison chaplaincy among the most unreformed. There was no answer on the other end of the phone, and as the Bishop hung up, he wondered if he dared dump the man on another bishop—somewhere out West, perhaps; and the thought occurred to him acidly that the Bishop of New York may have already dumped Tom on him.

Despite his suave assurances to the contrary, Crowley was disturbed by Tom's behavior, the alleged desecration, his statements on the Church, Christ, and race, and the upheaval now in Naughton. He was especially concerned at the prospect of a drop in church revenues. The total membership of Trinity was rising, but if Carolyn and Butch carried out their threat, the Diocesan mission quota, the "asking" as it's called, would drop. It was the Bishop's income. He called the suffragan bishop, his colleague in Alexandria, and it was Ben Cochrane who reached Tom later that evening.

"Listen, I have talked to Dick. You are to resign immediately."

"Ben, I'm not going to."

"I have charges against you. There's a letter here that claims you endorse free sex."

"Nonsense. Who said it?"

"It doesn't matter."

"Of course it matters. I have a right to see my accusers."

"Listen, Tom, you are causing us a lot of problems. This whole thing is embarrassing."

"I imagine it is. But what about me? You're supposed to support me."

"I am. I'm giving you a chance to resign. We'll find you a new parish."

"I don't want a new parish. I belong here. I have a calling here. Come on, Ben, do you believe all that about me?"

"It's you I'm thinking about. Resign. Be graceful about it. Accept defeat. If you fight," Ben said, "you throw yourself into conflict with the Episcopal Authority. You'll be tried by the Council, and the Council does what the Bishop wants. You'll only lose."

It was in this conversation that Tom told Ben he wanted to divorce Priscilla.

"Good God! What's the matter with you young clergy?"

"Young!" Tom gave a laugh. "Do you know how old I am?"

But Ben was disgusted. "I just heard of a minister up in Massachusetts who was kicked out of his parish on morals charges—doing it with the organist right in church, behind the organ, in the House of God. Another was a homosexual pederast—caught with a thirteen-year-old altar boy. What's happening to the Church? I met your wife. She seems like a decent woman, a strong hand at your back. Have you prayed for guidance?"

"Oh, Ben. Of course I've prayed."

"Well, why would you do such a thing?"

"Because I'm not happy with her!"

"Not happy—as if that's reason for divorce! Good God! You're an embarrassment to us all. The next time I hear from you, I want it to be a phone call to tell me you've mailed your resignation. Do you hear me? That's an order!"

And meanwhile Carolyn was quarrelling with Elizabeth.

"You were raised to be a woman of leisure," she said. "I don't see why you have to drag the family name through the mud just to make your point. A dress shop indeed!"

"If I had a college degree, I'd get a better job," snapped Elizabeth. And then Carolyn said:

"A college degree! As if I haven't heard enough. What do you need with college, I ask you? I never went to college. No one I know did."

And Elizabeth said, "No *woman*!"

And Carolyn said, "Well, of course, no woman. What a lot of rubbish you talk. Now, Lizzie, be a good girl and give up

your job. We'll support you, for heaven's sake. We aren't going
to throw you out on the street."

"I don't want to be supported. I want to do it myself," said
Elizabeth. She was close to tears.

And then Carolyn said, "You make me so mad. Well, don't
come to me when you run out of money, then. I've given you
your chance." So they parted angrily.

It's time to speak of me, for I was as shocked as the rest of the
Valley by the widening gyre, the collapsing of our center, when
the best lacked all conviction. One Sunday a Negro family
came to church, a man, his wife, and two small daughters
dressed in frills. Strangers, they weren't known to Naughton.
They sat at the back, and instantly the presence of rough white
farmers was reduced to nothing. Things were falling apart. I sat
through the service without hearing a word. In that moment I
understood Elizabeth's talk about electrical energy, for I felt it
flaring off my hands. Adrenaline. I didn't want them there.
What would happen to our congregation? I'd thought I was
liberal. I hadn't cared about one pickaninny at the school or
Tom's friendship with the Lunts. Hell, didn't we have the servants to Christmas carolling at our house, and remember their
birthdays and help them out of jail and loan them money when
they needed it? Didn't we love and care for our own? But Negroes had their own churches and they could worship there. I
tried to remind myself that Our Lord had talked to Gentiles
and Samaritans—the Negroes of his day—and then I remembered my mother, born during Reconstruction, saying, "If God
had wanted darkies to be our equals, He'd have made them white."
I'd been scornful of her bigotry, but even so, I was not so far
removed from Reconstruction, one generation from the war.

All these thoughts came rushing through my head. When the service was over, Tom shook their hands respectfully, even down to the two little girls, and made them welcome. I greeted them, too, my hands in my pockets. Some of the congregation also nodded politely, those that didn't slither out the side door.

The next day I asked Tom about it. His eyes grew hard; his smile flickered like lightning at the edges of his lips. He said our reactions came from fear alone. We were brothers, every one, he said.

I tried to move the discussion to national sovereignty—less threatening perhaps than color lines. I asked if he didn't see the difference between Germans and Italians, or Americans and French. But he only said he didn't, actually, and he felt such thinking immature.

But listen, horses in a field will congregate by blood, and so do people. It's a biological fact. It can't be ignored. You take the colt of a particular mare and put him in a field with other horses, including his half-brothers—offspring of that mare by different stallions—and in all that herd, you'll see the half-brothers move to graze together. They feel comfortable with their own.

Tom had no regard for rules. He had a theory about reaching God by breaking the barriers. He said you do not find IT (that Formless Order) in the known and comfortable, but only in a state of shock. Or pain. In shock the soul leaps up, ecstatic, and only afterwards can you return to stasis and discipline, find God in mankind's tight and ordered law.

But I believe in Form.

The rules are all we've got!

Withoutrulesallthewordsruntogetherhiggledypiggledy. And music without its silences is only noise.

Without rules all drivers would run stop-lights. We'd kill each other. Without rules banks would steal their depositors' money automatically, and gangs of thieves roam wild, slitting throats and filling us with fear. The rules, the law, the structure and discipline, are what create an ethical society. I've based my life on that.

Now Tom was telling me that virtue must come first. Right action develops organically, he said, from right thought. When you're in God, you don't worry about form or virtue. But I say, who knows when he's in God?

Tom had his own ideas of right and wrong. His guilt seemed directed at the feeling of guilt itself, because guilt, he said, or fear, or any feeling except love, separated him from God.

It was bizarre. I've never trusted a man who doesn't feel guilt. Yet here was Tom feeling guilty at feeling guilt.

One day, driving up to the church, he saw Priscilla's stiff back hurrying toward the parish hall. He felt his mouth go dry. Duty lay on her like a weight, and Tom felt he was being pulled down by her chains.

He felt shame at committing adultery, but more at the hardening of his heart that he felt on seeing his wife.

Where was her trumpet-call to simplicity and laughter, he thought, to lightheartedness? She disappeared into the parish hall, shoulders high, one hand pressed to her abdomen just where her belt cinched her carapace in two. Tom drove on, feeling dislike, and guilt for his dislike, and dismay at feeling guilt, and then more guilt at being unloving and therefore separated from his sense of God.

We talked often that summer of the New Church Tom

wanted to build. The old imagery no longer worked, he said. You might have to pull down Christendom itself in order to reach the essence of Christ's openness and joy. I didn't understand one-third of what he said.

I don't want to give the impression he had no emotions, either, no flaring up of indignation, because he did. One night he came to my house, his face drawn. I gave him whiskey. He swallowed it in a gulp and poured himself another. He told me he had just come from the hospital where Pinkie Stephenson was dying of cancer.

"His brother came in while I was there," Tom said. "He lives in Texas now. You know what he said?"

"What?"

"You have sinned." Tom came to his feet like an Old Testament prophet, his hair flying wild. "That's why you have cancer. This cancer is caused by sin."

"Good Lord."

"What kind of talk is that?" cried Tom. "To his own brother, dying. I wanted to throw him out of the room. Instead I stood like an imbecile. I never said a word. The same thing happened last May, when the Gibson boy swallowed a can of Drāno. Remember? He was lying in the hospital, his breathing so labored he could barely bring the next breath to his lungs. His sister and mother came down the hall. They were dressed in silk dresses and stockings, even in that heat, and their white-leather shoulderbags, like twins. And this twit of a girl—do you know her?—she looks at her brother lying on that bed and chirrups: 'Poor Peter, he's going to miss the Kentucky Derby.' I wanted to strike her. Peter died that night. That's the kind of people in this parish."

I tried to comfort him. "What could you have said?"

"Oh, I have things to say. Listen—we are all dying, I could have said. In the blink of God's eye our lives are over. We must use every minute. Christ! If I were good enough, I would write a work that rang out that single message. It would toll like a bell; and people reading it would be so moved that they would turn to one another—people who have been married to each other thirty years, and mothers to daughters, brothers to sisters and fathers to sons, and they'd say, 'Listen, I never told you this before. I've always been afraid. I love you. You have given me so much. In you I meet those parts of myself I otherwise would not have known. You have enriched me.' Oh, if I had the power, each person would turn to another on this earth and say, 'I only came here for an instant of life. Before I go, before you go, I want to tell you thank you for being with me on the journey. I don't know what I would do without you. Thank you.' "

"Yes."

"That's all we have to do. Say *thank you* to one another. *Thank you* to God all day long. Thank you to your enemy even. You don't need to send out prayers to God. You just say thank you for His having answered them."

"Do you say thank you to Priscilla all day long?"

He jerked as if I'd hit him, and stared into his drink. "Yes, I even say thank you to Priscilla," he answered between gritted teeth. "But she can't hear. No. Maybe I don't. Don't joke with me, John. I can't bear what I have seen today."

At the time I couldn't think of anything to say. I didn't think of the right response for months, and by then it was too late. I've said it over and over ever since in my imagination: *You see, you do need rules and form! You lay down rules yourself.*

But by then he had left Naughton. It was too late.

18

He brought up the limericks in church. He told us that we, the congregation, composed the Church. He was not *the* minister, he said, but each of us was a minister ministering to each other, and to any stranger anytime in need; and it was this that composed a Church. He said the poems represented a knife of hatred that would cut us apart. He asked us to pray, and especially for the person circulating the hate mail.

Carolyn stamped out, tossing her head, and Dutton followed two steps behind, staring pensively at the floor. Butch looked pleased as punch: the cat that ate the canary. The rest of us approved or disapproved according to our natures, but all of us discussed it in the sweltering, long afternoon.

Pris was shaking, she was so upset.

"How could you bring that up in church?" she asked as they walked back to the house together from the church. "Such filth should not be mentioned."

"I thought it deserved our prayers."

"And what did you mean," she continued, "standing in the aisle to talk?—not even in the pulpit like a proper preacher. You have no dignity. Like that time last spring—oh, yes, I heard about it, do you think I'm deaf?—when you paced up and down the aisles ranting—*ranting* was the word I heard. What's gotten into you?"

"The Lord perhaps."

"Don't be blasphemous! As if the Lord God would make anyone forget himself in church! That's the very place to re-member the Lord and behave. You know how to perform the service properly. I don't see why you—"

"Why, Priscilla, you're crying." He was concerned.

"Oh, leave me alone! I'm just upset, that's all, and who wouldn't be after what happened today? I don't know what's gotten into you. I don't understand you anymore, not at all." She turned on him, eyes glinting, and her body hunched. "There are others, aren't there? Dozens of others. Who are they? Tell me who they are."

"Priscilla."

"Don't touch me!" she cried. "Filth! Filth! This is all your fault." He was shocked. "Don't you see? It's crawling all around us. I have to wash my hands. I can't bear it. I don't see how you can."

That night he approached her, as he had on other occa-sions, about their lives.

"We could separate," he suggested. "You could live with your mother."

She reacted violently. "How can you think of such a thing? Married people don't live separately. I try to live a godly life. I don't shirk my duty. You'd put away your wife!" Once started, she could hardly stop. Tom suggested that she see a doctor, talk to someone—the Bishop perhaps. He knew she was unhappy. What could he do to ease her mind?

"Unhappy? What do you know of unhappy! I'm fine. It's your soul you should be looking after, not mine." Whatever he said incited her further, and that night he retired to his separate bedroom, touched by her pain. But what could he do? He prayed. The center would not hold, as Yeats said. The worst have most conviction.

Priscilla was ill. Moreover her rigidity was influencing Daphne and little Philip as well. Locked in his own unhappiness, Philip spent hours riding alone on his bicycle. He wanted nothing to do with his parents, the Church, the life they led. He had one friend, Darcy Bird, a boy as thin as a snake with gaunt bones, a thin, sharp nose, and a blond hank of hair falling across one ear. He was the son of a farmhand, common trash. He led Philip to the cow barns, where he talked of which bull inseminated which milk cow best and described in vivid detail the heaving, thunderous meetings of the beasts:

"Onct I saw a bull clapped inside a cow and the cow trotting crost the field, and the bull was running after her on his two hint legs, keeping up and slamming her all the time."

He took Philip in the cold, dark, secret hold underneath the high-standing clapboard house, where the damp smells of earth filled Philip's nostrils and the possibility of feeling a snake or spider under his hand made him cringe. Darcy gave his strangled laugh, the same high-pitched series of swallowed squeaks that drove his teacher mad; and Philip, on his mettle from the dare of that chuckle in his ear, would crawl deeper under the house until he could hear the very heartbeat overhead, the silent sewing of its vibrations into space. Over their heads they could hear the hollow footsteps of Darcy's mother and two older sisters (one of them cross-eyed) and the *chunk-a-chunk* that indicated the deadened rocking of Darcy's grandmother in her chair. The two boys listened, huddling in the dark amongst thick, dusty cobwebs smeared across their faces, avoiding the

corners where they both imagined lurked the nests of snakes—
we had rattlers, cottonmouths in our neck of the woods, though
likely not under the cool, hard dirt of a lived-in house; they lit
a match and by the glow (the sigh of relief: no snake) found
behind the cinder-block foundation of the front steps the small
bag of gold dust that Darcy's father had hidden there. They
pulled it from its hollow in the earth, weighed the cotton bag
in their hands, gauging the weight with glittering distrust; and
licked their lips, whispering of filching it. They could run away
together with the gold dust. They could get to California or
Mexico or New York. Drive eighteen-wheelers across the desert. Drift up to Alaska, thumbs hooked in their belts and their
pockets full of the stuff that makes men fall to their knees.
Replacing the gold dust, they'd crawl out from under the green
lattice skirts of the Baba Yagi house, high on its chicken legs,
and run down past the pigpens to the mushy brown creek, Dead
Run, wading until they'd collected black leeches all over their
legs. Then they'd come into the dry grass (avoiding cow pies)
and with a penknife slit the bloody bellies up. The leeches
would let go. Their legs would be smeared red with the blood
of leeches. Sometimes they pulled down their pants and compared their parts. When Darcy didn't have to work at farm
chores, they rode into town, both boys on the one bike, to
hang out. They broke into the new houses being constructed
on the Joppa Road; and once they broke into Stuart Redmond's
place, looking for liquor. They were run off by the dogs. The
local police watched the boys for some wrong move. So the
summer wore on for Philip, angry and rebellious. He avoided
his father, God's queer minister. For his mother he felt contempt. His sly, cold eyes cut into her offerings: the passing of a
plate of meat, the heaving, breathless laugh forced from her

lungs as she sat proud, the mistress of her table, trying to make small talk. Philip recognized only her cloying sweetness or her manipulative control.

"Dinner at seven, Philip." She would smile and nod, as if dinner had not been served at seven all his life.

Once he said, "I won't be there."

"Of course you will," she answered. "Where else would you be?"

"I've been asked out tonight."

"Where?"

"Darcy Bird's."

His mother smiled over him like a great gangly crane, her black hair sleek as a fish's scales, glimmering with scaly light: "Well, you must tell him you can't come."

"I can't do that!"

"Yes, just telephone."

"They don't have a phone. I'll have to go."

"You didn't check with me first. You know you can't go out until you check with me."

"And if I do, you won't let me go."

"Don't talk back, Philip."

"I'm not talking back. You never let me do anything."

"Go to your room."

"I won't."

"Go to your room, Philip."

He couldn't stand against her. He tried. He hated himself for not winning at the game. He crawled to his room and lay on his bed, despondent in the dark. The Birds would never know why he hadn't come for dinner. They would think that he was rude. He spent less and less time home that summer, though his father tried to talk to him. His father offered to take him swimming at the Seattle Quarry lake—with a friend if he wished—or into town for an ice-cream cone. Philip found those occasions only painful.

"It's hard growing up," his father would say, putting one hand on his shoulder. Sometimes the boy would shrug it off.

"What's wrong, Philip? I wish you'd talk to me."

But Philip pulled away, head down, a turtle sunk into the dark safety of his shell. "Nothing," he said, eyes blank. Nothing, he would tell his father, man of God.

Once he came across his father at Mrs. McEwen's house. He hid in the shrubbery at the roadside and watched his father and the pretty woman standing at the open door. She leaned against the sill, and Philip (crouched watching through the underbrush, one hand on his bicycle in the ditch) saw her pass her hand down her neck, down the open collar of her shirt—then wave away a fly. Tom rested one hand on the doorjamb just beside her head. He was holding the screen door open with his other arm, and they talked, talked, with total concentration. Or did they talk? He couldn't hear their voices. They stared into each other's eyes. Finally she shifted her weight with one fluid movement of her hips, slipped back into the house, and his father followed after, into the dark cool. The screen door slapped behind his heels. Philip waited for a time, but they did not come out again. It was hot beside the road, and dusty in the wake of passing cars. He got on his bike after fifteen minutes and rode down to Darcy's farm, wondering what his father did at work. He knew only the things he'd seen at church—the acolyte duties he'd performed for years, pouring the wine, and lighting and snuffing out candles, carrying the cross and bowing and turning with formality before the dead altars of an Episcopal god. He pedalled, pedalled with the sun in his eyes, the sweat running down his neck and beading his forehead and eyelids; pedalling, pedalling, trying to forget that gesture, her fingers stroking the soft skin of her throat and into the open V of her white shirt.

So the summer wore on. One August day, the heat waves shimmering off the macadam, making mirages on the road, I met Elizabeth as I hurried, head down, past raging jackhammers that tore up the street to put in power lines.

"John, aren't you going to speak?"

I was astonished at the change in her. She had gotten thin, and large blue circles underscored her eyes. But her smile! How can I describe it? She was a rose unfolding. For a moment I had a sense that she was totally complete. We stood on the corner of Madison and Lee, holding hands and shouting above the fury of the hungry drills.

I had not seen her in weeks. I'd heard that Angus was out of Willowhill, and she nodded and shouted confirmation of his new sobriety. He kept to himself, she said, drank quarts of coffee, and went to AA meetings five nights a week.

"He's not drinking," she yelled. "He has support."

"Come on." I took her arm. "I'll buy you an ice-cream soda." We went into Doc's to be slapped by a cold wall of air-conditioning.

"Brrr. I think I prefer it on the street."

"Ninety-eight and rising," I answered. We sat on twirling red stools at the counter. I had a strawberry soda with vanilla ice cream; Lizzie ordered a coffee shake. She had big news:

"I've decided to bring Duncan home."

"Elizabeth, why?" I was shocked. I could only see problems, both for the child and for herself.

"He's my child. He's the only one I'll ever have—"

"You don't know that," I murmured.

"Oh, I'm getting on. I'm middle-aged. If I remarry . . . well, fine." Her voice had a hard edge, more akin to the old Elizabeth I'd known, with her sharp, quick wit.

"What about Tom?"

She smiled and shrugged. "It's not likely anymore. Look, I'm an old woman, almost. I have one retarded child, and if he embarrasses people, that's too bad. I'm not going to hide him anymore. Do you know, I love him. I want to make him well, or if he can't be well, at least give him some taste of life." She told how Tom had accompanied her several times to Briarose, and her admiration for Tom, her delight in seeing Tom walk among the children, touching one, bending to another. He'd picked up Duncan and carried him with him as he inspected the wards and asked questions of nurses and administrative staff. He was organizing a group at Trinity to help Lizzie's volunteers. I'd heard of that, but hadn't reflected on what it meant. Of *course* he'd gone to Briarose! Of *course* he'd talked to Lizzie about her little boy.

"All my life everyone has told me what to do—my mother, my father, my husband. Everyone telling me to move here, dress like that, use this fork, go to that person's party—even telling me to put my child away. Well, I won't do it anymore. I'm responsible for my own actions. As for Dunks, he'll be fine. Just you wait and see. I've found a girl, a niece of Eleanor Lunt, a lovely girl. She's nineteen. She'll come live with me and help with Duncan when I'm not there."

"Are you doing this because of money?"

"Well, sure," she answered with a glowing smile. "Yes, it will be cheaper, but that's only part of it, John. Don't you see? He's my child. I want the privilege of loving him. He's so dear.

John." She touched my arm. "When I go to Briarose, he knows me now."

I was still afraid her motives smacked of sacrifice.

"You're going to earn a living by yourself and take on a handicapped sick child? A little martyrdom?"

"Don't you talk negative to me, John Woods." She tossed her head.

Did I sound negative? I looked over at her, her color high and her fine air, and that delicious, blooming smile. What had Tom given her? A year before, she had been beautiful, but hard and brittle. She'd had courage and high-spirited wit, but now she had some extra quality I can't name. Her hand, resting on the counter, was all bones, her fingers clasping her soda straw.

"You're trembling." The sound of the jackhammer outside the window cut like a chain saw through my flesh.

"I'm cold," she smiled.

"It's cold in here," I agreed, then came to the point: "You've changed." She looked up at me with a sidewise smile, and tossed her head in the old way.

"I know, John. I'm so happy." My thoughts flew to Tom with his magnetic spiritual joy, and here was Lizzie, her strong fingers quivering, her bare arms covered with goosebumps, yet inside firm as an oak. Suddenly I felt alone. Sitting on that stool that my own backside had helped shape for over forty years, sitting at the drugstore counter owned by George Stick, my friend, whom I'd gone to elementary school with, sitting in the town where I'd grown up, and a moment later counting out the sixty cents for sodas, even joshing with Maysie behind the counter about the difference between a nickel and a dime, I felt the cold hand of terror grip my heart. I was alone.

Instantly it was gone. I caught myself on the nasal edge of Maysie's voice. "Y'all come back now." She pulled me up short.

"Abyssinia," I said, my voice this time too loud in my attempt to curb my fear. We stepped into the jackhammer blast of scorching heat.

"Thanks for the milk shake," Lizzie shouted above the din. "Give my love to Margaret and the kids."

She stood on tiptoe to kiss my cheek, and turned away. I stood blinking against the glittering sidewalk on that sticky afternoon. The heat rose shimmering off the street, the air reaching to my knees like the fires of Hell in a medieval print. I could feel the heat burning through the soles of my shoes, licking at the back of my neck. I removed my glasses and wiped my eyes and neck with my handkerchief, polished my lenses and replaced them, tipped down my straw hat—the only shade in sight—and stood a moment squinting against the ferocious light. People jostled me, some hurriedly and others coming by with their hellos:

"John, harr you?"

"Nice to see you." A pat on the arm.

"Hot enough for you?"

I heard them through a tunnel of despair. I was empty, drowning in the meaninglessness of . . . of what? I could not say. Of it all. I barely could attend. Here was Miz Gibson at my elbow, chattering up at me with her buck teeth and shiny black eyes, her handbag tucked against her breast. I had no idea what she had said as she cocked her head, waiting for my reply.

I jerked awake. "I'm sorry, Miz Gibson. I'm afraid this heat. . . ." I stumbled away.

I had the green van that day in town. I remember sitting

in the cab, my forehead beaded with sweat, my shirt stained dark under my armpits. It dawned on me that it was not just heatstroke that was bothering me, but sanity. This flowering was going on all around me, everyone carrying the torch of sweetness and light, and where was I? I was the workhorse carrying all the load. I was the one who had Tom's confession that he had fucked the girl, was practically living with her—and I'd been protecting him. For what? I wasn't sure. All around me people were popping up like wildflowers, glowing. But what did I get out of it? My church defiled. My self-respect destroyed. Tom and Elizabeth bedding down without a grain of guilt. Here was Elizabeth divorcing her husband for Tom, and he with two wives in effect, one to keep his house and kids and one for intellect and sex. I was his donkey-mule, harnessed to the wheel that grinds out grist, grinding, grinding down my hooves in this interminable journey, day on day, and night on night, circling round my stone. I was defending Tom at every turn. I didn't even believe in all his stuff. I didn't like it. Moreover I wasn't getting any. Then sitting in that sweltering, silent cab, parked on a Naughton side street, I felt my eyes burning behind my glasses—I, who hadn't cried since I was eleven years of age and fell off the rope at the Seattle Quarry lake, landing on my back right on a rock. I felt the tears rise up. I swallowed the frog that was leaping in my throat, choking me with memories, because I had done the right thing, hadn't I? I had torn my heart right out of my chest, refused Flossie rather than live in sin. I had turned her down, gulped manfully, and done what needed to be done. And, yes, gone on, reminding myself through gritted teeth that time heals every wound, that one of the gifts of Pandora's box is forgetfulness, and that each passing minute of my life would lessen the hurt, until it never came to mind at all. Do not worry about a misfortune for three years, says the wisdom of the Brahmans, and it will become a blessing. There would come a time (I'd told myself, in those terrible teeth-gnashing times) when I would forget her for days and weeks together, and later months, her laugh not pealing through my mind, her body not lurking in the shadows of my consciousness. There would come a time when I'd not notice loss. So I had comforted myself. And it had happened. Until just now, when I sat in my green van after that ice-cream soda with Tom's mistress and felt the wounds open in my chest. What did I get out of protecting him? The truth was, I was jealous. I said I loved him. Lies, for how could I love someone whom I hated so? There were times when I had deceived myself that he was even a *great* man, a man of exceptional insight and purity, a saint, almost. But that was hogwash. Saints operate out of guilt. Saints are the *last* to think of themselves as pure. Saints know their insignificance before God's grace, acknowledge how un-deserving they are to have received so much as a glimpse of the Holy way. Everyone knows about saints! I wondered how I could have believed Tom's . . . yes, his *arrogance*, his pretty laugh and light soft-shoe: "Who is to say he's not deserving of God's grace?" That's what Tom told me. "If God gives you a peek behind the curtain, into the mysteries of eternity" (that's how he talked right after his epiphany), "then who are you to say God's wrong? Now *that* would be arrogant. 'Hey you, God, I think you're wrong. I don't deserve your grace.' Oh my, dear me, no," Tom had laughed. "Our task is very simple. It's the work of a child. It's simply to say thank you all day long. That's enough. Just joyfully praise God, sing worship to His name, and dance in love, the praises of His holy world."

I admit it: he'd unmanned me with his words. What he

said had nothing to do with the presbyterian *earned* grace that
I'd been taught, that God might come or not but you jolly well
did your duty and *earned* His love. Tom had been saying all
summer that it was enough to sit around and sing. Guileless as
an infant, fearless as a fool. I sat on the hard, green plastic seat
in my truck and sweated. What did he mean, no guilt? By that
standard I could have kept right on with Flossie and had my
pleasure of two women and just sung praises to the Lord!

I drove out to the church. I couldn't get the image of Flossie out of my mind, floating in the August heat, her moist body
steaming in desire for me, and mine for her. I could almost feel
her under my hands in my imagination; my legs twined round
her hips, my lips sucking at her skin, each kiss down her neck
leaving its mark of possession. I kissed her tiny breasts under
my hands. I kissed each foot, each fingernail. I drove my tongue
into the tender cleavage of her eyelids, and my mouth embraced her gullet, until her neck arched under my desire, her
head thrown back in partial and delicious panic at the threat
to the jugular, all vulnerable, all exposed, I—ah! then I would
be deep inside her, driving home first with long, slow, then
increasingly quick stabs; she moaning under my hands, under
my lips, my tongue, the scorching kiss of fingers on her flesh.
In the van in my imagination.

The limericks were right and Tom was right. Take it. Gulp
what you can of God's green paradise, where the coupling of
bodies constitutes the best and maybe only union we can know.
Did Tom say that? Or did I twist his words? I loathed the man
who—who what? It was all confusion and contradictions: who
had given Elizabeth that look, who denied that look to me,
who threw my life, my values, in my face—who left me thinking
I had thrown away—what? I didn't know.

I took the parish-hall steps two at a time, the sweat gleaming on my skin, my shirt soaked dark. I was babbling in my despair. I wouldn't mention Flossie, but I would tell him—I didn't know what! I burst into his office.

He was leaning against the window, his forehead pressed against the glass, then turned as I barged into the room.

"Oh," he said, as if disappointed. "It's you."

His eyes were hollow. Dead.

I was brought up short.

"The Bishop called," he said after a moment, and his voice was so low I had to strain to hear. "He's decided to take me to trial."

"To trial?"

"I'm being tried in ecclesiastical court."

I turned away to hide my righteous joy.

19

I can't write anymore. Days pass and I can't attack the last part of this story. I know why. I don't want to face Flossie again. Or my sins.

Margaret knows I've stopped. She watches me with sharp, darting glances out of the corners of her eyes, and I have come to hate her too.

I take long, solitary walks. The exercise clears my head, relieves my rage. I walk for miles and come back worn-out and limp. I feel old. Then I sleep. I realize I'm not being nice to Margaret. My voice is too hearty, my optimism forced.

We're making plans to go to Hawaii next February. It was Margaret's idea. "I think we ought to get away," she said, after one of her excursions downtown, and she pulled a stack of travel folders from her purse and dropped them on my desk. So I've been reading about Hawaii and Pele, the goddess of fire, who got in a fight with her sister goddess, the sea. Pele spewed out her anger in a volcano that rose above the ocean, making land. But her furious sister retaliated with tidal waves that swept the land away. Again and again Pele built islands, and each time the sea destroyed them. That's the Hawaiian legend. Now Pele is still alive, rumbling on the big island of

Hawaii in the volcanos of Mauna Loa and Kilauea, vomiting molten lava from the center of the earth, building up land to fight the sea. . . .

Last night I dreamt about Flossie again, only this time she came as Pele, and her red hair flowed like fire round her face, and from her mouth came flames.

The trial was set for October 15. From August 29, when Tom received the registered letter announcing that a trial would begin in six weeks—from that instant he was suspended from his duties.

The charge was disobedience to the Bishop.

The whole Valley buzzed with confusion, horror, delight. Nothing like this had ever happened in Naughton before. Phones were ringing and people dropping in on one another to relay the news and talk it out, which is how we adjust to change.

For Priscilla it was scandalous that Tom should be charged before the Bishop. Suspended from her church.

"How could you do this to me?" she cried at dinner the night the letter came. "It's not enough that you embarrass me with your queer ways—laughing out loud in church, touching people with your hands—you think I don't see? Shame!" Her voice, charged with emotion, reached toward a whispered scream. Philip sank lower in his chair, kicking the slats, his eyes closed, his thin lips quivering. Daphne was out that evening, as she usually was. "Even the Bishop . . . I'll never raise my head."

"Priscilla!" He threw his napkin on the table. "I'll not have you talk like that."

"Not have it. I won't have it! Why don't you change? That's all you need to do. Or apologize to Bishop Crowley. You *want* a trial. A public display—I can't bear it!"

"Philip, go," said his father in an undertone. "Duck out of here." Philip shot from his chair as his mother's voice lifted behind him—

"Don't you leave this room! Dinner's not over. You can't."

The door cut her short, and Philip ran, ran down the drive to his bike and pedalled and pedalled to the weird protection of Darcy Bird.

In the dining room Priscilla's eyes glowed with hatred. "You had no right to send him away. It's one more way you undercut authority. He has to eat his dinner."

"Priscilla," said Tom. "I want you to leave Naughton, at least for the duration of the hearing. And after that . . . well, we can talk then."

"Go away? Leave my husband in his difficulty?"

"Yes. There's nothing you can do. I don't want you to be hurt. Take Philip with you. He shouldn't have to undergo this at his age."

"And where would I go? You'd just turn me out? Just *go?*"

"You'd go to your mother's. You don't have to stay here, Pris. You're not happy here."

"Happy! Life's not for happiness. I do my duty—which is more than you know how to do—my duty to my God and Church. I try to remember who I am and stay unstained. You don't know the meaning of the word. Filth! Filth hangs over you, and now you drag us into public trial. Why? To test your will? You are the devil himself. The Anti-Christ, set against the Bishop's word."

"Woman, leave me alone!" he roared. "What can I do to get rid of you?"

"Get rid of me? Oh, you'd like that, I know. Cast off your wife when she gets old. I've served you all my years. I've borne your children. Now you'd cast me off, in poverty, old and ugly."

He squirmed in torment.

"You want some younger girl. Don't think I don't know! I see through you. You love the way they look at you, adoringly, all these women, but your thoughts are filth. I see you with Natalie Williams, leading her on. Or Mimi Foster, or that girl in the choir, or pretty Elizabeth McEwen."

"Enough!" He grabbed her wrist. "We shall separate. You're going to your mother's. I'll telephone your mother now and make arrangements," he said. "Daphne will be back in school. Philip can go with you for the duration of the hearing. But no matter what, when we divorce, I want Philip back."

Later, when it was all over, Tom dreamed another solution for Priscilla, had he only thought of it: Pris in a convent. He knew of one up in New York State. Imagine if she had gone to that gentle spiritual retreat surrounded by the orderliness of silent women praying from four-thirty in the morning until ten o'clock at night, moving in silence, eating in calm. What if he had gone to the Bishop months earlier? She respected Crowley. What if the Bishop had asked her to enter and pray for Naughton and Trinity Church, because her prayers were needed? Would she have gone? Tom wondered.

The next morning Margaret drove up to the rectory.

"I've just heard the news," she said, touching Priscilla's cold, white arm. "If there's anything we can do. . . ."

"What news?" A shock ran through her. Did the whole Valley know that Tom had cast her out?

"About you all, Tom," Margaret blundered on, meaning Tom's suspension, nothing more, and the date now set for the trial. "John told me. I came as soon as I could. Because it's going to be hard, and I want you to know that we're with you. If you need a place to stay, Priscilla, you can come to us. I want you to know you have friends. We have plenty of room. You can all stay with us."

"Philip too? And Daphne?"

"Of course."

Priscilla's black eyes glittered. Her quick mind snapped the offer up. An alligator's jaw could not clamp shut so fast.

"No, no," she answered with an awful grin. "You're so kind. Thank you, but there's a lot to discuss still. . . ."

"Priscilla, a trial is serious. You'll need your friends. Don't turn your back on us."

"A trial?" Her voice shook. It was Margaret's turn to be surprised.

"Well, the hearing, I mean, Tom's hearing before the Bishop. Priscilla, don't look at me like that. You act as if you haven't heard."

"Of course I've heard. Tom and I were just discussing it." Her voice was shrill.

"Priscilla, oh, honey, what have I done?"

Two tears rolled from Priscilla's immobile face. Stolid as marble, she accepted Margaret's embrace. Suddenly she turned on Margaret:

"What did he do? What's he on trial for?"

Margaret was stunned. "Oh, honey, don't you know?"

Pris grabbed her wrist. She bent down, black eyes boring into Margaret's. "Tell me. You have to tell me now."

"It's for refusing to resign when the Bishop ordered it."

"It's for sex," Priscilla whispered. "It's for the darkness closing in on us, and evil thoughts, and pain. Did you see the poems? Vile! Vile! Sacrilege and blasphemy! How can we live?"

"Priscilla."

"Don't touch me." She pulled back. "I want to be alone."

She straightened, one hand smoothing her hair. "You know, I won't let him touch me. I save myself for Christ. I would not fornicate in the shadow of the ch—" And then, instantly, she was formal as a tea party: "Thank you, Margaret, for coming over. I'd like to be alone now, please."

"Oh, Pris, what have I done? I came over to offer you help. I feel I've only made things worse."

Priscilla smiled her stiff, masked grin. "Not at all. Don't be silly."

"You're not alone in Naughton," said Margaret weakly. But the more she talked, the more removed Priscilla grew. "I'm so sorry," she finished lamely. She tried to embrace her at the door, succeeding in throwing a clumsy arm around Priscilla's rigid back, a lamentable kiss to her rejecting cheek. Priscilla stood at the door, imperturbable, watching her drive away, and Margaret felt so bad about the encounter that she almost went back. She did not. Pris was an acquaintance, no true friend.

And now we can imagine Priscilla left alone. It was eleven A.M. on a lovely summer day, and already the temperature in the nineties. She stood in the living room, and her hands began to shake. It was hot in the house. Her teeth were chattering; her body was racked with shuddering. The heat broke over her, producing a fine beading on her upper lip, and then like diamonds on her arms and shoulders, all across her skin. Which was worse? The filth and desecration? Or excommunication for his sins? How hot it was.

She unzipped her dress.

Philip was away at the time, as he usually was. She unbuckled her girdle and stripped off her terrible hot stockings. Daphne was in her room upstairs. She paid no attention to her mother's day. So it was natural that no one noticed, when

Priscilla floated out the door, her slip trailing in one hand behind her. Her feet were bare, as were her breasts, her buttocks.
She stood stark naked, and as she crossed the threshold (the
screen door's *slap*), the nylon slip dropped from her fingers to
the grass, billowing slightly in its gentle, parachuted fall. Her
head was high, her barren smile sliced hard across her face,
stretched by the black hair still drawn into a bun. She took a
few steps down the drive, stopped, sighed, turned as if to sit a
moment on a rock, then stood again. Her arms lifted to the
pins in her hair. She removed them with slow, dreamy gestures,
captured from the cobwebs of her practiced years, until her hair
loosened, black as soot across her shoulders, hanging dry and
limply toward her full breasts. The pins fell to the grass. Listlessly
she wandered across the field. Naked she was under a cornflower
sky; her eyes, unfocused, settled idly on the Queen Anne's lace
just coming up, on field daisies in the grass. She did not pause to
pick them, but moved on toward the center of the field, then
stopped. The stubble hurt her feet. She could not remember where
she was going or why she had come. Her fingers plucked at the
long stems of unmown grass. Then she threw back her head, as-
serted herself again, and with her proud, fixed smile at the humming summer world, set out again on the brave journey of her life.

It was Natalie who spotted her from her window. She
thought she was seeing things. She flew to the window. Yes,
Priscilla, naked as the moon and coming toward the church.

She screamed. And Tom, in his office, leapt to his feet in
fear, running to her assistance. "Mr. Buckford, look!"

So Priscilla was in an asylum then, and Tom on trial. Philip
was sent to his grandmother's in Chicago, and Daphne was
back in boarding school, laughing too brightly, pretending there

was nothing wrong. Curious. You'd think a revelation would unite, not tear a family apart. Duncan was living with his mother, but Angus had gone to Reno for a divorce.

Tom was suspended, but he met his supporters in the churchyard or at his own house or in the meadow up above the church. He preached to them as if he had the right. He prayed. I know he did healings, with laying-on of hands, and once (dear Lord!) he celebrated the Holy Eucharist in the meadow, at the grove where he and Lizzie used to meet. He celebrated the Eucharist without the Bishop's authority, using pieces of French bread and Gallo jug wine. And people took it. They came to hear him preach and went home moved to tears and moved also to his defense—which created further fights.

Tom said all things worked to the good. The trial gave the lie to that, for here was brother against brother and father against son. What could it mean that out of goodness, God-ness, his vision of a finer realm—what did it mean that out of this could come such discord? At those sermons in the hills he did not mention the coming trial, or his personal suffering, or the attacks on him. Instead, he talked about people caring for one another, forgetting, forgiving. He talked about trusting a beneficent Source. He held out, again and again, his vision of an evolution of the species, in which no one would worship or fear God the judge, or believe in God by faith, or look up awestruck to Christ as unattainable glory, but instead we would *become* like God, each one of us touched by the God inside. Light of the World. That was our destiny, he said. And he said that already we each caught occasional quick glimpses of this loving God-ness in ourselves. We held it for brief moments, and our task was to extend these into longer and longer inter- vals, until we existed only in that Light. Light of the World.

He said we were creating God, that God was evolving, too, and needed us.

He preached all that, while horror, violence rose around us. Did he know what he was doing? Why didn't he just go away when asked to? Run away with Elizabeth? He was so stubborn. I think he would have openly laid claim to their relationship, moved in with her publicly, except she wouldn't let him.

They argued. They fought. They felt they were being wrenched apart.

"Worst-case scenario: You're excommunicated," Lizzie teased one day. "Then we'll run away and elope." She laughed, yet she knew his reputation was at stake, and somehow his identity. He intended to fight the charge . . . and win. She wasn't sure she understood just why. Nonetheless she stood fiercely by his side.

It was Elizabeth who found him his defense attorney, George Tooey, one of the sharpest intellects in Virginia and, ironically, an atheist. But I'm ahead of myself again. There are a few domestic scenes with Lizzie and Duncan and Carolyn to play out before the final act.

Once Duncan had come home, he followed his mother with his eyes. He tried to pull himself after her on unsteady legs. He burst into tears when she left the room, and when she picked him up, he reached out for her hair, grasping it with unsteady, tender hands. He was crippled and retarded, yet he was so innocent! Already the sunlight streaming into his room, and the cat who stretched and yawned on his bed, whose fur he loved to touch and whose dignified removal, tail high, he strained to follow, were having their effect on him. His skin looked healthier. His eyes could focus for short periods, and by struggling after the cat his muscles seemed to be taking on new tone.

Carolyn, of course, was scornful of the whole, appalling experiment. "What will people think?" she said.

And then she said: "You're so stupid, Elizabeth. You never think of anyone but yourself."

And then she said: "At *least* get some decent help. Would you like me to loan you Mary or Bermuda once a week? They won't charge you much."

I was there one day when Carolyn brought little Duncan a present. "Here." She thrust a brown paper bag into her daughter's hands. "This is for Duncan. Since you've insisted on bringing him home, I suppose he can use this. I didn't get a big one because it would only be a waste of money. He's never seen a big one anyway, so he wouldn't know the difference."

Carolyn's gifts were usually wrapped in thorns.

"You give it to him," said Elizabeth. "It's your present."

Carolyn awkwardly pushed it at the child, and then the two of them tore off the wrapping paper, Duncan with increasing excitement and shrieks of laughter at the game. It was a polar bear, its hands and feet stuck out at rigid right angles from its body. Carolyn was satisfied with the child's delight.

"Now, don't let him do whatever he wants with it." She cut off Elizabeth's thanks. "It cost money. You'll notice it's washable. There was another, nicer bear, but it was the kind you can't wash, and that's no bargain."

Carolyn, in fact, dropped over frequently. "He is my grandchild, after all," she said. She liked to tell Lizzie how to raise the child and how she was doing it wrong.

It was one more strain on Elizabeth, who tried to maintain a determined cheer. In actuality she was scared. Duncan was more work than she had anticipated, and the nineteen-year-old baby-sitter, Eleanor Lunt's niece, less helpful and certainly less

experienced than she had implied. All summer Elizabeth had
nudged away her worries about money: that she couldn't earn
money without a college degree, but couldn't go to college
without money. She hated herself for having wasted the years
of her marriage, when she could have finished her schooling.
She scolded herself, lashed out at Duncan, burst into tears. She
could not sleep. She woke up in the middle of the night and
lay awake fearfully, forgetting to pray. Or she turned on the
light and tried to read. She didn't have Tom's faith.

Meanwhile she couldn't eat. Food nauseated her. She was
growing thinner. She knew poor nutrition accounted for her
irritability, but, when she tried to cook or plan a meal, her
stomach heaved. She would choke down half a sweet potato
for dinner, or a tomato and part of an ear of corn. At breakfast
she would force herself to chew a piece of toast as dry as cotton
in her mouth. HALT: Hungry, Angry, Lonely, Tired. That was
the AA acronym she had learned from Angus, the four Horse-
men who swept the alcoholic to the bottle. HALT. Alcoholics
were taught to search their emotions and, if they found one of
the four, to do something about it. She had all four. If she were
not so tired, she could handle her loneliness. If she were not
so angry, she could eat. If she could eat, she would not feel so
tired. It flowed in circles. If she were not lonely, she could draw
on an inner calm. But she found herself surrounded all day at
the shop with people, yet drained by their superficial talk.

Then there was Carolyn. Ever since she had surprised the
two together, Carolyn had known of Lizzie's affair.

"I don't know why *I* should feel guilty," she confessed to
me. "*He's* the one who's in the wrong."

"Have you told Elizabeth you're masterminding his disgrace?"

She gave me a scathing look. "Everyone's being subpoenaed. I suppose I will be too. *Then* what do I say, with Lizzie looking on? A child has *no* idea what influence she has over a mother—a parent, I should say. We're just at the mercy of our children's opinion. Don't you find that, John? I don't remember it with my mother and father, but people were stricter then, I think. Well, I had nurses and governesses. I suppose that makes a difference."

"So what are you going to say?" I brought her back to the subject. "When you're on the stand?"

"Oh, I have no idea, but I'm good on my feet. I'll manage. The thing I worry about is Lizzie. Whatever will happen if she's subpoenaed? She hasn't the brains of a goose. She looks awful, have you noticed? She's just a bag of antlers. It's taking care of that sweet boy. She never thinks of herself. I wouldn't be surprised if she collapsed on the stand. The strain could be too much for her. What if she says the wrong thing? That's what I worry about. She could hurt the reputation of the whole family."

"There's nothing I can do about it, Carolyn."

"Well, you're on the vestry."

"I'm not in charge of these proceedings. I have no influence at all."

But Carolyn's mind could not rest. A few days later she approached me again.

"I've told Lizzie she should go away. 'You look awful,' I said. 'You need a rest.' "

"What did she say?"

" 'Keep your money,' she said. Very haughty, my daughter. 'I intend to stay.' "

" 'You're such a mule,' " I told her. And then I said—

cunningly, don't you think?—I said, 'John is afraid for Tom Buckford if you stay.' "

"Oh, you brought me into it?"

"It got her attention. She wheeled around. 'What do you mean?'

" 'You should think about Tom Buckford,' I said. 'He'll be looking over his shoulder all throughout the trial to see how you react. If you cared one jot for him. . . .' Then, just dropping an idea into her ear, but it was true, I said I'd read about a doctor at Johns Hopkins up in Baltimore who specializes in rebuilding the inner ear. 'I wonder if Dunks could hear if he were operated on?' "

"Do you think that's possible?" I asked.

"John, I just want her out of Naughton for this trial."

Still, Elizabeth wouldn't leave. And so we waited for the proceedings to begin.

One day Carolyn arrived at the gatehouse waving a letter and breathless with her news. "Elizabeth, I've been subpoenaed for the trial. I'm supposed to give evidence."

Elizabeth tore the paper from her mother's hands. "What for? What are you supposed to say?"

"I have no idea," she answered guiltily. "Did you receive a notice?" She felt a wave of relief at the shake of Lizzie's head.

But the next day Elizabeth received a notice too. The congregation at large had been asked to write the Bishop with their opinions and information on Tom; and some wrote in support, and others in opposition; but we who were involved were asked to testify in person, including Mimi and Margaret and Natalie and General Shriver and Emily and myself.

20

MARGARET WANDERED BY JUST NOW, LANKY, A LITTLE AWKWARD
since her hip operation two years ago. She was wiping her hands
on a dish towel. "Where are you in it now?" Sometimes she re-
minds me of pieces of the story. "Don't leave out Duncan," she
said at dinner last week (which is why I remembered that part). Or
she'll pop out unexpectedly with a remark: "Do you think Elizabeth let him down?" She doesn't know about the Judas Iscariot.

I write now in red ballpoint, my Waterman having broken
months ago, and sometimes I try an osmiroid, which leaks black
ink on my fingers. My second finger has grown a knot on the
joint. The pages rise several inches high on the left-hand corner
of my desk, weighted with a black rock cut by a white-quartz
vein. Is there anyone alive who will want to read this? I write
it for myself. It started as an amusement; it has become the
monkey on my back. Who was it who said, "We write to discover ourselves"? I write to discover Tom.

When I look back over the events of that year, I can see
Tom pushed us to the trial. No one wanted it. Bishop Crowley
refused even to dignify the occasion with the title "trial." It
was a *hearing*, he declared. "We do not have trials in the Episcopal church."

Nevertheless we all knew it was a trial. We called it a heresy trial, for trial it was and the cause was heresy. There were lawyers for the prosecution and the defense, an order of procedure, a jury of five clergy, and the Bishop acting as president of the court. There were the finest minds in the Virginia presbytery, a recording clerk and all the rules of law, presented with the ecclesiastical splendor of black robes and purple shawls and white lace. The proceedings were held in Trinity Church itself, before the altar. Imagine the pulpit pushed back and the two banks of choir stalls removed, so that the entire chancel— the area before the altar—was free, and here on the crimson rug stood a library table spread with green baize, and the green covered with papers. At one end you saw the bishop's high, curved throne, a monster of black wood, the seat softened with scarlet cushions we'd brought in. It was red and green, the colors of Christmas, in the church, and heads were bent over pencils, scribbling, and faces contorted with their efforts at wisdom, and the long silences, and the rustling of papers and whispering of legal counsel and shuffling and dry coughs, while the pews were packed with those of us who had tickets for the show.

The canons prescribe no procedure for a trial. We had no precedent. The Bishop, therefore, acting as president of the court, made certain arbitrary decisions. He followed Virginia common law. The fingers of the court stenographer flew over the keys of his little black box. In a general way, the Bishop had chosen the proceedings of the lower civil court, but he bent the rules, and testimony was very free, for, as Dick Crowley kept reminding us, the audience, seated watching in the pews, this was *not* a trial. He could have saved his wind.

How hard it is to write of this. My mind keeps leaping ahead. I want to run away from my memories. I see the whole without chronology, like a painting in which you take in all the parts at once; and already I see parts I've left out.

The trial began, and suddenly the Valley erupted with violent acts.

Nothing was going as it used to, and all tranquillity was gone. People took sides about the coming trial and came almost to blows, literally fighting at their dinner tables over the rector's innocence or guilt. One teller at the Farmer's and Mechanic's Bank ran away with funds; and the streets were filled with strangers window-shopping as if they'd never seen clean towels and china displayed, or nice restaurants where people sit down with table mats and plastic flowers in milk-glass vases. When the trial started, it got worse, and you could hardly walk in comfort for the people on the streets.

It was the farmers, those wall-eyed, slack-jawed, t'backer-spitting backwoods poor white trash who had received Tom with the Amens and Alleluias that the Messiah might expect, who turned on him most viciously. Once the trial began, a handful gathered outside the church door, shouting and shaking their fists at almost anyone; and the sight of Tom escorted by a bodyguard loosed bloodcurdling yells. Some of the women carried signs—SATAN'S PREACHER or GLORY TO GOD—and one, more educated than the rest, held her placard—IMPEACH THE PREACH—up to one of the glass windows of the church, until the Bishop, who sat as the presiding judge, ordered that sheets of plywood be placed to cover the glass of the two lower windows.

Once, the noise outside grew so loud that the Bishop ordered everyone back beyond the churchyard gate; and then two men went outside, and, with the help of the sheriff's boys—big, burly men—they scattered them. They flew up, squawking like crows, flapping their coats and complaining. During the trial one threw a stone through an upper window, shattering the glass on screaming viewers, and stopped the trial outright. One man caught splinters in his eye and was rushed, bleeding, to the hospital, where, despite an operation, he lost partial sight. Then there was true blood on the pew cushions and on the floor, mingling with the blood-red stained-glass light; we crunched the broken glass beneath our shoes.

Imagine our church a court. Each morning the participants entered in parade—a stately, ragged ceremony filing up the aisle. In the background, we could hear the smothered noise of those outside, and, when the door opened, the voices cut in sharp and clear as the October cold, and then were shut off with a bang and muffled again.

First you saw five working priests enter from the sacristy and take their seats, black cassocks somber against the wall. And also from the sacristy the court stenographer slipped in and various bailiffs and court officers, but these were hardly noticed, for at the same time up the main aisle, heels hard on the bricks, came the main processional—the actors in our drama—and heads turned, necks craned, and hats bobbed among the audience. Here came the gray-suited legal consultant to the court and behind him three assistants, equally discreetly dressed, briefcases beneath their arms, their actions full of business and self-importance and their eyes flickering around the arches of this curious courtroom. They took seats at the green-baize table, whispering among themselves or passing papers back and forth—to what purpose no one could guess. But not all of us were watching anymore, for just on their heels, their entry trumpeted by another burst of sharp, high noise, swept in two favorites of our bishop—Graham Eric, the prosecuting attorney, blond and handsome and somewhat effeminate—and with him

another aide, Bo Zimmer, each in formal dress, their skirts
swishing at their heels, the eyes of the one lowered and of the
other raised to the carved altar behind the courtroom decor.
Just behind them came the Bishop himself, stepping up the aisle
in violet and black, with a touch of lace at throat and wrists.
His long skirts likewise brushed his shiny shoes, and his hands,
too, were folded before him in devotion. The public rose in
military waves on sight of him.

Then we saw that somehow Tom had sneaked in unnoticed
from the sacristy or some side door and stood at his seat, half-
hidden behind the lawyers. Only once, the first day of the trial,
did he come in like the others by the front door, pushing
through the throng outside, and with his lawyer walked the
length of that long brick aisle. Shocked he was, humiliated by
our eyes that noted his business suit—defrocked already. We
murmured to ourselves, a ripple running up and down the pews
as he hurried, head forward, shoulders hunched, as if to push
away the air. His face was drawn, lips taut. He felt the Bishop
had played a trick on him, to make him enter like that, like a
circus clown, and march exposed, alongside Tooey and behind
the prosecutors for the court. After that he never entered from
the rear, but managed somehow to come in from the altar. I
tried but never once saw him enter. Suddenly I would find he
had already arrived, sitting slumped in his chair, his chin on
his clasped hands, eyes closed, blocking out the whole. He was
always there by the time the Bishop arrived, and he stood with
the rest as Dick Crowley paced up the aisle, nodded to prosecution and defense, to us the audience, then paused before his
throne.

Crowley's first act every morning was to stand quietly till
not a sound could be heard, not a cough, not the rustle of a

coat or the shuffle of a shoe against the brick. Mind, you could hear a pin drop in that church; but from outside came the smoldering bee-hum of the little pack and the whistle of the October wind that whipped the autumn leaves—a fury of flame against the hard blue sky. When we stood in utter silence, Bishop Crowley said:

"Let us pray."

Each day he opened with a prayer for insight, justice, guidance, and an understanding heart, and each morning he charged us with the same directions on how he expected us to behave. He used terms reversible as raincoats, such as *reverent solemnity* or *solemn reverence.* We craned to see Tom in his chair, and if he straightened with interest or leaned over to whisper to his lawyer or write a note on his yellow legal pad—if he made any move—a stir ran through the church. It happened in the first hours of the trial, when Tom stood at his place, responding to the charge. His face was set, his eyes hollow. I couldn't see, but his lawyer, George Tooey, said he was gripping the back of his chair so hard that his knuckles went white.

It was George who came up with Tom's defense. "I stand on my conscience," he'd say. "My conscience is my guide." Some people thought it demonstrated weakness, and others that it cleverly undercut the prosecution, because a priest is *supposed* to stand on his conscience.

Graham Eric, speaking for the Council, read the charges in a loud, clear voice. They were cautious constructions of the canon law.

"Holding and teaching publicly and privately any doctrine contrary to that held by the Church."

Tom's head came up. "I have stood on my conscience," he said.

"Violation of the rubrics of the Book of Common Prayer."

There was the slightest pause. Tom looked over our heads, seeing God knows what. "I have acted upon my conscience."

"Refusal to heed the godly admonitions of the Bishop," read Eric, "which is a violation of the ordination vows."

Again there came that fragile, breathless pause. Tom's voice shook, but still it carried his special music and conviction.

"I stand upon my conscience."

Outside, the wind whispered, wuthering through the gutters.

Had he answered "Guilty" to any of the charges, there would have been no trial, the court moving instantly to punishment. Had he answered "Not guilty," the prosecution would have had to prove that he behaved as the Council charged. But he denied nothing. Instead he called on a higher authority than a bishop's—his own conscience or the word of God. A plea of Not Guilty was entered for each charge. The trial began.

The court could talk of disobedience to the Bishop or changing holy services, ignoring the rubrics or directions. But we knew his sin. He'd offended us. He was on trial for defiling all we held precious, for seeding doubt and conflict in our midst; and the people gathering at the Trinity doors attested to that offense.

The first day of the trial was Tom's. After the charges were read, he sat down.

Eric rose and motioned to him: "Now, you may make a statement, answer the charges."

Tom was taken by surprise.

"Before you call the witnesses? Before I hear an accusation?"

George Tooey came to his feet to object. The Bishop waved him down with a languid hand and then slumped back in his chair, listening, eyes half-closed and hands folded on his stomach judiciously. It was against the rules of law and took Tom by surprise, but he rose to comply, unprepared.

"I don't know what to say," he began, stuttering. "I don't know the specifics of the case. But—but I came here just about a year ago, called by the parish, to preach and teach, and also with the direct assignment to strengthen Trinity, bring it alive, to add new members and interest—"

"Well, he's certainly done that!" Margaret murmured beside me with a laugh.

"—because the church was dying. It was financially unstable. I know I made mistakes, and enemies. I apologize for that, but whatever I did was with good intentions, praying for direction."

He looked at George Tooey helplessly, then stared a moment at his feet before continuing, talking to the Bishop now as intimately as if only the two of them were in the room.

"I know nothing of teaching and preaching doctrines contrary to the Church. I have only said what I have seen.

"I know nothing about violations to the rubrics and prayers.

"But, yes, I have refused to resign. What I am being tried for today has nothing to do with these charges. This hearing is about offending people, calling their prejudices into question, teaching the Word of God. And, yes, God's word is dangerous."

The rest of the day, Tom was cross-examined about his life, marriage, schooling, work in former parishes, his studies, and the formation of his ideas. It was difficult for him. Questioned *before* the accusing witnesses, he could not tailor his remarks. He was walking across a mine field.

Eric skipped over the first charge—concerning Christian dogma—because it was too big a subject; and he skipped the second—violations of the rubric, as too petty. They were in-

cluded as charges anyway, not because the Council thought
they were important in themselves but because they were
needed as reasons for demanding Tom's resignation.

"Do you remember your studies in seminary?"

"Well, yes. It was some time ago, but yes."

"Can you name the courses you took, what books you
read?"

At first we didn't understand the logic of his questioning.
Then it became clear that Graham Eric was leading up to Tom's
revelation.

"And did you read the Christian mystics in seminary?"

"No."

"Or on your own perhaps? Out of curiosity? The works of
Saint Theresa, Saint John of the Cross, Meister Eckhart?"

"No. Not till just this year."

"This year?" Eric, pacing, paused with interest. "When
this year?"

"After my own . . . epiphany."

"Ah, yes," he said as if he had forgotten that landmark
moment entirely. He laced his hands behind his back and took
a turn around the chancel before returning brightly to the witness chair.

"But since then you've read them?"

"Yes."

"Tell us about your revelation, would you? In your own
words, what happened?"

When Tom said nothing, he prodded: "It was on the
twenty-ninth of March, wasn't it? Of this year?"

George Tooey made an objection—that the story was fully
outlined in the written documents submitted to the court; but
the Bishop overrode him; and then Tom also spoke up, stum-

blingly, saying that these were sacred and holy matters, which
he felt uncomfortable disclosing in this way before an un-
friendly and judging group. But the Bishop chastised him for
his fear, saying we were in the court of God. So the story was
forced out of Tom, pulled word by word, with prompting and
reminders from the court, while Tooey, the defense attorney
who should have been protecting him, lay back in his chair,
eyes closed, hands folded, to all appearances asleep.

It was the story I told earlier. And when he came to the
part about the cross—manure filling the silver salver with God's
dirt—Tom went silent, hung his head, and made no more answers, although he did admit that, yes, he had crawled to Emily
and kissed the earth before her and her feet.

Then came Eric's barrage of questioning.

"Does it seem curious that you never mention Christ?"

"How do you know it was a vision from God? How do you
know it was not from some other power?"

"Has it ever occurred to you that you might be insane?"

"Isn't it true, Mr. Buckford, that chemicals and drugs create similar hallucinations? Isn't it true that schizophrenics think
they talk to God?"

"Are people who see visions more godly than others?"

"Are those who haven't had a revelation less decent Christians?"

"Why were you chosen, do you think?"

"Your Grace," said Eric, addressing the Bishop, "I would
like to put into the record at this time the following documents." And he handed over several pages to the recording
clerk.

"Your Grace, we do not deny that the grace of God may
manifest itself in visions and revelations. This belief is a sacred

tenet of the Church and has been proven in the lives of many saints. Neither is anything Mr. Buckford saw in contradiction to these other visions. These documents, however, demonstrate a discrepancy in the story. When God appears, it is to the inner eye alone, and while the soul is soaring in limitless space, the body is paralyzed. It cannot move. Only when the visionary is coming out of the trance does he regain possession of his limbs, and to engage in any physical activity before that point is nearly impossible.''

He then read into the record various excerpts from the writings of saints.

"So the question is," cried Eric, "was it a true vision of God? Or not? And if so, are his subsequent acts and disobedience justified?"

A murmuring erupted in the pews. The Bishop had to gavel for silence. By then it was lunchtime and we had a few hours off before Tom took the stand again; so everyone filed out, talking and arguing over what had been said and what direction Eric and the Bishop were taking and how Tom had done, and some of the more lighthearted blades began to lay bets, as if it were a steeplechase they were watching and not a trial with the reputation and livelihood of a man and his family at stake.

After lunch we came back. I was interested to note that we all took the same seats—man, the territorial animal. I also noticed that we were divided according to our views—like the groom's and bride's sides at a wedding: those favoring the Bishop's prosecution sat in the left-hand pews, and those favoring Tom, on the right; and every seat was taken. Even the old choir loft—which had once been a slave gallery and which could not be reached since a fire destroyed the stairs—the choir loft was also full. Some genius had brought in a ladder to reach the rotting seats above. And people outside the church were pushing to get in, if anyone inside had to leave for any reason. Elizabeth, I should add, sat with Margaret and me, but her mother, Carolyn, sat disdainfully on the left-hand side. In the next days Dutton sometimes came for a few hours and sometimes not, but Carolyn and Elizabeth weren't speaking at all by then, and Carolyn was unwelcome in her daughter's house.

After lunch Graham Eric read various passages from the life of Saint Theresa on obedience, including:

> During this first stage, we have to go slowly and to be guided by the discretion and opinion of our director . . . we must always keep humility before us.

And also:

> My fear increased, to such an extent that it made me seek diligently after spiritual persons with whom to discuss this.

"After your . . . epiphany, Mr. Buckford, did you tell the Bishop what you had seen?"

"No."

"Did you tell another priest?"

"No."

"Did you confide in anyone?"

Tom flushed. "I told a lot of people."

"But not to check it out for accuracy, did you? Or to see if it conformed to church doctrine? . . . Wasn't that arrogant of you, Mr. Buckford, given that even the great saints admonish caution in that regard?''

Tom said nothing.

"I think it was arrogant. Self-important," Eric said. Then pacing to the table, he rested one hip on the edge of the green baize and held up two books: "These are from your library, aren't they? Do you recognize them?" He leafed through one.

"This book is underlined and marked with notations in the margins. Can you tell me if that is your handwriting?"

"Yes," said Tom numbly.

"And these scraps of paper, found in the pages of the books—are these also your writings? In your handwriting?"

"Yes," said Tom.

Now some of these notes were entered in this "hearing." Taken out of context, the words made no sense. Was Tom deranged?

The soul is the silence of a bell ringing.

In waiting all time ceased; in conversation the condition of an idiot prevailed: perfect.

Or this:

There is no good or bad, dark or light, right or wrong, war or peace, but all is God, as None is too. God is not physical and not spiritual, not sexual and not celibate, not male and not female. It is here and not here, everything and nothing. It is you and me without the "I." I am filled with God. I am less than

God, and even less am still entirely God, for there is
nothing else.

Eric read passage after passage aloud, questioning every
word.

"Would you care to explain to the court this entry?"

"Mr. Buckford, in this book I'm holding you made a mar-
ginal note that it is impossible to sin once you have seen God.
Would you explain to the court—?"

And: "Do you remember this entry?"

"It's my book."

"Answer the question, Mr. Buckford," said Bishop Crowley
dryly.

"Yes, I remember."

Oh, the questioning went on and on.

"Mr. Buckford, do you know what a mantra is? Is it true
that in repeating these sounds you are repeating the names of
Indian gods?"

"After seminary what happened?" asked Eric, surprising us
all with his change of subject.

"I graduated. I was ordained."

"What year did you take your ordination vows?" And when
Tom had answered: "Mr. Buckford, I am going to read you
another passage. I'd like to know if you recognize it."

He held a printed page at arm's length, disdaining glasses,
his head tilted, his wide sleeves hanging gracefully from his
wrists.

" 'Will you reverently obey your Bishop, and other chief
Ministers, who, according to the Canons of the Church, may
have the charge and government over you; following with a

glad mind and will their godly admonitions, and submitting yourselves to their godly judgments?' "

"Those are the ordination vows," said Tom mildly.

"Did you notice the direction to obey the Bishop, a promise and a vow that you admit you made?"

Tom flushed; his mouth twitched angrily. And Graham Eric turned away with a triumphant smile, then whirled back, his skirts swishing at his ankles.

"Yet, you refused the one godly admonition that His Grace has given you!"

George Tooey stood up. "May I?"

The Bishop nodded.

"Mr. Buckford," he said formally. "In seminary did you learn a code of behavior?"

"Yes, sir."

"And you learned a ranking of hierarchy of priestly orders— such as deacons, canon, priest, bishop—did you not?"

"Yes, sir."

"What is the highest authority in the Episcopal church, Mr. Buckford?"

"The bishop," said Tom. "He stands equal to the Bishop of Rome—the Pope."

"So there is no higher authority in the Episcopal church?"

"No. The presiding bishop in New York, but he's still a bishop."

"Is there any authority, then, higher than a bishop?" He smiled in a friendly, nodding way.

Tom stared at him and then broke into a grin.

"Yes. God."

"Ah," said Tooey. "And when you say you stood on your conscience, Mr. Buckford—?"

"I am invoking God's authority," said Tom. "For my conscience is the voice of God, if I listen carefully."

"Ah," said Tooey. " 'Be still and know that I am God.' That is all." And he sat down, to the annoyance of the Bishop and Eric.

That ended the first day of the trial.

Eric and the Bishop scheduled the strongest prosecution witnesses, the most damaging testimony, first and last—Tom's enemies sandwiching the rest; and I was interested to see that I was not on those lists myself, but would be called with the minor choir later in the week, after Emily but well before Carolyn and Butch.

Emily was the first witness called against Tom. "Do you swear to tell the whole truth in the name of God?"

"I do."

"Your name is Emily Carter?"

"Yes."

"Are you a member of Trinity Parish, Miss Carter?"

"Yes, I am, I was baptized in Trinity Church and confirmed here. I have always been a member."

"When Mr. Buckford first came to the parish, did you find him . . . strange? Was his behavior ordinary, let us say, in the beginning?"

"Well . . . he was never ordinary. No."

"Can you tell us about your first meeting with Mr. Buckford?"

Emily's story came blushing, stumbling out, drawn into public view by one horrible question after another: how she had locked herself in the rector's house and stewed in unseasonable heat . . . and how scared she had been and how odd Tom had looked and behaved, naked to the waist and beating on the door. She may have wanted to protect Tom, but her halting, confused testimony only damned him more.

"So you would say he seemed . . . um, *different* right from the start?"

Emily nodded unhappily.

Eric could not have been kinder, or gentler in his questioning. "Did it get better? Did you get used to his ways?"

"Well, yes. I made allowances of course."

"Do you remember occasions when he changed the regular services?"

"No, everything was, um, odd. You never knew what you were going to get in church."

"Can you give examples?"

"Well, one Sunday we sat in Quaker silence, I remember. We didn't even have a real service that day, just an opening and closing and a little direction on how to contemplate. And I remember another time he didn't give a sermon. We had a discussion instead, all of us."

"Can you describe what you mean?"

"Instead of talking to us from the pulpit, he strolled up and down the aisle and asked questions. We discussed whether Christ was the Son of God, and what the Resurrection meant. But it was the congregation doing the talking, not him. I mean, I liked it, but it was upsetting, because we're a traditional church. We're not accustomed to the little children running in the aisle or going to the Communion rail with adults, and strangers shouting Amen, and women—or even men—weeping out loud. He said strange things to us."

"Like what?"

"What?"

"What kind of strange things?"

"Oh dear, I can't remember now. That was a long time ago, and there were so many queer things in those days. Or maybe it was just me. I don't have the *best* memory anymore, unless it's about one of the dogs, it seems. I never forget anything about them, and I have seventeen, after all, so you'd think I'd confuse it sometimes, who got what medicines, or which one needs a walk—"

"Miss Carter, you were telling us some of the strange things Mr. Buckford said."

"Yes, well, you know. Well, I suppose, like 'You are God.' That sort of thing."

"He said that? That you are God?"

"Well, no, he meant *we* are all of us God, or else God is in us, I was never sure, but I'm not theological, you know. You should ask Carolyn Page. She'll remember. He meant that we're made in the *image* of God, I think, at least I took it that way. Because of course we're *not* God, are we? The world would be in even worse trouble than it is if *we* were God, as if it's not bad enough, I mean, and sometimes I think it couldn't be run worse and we *ought* to take control. But that's just silly thinking, isn't it?"

All through this speech Eric had been trying to interrupt, but Emily's eyes were wandering among the angels on the ceiling of the church, and she never noticed. Now she turned appealingly to Tom.

"Did I say it right? You *were* saying that, weren't you? Or else that we had to *become* like God. Or anyway to *try*."

He smiled fondly on her and nodded approval.

"It's fine, Emily."

"I wouldn't want to misquote. But anyway, he liked my dogs. He used to come out sometimes and feed the dogs with me. I never told anyone that, and the dogs all liked him, too, so he couldn't be bad, could he? Because animals always know."

I remembered that first party of Carolyn's and the black Lab laying her head in Tom's lap. He had told Elizabeth that any cat or dog or child would come to him, and actually it was true; but it was not what the prosecution wanted to hear just then. Graham Eric turned to another point.

"Can you tell us what happened on the day you found him lying on the floor of the church?"

The prosecution was trying to prove that Tom was mad. And here from Emily, fat and flustered, blushing, wringing her hands and squirming to look round behind her as if she could run into the sacristy and hide, came the hideous story of that day: of filth in the silver salver and on the holy vessels of the church—a donation to God's altar of earth's dirt; and Tom himself crawling on his knees to kiss her feet. But none of it was presented as I had heard or even as Tom had tried fumblingly to explain the day before: none of Emily's words indicated his exalted vision or the blinding light. Just facts.

"He had grass in his mouth, you say?"

Emily could hardly bring herself to nod. Tom, meanwhile, shrank down in his chair as the public twisted, gawking—some stood up—straining to see him. The Bishop's gavel pounded interruptions twice in Emily's account, to bring the place to submission once again.

"He was walking on his knees," the prosecutor prompted. "Did he say anything at that time?"

"No, only sounds. I stared at him. I couldn't think. I mean—" She paused.

"Go on, Miss Carter," said the bishop.

"Tell the court precisely what he did."

"He hugged my knees." It was the softest whisper. Even sitting in the front pew beside me, Margaret could not hear.

"What did she say?" she asked. One man in the crowd behind us called out, "Louder! Louder!" The Bishop's gavel banged. "Silence in the court!"

"I was afraid. He was holding my knees," Emily whispered.

"What were you afraid of, Miss Carter?"

"I was afraid he'd tear my stocking—"

The ripple of laughter was stopped by Crowley's gavel and his booming cry of "Silence!" Miss Emily hung her head, chins quivering. She was forced to finish her story. "I put one hand on his head," she whispered. The court stenographer leaned forward, fingers flickering over his black keys. "To push him away, you see, but he was kneeling and he dropped his head and kissed my feet."

A rustle fluttered through the church like pigeons' wings.

"My ankles were wet with his tears."

"And then?"

"Then nothing. My hand was on his hair. I thought—"

"What did you think?"

"I ran," she answered. "I pushed him off and ran because—" She stopped, appealing to the court, the door behind her, the ceiling, the floor, her lap.

"Remember, you are under oath. Why did you run?"

"Because he was so beautiful."

21

You will wonder what Tom was thinking all this time. He was living in our house, but he retired into himself. I imagine his moods: rejected, lonely, angry, humiliated. What would anyone feel? I know what disturbed him most: the times when he lost his living contact with the divine, with the juice of the Universe, as he called it. For long periods, interspersed with sudden shafts of light, he felt darkness, fear, doubt at the attacks of enemies, doubt at how he ought to act. He despaired at doubting, especially after all that he'd been shown, and this weakness tormented him. He felt he'd failed the test.

He lost his laugh, though occasionally that broke out too—a flash of good-hearted humor, quickly gone. He prayed long hours. I admit I did not understand the man in this period. My closest friend, and he was not available to me.

Trials have a way of being swallowed by silence for minutes at a time, while defense and prosecution collect their thoughts and shuffle papers or mumble to the judge. We've become accustomed on TV to courtroom dramas full of fascination and suspense. But boredom strikes a truer note. Trials often drain us to exhaustion by droning speeches, rifflings, readings, mutterings and mumblings at the bench, and long silences during which the public cough and scuffle their feet, ignorant of what's going on.

Into those silences Tom withdrew. His thoughts wandered from the trial to Elizabeth, to Daphne (busy at school, he hoped, and happy with her studies), or to Priscilla in the asylum and Philip with his grandmother in Chicago. Tom telephoned Philip every other night, and once he drove down to Miss Eu's to explain the trial to Daphne, who burst into tears of anger and fear, lashed out at him cruelly, and locked herself in her room until he finally drove away. Until a few days before the trial began, he had lived alone in the rectory. Then the attacks began—a car screaming up his drive at night and gunshots going off. A manifesto was nailed to his back door. Then his supporters came to his defense and patrolled the rectory at night as a vigilante force, until finally Tom agreed to come live with us, in our spare room. Why not? He was alone now—Priscilla and Philip gone and his daughter back in boarding school, her belly swelling secretly under her heavy corduroy uniform, poor child; and she jumping off of fences and trying starvation diets, too confused to confess. None of us knew her distress, and you can fault us for our ignorance, but our attention was on her father's trial.

The week of his trial Tom came and went in a car provided by the Bishop. The car had blinds. Tom was transported secretly, to protect him as much from his admirers as from his enemies. He felt himself a prisoner, a pawn being moved about the board to satisfy someone's secret whims. He sat and listened to the trial, but his thoughts were on other guilts and retribution. He shrank back in his chair in the courtroom-church, listening to the lawyers drone, eyes closed and fingers intertwined beneath his chin. The wind outside rattled the loose gutter. There is a passage in *The Brothers Karamazov*: *My brother used to ask the birds to forgive him.* Remember it? *For all is like an ocean, all things flow and touch each other; a disturbance in one place is felt at the other end of the world.* . . . It's an incredible passage, and Tom kept thinking of these lines. *Birds would be happier, and children, if you yourself were nobler than you are.* If he were nobler than he was.

The actual charges seemed petty to him, immaterial compared with those with which he charged himself. And one part of his mind turned over the situation he was in, guilty of these acts and worse. They had only to call him to the stand again and he would answer their queries. Instead they called one witness after another to prove undisputed facts. He moved the prayers around, or deleted them entirely. He skipped the readings, or denounced the angriest and most vengeful ancient Hebrew Psalms. Yes, he asked us (heretical view) to consider whether the Resurrection really occurred. He liked to drop the Prayer of Humble Access in the Communion service, in which, after confessing our sins and receiving absolution, we state that we are not worthy to gather the crumbs under His table but shall approach anyway for the Eucharist. . . . We heard testimony of his distaste for the cannibalism of certain passages. "Grant us therefore, gracious Lord, so to eat the flesh of thy dear Son, Jesus Christ, and to drink his blood that our sinful bodies may be made clean by his body, and our souls washed through his most precious blood. . . ." He had substituted a less savory version.

I'm not sure Tom even heard. He could have told them why the prayers were dropped. "We are not worthy . . . we do not presume to come to thy table . . . There is no health in us. . . ." Man's concentration on sin prevented him, Tom thought, from seeing, thanking God. The prayers reinforced the very qualities one needed to avoid. His lawyer dutifully made notes, and Tom, eyes closed, sat motionless.

Some witnesses shrank from the ordeal. Others basked in their power. Admiral Roen testified, and Billy Tyler. She threw back her head and answered with fine, clear declarations, remembering conversations we'd forgotten and one where he spoke privately to her.

She told how Tom had once told her the Church had grown lopsided in its patriarchal attention to the all-male Trinity. Where is the female energy in the Church, he'd asked, and somehow he had come up with the arcane fact that in Hindu belief God is masculine but impotent without his female side. The energy of God, the creative force, he'd told Billy, is female.

"Are you suggesting," Crowley himself intervened at this point, leaning forward to question Billy, "are you suggesting that Mr. Buckford did not believe in Christ?"

"I'm not suggesting anything," she answered. "I'm only telling you about this conversation. It was only one conversation, and I found it fascinating, but I don't know what it meant about Christ."

"Did he say anything more along these lines?"

"Well, yes, he did," she answered, with that characteristic rise of her voice. "He described how the yogis in the Himalayas sit in their caves and chant the names of God—a thousand names of God—over and over, year after year, until they achieve an actual *sexual union* with God. He said they make love to the feminine in God, to the Goddess, and then they enjoy sexual bliss for hours. I suppose women yogis do it with male gods. I thought that was very interesting, but it's not exactly Christian, is it?" She gave her quick, harsh bray.

At this point Tooey rose and inserted into the record John Donne's famous poem:

Batter my heart, three-personed God
Take me to you, imprison me, for I,
Except you enthrall me, never shall be free,
Nor ever chaste, except you ravish me.

"Christian mystics use that language too," he murmured, and also put into the record the passion of Saint Theresa, marked by Tom in one of his books:

I am God, says Love, for Love is God and God is
Love and this soul is God by condition of Love: but I
am God by Nature Divine. . . . This soul is the eagle
that flies high, so right high and yet more high than
any other bird, for she is feathered by fine love.

And finally, another Christian love passage of Saint Theresa's:

Thou givest me thy whole Self to be mine whole
and undivided, if at least I shall be thine . . . Thou art
in me and I in thee, glued together as one and the self
same thing, which henceforth and forever cannot be
divided.

The Bishop called a recess. We stood in our pews and stretched and talked softly among ourselves, waving to friends and laughing in low voices over testimony, or exchanging commentary. Joe Stappleton, who is a compulsive gambler, had so many bets on the outcome of the trial that he kept them on a list. I saw Angus at the proceedings that day. He tipped his hat. "Sir, to you," he said politely.

I couldn't help but notice how well he looked, how steady without the alcohol. A woman I didn't know was sitting with him. She was missing a thumb. I marvelled at the change he'd undergone in only eight or nine short months.

Like the others I was questioned on Tom's advent to Naughton, and his character, and what I'd seen the night of the revelation, and I won't bore myself repeating it. As senior warden I was also asked about the business affairs and workings of the vestry, about Tom's organizational skills (or lack of them), his ability to make enemies, and also the deep loyalty he inspired. You didn't come away neutral to the man. I told about his work for the town of Naughton, at the nursing home, for example, and his efforts to bring the different Protestant churches together to tackle poverty. What I didn't talk about was Lizzie or his personal affairs, though I did describe his hedonistic philosophy: take what you want from the world; eat it up; enjoy. Delight in it. God wants us to be free and happy.

And George Tooey, the brilliant lawyer, still asked almost no questions, but, lean and sinuous, bent over the table, doodling, or else stretched out in his chair, his long legs crossed at the ankles, hands clasped behind his head.

Then General Shriver took the stand.

The General looked very handsome there; his noble head, his flashing teeth, his military carriage, his dignity and presence, made him a good witness. He also knew what some others did not: that speaking in a low, clear voice, in firm, declarative sentences, answering only to the questions posed, made a better impression than long-winded elaborations.

Butch had kept records. He could consult his pocket diary and state exactly what prayers had been left out on which Sunday, what blasphemy expressed. He was a perfect witness.

"On May fourteenth he neglected the Creed."

"What do you mean neglected?" asked Eric.

"I mean, we never said it at all. He just skipped it."

"Did anyone object?"

"There isn't time to object. The minister is in charge of leading us through the service. Afterwards I commented on it. I told him what he'd done."

"Did he apologize or explain what happened?"

"He did not. He said, 'Oh, did I?' That's what he said. Like that. 'Oh, did I?' and not a word of apology or regret."

Butch continued: "On Sunday, June first, he reversed the order of the two Lessons. On June seventh, he entirely forgot the Prayer of Humble Access for the Eucharist. . . ."

"Do you remember other occurrences, General Shriver," said Eric, "that indicated his unusual state?"

"Unusual!" cried the General. "There were times you wondered if he was playing with a full deck."

The congregation laughed.

"Sure!" he said, ticking off points on his fingers.

"I've already told you about his moving the prayers around. He said the worship through Holy Eucharist was picked up originally from believers in Zoroaster—I'll never forget that—and that they had a Communion under Zoroaster using bread and water, and anointing with oil, and then baptized, too, with water, just like Christ."

"John the Baptist," Eric corrected him instinctively.

"Well, whoever. Anyway non-Christians. He liked to question the Resurrection. Emily told about the day we just *discussed* it in church—no real sermon at all. Yet *he's* supposed to be the preacher. He was arrogant, self-important. Ask him about the signs!" said Butch angrily. "As if he was the only person who knew anything."

"Signs?" said Eric, confused. I saw Tom lean over and whisper to George Tooey.

The General stared at Eric for a moment, then said, "Oh, nothing, it's not important." He flipped through his notes. "Let's see. Here, on July twenty-first, we have him dropping Humble Access again. And—ha! here, July third, at the eleven-o'clock service, he had us all stand in a circle for Communion, for God's sake, and hand the cup around ourselves."

"Yourselves?"

"He went round the circle with the paten, handing out wafers and saying, 'The body of Christ.' Then we passed the Communion wine and we each said—wait, it's here—'The cup of salvation,' and passed the wine without even wiping the spit off the cup.

"Here's another. He said *we*, the parishioners, were the ministers of the church, each one of us. He was just ducking his responsibility," he finished triumphantly.

But Eric made very little of it. Instead George Tooey rose quickly to his feet in one of his rare cross-examinations.

"General Shriver?"

"Yes."

"You are a general."

"You're darned right I am! SAC commander—"

Tooey interrupted. "So you know about hierarchy."

"You bet your ass," said Shriver, who was feeling confident on the stand. "Excuse my language, Bishop," he added graciously.

"Who has higher rank? The priest of a church or a vestryman?"

The question caught Butch by surprise. He stuttered momentarily.

"Well, they're not comparable. They're apples and oranges."

"Oh, come now, General."

"No, well, it's not in a straight chain of command, one below the other."

"Then the rector cannot *order* a member of the vestry to do a particular duty."

"He'd *better* not," laughed Shriver.

"And the member of the vestry—even the senior warden—cannot *order* the pastor to do something."

"No-o," said Butch cautiously.

Tooey rocked forward, hands clasped behind his back.

"So, technically the minister can't be called disobedient to the *vestry*, can he? Even if he doesn't carry out its will?"

"Well, he'd better watch his p's and q's, though. It's the vestry that pays his salary. And the members of the church," he added.

"You have been on the vestry for several years, haven't you? Since—"

"Five years, yes."

"So you were on the vestry when it voted in the rector."

"Yes, I was, and at the time, you see, he seemed all right. We didn't know."

"You are also treasurer, is that right?"

"I was."

"So you've had plenty of time to watch him over the last year, wouldn't you say? Do you consider yourself an objective observer? Unbiased?"

The General nodded modestly, and Tooey went on. "General, you mentioned signs a little bit ago. Last year Mr. Buckford and the vestry directed you to set up signs along various roads to direct people to the Episcopal church. Can you tell the court, did you put up the signs?"

"I was doing it—I was finding appropriate sites."

Eric rose to object that the questioning seemed irrelevant, but the Bishop waved him down.

Tooey continued: "How long had you been looking for sites?"

"Not long. It's a sensitive task."

"By my records it was a year and a half since you'd been assigned the task. Last fall Mr. Buckford took the signs away from you, if I am correct, and installed them himself."

"He didn't like the care with which I was approaching the job. Is that what you mean? And, yes, he took them and those are the three signs you see up now—one on Tuttle Road and—"

"Yes, we know where they are, General. You were so dissatisfied with the rector's action that you wrote a letter to the Bishop. I have a copy of this letter here."

"Yes?" The General was confused.

"I wish to place it in the record," said Tooey. "This is written to the Right Reverend Bishop Crowley, dated March twenty-eighth, the day before the defendant's revelation. It says:

Dear Bishop Crowley,

"This letter brings to your attention Thomas Buckford, rector, etcetera, etcetera.

"To ascribe malice as the motive for his arrogant disregard for the simplest proprieties would be un-Christian. To consider any other motive seems impos-

sible. You have only to ask around to see what people
say about his signs.

> "Sincerely,
>
> "G. Scully Shriver
>
> Major General, U.S. Army, retired"

Laughter came from the pews.

Tooey looked out at the audience, a faint smile flickering
on his lips. "You can imagine what the Bishop thought when
he got this. He thought it referred to visions and signs of God,
not to a personal vendetta from one dissatisfied parishioner. But
I wish to draw your attention to another matter," he continued,
and he began to pace in a lawyerly way behind the witness
table. "General Shriver, last year you gave Mr. Buckford five
thousand dollars for his discretionary funds. Did you specify
how this money was to be used?"

Butch went red. "I did." He pulled a cold cigar from his
pocket, clamped it in his teeth, and then removed it.

"And what exactly did you specify?"

"It was for a scholarship for some deserving kid."

"And did you also name a candidate?"

"He stole my money!" Shriver shot back. "He gave it to a
common nigger. He's crazy. He dances in the church, like Da-
vid. He eats with spades, with coons. He'd have us ask them
into our house. He wants our daughters to go to school with
them—with niggers, to marry niggers. He advocates free love."
Butch was shouting now. "He's always telling us to enjoy ourselves. . . ."

At this Tom tore a note from his pad and passed it to his
lawyer, who raised his eyebrows and pursed his lips.

"Ask about sex!" Butch cried, waving his cigar. "Ask if he

sleeps with his parishioners. He gives the women a taste of God. I know what he does. Ask him—"

He was on his feet, shouting over the Bishop's gavel, struggling against Eric and Bo Zimmer while the public in the pews came to their feet and the whole church erupted into noise. That was a question the Bishop had no intention of asking at a public trial.

He had once suggested to Shriver and Carolyn Page that sexual misconduct constituted grounds for firing a minister, and Carolyn had hurried to assure him Tom was clean. If he were not, the last place to take such scandal up, Crowley felt, was at a public hearing.

He banged his gavel in disgust. His annoyance at finding himself here, embroiled in conflicting politics, focused itself on Tom.

Carolyn took the stand next. George Tooey rested his chin on his hand and his elbow on the green-baize table and listened pensively. We all whispered in the pews, wondering why he didn't defend his client and whether he was any good; and Elizabeth's heart was breaking, as it had been now for days.

Carolyn had known for some time that she would be called to the stand this Wednesday afternoon, and she was dressed to the nines in a maroon-silk shirtwaist, her best pearl drops, and her pride. She had talked over with Dutton what she wanted to say and had also practiced before a mirror. She had decided to be firm, discreet, to the point. Calm, consistent. Especially she would avoid—nothing would make her mention—her daughter in the same sentence with this man. And she was pleased as the questioning began.

"How long have you lived in Naughton, Mrs. Page?" asked Eric.

"All my life. My mother owned Nacirema. I was raised here, except for boarding school."

Eric wanted to show her sophistication as well. "But I understand you travelled, too, and lived abroad?"

"After I married, we lived in Washington and San Francisco and then in Japan for one year after the war. My husband was on MacArthur's staff during the Occupation."

"So you would say you have seen the world?"

"Yes," said Carolyn with a self-congratulatory smile. "And then, of course, we've taken several trips to Europe."

"Mrs. Page, when did you first meet the rector?"

"Well, I don't really remember. I suppose it was at church. No, it was just after he had arrived in Naughton—at George Mitchell's funeral. I went to the service. Of course, he didn't know the man—you can't expect him to do a very good job, but I thought he could have done some research, asked around. I, for one, would have been happy to tell him about George, who was *not* the generous man that Mr. Buckford described in that impossible funeral oration, though I am not one to speak ill of the dead."

"Yes," Eric said. That line of questioning was unproductive, but before he could change course, Carolyn went on:

"But he came to a party of mine the first week he arrived, and there his true colors shone through, right at the beginning. You asked Emily Carter if he had done anything strange. The real question is whether anything he did *wasn't* strange. Even that first social event, you'd think the man would have been on his toes. I shall *never* forgive him for what he did that day. It showed, beyond a shadow of a doubt, his total insensitivity to his job, his inability to understand the Valley, *or* his parishioners, and I told John Woods so at the time. You can ask him if I didn't say so at the time, but you know John. He said, 'Now, now,' or something else inane, when anyone with eyes in his head could see that things would only go from bad to worse. So who could be surprised when he ended up with visions? Not I, for one. I suppose we should feel sorry for him now, having to go through all this. It can't be comfortable."

Tom looked over at her with the puzzled frown of an astronomer peering through the wrong end of a telescope by mistake.

She stopped and looked expectantly at Eric. For a moment a profound silence settled on the church while we all thought about what she had said.

"Yes," said Eric. And then he said, "What did happen at the party?"

"Oh." She waved one hand. "Nothing. Nothing. It's really not important. He offended me, that's all. It was nothing. A private matter."

"What happened?"

"Well, if you must know, it wasn't so minor. He was invited to the luncheon with some very important guests, and I found him in the kitchen talking to the maids. He preferred the company of the kitchen staff to our guests! I have *always* been taught—and hope I have taught my children—that a guest has as *much* obligation to work a party and help make it a success as a hostess does, and you are *not* to just go off with the black servants just because you're bored by the guests. It is self-indulgent and rude. Then to instigate a fight—well, he didn't instigate it exactly—but nothing like that has ever happened at a party of mine *before* or *since*, I can assure you. And the only thing different was this man in my living room sending out . . . *vibrations*. Of evil. An irreplaceable Chinese bowl was broken! It was my grandmother's, a gift from the empress of China herself. Irreplaceable! And I will never forget in the midst of all that chaos looking up and seeing him, sitting on the couch, patting the dog, as calmly as if he were all alone. As if he weren't responsible, and Elizabeth—''

She stopped.

"Anyway the party was not one of my better social efforts," she said with a bright smile at the Bishop. "And it just *symbolized* the rest of his time here."

There was a long, uncomfortable silence.

Graham paced the chancel thoughtfully. The lawyers shuffled their papers.

"Mrs. Page," said Graham in a quiet voice. "You say he was sending out 'vibrations.' Could you elaborate?"

For the first time the trial moved from misdemeanors and mistakes to malice. The demonic at play. We stirred on our benches. From outside in the windy air we could hear the voices of the people picketing.

Carolyn said, "Evil. Yes, well, I haven't thought of it before, but that is true. Whenever he walks into a room, practically, you feel a change. It is very subtle. It's like a—I don't know, an energy wave somehow, and you feel . . . odd. I can't explain it. You all call his vision a revelation of God, but I saw Emily Carter right after she left the church. I saw the state she was in, and I, for one, don't think God would scare people like that. And this nonsense about defiling the cross and pretending it's worship, you can't tell me that isn't evil. Now, I know very little about evil, but I have been a faithful churchgoer all my life, and I have *never*—never, I say—*never* seen the kind of disruption to the community that has come with the presence of this one man."

"Can you give us an example?"

"Well, look at his family life," she said. "Maybe you can't hold a man to blame for everything, but his wife is in an asylum. And—this!" she cried, sweeping her hand across the audience. "For heaven's sake, look at this trial, and everyone at each other's throats. If you're going to have a vision of God, it would pull people together, not tear them apart. It would bring harmony if it were real."

"Thank you, Mrs. Page," said Eric. "The court will take what you say to heart."

Now George Tooey came to his feet, a kind of balding Gregory Peck. He gave a great sigh and stared for an interminable moment at his feet before cocking his head at the witness.

"Hello, Carolyn." He smiled as if they shared an intimate secret.

"George," she answered cautiously.

"The day of the revelation you went up to the church after leaving Emily, is that right? Did you go inside?"

"No, it was locked."

"So you couldn't see inside?"

"No."

"Did you try the side door?"

"No, I didn't think of it."

"So you actually never saw Mr. Buckford that night, or the condition of the church?"

"No."

"Yet you say he's evil. That's a strong word," said George Tooey. "Do you really mean *evil*? Hmm. Look at this man, Carolyn." We all looked at Tom, sunk in his chair. "Can you honestly say that he's been possessed by the demonic?"

"Well—" she defended herself.

"What would the marks of the demonic be?" he asked.

"How would we recognize it, I wonder?" But it was a rhetorical question; he didn't expect an answer, and I noted with interest that we had moved from Carolyn's original thoughtlessly hurled out "vibration of evil" to demonic possession. I think he was pushing her damning testimony to the absurd, *reductio ad absurdum*, to undercut all allegations.

"The demonic," he continued. "I understand there is a Prince of Darkness. In the baptismal service reference is made to 'the devil and all his works,' and Christ, of course, cast out demons and sent them running off in a herd of pigs. I believe that in the Catholic church they still perform exorcisms, isn't that right, Your Grace? But we, in this enlightened age, generally relegate the demonic exorcisms to the ignorance and superstitions of the Middle Ages. Are you superstitious, Carolyn?"

"Me? No."

"You don't believe in astrology?" He smiled.

"Me?" said Carolyn, sensitive to any criticism.

"The humbuggery of astrology," continued Tooey, pacing thoughtfully, "whose practitioners assert that the configuration of the heavenly bodies control the individual destinies of men. And women too," he added graciously, staring at the palm of his hand with a little frown. "What about palm readers? Do you go to palmists, Carolyn?"

"No!"

"Ouija boards? Fortune-tellers? Reading the tarot cards?"

She shook her head, dismayed.

"I can see how it's easy to get carried away sometimes. But demonic possession—I could imagine that being slanderous."

"Objection," cried Eric, but Carolyn overrode him.

"I never said he was possessed! I don't even *believe* in demons or ghosts or any of that!" cried Carolyn in her own defense. "I just meant he had a disruptive influence on the community, and that's clear, isn't it? Why, we wouldn't be here at all, having this trial, if—"

"Hearing," Tooey corrected her. "An investigative, fact-finding hearing."

"Well, hearing, then. We're searching for objective facts," she said carefully. "That's all we're doing. I didn't mean to imply anything else. He is a good man, I'm sure. In fact some people adore him. I respect that fact."

"Thank you, Carolyn," said Tooey, and dismissed her.

Natalie Williams, Tom's secretary, took the stand. Once there, she seemed to change. She neither stuttered nor seemed shy but proclaimed her views with the conviction of Saint Joan. She told how one day, soon after Tom arrived in Naughton, she had found him in the church alone. He was on his knees at the communion rail, praying with absorbed intensity. When she entered the little church, she saw him shining with light. It flared from his hands and hair, she said, Saint Elmo's fire, radiant in the dusky church.

The audience stirred and whispered, fluttering.

Then Tooey inserted into the record a packet of letters of support for Tom written by members of the congregation, at which Eric put into the record the letters of dissatisfaction, including a large stack of the hate mail and anonymous poems.

After this the hearing was adjourned for that day, and we broke out into the cold October dusk with a wind that nipped under our coats and tore at our ears and necks. We bundled up and hurried to the safety of our warm, lit homes. The weather was unseasonably cold, when last year almost to the day it had been unseasonably hot.

22

THE STRAIN ON TOM BEGAN TO SHOW. HIS SHOULDERS SAGGED, and once when I walked in on him unawares, he was sitting in a chair, hands dangling between his knees, head down. He looked defeated, old. Usually he put on a face and made an effort to be cheerful or in control, but he was under stress. One night at dinner he suddenly broke into tears and sat there, shoulders shaking with distress. Annie and Johnnie both stared in horror. He wiped his eyes, pushing thumb and forefinger against the bridge of his nose, and after a moment excused himself from the table and went upstairs. We wondered then, Margaret and I, if we had done the right thing by bringing him home with us, where he had to cope with the closeness and bustle of a family. Maybe it would have been better for him to have remained in the solitude of the rectory. Would that have been more healing?

But even there he would have had no peace. He was always in demand.

In the evening people gathered at our house to hear Tom speak. Where he found the energy I cannot imagine. Standing before us, he was fire and flame. When the people left, he sagged into a chair, exhausted, his face white, the spirit draining out of him. Then he might begin to shake. Sometimes he went into another space, sitting perfectly still. He would not answer if spoken to, and once when Margaret touched him in concern (he was rigid as a corpse, she said), he responded as slowly as a fish rising belly-up from the bottom of a pond.

One night Dutton Page appeared. He sat in the back of the room, legs crossed. He never spoke or entered the discussion, and when the evening was over—the prayers, the talk—he rose as deliberately as he had come, put on his hat and coat, shook hands with Margaret and me, and drove home without a word to Tom. The following night he came again, and thereafter any night that Tom agreed to speak.

"I want to know this man my daughter loves," he explained. But he never joined the conversations.

Tom did not meet his followers every night. Sometimes he stared into the October fire, his face set, while the hours ticked past. I read a book, or pretended to, and Margaret brought in her knitting or the quilt she was working on—this, after Annie was in bed. What did he think about but guilt and retribution— sometimes of Priscilla, and the part he played in that, his trial, his sense of failure in the face of persecution? What did he think about but God?

Sometimes Elizabeth came over and sat with us until it was ten P.M. "I have to leave," she'd say, and Tom would walk her to the door. We could hear the murmur of their voices, and then silence, and more murmuring, and then Tom would return to the living room, say good night, and climb the stairs to bed.

Finally Dutton brought Carolyn to one of our evenings. They sat at the back of the room. Dut observed stoically, as usual, one leg crossed over his knee and his chin tilted in

that deliberate tilt that had served him so well in the navy and
later in his legal work; Carolyn sat, back straight, on a slat-
backed cane-seated chair. Her bag rested on her lap. Her mouth
worked. Tom stood at the fireplace, his hands thrust in his
pockets and his eyes turning from one to another in the room,
as we talked—sharing our experiences, hope, fears, strengths.

Someone asked him about the Gospel story about the wise
virgins and the foolish ones. The foolish virgins forgot to fill
their lamps with oil, and when the Bridegroom came, their
lamps were out. The foolish virgins asked the others, "Sisters,
lend us oil for our lamps," but the wise ones refused and went
inside.

Tom smiled around the group.

"I don't think Christ said that," he said. "God is not so
stingy. Actually when the Bridegroom arrived and saw the foolish women had run out of oil, he said, 'Sisters, give them oil
from your lamps, for we must celebrate the wedding. Sisters,
give them oil, because there is always enough for everyone. We
have Light in abundance, for anyone who wants it.' "

As he spoke, he walked across the room until he stood in
front of Carolyn. Her ankles were pressed tightly together; her
fingers clutched her bag; she could not draw back from him. As
he came to the last lines—"There is always enough for everyone. We have Light in abundance"—he looked directly at
Carolyn.

"Don't touch me!" she cried, and started to rise, then sat
down again and, fumbling, dropped her purse. He did absolutely
nothing. He stood watching her, glowing (as Emily put it).

"Don't touch me. Go away," said Carolyn again, and then
burst into tears. "Oh!" She came to her feet. Her chair tipped
over backwards.

"Caro," Dut called, and Emily and Margaret both sprang up, but Tom prevented their approach.

"There is abundance," he said, "for everyone." She stared at him, frozen, and tears ran down her working, red-nosed face.

"Don't *look* at me!" she cried, and fled the room. Tom turned back to us. We sat, concerned and frightened, but Tom, back at the fireplace, continued as if nothing had happened.

"Leave her alone," he said to Margaret, who started to get up. "She's fine now. She needs to be alone."

All this time Dutton sat, stunned, in his chair. Margaret sank back on the sofa, and the people gathered in the room shifted uneasily while Tom continued to talk with us. That night Carolyn telephoned Elizabeth, and the day after that Carolyn was sitting beside her in the third pew on the right when Tom entered for the trial.

Each day the crowd grew larger, louder. You could hardly push your way into the church. By Thursday morning, when Tom was scheduled to testify again, you'd think the whole world knew of it. The parking lot was full before eight A.M., and people stood jammed at the door. Some had waited an hour, ready to barge into the sacred courtroom, first-come, first-served. They brought pillows with them, thermoses of hot coffee, and homemade sandwiches. One man was trying to buy his way into the church with offers of ten dollars a seat, or twenty dollars— if anyone inside was willing to relinquish a place.

Early on, the crowd turned ugly. Some people said that Tom had exorcised a ghost for a widow named Edna Stubbs, and more than one person claimed miracles of healing, at which two fights broke out—though Tom expressly forbade his followers to fight. He asked for discipline.

And then the day I want to talk about. The Bishop had asked us to act as bodyguards for Tom—myself and a guy named Carter and Rod Cameron, our former vestryman, and George Tooey—ushering him in by the back door. We thought our lives at stake! By now the crowd had learned how Tom sneaked in and out. Young boys were keeping lookout, and when he was spotted, the crowd surged like a wave around the corner of the building and down on us. I put one hand on Tom's elbow to hurry him along. Hands reached out to touch him, and voices called out. I swear I heard the word *Master*, but maybe it was *Mister*, who knows? "Good luck," some shouted, and "We're with you." Others called out for his healing hands. "Help me," cried one woman, "bless me." Back in the churchyard or standing with their placards on the path surged his enemies, shouting out obscenities. I've never seen anything like it.

The crowd surrounded Tom. One woman wrenched the buttons off his jacket. The other bodyguards and I formed a circle around him, moving with elbows out and crushing anyone in the way.

There were cripples in the crowd and old people staggering on canes, and in our hurry to get Tom safe inside I knocked an old man down, but I could not stop to pick him up, for Tom was being mauled. We threw ourselves inside the sacristy hall, and the doors closed behind us. We passed into the welcome warmth of the heated church, to see the people packed in the pews shoulder-to-shoulder and chairs set up in the aisles; so, everywhere you looked were the white moon faces, and interspersed with them some black moons, too, darkies and whites sitting side-by-side, too absorbed in the proceedings to care that for this day they sat together in a church. Friends and enemies were all mixed up together, no one having time to choose where they would sit. Outside rose the muffled noise.

Then came the processional, the prayers for guidance. . . . Tom took the stand, and they went through his revelation again.

"Did Christ appear in your vision? Did any Christian imagery? The fish? The cross?"

And then: "Mr. Buckford, do you believe in Christ?"

A ripple of surprise ran through the church.

"I don't know what you mean."

"Do you believe in the existence of the living Christ, the embodiment of God, His only begotten Son, who died for our sins and on the third day rose from the dead? Can I make it clearer?" asked the prosecutor.

All eyes in the church were riveted on Tom, waiting for his response.

"I have not had a direct experience with Christ," said Tom. "I have to take Him as a matter of faith."

"That's what most of us have to do, isn't it?"

Tom glanced up with a quick, appreciative smile. "But that's nonsense, isn't it?" he said. "No one should believe something just because someone tells him to. It's direct experience we use. A man would be a fool to believe in God until he's experienced the Presence in his life. Then he cannot get enough. He's drunk on the liquor. Then he doesn't believe. He *knows*."

"Mr. Buckford," said Eric. "The question before the court is whether you believe in Christ. Would you prefer me to use the word *know*?"

Crowley's hand was covering his eyes, his head bowed. He

was in agony, but he did not stop the questioning. His right hand doodled furiously on his pad, marking small crosshatched boxes, as I discovered later, dozens of tiny crosshatched squares.

"Certainly I believe he lived. He was a great prophet, the son of God, and filled with holy Light."

"That's enough," Crowley interrupted. "That constitutes belief."

"Your Grace," said Eric. "I beg the court to permit me to proceed. It leads somewhere."

The Bishop beckoned him over and whispered something, and listened with soulful eyes as Graham Eric responded in his ear. Then—you could see his reluctance—the Bishop nodded, and Eric returned to his place at the table. He paused. But Tom's head came up, alert, and the entire church was straining. Outside, the wind rattled a loose gutter; the final question came:

"Mr. Buckford, the question I am asking is do you believe in the glory and Resurrection of the Christ?"

It's so simple a question. It is answered in the Apostles' Creed:

> The third day he rose again from the dead: He ascended into heaven, And sitteth on the right hand of God the Father Almighty.

Or it is answered in the Nicene Creed:

> I believe in One Lord Jesus Christ, the only begotten Son of God . . . God of God, Light of Light, Very God of very God; . . . And the third day he rose again . . . and ascended into heaven, And sitteth on the right hand of the Father.

Or in the catechism—there are forms for the response, and even if they are babble words to some of us, a kind of nonsense code, Tom had only to repeat those words. He must have known them by heart: "By his Resurrection Jesus overcame death and opened for us the way to eternal life." Or he could have said Christ "took our human nature in Heaven, where he now reigns with the Father and intercedes for us." Or perhaps he could have spoken of the Trinity—Father, Son, and Holy Spirit—one force, all three.

Instead Tom stared out across the church, over our heads, for a long moment, while we held our breath. If he couldn't answer, could he honestly be an ordained minister of the Church? When he spoke, his voice rang strong.

"I believe that Jesus was a great and holy man, the purest spirit of a living God, and that he understood the God-ness of the holy river that runs through us and every living stone. He was trying to tell us something without having proper words, because there are no words for what he knew. Did Christ die? I know there is no death, unless you care to use the term for the shedding of the physical shell that brings us life. No one dies. Did he go to Heaven? I know that Heaven is the state right here on earth of those who live in God, and Hell is the absence of that connection. And they exist inside us, Heaven and Hell, side by side and a million miles apart.

"About the Resurrection of Christ, I think it's the wrong question. What you want to ask," he continued, voice trembling with impatience and anger, "has nothing to do with Christ. You want to know how a man who claims to have seen the Divine can offend you, commit acts that defy your rules. Which are said to be the rules of God. Why don't you ask me outright what you want to know? I'll answer your questions.

General Shriver made the accusation. You want to know about the female nature of God and how I see God in a woman and love of God in her. Why don't you ask me about se—"

At this moment came the stone—the crash, the splintering of glass from the southwest window and the church was filled with screams, and a man's howl as the blood spurted from his eye. It was pandemonium, and blood on the pew cushions and people shrieking, struggling to the aisle—but there was no room to move. The Bishop pounded his gavel, and one of the priests rushed for a phone. People cleared a space about the man. Some were calling, "Stand back, give him air," while others pressed forward to see if they could help, until the wail of the ambulance was heard in the distance; and then the fire siren going off at the Valentine station three miles off.

The trial recessed. At the Bishop's orders the police called in reinforcements to push the restless mob back from the church and beyond the outside wall. Gradually things died down, and when the Bishop led us in prayers to still our fears, some semblance of order returned. The window was taped with a shirt board against the bitter wind. We broke for lunch.

I would gladly skip over what happened next. I am not proud of it, my betrayal. I look at that sentence and think, betrayal of whom? Was there only one or many, and which was worst? Betrayal of Flossie, Margaret, Tom, myself. Of everyone. Of God. "For all is like an ocean. . . . A disturbance in one place is felt at the other end of the world. . . . Birds would be happier . . . and children and all animals if you yourself were nobler."

If only we were nobler than we are.

So we come to what this story has been leading up to all this time.

It was after lunch. I was up at the conference table with Tom's lawyer, head bent in conversation, had just turned away—and found myself face-to-face with Flossie.

"Flossie." She stood before me, a guarded smile on her lips. I was eating her with my eyes, for I had not seen her in a couple of years. And what was strange—it was I who had rejected her, yet there I stood breathless, my legs turning to water, my stomach dropping, and I could feel the blood rushing to my face. She looked beautiful with her full red hair against a wintergreen blouse.

"Hello, John."

Our fingers touched and pulled apart, and I was trembling. "You look wonderful."

"I heard about the trial. I thought I'd see the fun."

"Fun," I repeated, trying to prolong our meeting. "How long are you here for? Where are you staying?"

She laughed. "Do I get to choose which question to answer?"

Only, she said it in that lovely, soft, Virginia drawl. "Do Ah get to chu-use . . . ?"

"I'm staying with Dut and Carolyn," she continued. "And I'm leaving tomorrow. I just wanted to see this new saint I've heard so much about."

"Have you? From whom?" I didn't care. I was trying to keep my heart in my chest and not act like a total ass.

"Everyone's talking about him. Isn't he wonderful?" she said. "I can't stop watching him. He gives me chills. I understand you know him. Can you introduce me?"

"Of course." Then: "Will you have lunch with me?"

"Oh, I can't. I'm having lunch with Carolyn and Dut. But why not dinner?" She laid two fingers on my wrist and looked up at me hesitantly, utterly vulnerable, and I would have laid down my life for her right then.

"Just the two of us?" I said cautiously, still trying to hold on to myself. "I think I can manage that." I glanced over and saw Margaret. Had she dropped her eyes at the movement of my head? I couldn't tell. She was deep in conversation with two friends.

"Oh, good," said Flossie. "Just the two of us."

"I've wanted to see you many times." I took her arm and wove her through the throng to Tom, who stood listening, head bent, to Emily. Beside him, a little possessively, stood Elizabeth.

"Tom, I want to introduce you to an old friend of mine."

Flossie held his hand in both of hers. "I have wanted so much to meet you. I can't tell you how much you've done for me."

Whatever did she mean by that? A lash of jealousy stung me.

Tom smiled gently. "Why, thank you. I appreciate your support."

"No, it's not support," she insisted. "I see what you've done for Elizabeth and Angus. They're my family. I want you to know I'm praying for you."

I was impressed. I didn't know she prayed.

"Miss Emily," she said. "Lizzie." And waggled her fingers at Elizabeth with a pretty smile.

We turned away. "Will you pick me up at the Pages', then, for dinner?" she asked softly.

"Well, that might be hard for me to do." I was embarrassed. "Could you meet me after the hearing this afternoon? It breaks up about five, and I'll have to stay a few moments.

But if you could drive back up here around six . . . I have to be discreet," I said.

"Why, of course! We always are." And looking back now, I can hear the high, harsh note in her voice, a little too loud perhaps, but I didn't notice then.

I should have known about Flossie. She was always crazy, joyous, mixed up, wild. One night she took off all her clothes as we drove in my convertible. I tell you, anyone could have seen her. She leaned against me on the blue plastic seats, shining in the moonlight, and her head back laughing at the stars, her breasts and belly open to the moon, and her russet pubic hair exposed. Her hair flew around me, swatting at my eyes.

"Put your clothes on," I told her. "What do you think you're doing?" She only hunched closer, rubbed her bare breasts on my arms, her lips nuzzling my neck, her fingers tickling through the buttons of my shirt—until I had to stop the car. I found a logging trail in the woods. Crazy woman. She tore off my pants and fell on me in the leaves, and then we dressed and ran on to Nacirema through the night.

But she wasn't marriage material, I thought, not steady, as Margaret was. I loved her, God. And she loved me. I suppose I led her on. I don't know. I know nothing anymore. I'm almost eighty, and I don't know one goddamn thing—less now, I sometimes think, than I did when I was young and called my motives clear. But I loved her; I know that, though at the time I called it lust.

That afternoon the Bishop rearranged the schedule. Tom came off the stand while the defense called scholars and Jesuits to debate abstract questions of the historical context of visions and prophecy or belief in Christ, and other questions of Tom's defense—this stand on his own conscience in defiance of the authority of the Church.

All afternoon my eyes trailed to Flossie in her pew. I watched her auburn hair, her high, arched nose, the line of her throat. The trial meant nothing to me then. Rain lashed at the windowpanes, wetting the cardboard and dripping down the inside plaster. The crowd outside crept off to warmer, drier spots, and suddenly the lawyers were droning. The clerks shuffled paragraphs, and priests coughed behind their sleepy hands. But my heart was a bird flying in the rafters in my joy.

When court broke up, I told Margaret I had work to do and not to expect me home till late. I stood before the altar of the church and told that lie at the cross without even blinking. Margaret gave me a queer, searching look, though I'd served on the vestry for years and more than once had conferences with the clergy that ran late. Well, Peter denied his Lord three times. I'm only human, but to this day I carry that defiant lie, though God knows how I've paid for it.

"I'll leave the door open," Margaret said. "No telling what time you'll want to come home."

Easy as pie. People were milling about, bundling into coats and hats and gloves and picking their umbrellas from the racks. Flossie ran out on an errand, saying she'd be back. I buttonholed the defense attorney to ask where he and the boys were going for drinks—for fear I might choose the same spot. And then, manipulative, I said I might be along, though it was never my intent, and then I hung around until the church cleared out.

Tom left, the crowd dispersed.

The cars outside had disappeared, and night was falling when I saw her Chevy pull into the parking lot.

"Well, now, Lady." I opened her car door. "It's very kind of you to come."

"Where are we going?"

"Someplace alone." I stood like an oaf beside the car. "I want to look at you and touch you."

"How about the Robert Morris Inn?" she said, and I felt my cup was running over.

I trailed my fingers under her hair, along the back of her neck. The inn is up the mountain road. We'd be safe there. Moreover they rented rooms.

"Let's take my car." Her voice had a hard, bright edge. "I'll drive."

"Good." I could hardly speak. "You drive. I want to look at you."

And so she did, steering skillfully with one hand, the other resting lightly on my thigh. I could feel the increasing tumescence in my pants. I kissed her hand. I kissed her neck. She pushed me away with a laugh and asked about Johnnie and Annie. How was Margaret? Business?

I asked similar questions. How was Jack? How many children did she have by now? Two. And how old were they?

"I've missed your smile, your beautiful mouth," I said. "You are a beautiful woman, Flossie Foxwell."

"Now, stop that, John Woods. You are not to make love to me tonight," she teased, though we both knew that it was untrue. She changed the subject. "Tell me about the trial."

We kept on neutral ground all through dinner. But I couldn't eat, for looking at her. I took her hand. She pulled it away.

"No, you mustn't, really."

"Why mustn't I? Do you think there's anyone else in the world for me?"

"I think you love your wife, your kids."

"Not the way I love you. Oh, Flossie, there was never anyone for me but you."

She turned away, scanning the dark room with its oak tables set with fat candles held in red webbed glass. In the far corner a fire burned.

"I'm very happy with Jack, you know. He's a good husband."

"I'm glad," I managed, then: "No, I'm not. I want you to think about me sometimes. I think of you. I want you to be happy, but I also just want you."

"Oh, John, I think of you all the time," she said. "In fact, I've planned this evening. I've thought of it for years, and how I'd have you bring me here, and what I'd do when we came. I think we should go get ourselves a room, don't you?"

My body was afire. I remembered how she used to sit on me. Her juices gushed on my belly and my loins. Sometimes she reached down and dipped her fingers in her secret place and brought out handfuls wet with her desire; then she smeared her soft jewels on my skin, fingerpainting up my belly in long streaks and dipping in for more to mark me—"Mine," she said. "You're marked. You're mine."

I rose from the table. "I'm going to get a room," I said.

She looked at me under her lashes. "Yes."

We went upstairs. She was excited.

"Your hair has gotten gray. You're still handsome though."

"Aging, aging." I felt like a boy. "You don't look any different," I said. "You look about twenty-two."

She laughed. How could I be so happy? I shut my eyes, the
better to breathe in her delicious scent. I clasped her naked
body in my arms. "Darling, darling," I murmured in her ear.
"My dearest one."

Her laughter bubbled in her throat. "I have a surprise for
you. I told you I've thought of this night for years."

"It's you; that's the surprise."

"You were surprised when you saw me, weren't you?" she
asked.

"I almost fell down, it was so unexpected. Why wouldn't
you write me? You're so beautiful. Tell me you love me. Tell
me you've missed me."

"Now, hush, it's time for your surprise."

"I love your Virginia accent. I love the way you make your
words."

"Now, close your eyes."

I complied. We were lying naked on the bed. She pulled
away, leaving my arms empty.

"There."

"What is it?"

She was holding a handful of elastic strings.

"Just you watch. I brought this just for you. It's fun." She
was giggling, squirming over my body, her breasts against my
chest, her feet stroking up and down my legs. I grabbed her,
kissing her. "Now, you be still," she said, slipping one of the
elastics over my wrist.

"What is this?"

"Bondage."

Now it was my turn to laugh. "Nu-uh."

But her mouth was on mine; I was putty in her hands.

"I want my arms around you."

"Wait till you try this. Come on, John. Let me do this. I want to."

What could I say? I helped her slip the elastic on my wrists and watched as she tied it to the bed. "Can you get free?"

I pulled, twisting with my hands. "No. It just tightens if I pull."

"Then let me get your feet."

"I want my legs free. I want to throw them round your back."

"Hush," she said, and drew my penis into her mouth. I quivered. She slipped the bonds over my ankles with no more protests, and I was then spreadeagled at her command, my eyes closed. It was ecstasy. She lay on top of me, kissing me everywhere, beginning at my eyes, dropping to my lips, then chin, then neck, and moving slowly down. I thought I would explode.

"Loosen me." I couldn't move. She was sitting on me now, her sweet juices pouring over me.

"Do you want to marry me?"

"Yes."

"Say it."

"Marry me, Flossie. I want to marry you."

"Yes?"

"I adore you, yes. I want you always with me."

"Beg me."

"Please marry me. Say you love me."

Then suddenly she slipped away. She ran into the bathroom, and I lay spread on the bed, bound hand and foot.

"Flossie?"

There was no answer. "Flossie?" In a moment she reappeared, fully dressed, right up to her hat. My erection flattened instantly. "What are you doing?"

"I'm going home now."

"You're going?"

"I'll leave a note at the desk to come untie you."

"Flossie!"

"If you pay them enough, they won't talk too much. Your reputation won't be hurt."

"Flossie!" I struggled against the elastic, but each pull stretched it tighter. "You're teasing, aren't you? Why would you do this?"

She laughed down at me. I recognized that high, crazy laugh.

"Why? Do you really mean to tell me you don't know? Because I don't like being used, that's why!"

"I never used you, Flossie."

"I gave you everything. I gave and gave, and you took. I don't know why I didn't see it at the time. You lied to me. You held out promises you wouldn't keep. I waited three years for you, and I really believed you'd leave your wife and marry me. Silly Flossie. I was kept in bondage by those promises. You wouldn't leave me alone—remember how you called me all the time? And I was too dirt-dumb to see the trap. I was bound hand and foot to you."

"Flossie, listen—"

"Now I'm a virtuous married matron, mother of children, and you think you just crook your finger and I'll come. But I won't. I won't ever let you do that to me again. You will never have a hold on me again."

"Flossie, it wasn't like that." She paid no mind.

"For years I've thought of what we'd do tonight."

"Don't leave me here."

"Ta-ta." She wiggled her fingers at me. The door closed, and I was left naked on the bed, the hollow silence ringing in my ears.

I strained against the cords. She said she'd leave a note at the front desk, but no one covered it this time of night. It might take hours before anyone found her note. Margaret was expecting me at home. Which was worse? To be discovered, ridiculed, and publicly exposed, my name a laughingstock? Or to lie here for hours naked, bound with elastic to the bed?

One snapped.

My wrist was bleeding where I'd twisted free.

With one hand I could release the others. I was dressing when the manager knocked on the door.

"Just a minute," I said through clenched teeth, fumbling for my glasses.

"Are you all right?"

I opened the door. "Is there anything I can do?" I know how to put on the chill of superiority. The manager was a heavy, stocky blond. He looked at me curiously. The elastics were in my jacket pocket, the bed pulled neatly up. He could not see my bruised, whipped wrists, hidden by my cuffs.

"Yes?" I asked.

"Are you all right? I got a note downstairs that you might need some help."

"No, I'm fine. What sort of note?"

"It didn't say," he said. "Just asked me to look into the room." Thank God! She hadn't told!

"You're perfectly welcome to look in. I'm leaving now. I think you'll find everything in decent shape."

Outside I realized I had no way of leaving. Damn the woman! She had driven me in her car. The whole thing had been a premeditated plot. I was shaky as I returned to the inn to call a cab. I went in the bar and downed two brandies straight. My wrists hurt and I felt sick. It was past eleven at night, and it would be midnight by the time I got home. Explanations would be needed. But that wasn't what upset me most, no, but the significance of this thing. I rested my head on the wooden post of the dark bar. I could feel a stone pressing on my chest.

"Mr. Woods, your cab is here."

"Thank you." I strode directly to the car. "I want Trinity Church," I directed the driver.

"Nice night."

I grunted.

"You been going to the trial?"

I grunted again, remote as the stars in the jet-black autumn sky.

"That's unusual stuff," he tried again. "I think they're nuts bringing the man to trial. I mean, what could anyone have done that would be as bad as that? If they don't like him, they should just ask him to leave. I met him onct. He seemed like a nice man. Not the least bit pushy, you know what I mean?"

I tried to get a grip on myself. I was shaking. I don't know when I've felt so weak, so lonely, exposed, and vulnerable.

The cab left me at the entrance to the parking lot. The stars wheeled in a night as black as pitch. My wrists were throbbing, and my feet groped over the stones. I stumbled toward my car.

"Who's there?" I saw the figure, nothing more. My heart stopped. I felt sick. "Who's there?" I said again.

"John?"

"Oh, Tom. Is that you?"

"Yes."

"What are you doing here?" I asked, and I was aware that my knees were trembling. I thought in a moment I might collapse. He came up to me.

"Dark, isn't it?" He put one hand on my shoulder. "I was sitting in the church." I'm a big man, taller than Tom, but when I felt his arm across my back, I gave a sob and broke. My arms came around him then, my head on his shoulder, and I was crying as I hadn't done since I was a boy, my body racked with sobs. I hurt. I hurt.

"John, John." His arms were around me, one hand on the back of my neck. I could never explain what happened then, or how—I say it was an aberration, the way the mind goes blank sometimes. I'm ashamed even remembering it now—my heart beating loud—but all I wanted was to crawl into his embrace. My lips were pressed against his neck, his cheek; and then suddenly I was kissing him full on the lips, like a woman, my hands at his head, my fingers in his thick coarse hair. I didn't think. I couldn't think. And when we broke apart for air, I grabbed at him again. I couldn't let him go. He turned. My kiss landed on his cheek, and he rocked me gently side to side.

"There, there."

I was crying in his arms, a baby bawling in the night. I wanted to be held by him and comforted. I wanted to lie beside him in the dark, with my whole body stretched on—

Horrified, I wrenched free. Thank God I'd been protected by the dark. No one had seen me in that dreadful act. Tom put one tentative hand on my sleeve.

"John?"

I pulled away. "It's so awful." I stumbled off to lean against a tree. What would we do without good, decent trees? I put both arms around the tree and felt the hot tears scald my eyes; my shoulders shook. At least it was a tree I was embracing and not another man. The rough bark bit into my cheek. With my open mouth I bit it back, my tongue and teeth crushing, sucking on the lumpy bark.

"Come on, I'll take you home."

"Yes, I guess I should. I don't—"

"You're not well. Easy. John, do you mind if I stop at the rectory for a moment? I won't be long."

"No, why?"

"I want to say good-bye."

He caught me off guard. "Say good-bye?"

"It's foolish, isn't it? Walk through it one more time. It's nearly finished—"

I didn't listen.

Now all my manipulative self-preservation came leaping to the fore, my little mind churning with the cunning idea that, yes, here lay the excuse for Margaret.

"Yes, let's do that," I said. "That'd be nice." That would be nice; I could tell Margaret I'd been sitting up, drinking with Tom in the rectory, and that's why we didn't either one get home till after one A.M. While that craven suggestion was scurrying through my mind, I was also thinking I would carry myself with such dignity and reserve that Tom would forget I'd lost my head, embracing him in my lonely and repulsive need. And another part of my mind was judging me, wondering if I were a closet fairy all this time.

We walked into a cold, empty house. We flicked on lights and the oil burner and tagged through the hollow rooms, al-

ready smelling with a musty, unused odor. He fixed us each a
drink. We sat in our coats at the kitchen table and ate sardines
and crackers.

"Do you know about round tables?" he asked.

"No, what?"

"Miss Eugenia at Daphne's school says you spill secrets in
round rooms and that conversations are always livelier and more
intimate at round tables."

"Is that so?"

"The oval is a compromise."

"So, we'll tell each other secrets, will we?" My heart was
a living ball of pain. "Since we're sitting at a round table, what
were you doing at the church?"

"I went in to pray. I prayed for guidance and for help. I
prayed for all of us."

I couldn't think of anything to say. At that moment I didn't
give a damn about his nonsense—his God-knowledge and spirit
planes. What of acts and doing?

"I prayed also for Elizabeth."

"Well, maybe you're better off without her," I said, though
whether I was talking about Elizabeth I could not have said.
"She can't be worth that much, can she?"

"What's happened to your wrist?" He reached for my hand.
I pulled back. "No, let me see. You need some ointment on
that. Why, that's a brand-new wound." He looked at me, appalled. "What's happened?"

"It's nothing."

But his eyes were on the red and bleeding burn. He bathed
it, treated it with ointment, and all the time I was close to
hysteria, I think. We began to talk about flagellation and the

physical abuse of the body. I remember laughing a great deal, for there's a time when if you laugh enough, you cover up the tears.

It was two o'clock when I got home. Tom decided to stay in the rectory. He wanted to be alone, he said, and it was only later that I remembered his words. "No one will trouble me tonight," he said. "Anyway we're coming to the end. Tomorrow's my last day. I need to be alone. Tomorrow will be. . . ." His voice trailed off, and his eyes seemed far away. Did he have some second sight? But I was self-absorbed and didn't heed him until later. Even now I wonder: How did he know the next day would be the last, when the trial was scheduled for two more days?

Anyway I crept back to my own bed, careful to ease myself onto the mattress slowly lest Margaret wake up. I was exhausted and also wide awake. It was hard to know which part hurt worse, my hands or pride or aching heart. I forced myself to lie still, eyes closed. It took a long time to get to sleep. Out the open window I could hear the wind whipping the trees, a rattle of bare branches, drear sound, precursor of winter chill. I was alone in ways I'd never thought about before. Surrounded by people, and so desperately alone! My isolation hit me with incredible force. When I was young, in my twenties, I had felt myself alone. I had even wallowed in the sensation of my uniqueness. I was alone then because no one understood me or could possibly experience the depths of what I felt; being alone was worth that sense of superiority. Later I had felt separate, enclosed in my own shell, unable to reach out or join in a moment of deep unity. I didn't comprehend that isolation: I had my neighbors, friends, church, my family, mother, children, wife, and an occasional forbidden woman to stir my heated blood. In the midst of plenty I'd denied my loneliness. But now. . . .

Eventually I slept, restlessly, with multiple images of Flossie, and of running feet and panting breaths. I was naked on a crowded street, looking for my clothes. I was being followed, and I could sense a black cloud following me. I was in a house, and the cloud was seeping in through the cracks. I was trying to close up all the doors and windows, but the blackness was drifting in around the window frames and behind the hinges of the door, filling up the rooms. I fled, from one room to the next, closing doors behind me, running; the billowing black cloud pursued me, until there was only one small attic window at my hand. If I did not squeeze through this window, too small for my frame, I would be consumed by the pursuing clouds. I pushed the window out and then thrust my head through the opening—only to see the glass and wooden frame falling, falling, falling, falling into limitless emptiness, while behind me pressed the cloud.

I woke up with a cry.

"Are you all right?" It was Margaret. Perspiration was beaded on my brow, my hair wet with sweat.

"I'm fine." I patted her hand, but I was trembling from that dream. To dispel it, I got up and went to the bathroom.

It was four A.M., still pitch-black outside. My body felt as if it had been beaten with sticks. I threw myself back on the bed.

This time I dreamt of Tom. I saw him in his surplice and cassock slipping through the black night to her house. He was walking furtively, and as I watched, he lifted his skirts to reveal big muddy work boots, just the thing for trudging through the mire. I've never seen such mud. It was boiling like black milk at his feet, gray muck and ooze. But Tom was grinning at me, exposing Shriver's strong, white, even teeth. The hot mud bubbled at his boots, and I saw one tongue of gray mud erupt just at his booted toes; it was an erect, smooth penis. . . .

I woke up sweating. I had to remind myself what was dream and what reality: that Tom only wore his skirts in church. I had to remind myself that we had no such mud pit in Naughton—not anywhere in the world had I seen such a pool of thick, gray, oozing slime.

It was beginning to grow light outside. I got up. I'd had less than four hours' sleep. I took a long, hot shower, growling at Margaret with undisguised ill temper. My wrists were swollen and so painful I could hardly bear to let the water touch them. Both ankles were rimmed with a red cord that stood up from the flesh. A tree ringed with a barbed wire will grow upward and around the wire in the same way. But the physical wounds were the least of my pain. My face was puffy, my eyelids swollen and white. I looked a hundred years old.

I got my own breakfast and buried myself grudgingly in the newspaper.

"Are you all right?" Margaret questioned.

"I'm fine," I grunted. "I was just out too late last night."

"Well, don't forget to take the laundry to Mrs. Paterno on your way."

I glared at her.

"In fact," she continued, without noticing, "why don't you drop Annie off at school. It's not too far out of your way. Annie, do you want pancakes, honey?"

So this was what my life had come to, a drudgery of taking the laundry to Mrs. Paterno and watching my daughter push pancakes down her throat? I couldn't bear it!

Forcibly I made my clenched fist open and rest relaxed on the table. All this played out like a fishing line to the end, the emptiness of my life. It was all meaningless. Why do I exist? Why be alive? I had a terror sitting on me. What were we doing but walking through the horror of life waiting to die? For the first time in my life I was mortally afraid.

My shell had cracked. Moreover (here lay the paradox) Tom had nothing—and yet everything. While I—who had everything—my wife and kids, my big historic house, and friends and respectability—I had nothing. I felt betrayed by Flossie; no, by my own self. I'd betrayed my family, kissed Tom. I'm no pansy. I'd wanted comfort, that was all. I'd forgot he was a man. My thoughts would not stop circling. I felt I was toppling over a cliff.

"I have to be up at the church." I could hardly control myself. "I'm leaving now. Annie, are you ready?"

"But it's so early," Margaret protested. "She'll just have to wait around the school."

"Well, I can't wait," I snapped. "If the laundry's ready, I can drop that off."

"It's in the hall. Oh, all right, never mind about Annie. I'll run her up later, but I really don't see why you can't wait a half an hour. It's not much."

23

THAT WAS A PERFECT AUTUMN MORNING, ALL SCORCHED COLORS and hard, blue-granite skies. The wind tossed the trees; I had to hold my hat to keep it on my head; and the crowd, just beginning to gather outside the churchyard wall under the watchful eye of standing troopers, braced themselves against the wind or turned their backs. No one bothered to hold up signs: they would have been snatched right from their hands. The dry leaves blew around our feet, caught on gravestones, twisted in the air. And everything was hollow. Empty. False. A piece of cardboard covered the window of my beloved church, and people were everywhere—great, noisy ragtag throng, trampling down my grass and sitting on the gravestones. "Hey! Get off!" I shouted to one young man. They'd pull them down, these ancient markers, some 100 or 150 years old. Everything about the church looked shabby and unkempt in that glaring, brilliant autumn light. The teenager (how he got past the police I can't imagine) pulled his bulk reluctantly off the stone and, jaws moving on his gum, slouched toward Bethlehem.

I was early enough to go get coffee in the parish hall, and there the Bishop met me in the hall.

"Good morning," I said.

"Good morning, indeed. This is your fault, John."

"My fault?"

"If you all on the vestry had done your job in the beginning, none of this would be happening. You wait. That man will destroy this whole community."

Silently I poured myself a cup of coffee.

"You know the subject today, don't you? It's more on the Resurrection. Now he'll spout God only knows what. Nothing would surprise me anymore. I suppose he'll say he doesn't believe at all."

"Isn't it tangential?" I said. "The charges don't pertain to that. Why can't you keep to the subject?"

"It is the subject, his belief—or lack of it. His stubborn insistence on doing things his way, defying all authority."

"Then kick him out," I said. "I'll support you."

"I would, I would. Look at that mob out there. He has as many supporters as enemies, and the more he talks, the worse it gets. The man has presence. He has some quality. I believe he did see God. That's why he's dangerous. God save us from the saints," he said. "We can handle the sinners. It's the ones who think they're saints who do the damage. There's no way we can get out of this now without tearing the whole Virginia Church apart."

"You really think it threatens the Church?"

I had never seen Crowley so angry. "He's a threat to my authority, and there's nothing I can do. Look at his defense: 'I stand on my conscience; I did what I did because of conscience.' Good Lord, he's *supposed* to stand on his conscience. But it's not supposed to cross *mine*. With every word he tears down our authority. He's dangerous."

For years I've excused what I did then with the remembrance of the Bishop's words. Today I wonder: Did I have a choice? Free will? Or was it all predestined, in the Calvinist sense?

"Look at this hearing—it's a circus!" cried the Bishop. "Now we need police." Crowley turned on me. "You know that businesses have folded because of this? One, at least—the Staunton Company; the two partners can't stand the sight of each other. They've decided to dissolve the partnership." I shook my head. I didn't know, though I knew that Carolyn's farm manager had walked off after fifteen years, leaving her to feed horses and find workmen; and the sole reason was that with the nervous strain from the trial and her husband going up to hear Buckford at our house, and Elizabeth not speaking to her, she'd lashed out at him, saying words that couldn't be taken back. But that's another story. The Bishop threw himself in a chair, his fingers tapping, one foot jiggling, until he burst out at me, repeating himself again:

"There's no way we can pass judgment on the man and not feel repercussions rippling through the Church. He's either insane or a saint. If I make the wrong move, I start a riot." He gestured toward the window with his head. "If I suspend him, he'll take it to the next level on appeal."

My wrists were throbbing. I could feel arrows of pain shooting toward my elbows. My fingers were swollen, red and stiff, and my socks chafed against my ankle sores. But what I remembered was Tom's look as he bent over my hands last night, applying ointment—for suddenly I realized he *knew*. He knew everything about me. He knew my secrets.

In agitation I turned to the window. Now three things happened—three trivial images smashed against my mind, for it was the combination of the three that made a difference. One was

a memory, the merest glimpse of Tom and Elizabeth greeting
each other one day, weeks before. He had stood very straight,
looking down at her, her dark head tilted up to him. But it was
their look I'd intercepted, a fire coal, a flash of angel fire that
passed between them. My knees shook, it was so intimate. I
remembered also how Elizabeth had jumped up one day, months
earlier, at my house. "Tom's coming!" she had said, as if they
were joined by invisible threads. She had run to the window,
pulling back the thin white curtains to spot the Plymouth turning up the drive. Yet she'd known he was coming long before
the car appeared.

To the casual observer Tom and Elizabeth seemed to be
just friends, but I (standing at the diamond-paned parish-hall
window, the blood pounding in my wrists, and pain shooting
halfway to my shoulder), I was helpless with anger. Who did
he think he was, getting his rocks off at our expense?

The second and third sights unfolded before me as I looked
out the window on the churchyard. One was little Angie Reischetz in a red coat. She stood, feet together, leaning forward
myopically, looking, I suppose, for her husband, Tony. The
other sight was Storey and Eleanor Lunt. They stood modestly
off to one side, Eleanor clutching her black purse in both arms.
At that instant everything fell into place.

"Then make him be the one to leave." I crept up behind
Dick Crowley and whispered—yes, whispered in his ear. I hated
Tom. "I'll show you how to make him leave by his own free
will."

"How?"

"Ask him what caused his vision?"

"What?"

"Ask him what triggered it," I said. "He's under oath. He'll answer. He's itching to answer. He started to yesterday, when he was interrupted, but he was going to bring it out."

"Bring what out? What will he say?"

"Ask him who the woman is."

"Jesus Lord! *Cherchez la femme.* We went through all that. I asked him once in my office, and he denied it."

"He was lying."

"Who is it?"

"Elizabeth McEwen."

"Carolyn Page's daughter?" He shook his head with distaste and sighed, thinking of Carolyn's financial contributions. "Can you prove it?" he said bravely.

"Ask him. He'll tell you everything."

"I won't ask that in public court. I want him to leave, not stir up more trouble. Good God! If he admitted that, can you imagine what would happen? We'd have everybody fornicating in their search for God. Do you think they wouldn't? All people want is license anyway to indulge their lust. They'd crucify him first and then raise him to martyrdom and start some secret rites, my God, to satisfy their appetites, and say that it was demonstrated in public hearings that—good God, no! I don't want that."

"Then leave it to me," I said. "I'll make him resign. Don't start the proceedings this morning. Just stall till I get back to you."

Then I told him my other plan.

Dick Crowley did not come to a decision easily. He listened with interest, questioned me intently. Then he settled into himself for a few moments, eyes half-closed. After a while he said, "Leave me alone, I need to pray about this. Don't go too far away. And, John, if anyone wants me, I'm not here."

So I went out while he prayed, and I don't know what communication he felt he had with God, but a half hour later he opened the door and called me in and told me he agreed and asked me to set the wheels in motion, and then it all began.

Dick Crowley closed the church to the public. He sent everyone away except his own two aides. His gavel banged on the wooden arm of his chair. The public trailed outside, questioning and complaining all the while.

"What's happening?"

"Do you know what's the matter?"

I caught sight of Tom's drawn face. I don't suppose he'd slept at all that night, for hadn't he said he'd had a premonition? Dick Crowley tried to be discreet, but afterwards word swept through the Valley. There are no secrets in Naughton. Damned few.

They stayed in the empty church—Dick pacing in his lace and robes, Tom dressed in sweater and tie and tweed jacket, seated in his place. Sometimes he drew abstracted circles on the table with one finger. Sometimes he leaned back. Once he came to his feet and sank back down again. Neither Dick's two aides, Graham Eric and Bo Zimmer, nor the defense lawyer, George Tooey, were present. But before the day was out, a lot of us knew what had taken place.

Tom made no effort at defense. "The truth can't hurt anyone anymore," he said.

Crowley was furious.

"Are you saying a woman led you to God? Like Dante and Beatrice, I suppose?"

"I say that my heart was opened through her soul so that I was able to love—which means able to reach God, for God is love and is only found in—"

Crowley cut him short. "You had sex with this woman?"

"Yes. For love demands union with the beloved."

"You took her for your mistress?"

"I don't use those terms."

"You continued carnal knowledge of her over a period of several months—is that correct?" demanded Crowley, and Tom nodded stubbornly.

"You enjoyed her for a year. . . . You betrayed your wife, your congregation, your marriage vows, your vows of priesthood. Have you anything to say?"

"No, sir."

"No defense?"

Tom said nothing.

"Yet all this time you claim to be chosen by God, serving God, doing the work of God. You violate your vows to your Bishop, your church, your congregation, your wife. . . ."

Meanwhile I went to find Storey Lunt. I did not do the deed myself. I didn't want traced to me that luckless kiss. Ah, sins. Tom would say there are no coincidences, that I was also acting out the part assigned by God, but that day I only knew of my need for vengeance and my hate. I called it justice. Necessary.

The sheriff was leaning on the low stone wall with two of his men. Above them a maple raged against blue sky. They had posted themselves where they could watch the crowd, which still billowed around the church and overflowed onto the graves.

"Ed, can we talk privately?"

We strolled through the churchyard while I played out my part.

———

Inside the church the Bishop raked Tom over the coals. "You
lied to me."

"I am ashamed of that."

"You're a disgrace. You should be defrocked. Is nothing
sacred to you?"

Tom looked up at him, then down at his hands. His face
was white. "I am ashamed of many things. I'm ashamed of
having lied. That was wrong. But I am not ashamed of what
has happened, which came to me through God. For I don't
understand it, but I believe I am serving the will of God."

"You disgust me. You disgrace my Church. You're not fit
to be a priest."

His hand reached down with the speed of a snake and
gripped Tom's silver cross. He yanked it from Tom's neck.

"You degrade anything you touch." He was breathing hard,
his face contorted. Tom half-rose, but the bishop held the cross
high out of reach.

"Now, you are going to resign," he said. "And I'll tell you
why."

Outside I wove through the crowd, looking for my man. He
was with the other Negroes in the parking lot. I paused on my
way to the parish hall and stopped, in passing, to tip my hat.

"Eleanor," I said. "Storey Lunt. How are you?"

"Mr. Woods."

We shook hands. Easy as pie. I went on into the parish hall
then, and no one knew, when the sheriff ambled up a few minutes later with his burly troopers bandoliered, hats low on their
eyes and faces grim, that I had led them to the prey. Now the
crowd surged forward, hurling itself from the churchyard into
the parking lot, for it's not every day we saw a black man

thrust, arms over his head, against a pickup truck, and his shirt and trousers frisked like a common criminal while his wife hops helplessly from foot to foot protesting to Mistah Sheriff, suh. The other Negroes backed away as Lunt was pushed into the back of the sheriff's car. They huddled in their fear.

"You'll resign," said Crowley, "because I tell you to. It's your sacrifice. Right now a man named Storey Lunt is being arrested."

"For what?"

"Assault! And possibly for the rape of Mrs. Anthony Reischetz last winter."

"But he didn't do that. He's innocent," Tom protested.

"I know."

"You know? I don't understand." Tom was confused. He looked down and saw his hands were shaking.

"It's simple," said the Bishop. "I want you out of Naughton and out of my diocese. And I am determined to do anything to get you out and this township quiet again. Now it's up to you. You choose the fate of that black family. Because of you that man will be charged with this crime, jailed, and held without bail. I understand he's your friend. He'll probably get off in the end, but meantime he'll lose months, and maybe years, of work. His family will suffer. The legal fees alone will ruin them. He'll lose his farm. His son won't get his schooling at Trinity. And the blame will rest entirely with you."

"With me?" Tom murmured, and he was trembling all over now.

"Because you alone can save him. All you have to do is hand in a resignation. Resign and go away and leave us all in peace."

"You'll let him go if I resign?"

"These are my terms," said the Bishop. "You are to sign this letter of resignation, admitting all the charges. You are then to leave Naughton tonight. I'd have you leave this minute, but I'll give you until nine P.M. You are to leave alone. Moreover no one is to know you're skipping town. And no one—no one at all—is to know *why* you are doing this, or about my terms."

"I can't control that," Tom said. "People will learn."

"Not if you don't tell them. I won't tell the news of your resignation until tomorrow. By then you'll be far away. You are to drive to my house in Richmond and stay there tonight."

He paced up and down the chancery. "You will not set foot in Naughton ever again. You will not see or speak to or write to this woman of yours, Elizabeth McEwen, for one year, is that clear? I am going to find you a post abroad, as far away as I can get you, and you will stay out of the country for one full year. Is that clear?"

Tom's jaw worked. "I'll resign from the Church."

"That's up to you. But you are never to tell *anyone* these terms. You stand on your word."

"You trust my word but treat me like this? That's illogical."

"I trust you," said Crowley. "I trust your honor. I even trust your vision was a true one, coming by the grace of God. But simply, these things have to stop now before they tear us completely apart."

"And if I don't resign?"

"Tom, don't make things hard on me."

"I'll write her," protested Tom. "I'll call her on the phone. I refuse that stipulation."

"I'm sorry, you can have no communication of any sort for

one full year. After that I don't care what you do—run away
with her if you want, but for one year you may not write or
speak to her. And I expect you to keep your word."

Tom flinched. "And if I refuse your terms, you'll put an
innocent man in jail?"

"Your resignation is entirely voluntary, of course."

"The boy will stay in Trinity School?"

"I'll see that he stays in school. I'll see that his schooling
is paid straight through twelfth grade, and I'll see that the father is released the minute you leave town. All charges will be
dropped. There will be no repercussions."

Tom looked up in anguish. "Blackmail."

"Yes." Crowley stared at him. "I believe in what I'm doing
and in the reasons why."

Tom said nothing, but again his mouth worked as he tried
to control his emotion.

"I use blackmail," said the Bishop softly, "because I see no
other way to stop the conflict. If I can't make you leave by my
authority, or your good conscience, then I'll use whatever means
God brings to hand." He grimaced. "It's unorthodox, but I
stand on my conscience too."

"Why don't you bring a judgment against me?" Tom
shouted. "That's what the hearing was about. Don't you want
straightforward punishment? This way is cowardly."

"I'd use the word *cautious*," said the Bishop. "I need a
sacrifice. To bring a judgment against you now will only incite
further trouble, maybe a riot. Look out there. Can you see them?
They're yours. I can't reinstate you as rector. I can't suspend
you. If I excommunicate you, and frankly, Tom, that's what I'd
like to do, I only aggravate the situation. I don't want people
to hear about your adultery. That's not good for you or her or

for the Church. I want people to forget, and for that to happen, you have to resign and go as far away as I can get you. Frankly, since you refuse to obey my wishes, I don't hesitate to force your hand. But," he continued, his voice hard, "if you still refuse, then I promise I will not only send an innocent man to jail, I'll see your whole family humiliated and Elizabeth's reputation ruined. You'll see this black man suffer, and all your efforts at racial integration will be lost. Do you want that on your conscience? Get out of here. It's a small enough sacrifice I am asking you to make."

He pulled a sheet of paper from the desk drawer in front of him and twirled it round for Tom to read.

"And Priscilla?" said Tom.

It took all morning, the negotiations. Finally:

"Your resignation," said Crowley. He set a pen on top.

Tom read it quietly.

"You think of everything."

"I try."

"The sheriff will be at the Woodses' house waiting for you at . . . shall I say eight o'clock? When he sees you across the county line, he'll release his man from jail."

"Your hostage," murmured Tom. "And you'll see that Priscilla—?"

"I promise she'll be taken care of," the Bishop repeated.

Outside, a police siren could be heard. The Bishop cocked his head. "Well? What are you going to do?"

"I'll sign," said Tom. "It's over now."

When Tom had signed the resignation, the Bishop bowed his head and said a prayer of thanks. "May this agreement be good, Lord, in thy sight. And now, O Lord, forgive us all!"

And that was the end except for details. I got back to the house at four o'clock. Elizabeth was there, beautiful as ever. She had stepped outside when I drove up and stood highlighted against the fan door (our pride: designed by Jefferson), hugging her arms across her thin blouse. When I reached the foot of the steps, she ran down to give me a kiss and take my arm back up inside.

"What's happening? I can't find anyone."

"It's over now. He's leaving."

"Leaving!"

"Come inside." I held the door for her. I wasn't about to admit what I had done. "He's made a deal."

"Tom wouldn't stoop to make a deal."

"Is Margaret in?"

"In the kitchen."

"I need a drink."

Later Tom arrived. His face was haggard. He caught Elizabeth and hugged her wordlessly.

"I have to leave tonight."

"Tom."

"By nine." His eyes met mine, and they held open pain. "I must be out of Naughton by nine P.M. and alone. He made me give my word. I cannot see you, Elizabeth, or write you. I can have no contact with you for one year."

"One year's not long. I can write to you. I made no promises."

He groaned.

"You made a similar promise for me!" She accused him. "I won't do it! You can't bind another party without that person's consent. It doesn't count."

"Don't make it harder on me, Elizabeth. I'm being sent to South America. I may never return." Their emotions poured from their eyes.

"Come upstairs with me. I have to pack." They went up, clinging to each other.

Margaret came in. "Where's Tom?"

"Upstairs, packing, I think. Lizzie's with him."

"That's good, then," she said. "Dinner will be ready in an hour."

There were a dozen details to be taken care of: a call to Daphne at Miss Eu's, to Philip at his grandmother's in Illinois, and four calls to the Bishop alone. Crowley was sending him to an Anglican mission in Lima, then into the high Andes. Dick wanted him right off the Northern Hemisphere. Tom decided to take Philip with him and to leave Daphne in school.

At dinner the phone rang incessantly, jangling our nerves. Margaret fielded calls. She said Tom was exhausted and not available that night. He needed to be alone, she said. No one knew what had happened, only that the Bishop and Tom had met for several hours without George Tooey being present and that the hearing had been postponed until Monday, when an announcement would be made. But somehow word still got round.

Emily came over.

She burst into tears in our hall, holding both Tom's hands.

"Don't be afraid," he said.

"I'm not afraid. I don't want you to go. Oh, Mr. Buckford, I'm so ashamed."

"Hush."

"I feel it's my fault."

"It's not. It's no one's fault, Emily. God is working things out in His own way."

"You mean there's no Free Will?" I interposed angrily. It was important to me, this question, though I was still hot with righteous indignation and convinced I'd done the only right thing possible.

"I think we have less will than we think," said Tom. "So don't cry, Emily, it's going to be fine." And then he burst into tears himself, tears running down his cheeks. "But, God, it hurts."

"Oh dear," said Emily.

Carolyn and Dutton arrived hurriedly, out of breath, at seven-thirty.

"I've brought you a cake," said Carolyn. "Mary made it. I thought you'd like it for your drive."

"Thank you, Carolyn. Will you tell her thanks from me?" Tears standing in his eyes.

"Well," she said.

Dutton shook his hand. "I'm sorry," he said. "You've taught me a lot."

"I don't know," Tom laughed. "But certainly you—all of you—have . . ." He shrugged wordlessly. "I am grateful to have known you."

It was insane, the whole thing. I hadn't made any agreement with Crowley that Tom had to slip away like a thief in the night. That was the Bishop's doing, and it caused added pain. At one moment Tom looked over at me with such anguish that I turned away. *The bastard, he deserves it*, I said to defend myself, and also: *Far be it from me to deprive him of his pain.*

At eight-fifteen the doorbell rang. It was the sheriff with two deputies. Annie would not let him in. Margaret and Lizzie both crowded to the door as well, and turned as if to block Tom's exit.

"Did you have to come get him? Can't he be trusted to leave?"

"I'm just doing my job." The sheriff removed his hat with a sheepish grin. "Hello, ma'am." He nodded to Elizabeth. To Margaret: "Miz Woods." To me he tipped his chin, but we were co-conspirators, exchanging guilty looks.

"We'll wait at the end of the drive."

"He'll be right out."

"As soon as I see him over the county line, the prisoner will be released," the sheriff said to me in an undertone. He ambled to his car, flanked by his bodyguards.

Then it was time for Tom to leave. "Write to me," said Margaret. "I'll send you news and pass on any messages you have, and then I'll write you back." So that was how they solved the problem of Tom's not writing to his love.

We walked him to his car. He packed his suitcases in the trunk and set of box of books on the front seat.

"I can follow you," Elizabeth whispered desperately.

"You can't. I gave my word." He stopped and swept her in his arms. She buried her face in his neck.

Beside me Margaret was in tears.

"I'll write you anyway," said Elizabeth.

"I'll be back in a year. Remember how we meet."

"At ten each night," she said. "The first five minutes are for me to send my thoughts to you, the next five to listen and receive. I'll begin tomorrow night."

"And pray for me," he whispered in her hair. "As I pray

always for you. John." He pulled away. "My dear, dear friend."
He embraced me too. I submitted to his hug, but my heart was
cold.

"Keep my church well. God, I'll miss you all. Dear Margaret . . ."

The night was black and moonless. Huge stars hung overhead.

"You have to go," said Margaret.

A groan broke from him. He jumped into the car. The
engine roared. He did not look back.

"Tom!" Elizabeth cried after him, and ran down the drive
behind the moving car. But he did not stop. She pulled up and
stood watching his headlights as they turned onto the main
road, picked up the sheriff's accompanying lights, wound round
three curves, and blinked out at a hill. They were gone. In the
black air a chill wind stirred my hair. I shivered.

Margaret walked to Lizzie, put her arms around the younger
woman, and led her back up toward the house. Their shoes
crunched on the pebbles of the drive, and I was struck, curiously, by the heavy silence of the stars wheeling in their des-
ignated paths.

"Don't worry, Lizzie," I broke the strain. "It will be all
right. You'll get over it in time"—though whether I was talking
to her or to myself I could not say.

Margaret shot me a look of contempt. "John, go away,"
she said. "Just leave us alone."

For years I punished myself. Elizabeth never joined Tom. Some-
how I hadn't expected that. When the year was up, she flew to
Peru and spent a month with Tom and then came back for
Duncan's next operation at Johns Hopkins. Twice Tom came

home on family business, and of course for Priscilla's funeral; and one of those visits lasted four or five months in all. After that the months turned into years. Tom and Elizabeth wrote to each other, telephoned. But Elizabeth would not leave Duncan, and Dunks could not be taken to the Andes, where Tom was working, and neither could Tom come back to the States, once he started that new ministry.

Five years later I came on Elizabeth in New York. We stood on the street with an icy wind tearing at our ears and making her dance in her thin shoes. She hadn't time to stop, she said. She had meetings all day long and that evening would be flying out again. By then she was head of the foundation for mentally retarded children that she had started and was flying round the country—the world—raising and dispersing money. She never did get through college, but it made no difference. She was smart. She became a force to be reckoned with in the health-services field, and I suppose our present treatment of the mentally handicapped is partly due to her.

Anyway, six days after our meeting in New York I got a letter in the mail. She sent a snapshot of Tom and herself in Peru. She knew Tom had given me his notebooks before he left—the scraps and fragments of his life. She knew I brooded over the affair.

"Someday I'll give you my journals," she wrote. "No one would want them but you."

But they did not come. Tom's notebooks sat for almost thirty years, until I saw his obit in the paper all those months ago. And finally Lizzie added her writings to his, and I've read them all to fashion the chronicle that's written here.

Bill Wentworth became our pastor. Once he arrived, I found I disliked the man. What I'd taken as presence turned out to be pomposity; what I'd considered intellect was posturing. After a time I disliked going to church at all. Yet Trinity was prospering by then, as was the school. In the following year two more colored children were added to the rolls, and parents who disagreed with the integration policy had the choice of swallowing their gall or removing their children to the public school—which, of course, had also integrated. This was the unforeseen result of the violence of the trial: that the Naughton schools had integrated and classes begun with a Negro boy—and hardly anyone had noticed. In the mayhem over the heresy trial we had forgotten the entire issue of desegregation. By the time the trial was over, both public and private schools had been in session several weeks. Everyone was tired; to picket seemed absurd.

Looking back, it's strange to see how everything worked out.

Sitting here now, trying to finish this account, I hear Margaret moving in the kitchen. The smell of soup is sifting through the house. There's the slam of the back door as she goes out. I think of poor, tense Daphne. Never will I forget that red-eyed child as she struggled down the aisle on my arm, her belly swollen perceptibly under her dress, going to her wedding with my son. It was a loveless match—no, worse, a match of two people who hated one another. Never will I forget my outrage at my son the night he learned of her pregnancy.

"Hell, Dad, it's midnight. You calling me at midnight to tell me I've knocked up some chick?"

"She's not some chick." I was enraged. "She's Daphne Buckford. She's the daughter of the former rector and my best friend, and I don't care what time it is."

"Listen, Dad. I'm not the only guy she's sleeping with. I'm not going to take a rap for her."

"Take a rap?"

"Well, that's what you want, isn't it? You want me to throw away my life on some hot chick? Look, we were having fun, that's all. It's her responsibility."

Then he dared quote Tom to me.

"Hey, her father said these things himself. You grab at life. That's what the padre said, isn't it? We're not responsible. Drink the cup. Worship at the sacred altar of the lord. That's all I was doing, drinking at the fountain of God." If he'd slapped my face, he could not have hurt me worse! "Hell, Dad, you're not going to make me marry her."

But we did. Daphne came to live with us, while Johnnie went back up to Yale. She attended Naughton public school and carried off her bulging belly with remarkably good grace. She was a ship under full sail, plowing before the breeze.

After the baby was born, she ran away. She left a note and Laurie behind, and she disappeared. We've never seen her since, though we tried for years to track her down. Laurie, our granddaughter, became our child, my rose of youth, a thorn in my flesh, brought to life by lust, and lusty in her life. She pricks me with her rebellion, her impatience with my limitations. Oddly she is the one I loved most, the one with the most power to hurt me. She's never heard of Daphne. She doesn't know she is her brother's child. She lives in a commune in New Mexico now and says that sex cannot be separated from a spiritual dimension—which is why she's lesbian.

Her uncle, Philip, still with those burning sullen eyes, came home for his mother's funeral, but returned right away to Peru. He married a Peruvian woman and has two children of his own. He went from one business to another at first, from windshield repairs to export-imports, then with his wife's money he opened a travel agency. He can take you to Machu Picchu, organize a jungle safari, or fly you over the Nazca lines. He has a bee in his bonnet about saving endangered animals.

Angus, likewise, did well. He managed a car dealership, invested in a restaurant, branched out into the garbage business, then into road construction. He remarried. He's worth millions today. So how can I say things didn't work out for the best? We grew or changed or hugged our limitations jealously.

And General Shriver? He grew smaller after Tom's departure, and dour. He retired into himself, grumbling about the world. I think he missed his fight. He missed Tom Buckford's enmity. He never did ask Billy Tyler to marry him, and neither did she propose to him. One day I saw that he'd grown old. He lived on war. Without an enemy of stature he would die.

That became evident at the memorial service for Tom. Shriver came creeping up the aisle on two canes, his bald head high, his eyes hot; and at the reception later at Walnut Grove he shouted at Emily until his face got red and he had to sit down on a bench. The new young Bishop had never known Tom. He read from the Sermon on the Mount:

> "Blessed are they which do hunger and thirst after righteousness: for they shall be filled. Blessed are the merciful: for they shall obtain mercy. Blessed are the pure in heart: for they shall see God . . . Blessed are they which are persecuted for righteousness' sake: for theirs is the kingdom of heaven. . . . Blessed are ye, when men shall revile you, and persecute you. . . ."

"He was a lunatic!" Shriver shouted at the reception afterwards. "A schizoid, mad as a March Hare. And if he were here, I'd kick him out again!" That day he recaptured a little of his fire.

484   REVELATIONS

And I? I suffered. Tom was the first person in my life to bring the message that everything is okay, that left to itself, the universe is working to the Good. He was the only one in my life to tell me that the task is self-discovery and not to be afraid to search. "It's all unfolding as it should." For years I'd hear his laugh booming through the hollow echoes of my dreams. In one we stood in the parish hall, looking at the church. That was the whole of that repeated dream. Us, standing together; but each time I would wake up in tears. In another recurrent dream he would be coming toward me. He would throw his arm around my shoulder and I would be filled with joy, my heart singing with delirium at the return of my friend. I would wake up with the words from the Apocryphal Acts of John ringing in my ears: "A lamp am I to those that perceive me. A mirror am I to those that know me."

Oh, Tom. For years I had that dream. I have not forgotten the things he taught me. "We are given bodily form," he used to say, "in order to experience the wonder of it all—love, hate, jealousy, anger, grief, all kinds of pain. You might as well enjoy it all."

"What, even loss?"

"Especially loss. I think loss," he wrote to me in one of his letters, "is partly an illusion too. I have come to believe that love never dies. Brecht says it in *The Threepenny Opera*—that the trick is not to make love stay; it's to notice that it's there."

Yet he suffered. I know he hurt for Daphne. God knows. For years Tom hoped she might turn up, vacillating between hope for her well-being and fear that she had died. He knew loss certainly. His visions and his service to his God did not protect him from one jot of pain. Not even from torture and that violent death in Guatemala.

Now I sit at my desk, struggling with the meaning behind these facts. Through the window I see Margaret in the garden. She bends at the hips, knees locked, head down and bottom pointing to the sky, weeding with quick jerks of her hands. I know those hands. I have watched them thicken, their skin grow wrinkled and blotched. Her fingers pull up weeds with quick, strong twists. I am filled with her awkward grace. Now she straightens her back and stares across the pond. We are like two trees, gnarled and grown together, the bark of one grown into the other until you can't tell where we divide. We are grafted by time. She has become so beautiful to me that I have developed a new fear: what will I do if she dies? I don't want to be alive without her.

So that was my journey.

I've wondered if she knew about Flossie. She never said a word, though once, before they'd healed, she traced the ridges on my wrists, the dry bark of Flossie's scars.

"That must have hurt." It was her only comment. I never proffered an explanation of the scabs.

So that was my journey: ending nowhere. When I was a child, I'd sit in class at school, the smell of ink in my nostrils. I'd sprawl across my desk, head on my arm in bored frustration at the columns of numbers before me, and outside the window the black crows would call: Caw! Cawm! they called. My eyes would swivel to the slit of sky, my shoes sputtering against the floor. Cawm! Come! I could have thrown myself from the second-floor window to join that noisy cackling black-backed crowd that flapped loose-shouldered across the cornfields and fluttered into the woods to settle on bare oaks. They chattered in derision at the static trees, stuck in perpetual place. Cawm! Come! They called. I never could.

Why did I think of that just then? So many hours, so many years have passed, the seasons turning and all of us playing at our conflicts and fears like the counters of a game—strife, anxiety, hate, with births and ends, and more beginnings and struggles toward an inner peace. It's all gone so quickly. In the blink of a god's eye. I'm eighty soon, nearly a year having passed in the course of writing this book. Eighty years. It's all gone so quickly. *Cawm! Cawm!* they called. Why do I have the feeling I was left behind?

Epilogue

What is heaven? A globe of dew.
    —PERCY BYSSHE SHELLEY

A MONTH HAS PASSED.

I never expected to write another word, but last night I dreamt of Tom again. He was running toward me, calling my name. "John! John!" with his face lit up in a smile. "John! *Look!*" And then Elizabeth was there and Margaret and Carolyn and Butch and crowds of others, and everyone was laughing, because in the dream we were actors taking bows, and I was bowing, too, with Tom and the others, while the audience resounded with applause. And I was bowing and laughing to applause.

In the dream.

Wasn't that queer?

I woke up. It was five-fifteen by the clock, and Margaret lay asleep beside me, her back turned, snoring prettily. I slipped out of bed, wide awake. Peed. Dressed. And walked downstairs and out onto the lawn.

The birds were singing up a storm. I stepped out onto the green grass, wet with dew and glistening under a slanting sun. The air was sweet, and I, wondering, still captivated by the dream, drew in a breath—and suddenly I saw the light fracture like prisms off the dew and glance into streams of colored rays. I caught my breath at that unimaginable delicacy, and I was swept by a gratitude so intense I almost cried aloud.

How good it was! How pure! How perfect! This pearling dawning day, this glorious creation. I was humbled by its innocence and generosity.

In that single moment I felt cleansed. I am forgiven!

I think I said the first true prayer of my life, and then I came inside to breakfast and wrote these last few lines to say that Tom was right. And I believe.

So end these revelations.

And now I'll make a breakfast tray to take up to my dear Margaret.

John Woods, Esq.